Evans Bell, Ross Donnelly Mangles

The Mysore Reversion

Second Edition

Evans Bell, Ross Donnelly Mangles

The Mysore Reversion
Second Edition

ISBN/EAN: 9783337418830

Printed in Europe, USA, Canada, Australia, Japan

Cover: Foto ©Andreas Hilbeck / pixelio.de

More available books at **www.hansebooks.com**

"Machiavel's errors arose not in consulting the principle of utility, but in making
false applications of it.   Bad faith is always bad policy."
JEREMY BENTHAM.

"I consider that, in fact, our Government is at the head of a system composed of
native States, and I would avoid what are called rightful occasions of appropriating those
territories.   On the contrary, I should be disposed, as far as I could, to maintain the
native States, and I am satisfied that their maintenance, and the giving to the subjects
of those States the conviction that they are considered permanent parts of the general
Government of India, would naturally strengthen our authority."
LORD ELLENBOROUGH, 1853.

"The House may dismiss at once all question of the annexation of territory.   There
are many reasons why I think we should not annex Native States.   It is for our advantages that such States should be left in India."
SIR CHARLES WOOD, now LORD HALIFAX, in the House of Commons, 26th Feb., 1863.

"Thirty years ago the predominant idea with many English statesmen was that our
interest in India consisted in extending our territory to the largest possible extent.
To that annexation policy the terrible disaster of the mutiny of 1857 must to a large
extent be ascribed.   But as time has gone on, that desire of increased dominion which is
the natural temptation of all powerful States has been overcome, and Statesmen of all
parties have arrived at the conclusion that we now hold in India pretty well as much as
we can govern, and that we should be pursuing an unwise and dangerous policy if we
tried to extend our borders or to lessen the power or the permanence of those native
rulers upon whose assistance we have so long relied.   I believe the native Princes were
formerly the objects of jealousy and distrust to English rulers, but within the last ten
years a great change has come over the spirit of our statesmanship in that respect; and
there is now, I think, a general desire to uphold them in the rights and honours which
they justly earned by their loyal support at the time of the mutiny, and to look upon
them not as impediments to our rule, but as its most useful auxiliaries."
LORD CRANBORNE, at Stamford, July 12, 1866.

THE

MYSORE REVERSION,

"AN EXCEPTIONAL CASE":

BY

MAJOR EVANS BELL,

LATE OF THE MADRAS STAFF CORPS;

AUTHOR OF "THE EMPIRE IN INDIA", "THE ENGLISH IN INDIA", ETC.

Second Edition.

WITH REMARKS ON THE PARLIAMENTARY PAPERS,
AND A FEW WORDS TO MR. R. D. MANGLES.

"Government is a practical thing, made for the happiness of mankind, and not to furnish out
a spectacle of uniformity."—BURKE.

LONDON:
TRÜBNER AND CO., 60, PATERNOSTER ROW.
1866.

The Rights of Translation reserved.

LONDON: T. RICHARDS, 37, GREAT QUEEN STREET.

PREFACE

TO THE

SECOND EDITION.

Since the first edition of the *Mysore Reversion* was published in January 1865, two events, calculated to affect materially the ultimate settlement in this matter, have occurred,—the Rajah's formal and public adoption of a son on the 18th June, 1865 ; and the appearance of the Papers Relating to Mysore, moved for by Sir Henry Rawlinson in the House of Commons, on the 27th February, 1866.

It may be gathered, as well from the contents of the Blue-Book as from general conversation, that there are four current objections to the restoration of a Native Government in Mysore. (1) The reversionary right of the Paramount Power to take that country by "lapse" ; (2) the duty of the Paramount Power to secure a good administration for the People ; (3) the great weight and authority of those who recommend the annexation ; and (4) the necessity of our Government maintaining at all hazards the consistency and inflexibility of its own well-considered decisions. In the following pages I have attempted to dispose of the two first objections. A few words must be said here as to the two last.

The argument of authority amounts to little more than this,—that five successive occupants of the Viceregal Chair, Lords Dalhousie, Canning and Elgin, Sir William Denison and Sir John Lawrence, have all returned adverse replies

to the Rajah's repeated applications; and that a majority
of the Council of India, the constitutional advisers of Her
Majesty's Secretary of State, have also decided against his
Highness's claims. This formidable array is, however, much
weaker than it appears at the first glance.

No one can have any doubt that Lord Dalhousie would
have annexed Mysore on the demise of the reigning Rajah.
But he would have done so by the same process that was
used to dispose of the Sattara, Nagpore, and Jhansi States,
and the mediatised Principality of the Carnatic; and as his
constant supporter, Mr. Mangles, has done in this instance,
he would have adduced the worst of these cases as satisfactory precedents. So that if we accept Lord Dalhousie
as an authority, we must approve in general the principles,
the procedure and the results of his territorial acquisitions.
And I trust that no British statesman, except perhaps the
Duke of Argyll, is at the present day prepared to go quite
as far as that.

Lord Canning was not really hostile to the Rajah's right
of adopting a successor. He admitted it in principle, and
withdrew from those false positions under which for some
years the unjust prerogative of nullifying adoptions had
been practised. He unquestionably looked upon Mysore
as a very desirable acquisition; but he had been misled
into the belief that the Rajah did not wish to adopt a son,
and would bequeath his dominions to the British Government. Lord Canning cannot be quoted as an authority adverse to the Rajah's rights.

Lord Elgin's lamented death after so brief a tenure of
office has left in doubt the course he would have taken.
It is understood that he was desirous of negotiating a settlement of the Rajah's claim of restoration by a sort of
compromise. Lord Elgin's authority, therefore, is by no
means injurious to the Rajah's cause.

Sir William Denison was called unexpectedly to take

provisional charge of the Viceregal office, and the letter of the 31st December, 1863, communicating the refusal of the Home Government to replace the Rajah at the head of his own administration, was obviously signed by him as a simple matter of routine. He could not have avoided explaining the Secretary of State's decision. The more important question of maintaining or destroying the State of Mysore arose at a later date, and did not demand the consideration either of Lord Elgin or of Sir William Denison.

Whatever may have been the views expressed by Sir John Lawrence since he returned to the latitude of Calcutta, he is understood to have been favourably disposed towards the Rajah, when he was a member of the Council in the more pure and free atmosphere of London. I think I have succeeded in proving in the succeeding pages that his altered opinions are not the result of a more careful scrutiny of the facts, or of a deeper consideration of causes and consequences.

The mass of Viceregal authority is thus reduced after our analysis to that of Lord Dalhousie and his most distinguished Lieutenant ; and the annexation of Mysore is seen to be a mere return to that policy which has shaken throughout Asia the belief in British honour, and which has been denounced, more or less plainly, by every leading statesman of Great Britain.

But let us turn to the other side, and read the list of those who are known to have supported, and who now recommend, the policy of good faith, restitution and solid reform. Lord William Bentinck, who, under the influence of exaggerated reports, assumed the management of Mysore, regretted the hasty step he had taken, and proposed the Rajah's restoration to the head of a more limited Government. His two immediate successors, Lord Metcalfe and Lord Auckland, concurred in the advisability of restoring

the Rajah to power, and the former characterised the suspension of his Highness as "a harsh and unprovoked measure." Sir William Hay Macnaghten, who was Foreign
Secretary at Calcutta, when that Report of 1833 was submitted which first revealed to Lord William Bentinck the
truth about Mysore, has left in writing his opinion that the
Rajah had been " visited with undue severity", and his wish
that " a portion of his country should be restored to him."
Lord Hardinge recorded his doubts of the legality of the
Rajah's supersession.

Lord Glenelg, who had been President of the Board of
Control when the Government of Mysore was taken out of
the Rajah's hands, was always of opinion that our action
ought to have been curative, not destructive of the dependent State ; and to the last day of his long life the
venerable statesman was anxious to hear of the Rajah's
full restoration.

The late Mr. Casamajor, who was Resident at Mysore
when the Rajah was superseded, and General Briggs, who
was the first Commissioner for the government of Mysore
after the supersession, have both declared that the total
exclusion of the Rajah from public life was unnecessarily
severe, and has been unwarrantably prolonged. General
Briggs, who after a long and distinguished career in India,
has won a reputation in Europe by his labours in Oriental
literature, history and statistics, has signed a petition to
the House of Commons, (presented on the 10th August,
1866,) praying that Mysore may not be annexed, but that
a native government may be reestablished, " with every
possible security for British interests, and for the prosperity
and happiness of the people of the country."

That petition was also signed by General Sir John Low,
late Member of the Supreme Council of India ; by General
J. S. Fraser, for fifteen years Resident at Hyderabad, and
previously Resident at Travancore and at Mysore ; by

Colonel Haines, late Judicial Commissioner of Mysore; by Major-General White of the Madras Army, who was Assistant to the Resident of Mysore, when the Rajah's personal government was suspended; by Sir Robert Hamilton, late Governor-General's Agent in Central India; by General Le Grand Jacob, whose influence and popularity with the Chiefs and leading men, and his abilities both as a soldier and a civil ruler, alone prevented the flame of rebellion from spreading in 1857-8 over Kolapore and the Southern Mahratta Country; by Mr. W. H. Bayley, late Secretary to the Madras Government; by Colonel French, late Resident at Jodhpore and at Baroda; by Mr. T. L. Blane, late a Member of the Madras Board of Revenue; by Colonel G. Williams, formerly Commissioner of Military Police, and who was by Lord Canning's side throughout those critical months of the insurrection, when the government of the North West Provinces was conducted at Allahabad by the Viceroy himself; by Captain Felix Jones, late Resident in the Persian Gulf; by Captain Frushard, late of the Indian Navy, and by about fifty other gentlemen, many of them having served in the Civil and Military Services of India, and many being well known as authors and men of science.

Only two of the majority in the Council of India, Mr. Mangles and Mr. Prinsep, have attempted to put into writing some answer to the powerful arguments of their five colleagues, Sir George Clerk, Sir Henry Montgomery, Sir John Willoughby, Captain Eastwick, and Sir Frederick Currie. My readers must judge how I have dealt with the Minutes of these two Councillors, who, as I have shown, are so deeply committed by their antecedent acts and pledges, that a strong bias about the Rajah's claims could hardly fail to be entertained by both of them.

It can scarcely be said, after due consideration of these facts, that the balance of authority inclines against the opinion held by the minority of the Council of India.

There remains to be considered what may be called the argument of *prestige*. It has been urged that the reversal of a decision, deliberately and repeatedly promulgated by the Viceroy of India in Council, and approved by the Secretary of State, would ruin the *prestige* of Government, and—to make use of words attributed to an official of rank at Calcutta—would shake the very foundations of British power.

This argument appears to me not only to be devoid of all moral principle, but to be directly opposed to sound political science. The *prestige* of an Imperial Government —that awe and respect by which order and obedience are preserved among its subjects and its dependent Allies,—is based partly on a belief in its material resources, partly on faith in its moral superiority. The obstinate maintenance of an unjust decree, after its injustice has been publicly exposed, cannot augment material strength, and must destroy moral influence. Such persistent wrong does not even tend to strike terror ; it rather inspires disdain.

No doubt when the professional rulers of Calcutta have written " able" and " elaborate" Minutes, despatches, demi-official and private letters innumerable, in defence of a decision embodying all their traditional and characteristic prejudices, until they have set their hearts on the issue, the reversal of that decision must be extremely mortifying to them, and must diminish their personal *prestige* very much with the outer world. And I can fully understand and admit that anything which lowers the credit and dignity of the higher officials, especially of the Viceregal Government, in the eyes of the people of India, is so far disadvantageous and regrettable. But the counterbalancing disadvantages of refusing redress, would be very much greater in many cases, and eminently in this particular case. Such a refusal would not only lower the credit of the Government of India more than could possibly be done by the reversal of their decision, but would carry discredit into more remote and vital regions of the State : it would dishonour Her Majesty's Government ; it would sully the Crown. Loss of respect for the Crown would be much more hurtful to the Empire than loss of respect for any individual Minister or Lieutenant, however exalted in rank or station. The officials of the day, their exploits and their failures, their glories and their mortifications, come and go, and pass away ; but the Imperial Government remains ; and if it accepts and confirms a wrong, can never shift the responsibility, or shake off the stigma. The loss of credit to a Judge, when his decree is reversed on appeal, is very trifling ; but the general administration of justice would fall into complete disrepute if appeals were never heard, and every decree were irreversible. In political affairs, where there is no code of substantive law, an unlimited right of appeal is absolutely essential ; and if the appellate jurisdiction is seen in important matters to be no idle form, no real discredit need fall on the " Court below." And even if the Provincial Government be so deeply committed by its previous pertinacity that it cannot accept a defeat without some little show of discomfiture, the love and honour gained for the general system of Imperial Government, would far outweigh the temporary disparagement, if any there be, that is thrown on local authority.

When, for instance, the little Principality of Dhar was at last restored to the administration of its native Ruler, in consequence of the public-spirited efforts of the most vigilant and energetic of Indian Reformers, Mr. John Dickinson, no doubt the effect was by no means pleasant to the feelings of Sir John Lawrence and Colonel Durand, —more especially of the latter, who, in his successive capacities, as Political Agent in Central India, as Member of the Council in London, and as Foreign Secretary at Calcutta, had endeavoured first to secure the annexation of

Dhar, then its management for an indefinite period by a British officer, and lastly the imposition upon the Rajah of a Minister who was personally disagreeable to him.*   When the Government of India was driven from these positions one after the other, and directed to carry out a real restoration, in consequence of Mr. Dickinson's persevering exposure, and the firmness of Lord Stanley, then in opposition, who as Secretary of State had originally saved the Rajah from the dethronement recommended by Colonel Durand, that officer in particular, and several members of the Government of India, may naturally have felt as if a slight had been cast upon their judgment and discretion, and may have feared that their personal weight and credit would be lowered in the eyes of the public,   And to a certain extent this fear may have been well-founded.   But most certainly the prestige and popularity of the Imperial Government were not lowered but raised, nor was the cheerful allegiance of the Princes and Chieftains of Central India weakened, but, on the contrary, strengthened, by the restoration of Dhar, after a period of beneficial and frugal management, the credit of which is almost entirely due, as I willingly admit, to the judicious instructions of the Calcutta Foreign Office.   The successful examples of Dhar, Kolapore, and Travancore, restored to their native Princes after effectual reformation, will form better precedents for the settlement of Mysore than the disastrous cases of Sattara and Jhansi.

The generous concessions of the Sovereign, in a time of peace and prosperity, do not produce an impression of weakness, but of strength and confidence.   And a great work of restitution may easily be conducted as a royal act of grace and favour, so as to convey no ostensible censure or reproof to those who have hitherto opposed it.

* *Dhar not Restored*, and *A Sequel to Dhar not Restored*, by John Dickinson, F.R.A.S., (King, Parliament Street,) 1864 and 1865 ; and the Parliamentary Papers, *Further Correspondence Relating to Dhar*, 1865.

The real political danger in India is not what it has been recently represented. The danger is not that the Viceroy's authority will be despised, but the Queen's. There is no danger that the tributary and protected Princes and their Ministers and adherents will learn to look for orders to London instead of Calcutta in ordinary matters. The danger is that if in their extraordinary emergencies an appeal to Great Britain is found to be nugatory, they may say in their despair, " There is no Imperial Power ; there is no Parliament ; there is no Sovereign over us ; there is only a Collector."

PREFACE

THE FIRST EDITION.

I THINK that any one who candidly and carefully peruses the following pages, will find that they are not open to certain plausible and obvious objections—that they are not written to represent a mere isolated grievance—that no claim is set forth here of despotic power for an Indian Rajah, on "divine right" principles, and at the expense of an industrious population, contented and prosperous under British management. It will be seen that I do not ask for the toleration of old abuses in the face of accomplished facts and altered circumstances, or insist upon an over-scrupulous devotion to letter and precedent in favour of a Prince, without regard to the spirit of engagements, without protecting the interests of the people.

This book is not written merely to propose the reconsideration of this case of Mysore, but to suggest a reconsideration of all the relations of the Imperial Power to the minor States of India ; to show how, in Mysore, we neglected our earliest duties of instruction and guidance—how, grasping at patronage, we have hitherto thrown away the opportunity of establishing a limited monarchy as a model and exemplar—and how, by abolishing that Principality, we should, in all probability, throw away the opportunity for ever, and retard, or finally obstruct, the progress of Indian reform, and the relief of our scattered military strength.

I shall endeavour to prove, that although the expected Mysore Reversion is not by any means "an Exceptional Case", in the sense of the official document which I quote, it is so far exceptional that the appropriation of this State would be exceptionally unjust, injurious, imprudent, and unprofitable.

And while I argue that statements disparaging a Prince's personal conduct or mental qualifications—unless asserting crime or idiocy—are as irrelevant to a question of his sovereignty and his regal position in India, as they would be in Europe, I shall show that this Prince's derelictions have been much exaggerated, and that their origin in British neglect has been completely overlooked ; that his conduct was never so blameable, and that his abilities are not so deficient, as to warrant his permanent exclusion from power, or to offer the slightest excuse or pretext for extinguishing the tributary State.

But I have not written the following pages as an apologist or an advocate for the Rajah of Mysore. I do not plead for the Rajah's personal advantage and dignity, I plead for the advantage and elevation of his people, and of the people of India, and for the general good of the British Empire.

I will yield to no one in the admiration I feel for those eminent men in the Indian Services, whose achievements in days of war and convulsion, and whose earnest labours in the time of peaceful organisation, have conferred so many blessings upon India. Let the fullest meed of honour and gratitude be awarded to our great Indian administrators— but let them be confined to their own sphere. The field of Indian administration is the very worst training-ground for Indian government. I do not say that it is absolutely impossible for a Collector or a Resident to rise above the small successes of his official career to broad views of Imperial policy ; but I certainly think it is highly improbable. The exceptions, though brilliant, have been very few. I think, moreover, that in the present day, the work and associations of an Indian administrator are even less likely to inspire him with enlarged and tolerant principles, and more likely to fill his mind with narrow technicalities and contemptuous prejudices, than they were forty or fifty years ago. Native States were then substantive Powers in India; native Princes and Ministers were looked upon as worthy opponents or coadjutors.

I must confess to considerable distrust and dread of a purely professional Government,—composed of members of a close official guild,—untempered by a well-defined Imperial policy, unmitigated by the presence of a British statesman as Viceroy, unwatched by Parliament, unmindful of popular feelings. The professional ruler must magnify his office ; to him it always appears an incontrovertible position, that "whate'er is best administered is best,"—an opinion which is probably entertained by a great many people in Great Britain, with reference to India, but which seems to me to be opposed to the first principles of modern politics, and to be fraught with infinite mischief.

But, it may be said, there are certain facts that cannot be denied—they speak for themselves ; the results of British administration are beneficial, the revenue and trade of India are increasing, the people are contented and prosperous. No one can assert more strongly than I do that British rule has conferred and is conferring the greatest benefits upon India. I object to the progress of annexation and uniformity, because it neutralises and debases those benefits, and endangers the stability of our reforming operations. I admit that in most provinces of India the people are in a thriving and improving condition. But that the population in general, or the reflecting and influential classes in particular, are politically contented, indifferent or apathetic, I must distinctly deny.

It does not follow as a matter of course, that a period of material prosperity is always a period of political tranquillity. Jeshurun waxed fat and kicked.

Nor does it follow as a matter of course, that a period of material prosperity is to last for ever. Because we dare not predict disaster, do not you presumptuously prophesy smooth things. Twenty years, thirty years, fill up a small space in history, form but a brief term in the life of a nation. Can we not look forward so far ? We may have goods laid up in store for many years ; we may eat, drink, and be merry, but the day may come—a day of reckoning for our stewardship—when a soul shall be required of us ; and it may then be found that there is no soul in our Indian Empire, but that it is possessed of a devil.

CONTENTS.

APPENDIX.

THE MYSORE REVERSION,

AN "EXCEPTIONAL CASE."

CHAPTER I.

THE REVIVAL OF ANNEXATION.

"We hereby announce to the Native Princes of India that all Treaties and Engagements made with them by or under the authority of the Honourable East India Company, are by Us accepted, and will be scrupulously maintained; and We look for the like observance on their part.

"We desire no extension of Our present territorial possessions; and, while we will permit no aggression upon Our dominions or Our rights to be attempted with impunity, We shall sanction no encroachment on those of others. We shall respect the rights, dignity, and honour of Native Princes as Our own ; and we desire that they, as well as Our subjects, should enjoy that prosperity and that social advancement which can only be secured by internal peace and good government."—PROCLAMATION BY THE QUEEN IN COUNCIL TO THE PRINCES, CHIEFS, AND PEOPLE OF INDIA, 1st November, 1858.

FOUR years ago, about the time when Lord Canning's important despatch of the 30th April, 1860, on the right of Adoption by native Princes, was published, it did really seem as if the era of annexation in India was closed. The unequivocal and weighty assurances of Her Majesty's Proclamation were hailed as the Magna Charta of the minor States. And even those unconverted and unrepentant officials—some of them men of great merit and ability, such as the late General Sir Mark Cubbon—who deplored that solemn and public statement of principles, declared that its pledges must be scrupulously respected, that its Royal origin forbade all tampering with its terms, and that it constituted an absolute bar to any further territorial acquisitions, except by open war.

During the perilous crisis of 1857, the most serviceable
and timely aid in men and money was furnished by every
class of native rulers, by independent allies, by protected
tributaries, and by feudatory Chieftains ; but the value of
this material aid was far exceeded by the moral effect of
their firm and loyal adherence. Lord Canning then learned
to admit—to make use of his own words—that "the safety
of our rule is increased, not diminished, by the maintenance
of Native Chiefs well affected to us. Setting aside," he
continues, " the well-known services rendered by Scindia,
and subsequently by the Maharajahs of Rewa, Chirkaree,
and others, over the wide tract of Central India, where our
authority is most broken in upon by Native States, I venture to say that there is no man who remembers the condition of Upper India in 1857 and 1858, and who is not
thankful that in the centre of the large and compact British province of Rohilcund there remained the solitary little
State of Rampoor, still administered by its own Mahomedan
Prince, and that on the borders of the Punjaub and of the
districts above Delhi, the Chief of Puttiala and his kinsmen still retained their hereditary authority unimpaired.
In the time of which I speak, these patches of Native Government served as breakwaters to the storm which would
otherwise have swept over us in one great wave."*

The grand and terrible events of 1857 did rouse the
nation, the statesmen of Great Britain, the rulers of India,
to something like enthusiasm, and under its influence—and
in spite of the irresistible exasperation of the hour—many
noble principles were avowed, some of which were embodied
in the Royal Proclamation, and in other official documents.
But the excitement soon died away, upon the restoration of
order. When none but financial difficulties remained, and
when even these were surmounted, the season of self-com-
placent apathy set in once more. And now, in this time
of our wealth, security and pride, there is a manifest tendency to depreciate our obligations to the native Princes,
and to renew pretensions which, it may be said, have never
been abandoned, except by way of grace and favour.

Almost every statesman of eminence, of all parties and

* Adoption Despatch, paragraph 34 ; Appendix A.

in both Houses of Parliament, sought for occasions during the Sessions of 1857 and 1858, to condemn emphatically the policy of annexation; one and all concurred in attributing the rebellion in a great measure to the bad spirit which that policy had created. Even so late as the 4th of August, 1864, Lord Stanley made use of the following words in a speech before the Liverpool Chamber of Commerce :—"This he might say, they had never had an abler Governor-General, or an administration at Calcutta more thoroughly peaceable in its intentions, or with a more fixed determination not to carry on that policy of annexation of which so much was heard fifteen years ago." In short, every one would have supposed that the tide of greedy acquisition of territory had ebbed at last, and for ever.

But it is a painful fact that the present Governor-General and the present administration at Calcutta are actually engaged in carrying on that same policy of annexation, that they are carrying it on by the discarded and discredited process of ignoring an adoption, and that this process now menaces the most friendly, the most tractable, the most orderly, and to us the most profitable native State that still exists in India. The tide of greedy acquisition ebbed for a time, but it has turned again, and, if not checked, will soon commence to sweep away in its course many of our neighbours' landmarks, and the bulwarks of our own Empire.

Lord Canning recommended his measures in 1860, for securing to every Chief above the rank of a Jaghiredar the right of adopting a successor, according to the Hindoo law, because, said he, it will " show at once, and for ever, that we are not lying in wait for opportunities of absorbing territory, and that we do deliberately desire to keep alive a feudal aristocracy where one still exists."* "And," he added, in that same despatch, "should the day come when India shall be threatened by an external enemy, or when the interests of England elsewhere may require that her Eastern Empire shall incur more than ordinary risk, one of our best mainstays will be found in these native States. But to make them so, we must treat their Chiefs and influential

* Paragraph 26; Appendix A.

families with consideration and generosity, teaching them that, in spite of all suspicions to the contrary, their independence is safe, that we are not waiting for plausible opportunities to convert their country into British territory, and convincing them that they have nothing to gain by helping to displace us in favour of any new rulers from within or from without."

But I shall prove that we are now "lying in wait" for "a plausible opportunity" to absorb territory to which we have no manner of claim or title whatever; that when Lord Canning penned those lines he was, with strange inconsistency and instability of purpose, himself "lying in wait" for that same territory; that the British Government is now visibly "lying in wait" until the death of the Rajah of Mysore, who has passed the age of threescore years and ten, to pounce upon that Principality without a shadow of right or justice.

Among the distinguished officers who, under the Governor-General's instructions, negotiated the Treaties of 1799 with the representatives of the Rajah of Mysore and the Nizam, there was one great man, then known as Colonel Arthur Wellesley, who foresaw that a measure of resumption might be planned at some future period, and warned his brother, Lord Mornington, in the following emphatic terms, to provide against the possibility of such a breach of faith :—

"Colonel Kirkpatrick will have written to you yesterday respecting the 6th Article of the Subsidiary Treaty. We all agreed that that ought to be modified in some manner. As it now stands, it will give ground for the belief *that we give the Rajah the country at the present moment with the intention of taking it away again when it will suit our convenience.* Supposing that the candid and generous policy of the present Government should weaken that belief as far as it regards them, it must be allowed that the conduct of the British Government in India has not at all times been such as to induce the natives to believe that at some time or other improper advantage will not be taken of that Article. They know as well as we do that there may be a change of government immediately, and that there certainly will be one in the course of a few years, and the person then appointed Governor General may not have such enlarged systems of policy as those by which we are regulated at the present moment. This induces me to believe, that they will object strongly to that

Article, and I don't think that it will be very creditable to us to insist upon it."*

The Governor-General did insist upon that Article; an improper advantage was taken of that Article; in the course of years the candid and generous policy of Government did become weakened; and in the present day the intention is too clearly manifested of taking away the country of Mysore, because it is supposed to suit our convenience.

The policy of annexation flagged after the shock of 1857, and went out of fashion for several years, but symptoms of its revival have lately presented themselves. A decided reaction has set in; peace and prosperity have lasted long enough to restore the national complacency, and to reinstate in the public confidence those who are officially responsible for the local management of India. The reins of government are committed to the hands of an eminent Bengal Civilian, the most active and able participator in that process of annexing provinces and resuming large estates which for a brief time had seemed to be for ever discredited and abandoned.

The ultimate disposal of the Mysore territories at the demise of the reigning Rajah, will probably, and may very reasonably be made to depend upon the answers that are finally given to the following three questions :—

1. HAS THE BRITISH GOVERNMENT ANY RIGHT TO ANNEX THOSE TERRITORIES ?

2. WOULD THE ANNEXATION BE BENEFICIAL TO THE PEOPLE OF MYSORE ?

3. WOULD THE ANNEXATION BE ADVANTAGEOUS TO THE BRITISH EMPIRE ?

I presume that our Government would at present answer these questions in the affirmative. I shall endeavour to show that all three questions ought to be met with an absolute negative. I hope to produce a conviction so decided

---

* Wellington's Supplementary Despatches, vol. i, p. 244. This letter was written before the Treaty was concluded; and the Article which is here called "the 6th" can only be Article IV. The discrepancy may be due to a subsequent alteration of the draft, or perhaps to some clerical or typographical confusion between "IV" and "VI."

of the injustice, impolicy, and imprudence of the meditated annexation, as may lead to some decided action in the Cabinet or in Parliament, and may once more place the Home authorities in distinct antagonism to that policy of bad faith and disguised rapacity by which, during the last twenty years, the officials of Calcutta have destroyed the fair fame of Great Britain in the East, and undermined the foundations of our Indian Empire.

CHAPTER II.

MYSORE FROM 1799 TO 1856.

ABOUT four centuries ago two brothers of that tribe of
Yedava Rajpoots, to which Krishna, the deified hero of
Dwarka in Guzerat, is said to have belonged, left the great
Hindoo capital of Beejanuggur, and travelled South in
search of adventures. One of them is said to have married,
under very romantic circumstances, the daughter of a
wealthy landholder in the neighbourhood of Seringapatam,
whose Canarese title of Wadiyar, or Lord, adopted by his
son-in-law, when he succeeded to the estate, became the
hereditary distinction of their descendants. Such is the
origin of the Rajahs of Mysore, according to the annals of
their court poets and genealogists.

For many years the Wadiyars extended their possessions
by subduing the neighbouring chieftains ; they assumed the
title of Rajah, but paid tribute and homage to Beejanuggur.
But from the subversion of that last great Hindoo State, in
1564, by the four Mahomedan Kings of Dowlutabad, Beejapoor, Golconda, and Beder, the Mysore Rajahs may be considered as independent Princes. One of them commenced
to coin money in his own name in the year 1654 ; and another, during the reign of the Mogul Emperor Aurungzeb,
claimed and established the right of sitting on an ivory
throne. The Mysore State, though sometimes reduced to
ceremonial homage, and to the payment of ransom or tribute, always maintained its autonomy against the successive
pretensions of the Mahomedan Kings of Beejapoor, the
Mahrattas, and the Nizam ; and enlarged its boundaries
during the political convulsions attending the fall of the
Mogul Empire, which altered the whole political aspect of
the Deccan.

On the death of the Rajah Chick Deo Raj in 1731, his
successor, a minor, became a mere puppet in the hands of
the Dalway, or hereditary Minister, a veritable Maire du

Palais. A succession of military and financial exigencies, with which no one else was capable of dealing, at length threw all the power of the State into the hands of the celebrated Hyder Ali, who had commenced his career as a simple trooper. Hyder Ali always kept up the form of annually presenting the captive Rajah, as their Sovereign, to the assembled people at the Dusserah festival, while he took the place himself of Commander-in-chief and Minister; but this custom was discontinued by Tippoo, who himself assumed all the style and emblems of royalty, to which his father had never pretended.

Counting from the final ruin of Hyder's patron and rival, the Hindoo minister, Nunjeraj, in 1761, to the death of Tippoo Sultan in the storm of his great stronghold, in 1799, the Mussulman ascendancy in Mysore only lasted for thirty-eight years.

Lord Wellesley's first plan after Seringapatam was taken, was that of recognising one of Tippoo's sons ; but he was deterred from this settlement chiefly, by a dread of French influence, and partly, also, by a regard for the " antiquity" of the Hindoo royal family's " legitimate title." He writes to Dundas, the 7th of June, 1799 :—" It would certainly have been desirable that the power should have been placed in the hands of one of Tippoo's sons ; but the hereditary and intimate connexion established between Tippoo and the French, the probability that the French may be enabled to maintain themselves in Egypt, and the perpetual interest which Tippoo's family must feel to undermine and subvert a system which had so much reduced their patrimony and power, precluded the possibility of restoring any branch of the family of the late Sultan to the throne, without exposing us to the constant hazard of internal commotion, and even of foreign war."*

Sound policy thus forbidding the maintenance of the House of Tippoo, the Governor General naturally turned to the representative of the royal family of Mysore, whose rights had been usurped by Hyder Ali. " Between the British Government and this family," writes Lord Wellesley to the Court of Directors on the 3rd of August, 1799, " an

---

* Wellesley's Despatches, vol. ii, p. 36.

intercourse of friendship and kindness had subsisted in the most desperate crisis of their adverse fortunes." Lord Wellesley here alludes to the negotiations carried on in 1782 with the agents of Cham Raj, father of the present Rajah, which resulted in a Treaty of alliance, ratified by the Government of Madras on the 27th of November in that year; in consequence of which the Hindoo Prince's flag was hoisted on the walls of Caroor, when that fort was taken, on the 2nd of April, 1783, by Colonel Lang. The conspiracy of the Rajah's adherents in Mysore, which led to these negotiations, was, however, discovered and crushed by Tippoo; and in 1783 the Honourable Company made peace with the Sultan, and in the next year concluded a Treaty with him.* "They had formed," continues Lord Wellesley, " no connection with your enemies. Their elevation would be the spontaneous act of your generosity, and from your support alone could they ever hope to be maintained upon the throne, either against the family of Tippoo Sultan, or against any other claimant. They must naturally view with an eye of jealousy all the friends of the usurping family, and consequently be adverse to the French, or to any other State connected with that family in its hereditary hatred of the British Government."

"In addition to these motives of policy, moral considerations and sentiments of generosity and humanity, favoured the restoration of the ancient family of Mysore. Their high birth, the antiquity of their legitimate title, and their long and unmerited sufferings, rendered them peculiar objects of compassion and respect; nor could it be doubted that their government would be both more acceptable and more indulgent than that of the Mahomedan usurpers, to the mass of the inhabitants of the country, composed almost entirely of Hindoos."†

And his instructions to the Commissioners appointed by him for the settlement of Mysore affairs were to the same effect :—

---

* *Historical Sketches of Southern India and Mysore,* by `Colonel Mark Wilks, 1817, vol. ii, p. 488-500. A copy of the Treaty of 1782, for the restoration of the Hindoo dynasty of Mysore, will be found in vol. v of the Calcutta Collection of 1864, p. 183. (Longman and Co.)

† Wellesley's Despatches, vol. ii, p. 81-82.

"The restoration of the representative of the ancient family of the Rajahs of Mysore, accompanied by a partition of territory between the Allies, in which the interests of the Mahrattas should be conciliated, appearing to me, under all the circumstances of the case, to be the most advisable basis on which any new settlement of the country can be vested, I have resolved to frame without delay a plan founded on these principles."*

I have already quoted a passage in which Lord Wellesley describes the recognition of the Hindoo Prince as "an act of spontaneous generosity." This was the fundamental principle upon which that great statesman based the whole transaction as between the Allies and the Mysore family :—

"From the justice and success of the late war with Tippoo Sultan," he writes to the Court of Directors, "the Company and the Nizam derived an undoubted right to the disposal of the dominions conquered by their united arms. The right of conquest entitled the Company and the Nizam to retain the whole territory in their own hands ; the cession of it to any other party might be a consideration of policy or humanity, but could not be claimed on any ground of justice or right."

"A lineal descendant of the ancient House of the Rajahs of Mysore still remained at Seringapatam ; but whatever might be the hopes of his family from the moderation and humanity of the conquerors, this young Prince could assert no right to any share of the conquered territory."†

The investiture of the Rajah with the character of a Sovereign was deliberately treated by Lord Wellesley, not as the restoration of an old Government and dynasty, but as the creation of a new one. It appears from his letter of the 7th of June, 1799, that according to the original draft of the Treaty the whole of the conquered territories were to be considered as the Rajah's dominions, and the provinces to be retained by the Allies were to be accepted by them as if ceded by the Hindoo Sovereign. To this process the Governor General objected. "I think," said he, "the whole transaction would be more conveniently thrown into a different form from that which you have given to it. I

* Wellesley's Despatches, vol. ii, p. 19.   † Ibid., vol. ii, p. 72.

do not see any necessity for ceding the whole country, in the first instance, to the Rajah of Mysore, and accepting again as a cession under his authority such districts as must be retained by the Allies. I think it will be more convenient, and less liable to future embarrassment, to rest the whole settlement upon the basis of our right of conquest, and thus to render our cession the source of the Rajah's dominion. For this purpose the proceeding should commence with a Treaty between the Nizam and the Company."*

But while Lord Wellesley thus upheld, on behalf of the Allies, their right of disposing of all the conquered territories in such a manner, and in such recorded terms, as should be a perpetual acknowledgment of the Rajah's obligations, and a perpetual bar to the revival of any pretensions to the sovereignty of the districts allotted to the Company and the Nizam, he intimated no design of depressing the restored Prince into an insignificant and insecure position. On the contrary, he was avowedly desirous to welcome the Sovereign of Mysore as a distinct and additional Power in India, pledged to the reciprocal recognition and defence of our titles and possessions, for he instructs the Commissioners that " the Rajah, after his accession, may be made a party to the general guarantee."†

The infant Rajah's elevation was opposed at the time by several of Lord Wellesley's advisers, and by none more than by Sir Thomas Munro, who held that we should divide between ourselves and our sole Ally, the Nizam, the whole of the conquered districts. But all objections were overruled ; a separate government for Mysore was constituted ; Poorniah, the able Brahmin, who had been Tippoo's chief officer of finance, was appointed Prime Minister, and for eleven years managed the country with great skill and success, so far as relates to the augmentation and collection of the revenue.

Poorniah was a clever financial officer, and would have been invaluable as a manager to one of the by-gone type of " crack" Collectors who, in the first twenty years of this century, gained an ephemeral reputation by putting on the

---

* Wellesley's Despatches, vol. ii, p. 26.   † Ibid.

screw in certain districts of the Madras Presidency and the North West Provinces. He had practised his art in a severe school. During the last seven years of Tippoo's reign, when the Sultan obstinately insisted on keeping up enormous military establishments on a revenue reduced by Lord Cornwallis's Partition to one half of its former amount, Poorniah was driven to exercise his greatest dexterity in squeezing the unfortunate population. And until the end of the year 1804 the demands of the Honourable Company on the Government of Mysore, under Article III of the Treaty, for its contribution "towards the increased expenses" of the war with the Mahrattas, seem to have precluded any mitigation of the public burdens. During Poorniah's administration the pressure was never relaxed. No imputation seems ever to have been cast upon his personal integrity, and when, in the year 1811, he was compelled to resign his office, he left a sum of hard cash in the Treasury exceeding two millions sterling. This fund was not, however, entirely due to savings from the public income, but was swelled by the gradual sale of vast stores of sandalwood—the special produce of Mysore and monopolised by the Government—and of other superfluous stock which had been heaped up in every department during the reign of Tippoo. The people did not prosper under Poorniah's rule, and little or nothing was done by him in the way of public improvement. Sir Mark Cubbon, in his Report to Government, as Commissioner of Mysore in 1854, alludes to the accumulated treasure "which the dubious policy of Poorniah had wrung from the people."

After the departure of Sir John Malcolm, the first Resident at Mysore, in 1804, Poorniah was left to pursue his own plans, undisturbed and uninstructed by the Government of Madras, or their representative the Resident. The young Rajah was left to the enlightened tuition of his mother, his grandmother, and the other ladies of the harem. Systematic negligence, in its most culpable form, characterised the dealings of the Madras Government with the pupil State committed to their charge by Lord Wellesley's arrangements.

From 1799 till 1832, with a very brief interval, the British Resident at the Court of Mysore was in direct communication only with the Madras authorities, from whom he received his instructions ; while the Madras Government reported its proceedings to the Supreme Government in Bengal. The plan never seems to have worked well. The authority and the responsibility were too much divided. The Duke of Wellington—then General Wellesley—in a letter to Major Shawe, dated the 14th of January, 1804, gives us the strong opinion on this subject of a very shrewd observer of men and manners who had had the best opportunities of forming a judgment, and affords us another instance of his remarkable foresight as to the course of Mysore affairs.

"In respect to Mysore," says he, "I recommend that a gentleman from the Bengal Civil Service shall be Malcolm's successor there. The Government of that country should be placed under the immediate protection and superintendence of the Governor General in Council. The Governors of Fort St. George ought to have no more to do with the Rajah than they have with the Souba of the Deccan" (the Nizam) "or the Peishwa. The consequence of the continuance of the present system will be that the Rajah's Government will be destroyed by corruption, or, if they should not be corrupt, by calumny.* I know no person, either civil or military, at Fort St. George, who would set his face against the first evil, or who has strength of character or talents to defend the Government" (meaning clearly the Mysore Government) "against the second. In my opinion the only remedy is to take the Rajah under the wing of the Governor General ; and this can be done effectually only by appointing as Resident a gentleman of the Bengal Civil Service, and by directing him to correspond only with the Governor General."

This advice was acted on for a short period ; but soon after the departure of Sir John Malcolm's successor, Colonel Mark Wilks, the Resident was replaced in direct subordination to the Government of Madras, and, under their instructions, continued, down to the year 1832, to carry out that policy of masterly indifference to Mysore affairs—so long as the Subsidy was paid—that was best calculated,

---

* Only those who know some of the secrets of the "political" system in India, will appreciate the full force and significance of this prediction.

whether it was so intended or not, to lead to the Rajah's ruin, and to augment the power and patronage of the Governor of Madras.   And at Calcutta the salutary principles of control relied upon by Lord Wellesley seem to have been completely forgotten.

The most striking and critical instance of this cruel neglect—that to which all the subsequent disorders must be attributed—occurred in December 1811, when, after an unavailing struggle against the Palace party, Poorniah was finally deprived of power, and the Rajah, now sixteen years old, proclaimed his own majority and took the government into his own hands.   The young Prince and his personal followers were not entirely without excuse in effecting this dismissal; for the Brahmin Minister had very clearly evinced the intention of perpetually keeping his Master in luxurious seclusion, and of gaining for himself and his family, after the manner of the Peishwas at Sattara and after the recent precedents in the Mysore State, the position of hereditary Premier and actual ruler of the Kingdom.

Lord Dalhousie, in a Minute dated the 16th of January, 1856, says that the Rajah's "rule was scandalously and hopelessly bad, though he commenced it under every advantage." But what is the fact? Where ought the responsibility for the misrule of Mysore really to-fall?   The British Government, entitled by Article XIV of the Subsidiary Treaty to impose its authoritative advice in any matters connected with " his Highness's interests, the economy of his finances, and the happiness of his people,"* looked on with apparent unconcern while the Regency of its own institution was pulled to the ground; demanded no securities, imposed no authoritative advice, introduced no ordinances, but allowed a boy of sixteen to declare himself of age, and to seize upon absolute power.   Yet Lord Dalhousie says that the Rajah commenced his rule "under every advantage"!

The officials of Calcutta do not hesitate, by what we can only consider a cruel abuse of rhetoric, to call the misgovernment of Mysore "a flagrant and habitual violation of the Treaty."   It was never intended by the Treaty to bind

---

* Appendix B.

down the Rajah to a course of immaculate administration, under the penalty of immediate and perpetual suspension, and the ultimate extinction of the State in the event of failure. He was bound to accept any "regulations and ordinances" imposed by the Company; but none were imposed. He was bound by the very vague obligation of "paying the utmost attention to the advice of the Company's Government;" but he never refused to carry out any specific plan of reform; no such plan was ever laid before him. The controlling action of the British Resident and of the Madras Government was confined to desultory rebukes, and remonstrances in cases of individual grievance.

If the Rajah could really have been said to have failed to fulfil the obligations of Article XIV of the Treaty, by disregarding the advice of the Company's Government, the legitimate consequence would have been, not the total and permanent suspension of his sovereign functions, but that the Governor General would then have been justified in enforcing the obligations of that Article; in which case, as can be seen by the immediate submission of the Rajah to the still more severe measures of 1831, not the slightest obstacle or opposition would or could have been offered by the Mysore Government.

But, far from the obligations of this Article having been enforced by the East India Company, it stands on record that, in the year 1814, the Resident having tendered his advice rather more strongly than usual, the Rajah, then nineteen years of age, sent a confidential agent to Madras expressly to complain of the Resident's interference; the efforts of the young Prince's emissary were successful, and the Resident was instructed by the Madras Government, in a despatch dated the 3rd July, 1814, to receive no more complaints from the subjects of Mysore, to abstain from the avowed support of those whose grievances might become known to him, and "to endeavour to guide the Rajah by advice and admonition delivered in a private and conciliatory manner." Thus, instead of the strict observance of Article XIV being enforced, its relaxation was promoted by the direct orders of the Company's Government. A signal triumph was given to the young Rajah and his corrupt advisers by the moderated instructions which they succeeded in procuring from Madras. It was naturally assumed by the evil-doers that the British Government was not very much in earnest in its remonstrances, when it did not adopt the obvious and most easy mode for giving them full effect.

Sir Henry Montgomery, Member of the Indian Council, writes as follows in his Dissent of the 13th July, 1863 :— " The Maharajah is declared to have failed to have fulfilled the conditions of the Subsidiary Treaty by neglecting the advice of the British Government, though it is well known and officially on record, that not only was no advice rendered, but that it was systematically and purposely withheld."[*] And Sir Frederic Currie says :— " The conditions of the 14th Article of the Treaty the British Government had themselves, it must be admitted, " failed to fulfil," when they systematically withheld from the Rajah the advice which, by that Article, they are bound to give to him in the conduct of every detailed department of the administration. The withholding of that advice, and the withdrawal of the support of the British representative, with their results, are forcibly remarked on by the Commissioners in their Report as to the causes of the rebellion which led to the proceedings adopted by Lord W. Bentinck in 1831."[†]

In the year 1805 General Sir Arthur Wellesley had written to his brother the Marquis Wellesley in the following terms :—" I still fear the new Government of Madras, one of whose objects I believe is to overturn the existing system in Mysore, of which I have hitherto been the principal support."[‡]

The reputation of the Madras Government for purity, and that of Indian officials in general, improved very rapidly after the Duke of Wellington's departure from India, chiefly in consequence of more stringent regulations, and of a large increase in civil salaries ; but this latter reform of itself tended to enhance the value of patronage, and to stimulate the creation of new offices. The hostility to the local self-government of Mysore became even stronger than before in Madras about the year 1820, and seems to have been

---

[*] Papers relating to Mysore, 1866, p. 21. [†] Ditto, p. 22.
[‡] Wellington's Despatches, vol. i, p. 432.

strangely compounded of jealousy against native pretensions and partial independence, the greed of good appointments and a strong desire to obtain the salubrious and pleasant station of Bangalore either as the permanent seat of the Madras Government, or as an occasional residence for the Governor and his Councillors. This last consideration was even urged by Lord William Bentinck upon the Court of Directors in 1834, as an argument in favour of that plan for dividing the Mysore Territories between the Rajah and the East India Company, to which our attention will shortly be called.

A few years after the Rajah assumed the direct government, and while Poorniah's accumulations still supplied ample funds for the expenditure of the Court, the public revenue began to fall off, and serious financial difficulties began to make themselves felt; but these difficulties had their origin in other causes than the mismanagement of the native functionaries. Before the Rajah's accession,—as well under his ancestors as under Hyder and Tippoo,—Mysore was an independent and predatory State, continually enriched by contributions from the surrounding countries, while its entire resources were spent within itself. After the conquest and restoration all external tribute ceased, and the greater part of the seven lakhs of pagodas (£245,000) paid as Subsidy to the East India Company, was absolutely subtracted in hard cash each year from the capital of the country. During the administration of Poorniah this evil was in some degree averted by the large expenditure of the British troops stationed in Mysore. But as that force was reduced, the full extent of the change was felt. Very shortly after the Rajah's installation General Wellesley said of the Mysore administration :—" At this moment it goes on principally by the regular monthly expenditure within it."*

Another cause of distress, which about that time was felt throughout British India, arose from a fall in the price of agricultural produce, which at once caused a corresponding decline in the revenue of Mysore, where the land-tax was payable in kind ; while the annual necessity of finding specie to the full extent of the Subsidy was, as General Wellesley

---

* Supplementary Despatches of the Duke of Wellington, vol. iii, p. 165.

had foreseen, a heavy drain upon the internal wealth of a State which had no external commerce.

The great financial success of Sir Mark Cubbon's administration of Mysore after 1832, was almost entirely owing to his wise attention to improving the means of communication, whereby a constant example and increasing stimulus were given to corresponding improvements in the adjacent districts of Madras and Bombay; and the table-land of Mysore was gradually connected with the plains and the coast. But this development of public works was an idea far in advance of the period during which the Rajah was in power, for years elapsed after the assumption of his country before a single decent road was constructed in the Madras Presidency.

In the year 1825, Sir Thomas Munro, then Governor of Madras,—able and upright, but hostile from the first and prejudiced against the native State,—visited Mysore, and warned the Rajah, that if the disorder in his affairs were not checked, the direct interference of the British Government would soon become unavoidable. In a Minute which the Governor wrote immediately after the interview, he says :—" I concluded by saying that the disorder of the Rajah's affairs had reached such a height as would justify the Government in acting upon the fourth Article of the Treaty; but that as a direct interference in the administration, or the assumption for a time of part of the Mysore territory, could not be undertaken without lessening the dignity of his Highness, and shaking his authority in such a manner that it would be impracticable ever to reestablish it, I was unwilling to adopt such a course until the last extremity, and wished to give him an opportunity of restoring order himself. But if reform were not immediately begun, direct interference would be unavoidable."

The plan of persistently abstaining from active remedies, until the disease became inflammatory and dangerous, although maintained by so eminent an authority as Sir Thomas Munro, will, I think, be pronounced erroneous, even on his own showing, without appealing to its actual effects. Surely it would not have " lessened the dignity of his Highness," or " shaken his authority," if certain " ordinances," dictated by the Governor of Madras under the powers conferred on him by Articles IV and XIV of the Treaty, had been issued by the Rajah in his own name and as his own act, and if the due execution of those ordinances had been secured by the Resident's close supervision, and by the appointment of a trustworthy Minister.

But no decisive step was taken ; no ordinances or regulations were imposed upon the Rajah ; the Governor of Madras took his leave, and the Rajah was once more left to his own devices. The result was what might have been confidently predicted. After the Rajah's triumphant success in staving off interference in 1814, it may be easily understood that he was even less amenable to advice in 1825, and that the faults of his administration had by that time become of such a nature as could not be cured by the mere repetition of remonstrances, unaccompanied by a decisive and authoritative plan of reform. Those who flattered and fleeced the young Prince considered the Governor's inaction to have conferred upon them a fresh lease and a new license. Matters went on from bad to worse.

But even in the midst of administrative negligence, the Rajah's fidelity to the British Government was still conspicuous. The Marquis of Hastings, in an autograph Despatch to the Secret Committee of the Court of Directors, dated 11th July, 1825, finds great fault with the treatment which the Rajah had experienced from the Madras Government, and in prescribing a more generous policy, states that his Highness had performed good and loyal service :—" This policy," he says, " I have wished to see extended to the Court of Mysore ; and I have now augmented motives for the solicitude, in my sense of what is due to the Rajah for very zealous and efficient assistance contributed by him during the late military operations."*

The crisis rapidly advanced after Sir Thomas Munro's abortive visit. The vast hoards of Poorniah's administration had entirely disappeared. Funds were wanted to sustain the extravagant scale of expenditure that had become habitual ; while the revenue was actually declining, and remissions rather than exactions were urgently required.

The condition of the country gradually and steadily dete-

* Mysore Papers, 1866, p. 34.

riorated ; distress and dissatisfaction began to prevail. The Resident's counsel and support were withdrawn. Vague rumours of the expectant and passive hostility of the Madras Government spread over the Principality, and mainly contributed to promote the subsequent insurrection. The North-Western province of Nuggur was in open rebellion in the year 1830, and the disturbances spread to other parts of the country. British troops promptly quelled the revolt ; but Sir Thomas Munro, who had died at his post as Governor of Madras three years before, had left on record his firm convictions that no good could come of the administration of a Prince, against whose original elevation he had protested. The strongly expressed opinion of such a man, whose memory had been recently honoured with an official canonisation, and whose views now appeared as fulfilled predictions, was irresistible, when used by his successor to support his own proposal of superseding the Rajah's authority. Accordingly, Lord William Bentinck, who had become Governor-General of India in 1828, acting on the exaggerated representations of the Madras Government, despatched to the Rajah an intimation, couched in terms of great severity, that, under the provisions of the Treaty of 1799, the British Government had determined to take into its own hands the management of Mysore.* The letter, dated the 7th of September, 1831, was delivered by the British Resident. His Highness surrendered his authority without any altercation or resistance, and two Commissioners appointed by the Madras Government were at once put in charge of all the departments of the State ; a Resident continuing, as before, to maintain at the Rajah's Court the semblance of diplomatic relations between the two Sovereign Powers.

That the eventful restoration of the country was intended from the first by Lord William Bentinck, appears clearly, both from his letter to the Rajah, in which he terms the assumption of the government, " the course which the wisdom of the Marquis Wellesley established for a *crisis* like the present ;" and also from the instructions given by him to the Governor of Madras, that under the two Commis-

* Appendix C.

sioners whom he originally appointed, " the agency should be exclusively native : indeed that the existing native institutions should be carefully maintained." And the Governor General seems very soon to have perceived how little had hitherto been done on our side to instruct and guide the young ruler, and to avert the disorder in his affairs, for early in 1832 he took the step that had been so strongly urged by Sir Arthur Wellesley in 1804, relieved the Madras Government from further interference in the administration of Mysore, and placed it under the direct superintendence of the Governor-General in Council. Lord William Bentinck also appointed a Special Committee of four eminent officials,* to inquire generally into the state of Mysore.

The summary substitution of direct British management was a somewhat harsh remedy for any administrative abuses, when the Treaty gave us the power of dictating and enforcing the acceptance of such " ordinances" as might have removed all cause of offence.

But it must also be remarked that, according to the strict letter of the Treaty (Article IV), neither objections on our part to the Rajah's domestic policy, nor the occurrence of a revolt in his dominions, afforded sufficient grounds for even his temporary supersession, unless the payment of our Subsidy were endangered. Reasonable anxiety for the instalments of annual tribute, was the only cause laid down that could sanction our interference, whether by imposing ordinances, or by the open attachment of districts.

And it must be further remarked that, according to the strict letter of the Treaty (Article IV), when it should be thought necessary to have recourse to this extreme measure, we had no right to attach the whole of Mysore, but only " such part or parts" as should be required to render the funds of the State " efficient and available either in time of peace or war."†

---

* Generals Hawker and Morrison, Mr. John Macleod, and Lieut.-Colonel Cubbon, afterwards for twenty-five years Commissioner of Mysore.

† The whole Article stands as follows : "And whereas it is indispensably necessary that effectual and lasting security should be provided against any failure in the fund destined to defray either the expenses of the permanent military force in time of peace, or the extraordinary expenses described in the third Article of the present Treaty, it is hereby stipulated and agreed between the contracting parties, that whenever the Governor-General in Council shall

Nor did these difficulties long escape the observation of Lord William Bentinck. In a despatch to the Secret Committee of the Court of Directors, dated the 14th of April, 1834, he writes as follows :—

"By the adoption of the arrangement which I advocate, certain doubts will be removed which I cannot help entertaining, both as to the legality and the justice, according to a strict interpretation, of the course that has been pursued. The Treaty warrants an assumption of the country with a view to secure the payment of our Subsidy. The assumption was actually made on account of the Rajah's misgovernment. The Subsidy does not appear to have been in any immediate jeopardy. Again the Treaty authorises us to assume such *part* or *parts* of the country as may be necessary to render the funds which we claim efficient and available. The whole has been assumed, although a part would unquestionably have sufficed for the purpose specified in the Treaty; and with regard to the justice of the case, I cannot but think that it would have been more fair towards the Rajah had a more distinct and positive warning been given him that the decided measure since adopted, would be put in force, if misgovernment should be found to prevail."

The arrangements which Lord William Bentinck advocated in this despatch were, that the three districts of Nuggur, Chitteldroog, and Bangalore—yielding an annual revenue equal to the permanent claims of our Government for the Subsidy, pensions, and the body of Horse which the Mysore State was bound by Treaty to maintain—should be ceded to the Company, and that the remaining three districts of Mysore, Ashtagram, and Munjeerabad, should be restored to the Rajah's direct rule.

By this time Lord William Bentinck had begun to perceive, that the unqualified denunciations which had induced him to shelve the Rajah, were by no means corroborated by the detailed information laid before him by the Special

have reason to apprehend such failure in the funds so destined, the said Governor-General in Council shall be at liberty, and shall have full power and right, either to introduce such regulations and ordinances as he shall deem expedient for the internal management and collection of the revenues, or for the better ordering of any other branch and department of the Government of Mysore, or to assume and bring under the direct management of the servants of the said Company Bahadoor, such part or parts of the territorial possessions of his Highness Maharajah Mysore Kistna Rajah Oodiaver Bahadoor, as shall appear to him, the said Governor-General in Council, necessary to render the said funds efficient and available, either in time of peace or war."—Appendix B.

Committee of Inquiry. He felt that he had been deceived and misled. He acknowledged his error, and he regretted it to the last hour of his life. It is well known that after his return to England, he repeatedly declared that the supersession of the Rajah of Mysore was the only incident in his Indian administration that he looked back upon with sorrow. In the early part of 1834 Lord William visited Mysore, received the Report, which is dated 12th December, 1833, from the hands of the Special Committee, and had more than one interview with the Rajah. His Highness implored the Governor-General to have pity on his fallen condition, and especially challenged the closest research into his own private conduct, and into the personal share he had taken in the executive duties of the Principality.

That the effect produced upon the Governor-General's mind by his own local investigation, as well as by the Report of the Special Committee, was not altogether unfavourable to the Rajah, is manifest, not only from his having immediately addressed, from Mysore, that despatch to the Secret Committee, already quoted, in which he recommends the Rajah's restoration to a more limited sphere of power, but more clearly and explicitly from the following expressions occurring in that same despatch :—

"It is admitted by every one who has had an opportunity of observing the character of the Rajah, that he is in the highest degree intelligent and sensible. His disposition is described to be the reverse of tyrannical or cruel, and I can have little doubt, from the manner in which he has conducted himself in his present adverse circumstances, that he would not neglect to bring his good qualities into active operation, and to show that he had not failed to benefit by the lessons of experience. But lest this hope should be disappointed, the means ought undoubtedly to be retained in our own hands of guarding against the evil consequences of his misgovernment. The personal character of the Rajah has, I confess, materially weighed with me in recommending the measure above alluded to. I believe he will make a good ruler in future, and I am certain that, whatever may have been his past errors, he has never forgotten his obligations and his duties to the Company's Government."

The first attachment of the country by Lord William Bentinck was not justified either absolutely by the terms of the Treaty, or morally by any special urgency of outraged humanity, or of danger to the tranquillity of our own adjacent provinces. The first point,—that of the mere abstract illegality, according to the letter of the Treaty, of suspending the Rajah's authority,—appears to be proved by Lord William's own subsequent admissions that while the Treaty only warranted an assumption with a view to secure our Subsidy, "the Subsidy does not appear to have been in any immediate jeopardy;" that whereas the Treaty only warranted the assumption of such "part or parts" as should be sufficient to secure the payment of our demands, we actually assumed charge of the whole country.

The truth is that the case in favour of the Rajah, and against the hasty assumption of his country, is much stronger than would appear from Lord William Bentinck's frank acknowledgment. He says that the Subsidy was not "in immediate jeopardy"; but he was not aware of the fact that it had never been in arrears for a day. His Lordship, writing to the Rajah on the 7th of September, 1831, to give formal notice of the step about to be taken, and under the influence of the highly coloured reports of the Madras Government, asserted that "the Subsidy due to the British Government had not been paid monthly according to the Treaty of 8th July, 1799." The fact is that the Subsidy had been always paid with the utmost punctuality, and that not a single instalment was due at the date of the Governor-General's letter. The monthly receipts of the British authorities, carefully preserved at Mysore, testify to the unintentional inaccuracy of Lord William Bentinck's accusation, —and prove, moreover, that payments in advance to the amount of 210,648 Canteroy Pagodas (about seven lakhs of rupees, or £70,000) had actually been made, when the management of the Mysore Territories was assumed by the British Commissioners on the 18th of October, 1831.

Thus the grounds alleged for the original attachment of the country are not only unsustainable by the terms of the Treaty, but are found to be even more opposed to truth than Lord William Bentinck was ever made aware.

But we must now inquire whether any special urgency of outraged humanity, or of danger to the tranquillity of adjacent British provinces, can have morally justified the supersession of the Rajah. Lord William Bentinck, though quoting only the 4th and 5th Articles of the Treaty, and basing his intervention on their provisions, and on that apprehension for the Subsidy which he afterwards allowed to have been unfounded, proceeds in the second portion of his letter to the Rajah of the 7th September, 1831, to denounce the general mismanagement of Mysore as the exciting cause of the rebellion ; declares that in the suppression of the outbreak " the greatest excesses were committed and unparalleled cruelties were inflicted by" his " Highness's officers ;" and asserts that " from a regard to the obligations of the protective character which the British Government holds towards the State of Mysore," it was " imperiously called upon to supply an immediate and complete remedy, to vindicate its own character for justice," and " to interfere for the preservation of the State, and to save the various interests at stake from ruin."

And we may well concede the broadest scope to the action of the Protective Power ; we may allow of its coercive intervention to check flagrant abuses and savage atrocities, even though the insecurity of the Subsidy,—the only pretext explicitly supplied by the Treaty,—should be a very distant and doubtful contingency. But the grounds of any such extraordinary intervention ought to be very solid and very sure ; and it ought not to be enforced to a greater degree, nor for a greater time than necessary.

Lord William Bentinck's sweeping administrative sequestration was justified by no such conditions. The grounds of his action were not solid or sure, but fell to pieces on close inspection. The Special Committee, in their Report of the 12th December, 1833, undoubtedly condemn the Rajah's misrule, but they include in their censure the period of Poorniah's administration, and with the exception of a profuse expenditure—neither an unpopular nor an unprofitable fault for Mysore,—no new charge is brought against the Prince.

The Committee declare that the assessment all over the country had been screwed up by Poorniah to a height at which it could not have been maintained for many years

longer ; and that the decline of the revenue since the
Minister's dismissal had not "been caused entirely by misgovernment," but was "partly attributable to causes which
were beyond the control of the Rajah's administration."
They also observe that at the same time, and for the same
assigned cause, viz., oppressive taxation, there was an insurrection in the adjacent British district of Canara, where the
assessment of the land revenue was much higher than that
prevailing in Mysore.

The Committee also explain that the rebellion in Nuggur
was not a popular rising caused by intolerable tyranny, but
was chiefly the work of an ambitious pretender to a large
feudal estate, aided by some of the disaffected landholders
of the Provinces—whose predatory habits and separate jurisdiction had been recently checked and limited,—by British
insurgents who flocked to the rebel standard from the province of Canara and the Southern Mahratta country, and by
the intrigues of an influential Brahmin family at Mysore,
whose oppressive and corrupt practices were then under
investigation, and who hoped to evade inquiry amid the
turmoil of an insurrection.

And the Commissioners draw attention to the very
remarkable delusion, universally prevalent at the time
throughout Mysore, a firm belief that the British Government was in favour of the insurgents, and would not support
the Rajah's authority. It would be impossible to account
for these vague rumours, which unquestionably promoted
the uprising and fostered its growth, if we did not know
with what jealous and greedy eyes the Mysore administration had, from the first, been watched from Madras ; how
the Rajah had been in turn neglected, encouraged to resist
interference, and calumniated by the very officials who
ought to have guided and protected him.

Indeed without this knowledge it would be difficult to
imagine any sufficient exciting cause for the severe measures
against the Rajah adopted by the Supreme Government.
The mere fact of a local insurrection having broken out,
does not seem to justify the immediate degradation of the
Sovereign, nor does the mere fact of British troops having
been employed to quell that insurrection. We were bound
to employ that military force, which was amply subsidised

by the Rajah, for the maintenance of his rule, and for the suppression of public disorder.*

And so far from " the greatest excesses and unparalleled cruelties" having been perpetrated by his Highness's officers, it is the fact—a fact that can be proved by unimpeachable living testimony as well as by official documents,—that the greatest severities by which the suppression of the revolt was signalised, were inflicted by British officers, without the sanction or knowledge of the Rajah, and to his great horror and indignation when they were subsequently brought to his notice.

It is therefore quite clear that both the legal and the moral justification advanced by Lord William Bentinck breaks down on careful examination. It is certain, and is indeed admitted by his Lordship, that if he had known the true history and position of the case, as detailed in the Report of the Special Committee, he would never have suspended the Rajah's authority, but would have resorted to milder measures of reform.

In March, 1835, Lord William Bentinck left India, and Sir Charles (afterwards Lord) Metcalfe succeeded provisionally to the office of Governor General, which he held for a year. Shortly after his accession to the Government, he addressed a letter to the Rajah of Mysore, dated the 6th of April, 1835, in reply to one received from his Highness, in which the following passage occurs :—

" My Friend, you appear to be disappointed because the expectation held out to you by his Lordship, that the resolution relative to the affairs of Mysore would reach this country from England by the close of the past year, has not been fulfilled ; but you will readily admit that the realisation of this expectation depended upon circumstances wholly beyond his Lordship's control. I sincerely hope, however, that your mind will not be kept much longer in a state of suspense, and that the decision of the Home Authorities may be conformable with your inclination."

---

* Article X of the Subsidiary Treaty provides that " in case it shall become necessary, for enforcing and maintaining the authority of his Highness in the territories now subjected to his power, that the regular troops of the English East India Company Bahadoor should be employed, it is stipulated and agreed, that upon formal application being made for the service of the said troops, they shall be employed in such manner as to the said Company shall seem fit."
—Appendix B.

Lord Metcalfe decidedly favoured the reestablishment of the Hindoo Sovereign's authority ; and his deliberately recorded opinion is extant that the supersession of the Rajah of Mysore was a "harsh and unprovoked" measure.

Sir William Macnaghten also, when Foreign Secretary at Calcutta at this period, wrote as follows :—"My opinion has always been that his Highness" (the Rajah of Mysore) "has been visited with undue severity, and I shall be very glad to see a portion of his country restored to him."[*]

At last the reply to Lord William Bentinck's despatch of the 14th of April, 1834, arrived from England. The Court of Directors, in their letter, No. 45 of the 25th of September, 1835, distinctly declare their intention of retaining the charge of Mysore only for the specific and temporary purpose of establishing "a fair assessment upon the ryots, with security against further exaction, and a satisfactory system for the administration of justice." They object entirely to tarnish the prospective reinstatement of a Prince who "had ever been," as they observe, "the attached friend of the British Government," by even that limited project of partition recommended by Lord William Bentinck. They object to the division of a State, the separate integrity of which was guaranteed by the Treaty with the Nizam. The doctrines of annexation were not yet in vogue.

After alluding to the extravagance which had been one main cause of the Rajah's difficulties, the Directors go on to say :—

" We would not willingly, after having assumed the powers of government, place the inhabitants of any portion of the territory, however small, under the absolute dominion of such a ruler, until we had established a system which would afford security against the vices of his character, till we had secured protection to the people against extortion, and afforded them the means for a legal redress for their injuries ; and if this desirable end can be attained, the same reasons which served to recommend the restoration to the Rajah of a portion of the country, will, in our opinion recommend the restoration of the whole."

They advert to " the deferred and future possession of the whole Kingdom" by his Highness,[†] and in giving their

---

general suggestions as to the form and principles of the government to be constructed, they say :—

"We are desirous of adhering, as far as can be done, to the native usages, and not to introduce a system which cannot be worked hereafter by native agency when the country shall be restored to the Rajah."

It now became necessary to inform the Rajah that he was not to expect the immediate restoration of any part of his country; and, accordingly, in a letter dated the 28th March, 1836, the new Governor General, Lord Auckland, thus alludes to the instructions that had been issued by the Court of Directors :—

"I hasten to announce to you that the propositions of Lord William Bentinck, of which you were informed by his Lordship's letter of the 14th May, 1834, have received the most attentive consideration from the authorities in England, who have now directed me to communicate to you their decision in regard to them.

"The Honourable the Court of Directors have signified their commands that the administration of your Highness's territories shall remain on its present footing until the arrangements for their good government shall have been so firmly established as to be secure from future disturbance."

In reporting the delivery of the Governor General's letter, the Resident at Mysore, in a despatch dated the 5th May, 1836, observed :—

"With reference to that portion of his Lordship's letter which states that the administration in Mysore is to remain on its present footing until the arrangements for its good government shall have been so firmly established as to be secure from future disturbance, his Highness asked who was to be the judge of when this period had arrived? Were the reports of the officers employed in the Commission to be the guide to the Government,—of those whose employment would be lost by the re-transfer of the country? And he concluded this subject by asking how many years I thought it likely would be deemed by Government as sufficient to afford just ground for confidence that salutary rules and safeguards had been matured and confirmed by practice, and when I thought it likely he might look to receiving back the management of his country."

These proceedings were duly reported to the Court of Directors on the 31st of October, 1836, but in their reply,

No. 20, dated the 20th of September, 1837, the Court gave no instructions as to the restoration of the territory. But that it still continued to be their intention to retain the direct management only as a temporary measure, is apparent from a despatch of the Court of Directors, No. 20, dated the 30th of October, 1839, in which they review the course taken for organising the administration of Mysore :—

"We think it unfortunate that a country like Mysore, which has so recently come under our management, which we had it in view ultimately to restore to a native Government, and for that reason avoided any innovations inconsistent with the maxims and practices of the best native Governments, should have been made the subject of an experiment so embarrassing."

When the Commission for the Government of Mysore was established in 1832, Lord William Bentinck determined that the machinery of the administration should be that of a native agency, and that " the existing native institutions should be carefully maintained." Two joint Commissioners were originally appointed, but they did not work together harmoniously; and on the 5th of June, 1834, Lieutenant-Colonel Cubbon (afterwards General Sir Mark Cubbon, K.C.B.), was appointed sole Commissioner, with very large discretionary powers. And while the entire fabric of native institutions was for many years preserved in outline, the original plan of governing by " an exclusively native agency," was very soon abandoned as impracticable, and English officers were introduced into all the higher appointments. And though General Cubbon, with all his great abilities, was not in any respect a man of broad and liberal mind, was of the stiffest school with regard to distinctions of race and social rank, and was no friend to educated natives, it must not be overlooked that in the earlier stage of his operations there was an influence at work, which rendered the exclusive employment of native agency, especially of the old incumbents, almost impossible,—the opposing influence of the Rajah and his adherents throughout the country. Every innovation appeared to them to be a new turn of the screw, securing the English occupation, and making the restoration of the Rajah's authority more difficult and more unlikely. And, as we have just seen, the Court of Directors in London had themselves started the same class of objections. But the Rajah had an auxiliary more near at hand in the person of the Resident, Major (afterwards Major-General) Stokes, who, in his despatches to Government, gave a general support to all his Highness's demands. Between the Commissioner, one of Sir Thomas Munro's disciples, and the Resident, a friend and pupil of Lord Metcalfe, there was a complete antagonism of opinions and feelings. Their long continued official disputes were terminated in favour of General Cubbon in 1843, when Lord Ellenborough was Governor General, by the post of Resident being abolished. This was at first felt by the Rajah as a great blow, but he learned to acquiesce in its expediency. On the removal of the concurrent authority from his Court, the Rajah was brought into closer relations and more frequent communication with the Commissioner, and they soon came to understand each other better. The great advantages arising from General Cubbon's excellent administration, began to manifest themselves about this time, in the increased revenue and trade of the country. In December, 1847, the General finally reported to Government that the differences between himself and the Rajah were at an end ; and henceforth they continued to be on the most friendly terms.

Sir Frederick Currie, Member of the Council of India, in his Minute dated the 17th July, 1863, says :—" I dissent from the introduction of Sir M. Cubbon's statements about the Rajah's conduct and character, made upwards of sixteen years ago, as a pretext for the measure which this despatch adopts, when it is known, and is on record, that for very many years past the estimate of Sir M. Cubbon of the Rajah's character has undergone a complete change, and that he has on many occasions taken the opportunity of writing in high terms of praise of the Maharajah."*

The Rajah again brought forward his claim to the restoration of the country in a *khureeta,* or royal letter, to the Governor General, Lord Hardinge, dated the 15th day of February, 1844, in which, referring to certain measures that were in preparation for the payment of his debts, he said :—

* Mysore Papers, 1866, p. 24.

"When, in consequence of the mismanagement of treacherous hirelings, and the influence of their evil counsels, the resources of my country were found inadequate to defray its expenses; when those financial embarrassments gave rise to many internal disquiets, the British Government, to whom I was previously indebted for the restoration of my throne and Kingdom, could not remain indifferent spectators of this state of things: they interposed, not to wrest the country from my hands, but to heal it of its disorders, and return it to me in a healthy state. But as its principal disease, from which, as a common source, all its other evils engendered, was its involved condition, I saw the accomplishment of two distinct objects, namely, its restoration to a prosperous state, and when thus restored, the approximation of the prospect to myself of once more ruling my own country, that hereditary patrimony bequeathed to me by my Sires, the Sovereigns of the soil, and the perpetuation of which has been guaranteed for me by the Honourable Company, but of which I have been deprived for the long space of twelve years, in consequence of my misplaced confidence in unworthy hirelings. Hence, my Lord, this desire on my part for the speedy liquidation of the public debts of my country."

In another letter, dated the 10th of April 1844, his Highness thus pleads his cause :—

"I am now in the fifty-first year of my age; I have been relieved from the government of my own country for the last twelve years for my misplaced confidence in unworthy servants; these twelve years have been to me a season of the severest trials and afflictions; in this school of adversity I have acquired lessons of true wisdom, which remain legibly inscribed upon my heart by the fearful finger of experience; and thus initiated and instructed, I am anxious to approach your Lordship as the Governor-General of India, and by consequence my Patron and Protector, seeking, through your Lordship, the restoration to me of the government of my own country, of which I have been temporarily relieved."

About this time the Rajah's importunate applications, and the rumours of their probable success, excited so restless a spirit throughout Mysore, that it was officially suggested to the Supreme Government to remove his Highness from his own country, and place him in the Fort of Vellore, in a position little removed from that of a state-prisoner. This cruel proposition was totally disapproved by Lord Hardinge; but before it had been negatived at Calcutta it had reached the Rajah's ears, and in an indignant letter to the

Governor-General, dated the 9th of May 1844, referring to the Treaty of 1799, and protesting against his removal from Mysore, he writes as follows :—

"From these provisions your Lordship will perceive that the British Government reserved to itself the right, under certain circumstances, to bring under the direct management of the servants of the Company Bahadoor, 'part or parts' of my country, &c. ; but nothing is said about the power to remove me from the country. At the time of the assumption, my Lord, I did not solicit the trial of any mitigated measures of reform, but I readily consented to the extreme one of the assumption of my country ; nor did I, my Lord, claim the privilege of ceding only 'part or parts' of it, but I as readily yielded the whole. Thus, my Lord, have I conducted myself with grateful submission to the British Government, impressed by a lively sense of the obligations conferred by them in the original restoration to me of my country, in the full belief that, in the words of my Treaty, the British Government will act towards me and my heirs, even 'as long as the sun and moon shall endure,' as my Guardian and Patron ; and in the most anxious hope that they will, after making the necessary arrangements for my future prosperity, return my country to me, whole and entire, as I had committed it to their care."

A formal application for the restoration of his territory was addressed by the Rajah to the Governor-General, Lord Hardinge, on the 7th of September 1844. On the 7th of June 1845, the Maharajah wrote to complain that no reply had been made to his last letter, and after defending his character from misrepresentations, he observed :—

"I can call on those who now best know me to say whether at this moment I am not, as to mental and physical vigour, as capable of governing my country as any man of fifty years of age in India. I am not aware that it has been attempted to show that any other reason exists sufficient to render null the Honourable Company's Treaty with me, or to justify the withholding from me now the government of my country."

"I believe I could it make it plain that the assumption of the government of my country by Lord William Bentinck, was a measure both unnecessary and uncalled for by the exigencies of the time, not to speak of its being unjustified by the Treaty existing between the Honourable Company and myself. Disturbances there were in some districts of the country, but do not disturbances occur in portions of the Company's country without any blame being imputed to the governing authority ? I had contracted debts, it is true ; but what were they in proportion to the revenue of my country? And have not the best and most upright Governments in the world debts?"

In another part of this letter the Rajah admits his early extravagance and the mismanagement of public affairs, but asks if this is any reason that he should be "disinherited for ever."

" I appeal," he says, " to the Treaty existing between the Government and myself, that Treaty which I have never violated in the slightest particular or degree, and which I am sure your Excellency will consider the Government bound in honour to abide by. I have received repeated assurances from Governors-General that the British Government will do me justice. I ask no more, but, as human life is limited, I earnestly entreat that justice may be deferred no longer. It is more than nine years since Lord Auckland gave me a hope that, a short time longer being then necessary to perfect the measures in progress for the better ordering of my country, it would be returned to me ; but more than nine years have passed away, and, so far as I am acquainted, no steps have been taken to fulfil this promise."

" It may, and I daresay will be said that neither the debt of the country nor what are considered my own private debts, are yet paid, and therefore I should not yet think of asking for the government of the country to be restored to me. Your Excellency will not consider that man a bankrupt, or that country in a bad state, whose debt is not much more than one-third of his or its income for a year,—not to mention that there are funds accumulated in the Treasury nearly enough to clear it ; and as to the latter, my private funds are much more than sufficient to pay them off. And I could easily prove what your Excellency will, I doubt not, readily believe, that were the government in my hands during the last thirteen years, under any salutary regulations the Governor General might have thought fit to impose, and which I was bound by the Treaty to regard, all debts of every description would have long ere this been paid, considering only the difference, perhaps necessary, between the expenses of European and native administration."

No reply was sent to the Rajah's letter ; but Lord Hardinge, who, it is understood, had begun, after a careful examination of the case, to entertain grave misgivings as to our right of retaining the administrative charge of the country, called upon the Commissioner of Mysore for a return of the exact amount of the Mysore public debt ; and, on the required information being furnished, all these proceedings were reported to the Court of Directors in a despatch, No. 22, dated the 6th of August 1846, the purport of which was to express a doubt whether we ought to keep possession of the Rajah's dominions after our pecuniary claims were satisfied, and when there was no longer any cause for anxiety as to the regular payment of the Subsidy.*

We have seen, then, that from 1834 to 1847 the Rajah never ceased to claim his restoration ; that three Governors General—Lord William Bentinck, Sir Charles Metcalfe, and Lord Hardinge—admitted that his abrupt supersession was inconsiderate, unduly severe, and of doubtful legality ; that neither the Supreme Government nor the Home Authorities ever rejected or contested his claim, but only postponed their assent to a more convenient season, placing before him the prospect of reinstatement as soon as an orderly administration for the country had been effectually established. And I may add, that in no despatch of the Home Government, or of the Government of India, during that period, was any intention of permanently retaining the management of Mysore ever expressed or implied. But new views of policy were now beginning to prevail ; the Mysore Commission, under the able direction of General Cubbon, had effected great improvements in the twelve years between 1834 and 1846 ; the authorities, both at Calcutta and in London, began to be enamoured of their own achievements ; and the lust of patronage also lured them on to tighten their grasp on Mysore. The appointments in the Mysore Commission were among those most coveted by young officers in the Army, and the idea of not merely being unable to provide for the candidates already on the Governor-General's list, but of having to turn adrift, or remand to regimental duty, all those gentlemen actually in the enjoyment of those lucrative offices, must have been most unpleasant when pressed upon the consideration of the Council and the Secretariat by the Rajah's repeated claims for his restoration. Nor could the Commissioner and his Assistants be expected to under-estimate the value of their own labours, or to advocate their own abolition. The Rajah himself very naturally foresaw this obstacle

* I have not seen this despatch, but I am assured that its effect is as above stated.

when, as we have seen, he asked the Resident, in 1836, "who was to be the judge" of the period when the "good government" of Mysore "should have been so firmly established as to be secure from future disturbance ? Were the reports of the officers employed in the Commission to be the guide to the Government—the reports of those whose employment would be lost by the re-transfer of the country ?"[*]

The views, therefore, of Lord Hardinge, expressed in the despatch No. 22 of the 6th August 1846, not being in accordance with those that were generally accepted both in Calcutta and in London, were by no means well received at the India House. In their reply to it, No. 15, dated the 14th of July, 1847, after ten months' consideration, the Directors observe :—

> " The Rajah addressed a letter to the Governor-General in June, 1845, claiming to be reinstated in the government. In November following the Rajah was informed that the reply to his letter was delayed in consequence of the necessity of ascertaining the exact amount of the debt due to the British Government. We think this a most insufficient cause of delay ; first, because the most exact information on this point ought to have been at once accessible ; and, secondly, because such an intimation would naturally tend to make the Rajah believe that the only or the chief obstacle to this reinstatement was the non-liquidation of the debt. The real hindrance, however, is the hazard which would be incurred to the prosperity and good government which the country now enjoys, by replacing it under a ruler known by experience to be thoroughly incompetent."

Unfavourable as is the tenor of this despatch, it is remarkable as containing no positive denial of the Rajah's rights, no absolute refusal to consider some plan for his restoration to power under adequate securities. His alleged incompetence is only spoken of as an " obstacle " and " a hindrance," not as a final and insurmountable objection to his reinstatement. And the whole question is left open by the concluding sentence :—" We have not been apprised whether any definite answer has yet been made to the Rajah's application." No instructions for a definite answer are given. No definite answer, no answer at all, was in fact made to the Rajah's appeal.

<hr>

[*] Ante, p. 24.

This despatch of the 14th July 1847 may be considered as marking the turning-point in the Rajah's fortunes, after which the tide set in against him : it contains the first decided indication of a simple reluctance to part with the management of so rich and thriving a province, and to break up the administrative system of our own construction, under which the country had so signally prospered. The reluctance was natural, defensible, justifiable ; but the real difficulty, however disguised, was the patronage. There was not sufficient sympathy with the Rajah's claims and with native interests, to induce the British authorities, at home and in India, to seek for some intermediate plan, by which the Prince's power might for the future be limited by law, and by which an efficient native hierarchy might be gradually trained to replace their English instructors. It has been, throughout, the official theory that the Rajah's restoration must necessarily involve the total and immediate withdrawal of European agency—a theory manifestly erroneous, for ample power is conferred upon the British Government by the Treaty, to introduce "regulations and ordinances," and to offer authoritative advice on all subjects "connected with his Highness's interests, the happiness of his people, and the mutual welfare of both States." But this theory was at first, I have no doubt, sincerely held; an incongruity was conceived to exist in any plan for associating, even as a temporary expedient, a native Sovereign and English administrators in the government of a Principality; and the idea of a native ruler's power being limited in any direction by a Code or a Constitution, never seems to have presented itself—not even up to this day. The complete exclusion of the Sovereign and of all natives from power, the monopoly of all official honours and emoluments in the hands of Englishmen, are the only conditions on which our assistance has been afforded.

Somewhat perplexed by the problem of reconciling the separate and native Government of Mysore under the Rajah's sovereignty—as designed by the Treaties of 1799—with an effectual guaranty for the continuance of good order and economy, somewhat averse to relinquish a valuable field of patronage, and yet more than half persuaded of there being no longer any valid pretext for maintaining the sequestration, the Government subsided into the passive policy of letting well alone, and of gaining time by harping on the Rajah's incapacity. This excuse, when advanced by the British Government in India, amounts to a confession of its own incompetence as a protective and reforming authority. That system for the government of a Principality or of a Province, which depends for its success upon the personal abilities and moral character of one man, is not one that British statesmen in the nineteenth century could be expected to approve or to uphold, in a case where they were authorised to express disapproval or to suggest modifications. And why such a system was allowed by us to exist for one day in Mysore, why a boy of sixteen, supported by his minions and flatterers, was permitted by us to displace an experienced and faithful Regent, to possess himself of absolute power, and then to retain it uncontrolled for twenty years, is a political mystery that has never been explained.

What Prince in the world is endowed with sufficient talents, or with sufficient self-denial, to be safely trusted with uncontrolled and absolute power? It seems a waste of time to dwell, even for a moment, on so elementary a principle of modern politics. Yet, because the Rajah of Mysore, an absolute ruler at the age of sixteen, by permission of his British Guardian, failed to make a good use of the power which never ought to have been thrown into his hands, that negligent and incompetent Guardian turns round upon him, stigmatises his rule as "scandalously and hopelessly bad," denounces him as "thoroughly incompetent," and permanently suspends his authority.

And after fifteen years of government by an able and zealous Commissioner, who, in common with his Assistants, is remunerated by a liberal but fixed salary, who is controlled by regulations, and is responsible for every official act, and for every item of expenditure, to the Governor-General in Council—when Mysore has prospered, as might have been expected under this well-regulated scheme of administration —a most unfair and unreasonable comparison between the two periods of native and British rule, is accepted as a full and complete apology for the proscription of the Sovereign, and, as we shall shortly see, for the abolition of the sovereignty.

We may surely assume that the Rajah never was really incompetent for the legitimate duties of a constitutional Sovereign, when we find that Lord William Bentinck, after a careful inquiry, pronounced him to be "in the highest degree intelligent and sensible," described his disposition as "the reverse of tyrannical or cruel," and expressed his belief that he would "make a good ruler in future." Several successive Governors-General had held out the hope to the Rajah, with more or less of sympathy and encouragement, that as soon as securities for good government had been firmly established, he should be reinstated at the head of his own administration. But in the twelve years from 1835 to 1847 the replies from Calcutta became less frequent, and latterly their tone became less pleasant and more evasive. The facts had not altered; the merits of the case had not been affected; but the times had changed. Fifteen millions sterling had been sunk in the Affghan war; the conquest of Scinde was said to have entailed a heavy burden on the finances; the Sutlej campaign had certainly cost money; an annual deficit had for many years appeared in the accounts. Distant expeditions and the advance of our external frontiers were deprecated; but the short-sighted policy of internal acquisitions began to be entertained both at Calcutta and at home. The favourite plan for restoring the financial equilibrium was that of gradually extinguishing all those native States that were in the midst of or contiguous to our territories. The Rajah had no son, and in 1847 he was in his fifty-fifth year. Mysore, the valuable field of patronage, now began to be regarded, though in a vague and furtive fashion, as Mysore the rich reversion. In February 1848 Lord Dalhousie arrived in India to turn these vague predilections into a predetermined policy. In a letter dated the 8th of August 1848 the Rajah once more addressed the Governor-General on the subject of the restoration of his territory :—

"General Cubbon," he said, "in his letter to me of the 5th December 1845, informed me that the delay on the part of your Excellency in replying to my *khureeta* of the 7th June 1845, was occasioned by the absence of some information relative to the state of the debts, which your Excellency had deemed it necessary to call for. I trust your Lordship has received this information, and that

it has been satisfactory. Your Lordship will have heard from Mr.
Grant that all my private or the Soucar debts have been settled;
and in regard to the sum due by the State to the Honourable
Company, should there be any deficiency in the funds accumulated in the Commissioner's Treasury to liquidate it, I will make
it up, as I mentioned to your Excellency in my *khureeta* of the
7th September 1844, from my private funds. I trust also that
your Lordship will have had from the Commissioner such a
favourable report of the country, after fifteen years, as will satisfy
your Lordship of the efficacy of the arrangements made; and
that there can be, in your Lordship's mind, no reason to apprehend failure of the military funds provided for by the 3rd Article
of the Treaty; and that, consequently, the time has come when I
have a right to expect the fulfilment of the intimation given me
in the 5th paragraph of Lord Auckland's letter of the 28th March
1836, communicating the sentiments of the high authorities in
England as to the period at which I might expect the government of my territories would be restored to myself."

No orders were passed by Lord Dalhousie on this letter,
and no reply was made to it. A copy of it was sent to
the Court of Directors with the despatch, No. 27 of the 1st
of July, 1848, but their answer, No. 6, dated the 14th of
February, 1849, contained no allusion whatever to the
Rajah's requisitions. Less than a month before the date of
the last mentioned communication, their despatch (No. 4,
dated the 24th January, 1849), approving and confirming
the annexation of Sattara, had been transmitted to Calcutta.* The reign of terror for Hindoo Princes had commenced. Nagpore and Jhansi were annexed in 1854. The
smaller Principalities of Jaloun, Ungool, Jeitpore in Bundelcund, Bughat, Sumbhulpore, Boodawul and Chota Oodeypoor were also absorbed during Lord Dalhousie's tenure of
office.† In 1853 the Nizam was coerced into assigning to
our "exclusive management" some of his finest provinces,
producing about a fourth of his revenue. In January 1856
the appropriation of Oude had been finally sanctioned, and
the orders for deposing the King had been issued, and were
in process of execution.‡ On the 19th of December 1855

---

* Sattara Papers, 1849, p. 8.
† His Lordship also proposed, on various occasions, the annexation of the
Rajpoot State of Kerowlee, of Kolapore (whose Rajah now represents the family
of Sivajee, the founder of the Mahratta power), and of Adyghur; but these
were all disapproved by the Home Government.
‡ Oude Papers, 1856, p. 241.

Lord Dalhousie recorded a Minute denying to Prince Azeem Jah, the heir and representative of our faithful Allies in war and peace, the Nawabs of the Carnatic, that hereditary dignity and revenue which had been expressly secured to the Wallajah family by the Treaty concluded in 1801 with the Prince's own father, the Nawab Azeem-ood-Dowlah. During Lord Dalhousie's administration, all the evil influences of Calcutta were fully indulged, and strengthened threefold. The extension or restoration of native rule was the last thing thought of, and such a proposal would have been treated with derision. What were Lord Dalhousie's reflections on Mysore, in the full tide of his territorial acquisitions, may be easily conceived.

In one of his Minutes, dated the 16th January, 1856, reviewing General Cubbon's Administration Report for the preceding official year, occurs the following passage :—

"The Rajah of Mysore is now sixty-two years of age. He is the only Rajah who, for twenty generations past, as he himself informed me, has lived to the age of sixty years. It is probable, therefore, that his life will not be much further prolonged. He has no legitimate son or grandson, nor any lawful male heir whatever. He has adopted no child, and has never designed to adopt an heir. On the contrary, General Cubbon informed me that, when sometimes pressed by those about him to adopt, the Rajah has been used to reply, 'No, I have no male child of my own. I will not adopt. I will be the last Rajah of Mysore.'

"The Treaty under which Lord Wellesley raised the Rajah, while yet a child, to the musnud, and the Treaty which was subsequently concluded with himself, were both silent as to heirs and successors. No mention is made of them; the Treaty is exclusively a personal one.

"The inexpediency of continuing this territory, by an act of gratuitous liberality, to any other native Prince, when the present Rajah shall have died, has been already conclusively shown by the conduct of his Highness himself, whose rule, though he commenced it under every advantage, was so scandalously and hopelessly bad, that power has long since been taken from him by the British Government.

"I trust, therefore, that when the decease of the present Rajah shall come to pass, without son or grandson, or legitimate male heir of any description, the Territory of Mysore, which will then have lapsed to the British Government, will be resumed, and that the good work, which has been so well begun, will be completed."

This Minute was one of the legacies that Lord Dalhousie left behind him for the instruction and guidance of his successor, Lord Canning.

We have now arrived at a new stage in our downward progress. For the first time a Governor-General has now placed on official record, although in a secret department, a statement of his desire and design to incorporate Mysore with the British dominions, on the death of the reigning Rajah. Henceforth the question of reinstating the Rajah, treated with silent contempt in the Minute just quoted, sinks into a secondary place. Henceforth a suspicion cannot be avoided, that the true obstacle to restoration is not the Rajah's incompetence, nor the impossibility of securing good government, but an aversion to relax our grasp, to relinquish the visible advantage afforded by long continued administrative possession.

But though Lord Dalhousie avows himself to be prepared to rely, if necessary, upon the newly invented weapon, which he had just used with cruel effect in the Carnatic spoliation —to deny that the sovereignty of Mysore was hereditary, to declare the Treaty of 1799 "a personal treaty," made only for one life, and renewable merely at the good pleasure of the British Government, as a matter of grace and favour —he very plainly indicates a hope that this engine of destruction may after all not be required, that the conveyance may be quietly effected, without notice, dispute or scandal; that the Rajah, who had now outlived by three years the supposed family limit of sixty, may soon disappear from the scene, leaving no heir by birth or adoption, no possible claimant of the throne, to draw from us a premature or public disclosure of our expansive pretensions. And it is very remarkable how, in his eagerness to lay this flattering unction to his soul, Lord Dalhousie snatches at the veriest trifle, some petulant expressions attributed to the Rajah, and parades them as a proof of that Prince's acquiescence in the prospective extinction of his dynasty. The Rajah, we are assured, has "never designed to adopt an heir." There can be no question of this, because, when pressed by those about him, he has been used to reply, "I will not adopt. I will be the last Rajah of Mysore." General Cubbon himself, when he repeated this interesting piece of

Court gossip—probably after dinner—to the Governor-General, cannot have anticipated that it would be treasured up so carefully, and turned to such a purpose. There can scarcely be a better specimen of the enormous assumptions, the transparent fallacies, which, in the privacy of a compliant Council, Lord Dalhousie was permitted to pass off as arguments, than is shown in this short extract from his Minute on Mysore. A Treaty of "perpetual friendship and alliance," the obligations of which are to last "as long as the sun and moon shall endure,"* is pronounced to be "exclusively a personal one," good only for the Rajah's life, and providing for no heir or successor. The solemn formalities of a Treaty become mere idle words when they uphold the native sovereignty ; the recorded intentions, the written proposals of his predecessors are silently overlooked—I suppose because they are not legally binding— but the tittle-tattle of a Residency Moonshee, when it implies that the Rajah is resigned and even reconciled to the extinction of his family, is hailed as holy writ.

There can be, to my mind, no more evident mark of conscious moral weakness, than that exhibited by our authorities at home and in India, with strange uniformity, at every stage of the numerous acquisitive transactions between 1848 and 1856, in always grasping with manifest exultation at anything said or done, or omitted to be said or done, by the injured parties, that could be twisted into even the remotest resemblance of an admission or acquiescence on their part.

And even if we accept as accurate the reported version of the Rajah's exclamations, to what do they amount ? He had watched with dismay the recent destruction of so many friendly Principalities ; he had ascertained during his own interviews with Lord Dalhousie, that there was no hope of redress for himself, and he said in the bitterness of his heart, "I shall be the last Rajah of Mysore,"—not "I will," for the nice distinction between "shall" and "will", peculiar to the Teutonic languages, was unknown in his own vernacular ; and most certainly, as I shall show, the Rajah could could not and did not *willingly* abandon the hope of per-

* Appendix B.

petuating his dynasty,—but "I now see clearly," was his
obvious meaning, "that I am doomed by the present policy
of the Calcutta Government to be the last Rajah of Mysore.
I will not, like the Rajahs of Sattara and Jhansi, adopt a
son to be an outcast, a beggar, a pretender threatened with
the gibbet or the jail, or at the best a pensioner for life. I
shall be the last Rajah of Mysore."

But although it may be true that expressions such as
these, indicating an aversion to adopt a son whose succession would be assuredly forbidden, may, during the darkest
hours of the Dalhousie reign, have sometimes escaped the
Rajah, the assertion that he had "never designed to adopt
an heir", is positively contradicted by facts. In his letter
to Lord Hardinge of the 15th of February, 1844, already
quoted,* he speaks of his Principality as "that hereditary
patrimony bequeathed to me by my Sires, the Sovereigns of
the soil, and the perpetuation of which has been guaranteed
to me by the Honourable Company." In another letter,
dated the 9th of May, 1844, from which some extracts have
also been given,† he declares his belief "that, in the words
of my Treaty, the British Government will act towards me
and my heirs, even 'as long as the sun and moon shall endure', as my Guardian and Patron". At this time the Rajah
was upwards of fifty years of age, and had no son. And
in his letter of the 8th of August, 1848, to Lord Dalhousie
himself, he had confirmed these letters and renewed their
claims. And at a later period, when appealing to Lord Canning against the proposed retransfer of Mysore to the supervision of the Madras Government, he says:—"Moreover, my
Lord, I have grave fears that such a measure as this, if introduced, would possibly interfere with the claims that I *and
my heirs* have for the restoration of the Government of my
country." This letter, of which I shall have to say more
hereafter, is dated the 15th of March, 1860, when the Rajah
was sixty-five years old. On these two occasions he can
hardly be supposed to have written in these terms, without relying on his right of adopting an heir. This at least
is certain, that from 1832 to 1844, when he claimed the
perpetuation of his sovereignty, and declared the rights of

* Ante, p. 26.　　　　　　　† Ante, p. 27.

his heirs; and from 1844 to 1860, when he again protested against any infringement of their rights, the Rajah never, in any official document, or at any official interview, allowed any opportunity to pass away of asserting the hereditary nature of his dignity, he never expressed any doubt on the subject, and none was ever expressed to him.

And it is worthy of remark that Lord Dalhousie's aspirations for the completion of the good work of assimilating Mysore, do not seem to have called forth any response or approval from any other member of the Government. Not one of his predecessors had ever suggested such a breach of faith. Lord Auckland, when Governor-General, referring to an attempt made by the Supreme Court of Calcutta to enforce its process in Mysore, and quoting his legal adviser, the Advocate-General, wrote as follows in a Minute in Council, of July 1840 :—"The sovereignty of Mysore is exercised by the East India Company as trustees for the Rajah; and it is contrary to their duty to commit, or to allow others to commit, any violation of the sovereignty, which might disable them from restoring it, without derogation, to the person whose sovereignty they admit."

And, at a much later period, in the consultations on the disposal of Oude, during Lord Dalhousie's administration, Sir John Peter Grant, then a member of Council, in a paper dated August the 7th, 1855, made use of the following distinction :—"The case of Mysore differs from the supposed case of Oude, inasmuch as our management of that province is professedly temporary, and on account of the Sovereign of Mysore."*

And again, in a despatch dated 20th December, 1858, Sir John Peter Grant, when President in Council at Calcutta, instructed the Madras Government that Mysore was "a foreign State," and that land and houses in the military cantonment of Bangalore, must be held under tenure from the Rajah's Government, and not from any British authority. And in a letter of the 18th November, 1859, Sir Mark Cubbon observed that "the sovereignty of Mysore is still vested in the Rajah, and that the powers of administration are exercised in trust on his account."†

---

* Oude Papers, 1856, p. 213.   † Mysore Papers, p. 33.

General Cubbon was certainly not prepared for the absorption of this native State, for he wrote in the following terms in a private letter to a friend on the 23rd of June, 1859 :—

"I have received a tremendous wig lately from Bengal on the subject of duties, and shall have to point out more than one mistake on their part, besides insinuating that they have no right under the Treaty to reduce the revenues of a foreign State, and that they will have to make a corresponding reduction in the Subsidy. In truth they, or I should rather say, Mr. Beadon, have forgotten that the orders from England are imperative that the administration of Mysore should be so conducted that the country may be restored to a native Government at the shortest notice; and in consequence we are at this moment obliged to oppose many parts of procedure which a native Government could not administer."

Lord Canning himself, so late as the year 1860, in referring to the affairs of Mysore in the General Report on the Administration of India for the preceding official year,* treats the maintenance of the separate jurisdiction and distinct establishments of Mysore, as a matter of conscientious obligation.

"It has also been necessary," he says, "so to conduct the administration as to fulfil *conscientiously* the instructions laid down for guidance in a letter from the Home authorities, under date the 25th September 1835, and which states as follows :—'We are desirous of adhering, as far as can be done, to the native usages, and not to introduce a system which cannot be worked hereafter by native agency, when the country shall be restored to the Rajah.'"

---

* Published at Calcutta.

CHAPTER III.

WHEN Lord Canning succeeded to the Viceregal chair in 1856, the answers to the Rajah's numerous applications had all been either favourable or evasive. His claim to be restored to power had never been denied or rejected, but only postponed.

Throughout the terrible events of 1857 and 1858 the people of Mysore remained tranquil. Elements of mischief existed in abundance in various quarters ; emissaries of rebellion traversed the country in every direction ; but peace was never disturbed, and the Rajah's troops were actually detached into the adjoining British provinces to assist in preventing insurrection. Sir Mark Cubbon's own official statements to Government may be adduced to prove how efficacious were the example and exertions of the Rajah in securing to us the fidelity of his people. In a despatch, dated the 2nd of June, 1860, the Commissioner of Mysore wrote in the following terms to the Governor-General, Lord Canning :—

" To no one was the Government more indebted for the preservation of tranquillity than to his Highness the Rajah, who displayed the most steadfast loyalty throughout the crisis, discountenancing everything in the shape of disaffection, and taking every opportunity to proclaim his perfect confidence in the stability of the English rule. When the small party of Europeans arrived at Mysore, he made manifest his satisfaction by giving them a feast. He offered one of his Palaces for their accommodation, and as a stronghold for the security of the treasure ; and even gave up his own personal establishment of elephants, etc., to assist the 74th Highlanders in its forced march from the Neilgherries to Bellary, for the protection of the Ceded Districts, a proceeding which, although of no great magnitude in itself, produced great moral effects throughout the country. In fact, there was nothing in his power which he did not do to manifest his fidelity to the British Government, and to discourage the unfriendly."

The Viceroy acknowledged the Rajah's valuable and faithful services in the following letter of thanks.

" To his Highness the Maharajah of Mysore.

"Fort William, the 28th June, 1860.

"MAHARAJAH,

"I have lately received from the Commissioner of Mysore a despatch, in which the assistance received by that officer from your Highness, in preserving peace and encouraging loyalty in the districts under his charge during the recent troubles in India, is prominently brought to notice.

"I was well aware that, from the very beginning of those troubles, the fidelity and attachment to the British Government, which have long marked your Highness's acts, had been conspicuous upon every opportunity.

"Your Highness's wise confidence in the power of England, and your open manifestation of it, the consideration and kindness which you showed to British subjects, and the ready and useful assistance which you rendered to the Queen's troops, have been mentioned by the Commissioner in terms of the highest praise.

"I beg your Highness to accept the expression of my warm thanks for these fresh proofs of the spirit by which your Highness is animated in your relations with the Government of India.

"I shall have much pleasure in making them known to her Majesty's Secretary of State for India.

"It is satisfactory to me to know that, throughout the time of which I have spoken, your Highness has had the advantage of the support and counsel of so tried and distinguished an Officer of the Crown, and one so devoted to the welfare of your Highness's State, as Sir Mark Cubbon.   "I have, &c.,

"CANNING."

But even while these amenities were passing between Mysore and Calcutta, the Rajah was in the agonies of a fresh wound, one that touched him to the quick, that seemed to destroy all hope of recovery from his long political syncope, and to threaten him with the infliction of political death in the face of all India, before his natural term of life had closed.

Ever since 1832 the management of Mysore had been under the direct superintendence of the Governor-General of India, and was not liable to be interfered with by the subordinate and nearer Presidency of Madras. The Rajah had some pride in this arrangement, not, perhaps, unmingled with the feeling that the transfer had originally been made

with some intention of rebuking the Madras Government
for its neglect, and of thus casting upon it to a certain extent the blame of the misgovernment of his country. He
also knew that his supersession had been instigated by the
Madras officials, that gentlemen belonging to that Presidency enjoyed most of the lucrative offices dependent on
his continued supersession; and he believed that his prospects of restoration would be much more favourable, while
he was in direct communication with the higher and more
distant authority, than if he were left in the grasp of the
more contiguous and more interested minor Government.

In a despatch to the Governor-General in Council, dated
the 26th of January, 1860, the Secretary of State, Sir Charles
Wood, quite unexpectedly desired that the Mysore Commission should be placed under the immediate superintendence of the Government of Madras, to which Sir Charles
Trevelyan had been recently appointed. The grounds for
this sudden change are thus stated in the despatch :—

"The arguments which in 1832 were advanced by the Governor-
General of India, in favour of the transfer of the controlling authority over the Mysore Commission to the hands of the Governor-
General of India in Council, were of a temporary and accidental,
rather than of a general character, and do not appear to be
applicable to the present circumstances of the Mysore administration. On the other hand the territory over which political and
administrative control is exercised by the Government of India,
has been so extended, and the current business of your office has
so increased since 1832, as to afford full and ample employment
for the Foreign Department of your Government. It appears to
me, therefore, that it is advisable, partly with the view of relieving
your Government, and partly with the object of placing the superintendence of Mysore and Coorg under the Government which,
from its position, can most conveniently exercise it, to revert to
the arrangement which was orignally made, on our first assumption of the administration of Mysore, viz., that the superintendence should be exercised by the Government of Madras."

But the geographical position of the Mysore Principality,
which naturally suggests the Madras Government as the
centre of direction in the event of Mysore becoming a
British Province, was the very circumstance that made the
proposed transfer most alarming and offensive to the Rajah
and all well-wishers of his sovereignty. It seemed to them

to denote the beginning of the end, to be the preliminary measure of annexation. The Rajah prepared a firm but respectful remonstrance to be forwarded to the Governor-General, wrote to Sir Mark Cubbon declaring that " nothing would ever exact from him acquiescence in this measure", and implored the Commissioner not to leave him in the midst of these new difficulties. " I could ill afford," wrote the Rajah, " to lose your much valued friendship and counsel at any time, but just at present it is a positive calamity both to myself and to my country." For immediately on receiving information of the intended change, Sir Mark Cubbon had sent in the resignation of his office in the following letter to Government.

From the Commissioner for the Government of the Territories of His Highness the Rajah of Mysore, to the Secretary to the Government of India in the Foreign Department.

" Nundydroog, 5th March, 1860.

" Sir,

" Having received private but authentic information that orders have issued from the Office of the Secretary of State for India, that the control of Mysore shall be withdrawn from the Government of India, notwithstanding the declaration contained in the despatch from the Honourable the Court of Directors, dated the 31st May, 1838, No. 34,* I have the honour to request you will be so good as to tender to the Honourable the President in Council the resignation of my appointment as Commissioner, and to add to it my respectful solicitation to be relieved as soon as his Honour may find it convenient.

" I shall have the satisfaction of making over charge to my successor of the territories of Mysore and Coorg, in a state to all appearance (I say to all appearance, for I do not presume to be able to see beyond the surface,) of perfect tranquillity, and not dissatisfied with the present form of administration, and with a current revenue exceeding that of any former year in Mysore, that is to say, not less than 93 lakhs of rupees.

" I have the honour to be, etc.,

" M. Cubbon, Commissioner."

The motives and feelings by which General Cubbon was actuated in taking this step, may be gathered from the following extracts from two of his private. letters, both dated the 8th of March, 1860.

---

* I do not know what this declaration is, but I believe it would throw some light on the early history of this question.

"I have just had a little talk with —— (a native) 'and find that the late order is regarded as a great breach of public faith, as the first step towards the final extinction of the State of Mysore and its incorporation with Madras, and consequently tending to produce the most fatal of all results, the destruction of all confidence in the sincerity of the Queen's Proclamation. Viewed in this light it is a most serious affair, and in the present suspicious temper of the native mind, it is certain to give rise to the most unfavourable interpretation, and be made a party question of by our enemies, who will represent it as another proof of our intention to degrade the natives.'

"The Rajah's *khureeta* is most forcibly put; and whatever impression it may make on the Government of India or the India Board, it is almost certain to cause a sensation if read in the House of Commons. As for the adoption, they dare not refuse it. I had no idea it would have been so generally believed that this step was preparatory to the extinction of the Raj, but such appears to have been the impression that has got abroad, and which is openly avowed in the petitions that are coming to me."

The following is the *khureeta* or letter from the Rajah to Lord Canning, to which General Cubbon alludes.

"Mysore Palace, 15th March, 1860.

"My Lord,

"Having been informed that the Mysore country has been or is about to be transferred from Bengal to the Madras Presidency, I beg leave most respectfully to address your Lordship upon this subject, and to entreat that the reasons which induce me to protest against this measure will meet with your Lordship's consideration.

"2. The transfer of the management of my country from the Supreme to a subordinate Government, without any reference to me, as if I had no longer any interest in the matter, or any rights to uphold, fills my mind with apprehension and alarm.

"3. Consider, my Lord, I beseech of you, the degradation to which I should be subjected, by such a measure, in the eyes of all natives, and especially those of my own subjects. Pardon the boldness of my language, my Lord, but my conscience tells me that I am entitled to protection from your Lordship, in consideration of the loyalty exhibited by myself and my subjects during the recent sad disturbances, which permitted of two thousand of my Silladar Horse being sent to aid in the suppression of the Rebellion. I claim it, moreover, my Lord, in virtue of her Majesty's Proclamation.

"4. I cannot, my Lord, see how my interests, or those of my country, are to be bettered by this transfer. Perfect tranquillity reigned in my country at a time when a word of mine, or disaffection on the part of my people, would have thrown Southern India into a blaze; but my conduct, and that of my people during that dreadful period, exhibits the complete success of the administration as at present carried out.

"5. Moreover, my Lord, I have grave fears that such a measure as this, if introduced, would possibly interfere with the claims that I and my heirs have for the restoration of the Government of my country, as it is evident that the contemplated change is with the view of introducing alterations in the form of Government, which would render it difficult for me or my successor to conduct the administration hereafter with a native agency; and the recent conduct of the present Governor of Madras adds cogency to my fears on this point.

"6. I do not, moreover, my Lord, hesitate to state (and, from my position, I claim a right to be a judge in such matters, seeing how much I am interested in this question) that the condition of Mysore at this moment would contrast favourably with any other Province on this side of India. The revenue has increased, and is increasing; and that, too, without pressing on any class, or giving rise to murmur or complaint. There is comparatively little crime; and, what there is, is effectually met by a system, which, for efficiency and cheapness, is not surpassed by any in the country. The judicial system founded upon that most cherished by natives of all their institutions, the Punchayet,* operates with the utmost success, and I specially deprecate any innovation in the native system of judicial administration at present in force; the most sacred rights and privileges of the people are respected, and the utmost confidence exists in the minds of all that such will continue so long as the present system lasts.

"7. I now beg to bring to your Lordship's recollection, that Mysore was under the control of the Supreme Government for many years and prospered. It was afterwards transferred to Madras, and the result does not afford proof of the advantage of the transfer, for the insurrection arose, and the country was assumed while under the control of that Presidency.

"8. In conclusion, my Lord, I beg to remark, that it would require very strong reasons to justify the risk of making the change now proposed; and I most respectfully, at the same time most emphatically, deny that any such reasons exist.

"9. And now, my Lord, I have stated my case, and, fully relying on your Lordship's well-known sense of justice, I confidently leave the issue in your Lordship's hands. I am an old man, and have suffered much; and you, my Lord, will, I feel assured, save me from this crowning indignity.

---

* Trial by a jury of five members.

"With the assurance of my unaltered respect and esteem for your Lordship, I beg leave to subscribe myself,

"Your Lordship's most faithful Friend and humble Servant,

"MYSORE KRISTNARAJ WADIYAR."

It will be observed that the Rajah here lays claim to the restoration of his country, on behalf of himself and *his heirs*, and deprecates rash innovations, not only on his own account, but on account of *his successor*. No trace is to be found of that indifference to the interests of the family, of that determination to be the last Rajah of Mysore, upon which Lord Dalhousie relied in 1856. He alludes to the rights of his heirs in 1860 just as he did in 1844.*

Lord Canning supported the Rajah's application in the following letter to the Secretary of State, informed the Rajah and Sir Mark Cubbon that for the present the proposed change would not be carried out, a reference having been made to London ; and requested the Commissioner in the meantime to suspend the tender of his resignation.

"Foreign Department (Camp Hoshiarpore),
"No. 35, 30th March, 1860.

"SIR,

"I had the honour to receive, on the 8th instant, your despatch of the 26th January, directing me, at my earliest convenience, to place the Mysore Commission under the immediate superintendence of the Governor of Madras in Council. I thereupon called, by telegraph, for the papers showing the circumstances in which, in 1832, the Mysore Commission was placed on its present footing. Before the papers reached me, I received a telegraphic message from the Rajah of Mysore. The letter to myself, which his Highness announces, as well as a letter from his Highness to the Commissioner, Sir Mark Cubbon, reached me yesterday. Copies of these letters I enclose.

"I have received, too, a letter from Sir Mark Cubbon, tendering his resignation, on account of the change prescribed in the superintendence of his charge.

"Whether, if the opportunity had been allowed to me of being the channel of the communication to his Highness, I could in any degree have anticipated his remonstrances, and lessened the feelings of mortification and indignity which he has expressed, I cannot say. Perhaps it might have been so, although certainly I do not pretend that I could have made the change palatable to him.

* Ante, p. 33.

"But the question now to be considered is, how the appeal of the Rajah is to be dealt with, and I feel it to be impossible, in the face of such an appeal coming from so venerable and loyal a Prince, and couched in terms so dignified, but so respectful, to persist in the immediate execution of your orders without submitting the case for your reconsideration.

"Although no allusion is made in your despatch to the Sovereign of Mysore, it appears to me that that Prince possesses a very strong claim to have his wishes and feelings considered by us, and that we shall do that which is both ungenerous and impolitic, if we set these aside.

"I am, therefore, not surprised that the Rajah of Mysore should speak of the declared measure as being a degradation of himself in the eyes of all natives, especially in those of his own subjects, and an indignity.

"It is unnecessary for me to say, that the Rajah's allusions to the loyalty of himself and his people, and to the example and aid thereby given to the native subjects of the Crown in Southern India, are quite just. Mysore was traversed in all directions during 1857 and 1858 by Mahratta and Brahmin emissaries, but the people of that country remained tranquil.

"Also, the Rajah is well entitled to point (as he does point with pride) to the actual condition of his dominions. The system of administration which has prevailed there is in many ways capable of amelioration, but it has been repeatedly acknowledged to deserve the character given to it by the Court of Directors in 1838 of a 'beneficial and improving system'; and I cannot think that the nearness of supervision, or any other convenience which would result from a transfer of the superintendence of that system to Madras, is worth purchasing at the cost of offending and alienating the Sovereign of the country; especially when, by a little patience, the desired end will, in all human probability, be attained without any such consequences.

"As bearing on the price which we shall pay for forcing this measure upon Mysore, I invite your attention to the following facts.

"The Rajah of Mysore is an old man, past sixty, and of a family notoriously shortlived. He has no son, and has adopted no heir. It has been supposed that he will bequeath his Kingdom to the British Government. I say 'supposed,' because there is no formal or official evidence of his purpose; but I know for certain that such was his intention, because early in 1858, and whilst Upper India was still in full rebellion, the Rajah seized an opportunity of conveying to myself, through an entirely private channel, not only the strongest protestations of his loyalty, gratitude and and devotion to the Government, but a distinct and earnest declaration, more than once repeated, of his wish that everything that he possessed should at his death pass into its hands.

" I beg you to compare this declaration with the passage in his letter now enclosed, in which the Rajah expresses grave fears that the measure announced from England will interfere with the claims which he and his heirs have for the restoration of the Government of his country.

" It may be very little desirable that more Provinces should be added to those which are already under the absolute rule of the Queen in India; but the case of Mysore, lying in the midst of the Madras Presidency, and already bound to us in a way which is not convenient or satisfactory, is quite exceptional; and the bequest of that country in full sovereignty to the Crown, by the free will of the ruler, and in a spirit of loyal attachment to the British power, is a consummation which, in the interests of all concerned, no one would wish to see defeated.

" It will be the first measure towards Mysore by the direct Government of the Queen, and it may probably be the last to be taken during the present Rajah's lifetime. Surely it is to be desired that it should not be such as to draw from the Rajah an emphatic protest and refusal of consent, in which he will carry with him, reasonably or unreasonably, the sympathy of his fellow Princes.

" I have, &c.,

" CANNING."

The first point that demands notice in this very remarkable despatch, and which must be carefully held in remembrance, is that Lord Canning very properly describes the Rajah as " the Sovereign of Mysore." The people of Mysore are also said in this despatch to be " his own subjects." A subsequent letter of great importance, addressed, under his Lordship's signature, to the Rajah, carefully avoids the use of these terms, and claims the sovereignty for the British Government.

The next noticeable point is the admission that " the Rajah is entitled to point (as he does point with pride) to the actual condition of his dominions." In that subsequent letter to the Rajah himself, which I shall shortly have to produce, he is expressly debarred from the merit of having given any support to Sir Mark Cubbon, whose enlightened services he had eulogised, and is taunted with the counteraction offered by himself and his partisans to the improvements introduced by that officer. That counteraction, chiefly due, as explained in the last Chapter, to the rivalry of the Resident and the Commissioner, had been reduced to nothing on the Resident's departure, and had ceased

entirely since 1847.   For thirteen years the most perfect
harmony had subsisted between the Rajah and General
Cubbon.   The General himself, in the same despatch, dated
the 2nd of June, 1860, from which I have already quoted
his testimony to the Rajah's loyal services during the rebellion, acknowledges "the cordiality observed by him for a
good many years towards the existing administration."*

In the despatch to the Secretary of State, which we have
just read, no complimentary words are omitted, no consideration is to be withheld, no offence is to be offered to
the dignity of "the Sovereign of Mysore," that "venerable
and loyal Prince"—apparently because he is supposed to be
going like a lamb to the slaughter.   In the subsequent
letter to the Rajah himself, which we have yet to see, he is
a "hereditary prisoner," his ancestors were "vassal chiefs,"
his rank and possessions are not hereditary, the sovereignty
of Mysore is claimed for the British Government, and every
form of studied disparagement and reproach is aimed at
this unfortunate Prince—apparently because he will not go
like a lamb to the slaughter, because the hope of his quietly
submitting to be extinguished has been dispelled.

The main interest and pith of the despatch now under
consideration are concentrated in two paragraphs, which I
shall here quote separately :—

"The Rajah of Mysore is an old man, past sixty, and of a family
notoriously shortlived.   He has no son, and has adopted no heir.
It has been supposed that he will bequeath his Kingdom to the
British Government.   I say 'supposed,' because there is no

---

* With what flagrant unfairness the opinion of Sir Mark Cubbon is quoted
against the Rajah, may be seen from the following extract of Sir John Willoughby's Minute :—" I do not think that the Despatch can be said to give an
impartial account of our past relations with the Mysore State, or is altogether
fair towards the present Rajah.   It brings prominently before the reader
various extracts from the records of olden times which tell against his Highness, by referring to the errors and vices of his youth, sufficiently atoned for,
most people will admit, by the penalty inflicted in 1831, and continued up to
the present time.   On the other hand, it either omits or passes by with brief
notice, other public records, and for the most part of more recent date, which
tell greatly in his Highness's favour.   The state of Mysore in 1863, is far different from what it was when Sir Thomas Munro in 1825, and Sir Mark Cubbon
in 1847, recorded the opinions against the Rajah quoted in the Despatch (paras.
10 and 30).   But, as regards the latter officer, it is matter of notoriety that
his opinion had changed, and that had he lived, he would have advocated restoration to the Rajah of the management of his country."—Mysore Papers,
p. 32.

formal or official evidence of his purpose; but I know for certain that such was his intention, because early in 1858, and whilst Upper India was still in full rebellion, the Rajah seized an opportunity of conveying to myself through an entirely private channel, not only the strongest protestations of his loyalty, gratitude and devotion to the Government, but a distinct and earnest declaration, more than once repeated, of his wish that everything he possessed should, at his death, pass into its hands."

And then :—

"I beg you to compare this declaration with the passage in his letter now enclosed, in which the Rajah expresses grave fears that the measure announced from England will interfere with the claims which he and his heirs have for the restoration of the Government of his country."

And certainly if the supposed declaration and the actual claim, be compared, they will be found to be directly contradictory. The only wonder is that this utter incompatibility of the colloquial concession with the written claim before his eyes,—a claim consistent with all the Rajah's authentic declarations before or since,—did not suggest to Lord Canning that there must have been some strange misunderstanding in 1858, some mistake in reporting the Rajah's private conversation, some wrong interpretation of his words, some mis-translation of his Oriental compliments to that *entirely private channel* through which his supposed "wish" was conveyed to the Governor-General. It appears as if Lord Canning was so eager to believe, and so anxious to persuade himself, that the Rajah had expressed this unaccountable "wish,"—at variance with the whole tenour of his life—that, although he knew this private report must require some formal document to corroborate it, he never took the least notice of it in his communications with the Rajah, never acknowledged it, or returned thanks for it, or requested any explanation on the subject, as if he feared that a touch would burst the bubble. If the Rajah's alleged message appeared to the Governor-General to be of any public importance, it was surely his duty to make some further inquiry about it. Instead of that, the very incident which we noticed in Lord Dalhousie's Minute of the 16th January, 1856, so typical of the moral weakness and legal nullity of these acquisitive apologetics,* is exactly re-

* Ante, p. 41-43.

produced. No question is asked, no confirmation is required of the vague expressions informally translated and informally reported. After having been treasured up for two years, the Rajah's deferential protestations are brought forward by Lord Canning,—as a rumour of his desponding soliloquy was by Lord Dalhousie,—to prove his Highness's indifference to the rights of his family and the future existence of his State, at the very time that he was contending for them.

The despatch then proceeds thus :—

"It may be very little desirable that more Provinces should be added to those which are already under the absolute rule of the Queen in India; but the case of Mysore, lying in the midst of the Madras Presidency, and already bound to us in a way which is not convenient or satisfactory, is quite exceptional; and the bequest of that country in full sovereignty to the Crown, by the free will of the ruler, and in a spirit of loyal attachment to the British power, is a consummation which, in the interest of all concerned, no one would wish to see defeated."

For my part I do most positively declare, that if the Rajah ever had any such intention, which I do not believe, I should have wished to see it defeated. I believe that we cannot afford to lose Mysore as a dependent native State, and that we cannot afford to take it as an additional British Province. Mysore is indeed "an exceptional case." It stands as the last barrier against a policy of despair and defiance. It ought to be made our model Principality. But if Mysore be annexed,—if, in defiance of her Majesty's Proclamation, the rapacious system is to be reopened,—our promises and counsels will never be believed or trusted, and any suggestion of reform, or offer of administrative assistance, will spread consternation and rouse opposition throughout every native State.

Lord Canning, as it seems to me, betrays an uneasy consciousness that the deliberate appropriation of Mysore would be quite indefensible, by his extreme anxiety that the Rajah should not be startled or provoked into an assertion of his rights; by that unpleasant allusion to the short lives of the Mysore family; and by his strongly expressed desire for a free will bequest "in full sovereignty." He plainly enough declares a hope that the Rajah may be allowed to dic quietly without having adopted a son, but states no doubt whatever as to his right to adopt a son if he chooses.

The free will bequest of the country in full sovereignty was never offered, and will never be effected; the Rajah, as he always intended, has now adopted a son. The loyal attachment which Lord Canning acknowledged, will be confirmed throughout Mysore by the restoration of the Rajah or his successor, but will not long survive the destruction of the dynasty.

Whatever objections may be made to this despatch on other grounds, it was effectual in removing the immediate grievance of which the Rajah complained; and in the following letter the Governor-General informed his Highness of the favourable result of his remonstrance :—

To his Highness the Maharajah of Mysore.

"Fort William, the 28th June, 1860.

" MAHARAJAH,

" I have the satisfaction to inform your Highness that the expression of the feelings with which your Highness regarded the proposed transfer of the superintendence of the Mysore Commission to the Government of Madras, received, so soon as it was known to Her Majesty's Secretary of State for India, the immediate and respectful consideration of the Queen's Government.

" I am informed by the Secretary of State, that, in making this transfer, it was intended that the policy which has guided the administration of the Mysore territory should remain the same, and that its superintendence should continue to be subject to the general authority and control of the Governor-General in Council, but that now, as being more agreeable to your Highness's feelings, it has been determined by Her Majesty's Government that the orders directing the transfer should be cancelled.

" It gratifies me to think that this intimation will be agreeable to your Highness. I have, etc.,

" CANNING."

Matters were thus restored to their former footing, and Sir Mark Cubbon consented to remain at his post. But in the following February he was attacked with very serious illness, and was compelled to resign. He died at Suez, on his way to England, in April 1861, at an advanced age, having passed the whole of the present century in India.

So far, let me remind my readers, the amenities prevail. Not a disagreeable word has passed between Calcutta and Mysore. The Rajah's letter to Lord Dalhousie of the 8th of August 1848, still remained unanswered at the end of 1860. The Rajah's repeated application to be reinstated in the government of his country, had never yet been directly refused. The last communication on the subject which his Highness had received, was the letter from General Cubbon of the 5th of December 1845, informing him, by the Governor-General's orders, that the delay on Lord Hardinge's part in replying to the Rajah's letter of the preceding 7th of June, was caused by a pending inquiry into the state of the Mysore debt.

But the crisis was now at hand. Besides one copy sent by his Lordship for General Cubbon's information, several copies of Lord Canning's despatch had reached Mysore and Madras, and the Rajah was not long kept in ignorance of its contents. While it appeared to promise him relief from his immediate cause of alarm, it did so on grounds that were still more alarming. He was represented as a life tenant, and as a life tenant by choice—as the last in entail, quite willing to make a bequest of his Kingdom, from his own "free will" and "loyal attachment," to the British Government. And notwithstanding his frequent previous assertions of his "hereditary patrimony," of the rights of his heirs and successors, his latest allusion to the claims of himself and his heirs to the restoration of the country, was spoken of in Lord Canning's despatch as if it were something quite new and unexpected. Somewhat encouraged therefore by the favourable answer given to his request, and the courteous terms in which it was conveyed, the Rajah saw that he must take the first opportunity of once more distinctly setting forth his unrevoked pretensions, and of urging their consideration on the Government of India. An opportunity seemed to present itself when General Cubbon's illness compelled him to resign the office of Commissioner. It was while Sir Mark Cubbon was preparing for his departure, that the Rajah addressed the following letter to Lord Canning :—

"Mysore Palace, 23rd February, 1861.

"MY LORD,

"I have to crave your indulgent attention to, and serious consideration of, a subject of the highest importance, which I shall, as briefly as is compatible with the magnitude of the interests involved, now proceed to lay before your Lordship. In the year 1799, the all-powerful English nation conquered the armies of Tippoo, stormed the fortress of Seringapatam, and slew the usurper, and then that great statesman, Lord Wellesley, founded a noble and disinterested policy, which added immensely to the fame of the British Government, and did more to establish its influence and consolidate its power than many great victories. The Governor-General waived all right of conquest, rescued me, then an infant, the rightful heir to the throne of Mysore, and the descendant of a long line of Kings, from captivity, and restored me to the musnud of my ancestors. By an Article in the Treaty between the British and myself, it was provided, that, if at any time the affairs of my country fell into confusion, the British Government should have the power of assuming the management of the country until order was restored; and in 1831, Lord William Bentinck, then Governor-General, intimated to me that this provision of the Treaty was to be enforced, and it was enforced without being resisted in any way by me. I will not pause to argue whether the step taken was an absolutely necessary one. The character of Lord William Bentinck was a guaranty that he considered it so; but his views must have been subsequently greatly modified, for he proposed in the year 1834, two and a half years after the assumption of my country, that three-fourths of it should be restored to my control, on the condition that I assented to the temporary alienation of the remaining portion, as a guaranty for the payment of my Subsidy to the British Government.* I had previously been gratified by his Lordship's assurance that the assumption of the administration of my country by the Government had not been caused by the personal omissions of the Sovereign. In the year 1836, Lord Auckland received a despatch from the Court of Directors, in which their opinion was declared, to the effect that, instead of adopting the views of Lord William Bentinck, they considered it a better course to let the sole management of the country remain as it was, until such salutary rules and safeguards should be matured, as would place the affairs of Mysore on a safe and secure basis. In a despatch from the Court of Directors, republished by your Lordship in your last Administration Report of India, it is ordered, with reference to Mysore, ' that they are desirous of adhering, as far as can be

---

* This is a singular mistake of the Rajah's. Lord William Bentinck proposed a permanent cession, not a temporary alienation. Could the Rajah have misunderstood it at the time ?

done, to the native usages, and not to introduce a system which cannot be worked hereafter by native agency *when the country shall be restored to the Rajah.'* After a personal inspection, Lord Dalhousie, on his return to Calcutta, pronounced his decision, that the affairs of Mysore were all that could be desired. My Lord, I never hesitate to assert that the enviable state of Mysore is to be attributed to the enlightened services of Sir Mark Cubbon, whose acknowledgments of my support have received your Lordship's recognition. During twenty-six years he has carried on the administration of the affairs of my Kingdom, and has indisputably shown that whatever requirements there may be in other countries for introducing changes, Sir Mark Cubbon has established that Mysore needs none of them, for its native system of government has produced results that bear comparison with any that can be exhibited in any part of India, whether its material prosperity, the happiness of its people, or any other test be applied. But, my Lord, as you know, Sir Mark Cubbon leaves his office, and there is no successor who can occupy his place. He departs with the fervent prayers of the Sovereign and his subjects, that blessings may be showered on him.

"The universal desire of my people, and justice to my own character, require that I should now solicit the restoration of my sovereign rights, of which I was deprived, as has already been stated, as a temporary measure ; in proof of which, should proof be required in a matter so notorious, I beg to refer your Lordship to Lord William Bentinck's despatch to the Court of Directors, the Court's answer to Lord Auckland, also the Court's despatch, an extract from which I have quoted above. What I ask, my Lord, is not much ; the country is acknowledged to be mine ; all I ask, then, before I die, is that I may be restored to the position I formerly held, that the stigma which now attaches to my name may be removed, and that I may appear once more before my own subjects and the Princes and people of India as the Sovereign of Mysore in fact as well as in word.

"I ask for my country, not with the intention of making any great changes in the nature of its administration, for Sir Mark Cubbon has shown where the safe road to further improvement alone lies ; and I purpose, by the selection of experienced persons to conduct the Government, to prove that this State will continue to prosper under a superintended native administration, and be as heretofore loyal to Her Majesty and to her successors, be the consequences what they may to myself and my heirs. I have now only to request your Lordship to submit this letter to Her Majesty's Government, and to solicit your support of my claim ; and this, from the proofs I have already received of your Lordship's generous nature, and from the noble sentiments expressed in your Lordship's letter to the Secretary of State for India, on the question of the rights of native Princes, I feel assured I shall receive. And here I hope I may be pardoned if I express my individual opinion, as one of the Sovereigns of India, on your Lordship's just and wise treatment of the native Princes of this great country, in strengthening their hands, elevating their position, and consolidating their possessions. A day will come, my Lord, possibly not in my time, for I am now an old man, but probably at no remote period, when these Princes and Chiefs, bound to your Government by the double tie of gratitude and self-interest, will present a bulwark which neither the wave of foreign invasion nor the tide of internal disaffection can throw down; and then the wisdom and justice of your Lordship's policy, a policy which no Governor-General before your Lordship had the courage to avow, will become manifest to the world. In conclusion, I beg you to remember, my Lord, that I have never committed the smallest offence towards the British Government. I have ever been true and loyal; the avowed object for which the Government of my country was temporarily assumed has long since been accomplished, and there is no justifiable pretext for its further retention. Support, then, my prayer, my Lord; render me justice, and make the few remaining days of a Sovereign who has drunk so deeply of the bitter cup of affliction as I have done, happy, and you will add another jewel to that immortal crown which your Lordship has earned by your generous advocacy and support of the rights of the Princes of India."

The solemn appeal here recorded remained unanswered and unnoticed for thirteen months.

CHAPTER IV.

1862 to 1863.

THE letter dated the 11th of March, 1862, which I am now about to lay before my readers, with a few brief comments of my own annexed to some of the paragraphs,* did not, of course, come into the hands of the Rajah of Mysore until several days after Lord Canning's departure ; for his Lordship left Calcutta for England on the 12th of March, the very day after that on which this letter must have been signed, and, I suppose, despatched. In all probability, therefore, this was Lord Canning's last public act of any importance.

" To his Highness the Maharajah Kishen Raj Wadiyar Bahadoor,
" Mysore.

" MY HONOURED AND VALUED FRIEND,

1. " I have received your Highness's Khureetas of the 14th August and 21st October, urging, with reference to your own advanced age and my approaching return to England, that a speedy answer should be given to your Highness's Khureeta of the 23rd February, 1861.

2. " It is your Highness's request that the last mentioned Khureeta may be submitted to Her Majesty's Government, and that it may be accompanied by my support of the claim therein advanced—that claim being, that the management of the country of Mysore should be now restored to your Highness.

3. " This demand, based upon arguments which will hereafter be noticed, is one which it is as little my inclination as my duty, to treat lightly, or to set aside without the most patient and impartial consideration; and I regret the disappointment which may be caused to your Highness, when I now inform you of my inability to support your claim, or to admit the grounds on which it is founded, and which I regard as mistaken and untenable.

4. " My regret is the greater because it was my pleasing duty, in a letter of the 28th June, 1860, to express to your Highness

---

* I have affixed numbers to the paragraphs, which was not done in the original. I have also italicised certain passages.

my cordial thanks for your steadfast loyalty, prominently noticed by the late Sir Mark Cubbon in his letter of the 2nd June, 1860, and subsequently to make known to Her Majesty's Government the spirit by which your Highness had been animated, and of which you had given substantial proofs during the troubles of 1857. Your Highness, in your Khureeta of the 23rd February, 1861, after a candid avowal that the present enviable state of Mysore is attributable to the enlightened services of Sir Mark Cubbon, has referred to a supposed recognition by me, not only of the loyalty displayed by your Highness at the time of which Sir Mark Cubbon wrote, but also of support given by your Highness to that officer during his long and able administration. Had Sir Mark Cubbon ever acknowledged such support, your Highness must feel sure that nothing would have been more agreeable to me than to have had it in my power, on such good grounds, to attribute to your Highness a share in the credit due for the successful administration of Mysore. Under such circumstances there would most certainly have been no hesitation on my part in freely according to your Highness the merit which you appear to claim in your Khureeta of the 23rd February, 1861. But I cannot conceal from your Highness that throughout the correspondence between Sir Mark Cubbon and this Government, extending as it does over many years, *I have failed to find any such acknowledgment.* Sir Mark Cubbon has left on record opinions of an entirely contrary character. He has stated that any improvements which had taken place had been effected *in spite of the counteraction he had met with on the part of your Highness and your partisans,* and that the conduct of your Highness, during your suspension from power, would afford no security that the crisis which had induced your suspension would not recur in the event of your restoration."

PARAGRAPH 4.

It is strange that the Calcutta officials should "have failed to find such an acknowledgment". They might have found one, if they had looked for it, in Sir Mark Cubbon's despatch of the 2nd of June, 1860, in which he acknowledges "the cordiality observed by the Rajah for a good many years towards the existing administration."

As to the counteraction of the Rajah and his "partisans", suffice it once more to observe, that all such counteraction had ceased for nearly fifteen years. (*Ante,* pp. 30, 31.)

General Cubbon undoubtedly was opposed to the Rajah being restored to absolute power. And so am I.

5. "Your Highness observes that the Marquis of Wellesley rescued you when an infant from captivity,—this is true; but the Marquis Wellesley, when he released you from *a hereditary*

prison, and placed you on the Throne of Mysore, *far from waiving any right of conquest, asserted and maintained that right* in all its integrity and in a threefold manner. In the first place, after the fall of Seringapatam, and the death of Tippoo Sultan, the Territory thus conquered was made the subject of a Partition Treaty, in which your Highness was not otherwise a party concerned than as the notified future recipient of the liberality of the British Government. *The contracting parties were the Governor General and the Nizam.* The details of the Partition of the Territory were prescribed by Lord Wellesley, *the conquest having been effected by British arms.* This was Lord Wellesley's first and chief assertion of the right of conquest, and in it your Highness had no share whatever as a principal."

PARAGRAPH 5.

The Mussulman domination, which during the twenty-two years of Hyder Ali's rule never impugned the sovereignty of the old House, endured for no more than thirty-eight years, hardly long enough for the Rajah's legitimate rights to have been forgotten or annihilated. *We* had not lost sight of them, for sixteen years before his release we had made a Treaty with his father, and had hoisted the Mysore Rajah's colours on a fort taken from Tippoo. (*Ante*, p. 9.) Lord Wellesley, while unquestionably maintaining the rights of conquest, — not of British arms alone, but of the Company and the Nizam,—still respected and relied upon the antiquity and legitimate title of the Hindoo family. And this is recorded in the Partition Treaty and in all the contemporary documents, as one principal reason for the Rajah's elevation.

6. "In the next place, *ancillary to the Partition Treaty of Mysore*, was the grant, on certain conditions, of that portion of the territories conquered from Tippoo Sultan, which the Governor General thought proper to assign to your Highness. The instrument was styled the Subsidiary Treaty; *its subordinate relation to the Partition Treaty* being thereby indicated. The cession of territory in favour of your Highness, which comprised districts annexed by Hyder Ali, over which your ancestors had never ruled, *was based distinctly upon the British Government's*

PARAGRAPH 6.

The Subsidiary Treaty, by which the Rajah was placed in possession of his Principality, was undoubtedly "ancillary" and "subordinate" to the Partition Treaty. That is the strongest part of the Rajah's case. The cession or grant in favour of his Highness was not made by the Subsidiary, but by *right of conquest.* In one of the communications from your Highness, mention is made of that hereditary patrimony ' bequeathed to me by my sires, the Sovereigns of the Soil.' But when the grant was made by Lord Wellesley in favour of your Highness, you did not inherit any patrimony in the soil, and you could not claim a single village, for the independence of your Highness's ancestors, after the destruction of the Kingdom of Bijeynuggur, to which they had long been vassal chiefs, was short-lived, and they had entirely lost by the sword what they had gained by the sword. *Therefore, your Highness's title to authority in Mysore rests solely upon the cession made to you by the British Government;* and both in the Subsidiary Treaty, and in the despatches explanatory of the principles on which it was framed, Lord Wellesley was careful to assert that the only basis of your dominion was *the British right of conquest,* and the power of his Government to make the cession on conditions. This was Lord Wellesley's second assertion, and *maintenance of the right of conquest.*"

the Partition Treaty, and, therefore, is *not* "based distinctly upon the British Government's right of conquest." The Rajah was placed on the throne by the chief officers of the Allied Powers after the Partition Treaty was signed, but eight days before the Subsidiary Treaty was concluded.

Some districts over which the Rajah's "ancestors had never ruled," were ceded to him; and some districts which had formed part of his hereditary possessions were included in the Company's share.

If we add the name of the other contracting party, the Nizam,—never omitted by Lord Wellesley, but always overlooked in this despatch,—it is perfectly true that "the only basis of the Rajah's dominion," after 1799, was the right of conquest of the Allies, and their power to make the cession. And what better basis, what better title could he have? But the cession was made by the two Allies in their Partition Treaty, and not in the subordinate Treaty between the Company and the Rajah, in which no word of cession or specification of territory occurs, but in which the Rajah is treated as already Sovereign of Mysore under the Partition Treaty.

7. "Lastly, the fourth and fifth Articles of the Subsidiary Treaty show that *far from waiving the rights derived from conquest,* Lord Wellesley, in a very signal manner, *kept those rights alive* in the conditions which he attached to the cession. By the fifth Article, a wide discretionary power is retained to the Governor-General to assume, whether your Highness consent or not, the management of the Territories, and to provide for the effectual protection of the country and the welfare

of the people. Nor was the latitude of this discretion unintentional. In a despatch which accompanied the draft Treaty of Seringapatam, Lord Wellesley informed the Commissioners that the provisions of Article 5 were absolutely necessary for the purpose of precluding the embarrassments which had arisen in Oude, the Carnatic, and Tanjore, and that, in his opinion, it was a more candid and liberal, as well as a more wise policy, to apprise your Highness, from the first hour of your accession, of the nature of your dependence, than to leave any channel open for future ambiguity and discussion. His Lordship proceeded to state that this was a point which he held to be so essential to the very existence of the new arrangement, that if it should appear objectionable ' on grounds of which he was not then aware', he saw no alternative but that of dividing the whole territory between the Allies : in other words, of totally excluding your

PARAGRAPH 7.

The fourth and fifth Articles of the Subsidiary Treaty show that the Allies having, by their right of conquest, ceded Mysore to a descendant of the ancient Rajahs, the British Government could only secure to itself the power of interference in the government by a special agreement to that effect in the Treaty. The Rajah's right of sovereignty depends upon the Partition Treaty, and the British right of guidance depends upon the Subsidiary Treaty, and not upon "keeping the rights of conquest alive",—a very inaccurate rhetorical flourish, as I shall show.

Highness from the proposed liberality of the British Government, if there were any demur on the part of those acting for your Highness to accept the grant on the conditions attached to it. Nor was he less precise, when reporting his arrangements to the Court of Directors and to the Ministers of the Crown."

8. "Throughout these despatches there is *no waiving of the rights of conquest, and of the Supreme Sovereignty which it conferred upon the British Government.* On the contrary, there is repeated assertion in the strongest and clearest language, that in the arrangements made, it was had in view that the title of your Highness to the territory entrusted to you, should have no other basis than *the right and power of the British Government to assign it,* and that the grant of dominion over that territory was to be in en-

PARAGRAPH 8.

Here we have a perfectly new term introduced, a term quite unheard of from 1799 to 1862—"the Supreme Sovereignty" of the British Government over Mysore. This is a term to which the Rajah would certainly not object,—though I believe Imperial Supremacy would be more accurate,—if it were used without prejudice to his rights as

tire subordination to the *Sovereignty* of the British Government, and was conditional on the country being governed in accordance with the wishes of the British Government, for the good of the people, and in a manner that should leave no reason to apprehend failure in bearing such share of the burthen of military expenditure in peace or in war, as the Governor-General defined for the one, and left open to discretion in the other state of affairs. There is then no doubt whatever as to the intentions of *the Marquis Wellesley, when making the grant in favour of your Highness.* He has recorded them in the different stages of the arrangement; first, prior to its completion; next, in the terms and conditions themselves of the Treaty; and, lastly, when announcing to the British Government that the spontaneous act, by which conditional dominion was conferred on your Highness, was secured from being hereafter made a ground for assumptions such as those which I regret to see in your Highness's Khureeta."

Sovereign of Mysore. Since 1799 the Rajah has stood towards the British Government in the position of a subordinate, dependent Prince, a position by no means incompatible with that of Sovereign over his own dominions. But the term is clearly introduced here, in order to insinuate that he is not, and never was a Sovereign at all, but a sort of probationary Satrap or Hospodar, tolerated during good behaviour, but removable at will.

And this Supreme Sovereignty is said to be conferred upon the British Government by "the right of conquest"; and it is again asserted that the Rajah's title had "no other basis than the right and power of the British Government to assign it"; to which I must again reply that the right of conquest, as proclaimed by Lord Wellesley, belonged to the Company and the Nizam, and that the Rajah's territories were not assigned to him as a grant by Lord Wellesley, or by the British Government, but by the Allies, under their Treaty of Partition.

9. "But the Khureeta, passing from assumptions without foundation, proceeds on the strength of them to make an appeal for justice, complains of the further retention, without justifiable pretext, of your country, after the avowed object for which its government had been temporarily assumed, had long since been accomplished; and claims the restoration of sovereign rights, the suspension of which, it is asserted, was always stated to be a temporary measure. Your Highness thus challenges the justice and the good faith of the British Government. Thereby your Highness compels me to point out to you, that the British Government did not interpose to enforce the remedy provided in the Subsidiary Treaty, until the obliga-

tions which attached to the cession had been for *twenty years flagrantly and habitually violated*, in spite of repeated warnings and remonstrances by the British Government and its agents; nor until the country had been driven into rebellion by misgovernment of the very worst description, and when, but for that interference, most of the provinces of Mysore would have effectually shaken off your Highness's authority."

10. "It was under these circumstances that the British Government, sensible of the responsibility which the *rights of conquest* and of *sovereignty* imposed upon it, acted upon the provisions of the Treaty; and having made ample provision for your Highness's comfort and dignity, *cancelled the authority it had conferred*, and re-entered on the possession and the administration of the Mysore territory, in order to retrieve its public resources, and to rescue the country from anarchy and ruin. When thus reluctantly forced to supersede your Highness's authority, no expectation, direct or indirect, was held out that that authority would be restored in your Highness's lifetime, *under its former conditions*. The Government of India carefully held itself free to act as future circumstances might show to be the best; and it abstained from all pledge to Prince or people, that an administration which had so signally failed, would ever be re-established."

PARAGRAPH 9.

The misgovernment of Mysore was due, as I have shown, to the fault of the British Government, which allowed a boy of sixteen to assume absolute power, and neglected to employ the efficient means provided by the Treaty for the regulation and control of the native administration. It is therefore the worst abuse of language to call the misgovernment of Mysore "a flagrant and habitual violation of the Treaty". (*Ante*, p. 15-16.)

PARAGRAPH 10.

The British Government is said to have "cancelled the authority it had conferred". Nothing was cancelled; no permanent change was declared or intended at that time. And thus Lord William Bentinck writes in a Minute dated 14th April, 1834: "Is the Subsidiary Treaty of Mysore virtually cancelled, or is it still in full force?"

"The answer must decidedly be that the management has been assumed for and on behalf of the Rajah, and that the Treaty is in full force." (Mysore Papers, 1866, page 26.)

It is said that the Rajah was never led to expect that his authority would be restored, "under its former conditions." The Rajah has never asked to be replaced at the head of affairs under the former conditions of lawless power. On the contrary, he has proposed the imposition of regulations and ordinances.

11. "Your Highness has adverted to certain proposals made by Lord William Bentinck, subject to the approval of the British Government. As the latter withheld its concurrence, the proposals of the Governor-General fell to the ground. In the course of the correspondence, the Court of Directors used language which was consistent with a purpose, at some future period, *and under conditions left undefined,* to restore a native Government, but *not specifically that of your Highness.* The expressions of the Court of Directors were simply in the way of caution, to prevent anything being done which could interfere with the future free action of the British Government, as to the form of administration to be organised for Mysore. There was nothing in them which approached to a pledge to restore your Highness' share in the administration, even if administration by a British Commission should fail. That which the Treaty promised, the British Government scrupulously performed; and your Highness is now enjoying the personal provision which was secured to you in the event of that Government resuming the administration of Mysore. *This provision is a personal right, not an heritable one. It is not claimable as a right, even by a natural-born heir,* however liberally the Government might, of its own grace, be disposed to deal with a claim from such a quarter; and as your Highness failed to fulfil the obligations of the authority which had been ceded to you, it is the only right which remains to you; and your title

PARAGRAPH 11.

The writer of the despatch says that the Court of Directors spoke of restoring a native Government, "under conditions left undefined," and "not specifically that of his Highness." Yet the Court of Directors objected to "a system which cannot be worked hereafter by native agency when the country shall be restored *to the Rajah.*" (*Ante*, p. 46.) This mention of the Rajah is surely quite as specific as his Highness himself could desire.

The sting of the whole letter lies in the latter part of this paragraph, which proves too clearly that it is not merely the retention of the management that is sought to be justified, but the eventual extinction of the native State. The Rajah's share of the revenue is declared to be "the only right which remains" to him, and this is "a personal right, not a heritable one." The only reason that is given for declaring the sovereignty not to be hereditary, is that he has "forfeited" his "title" "through misrule," and that he has "failed to fulfil the obligations of the authority which was ceded to him"—penalties which are unexplained and unjustified either by the facts of the Rajah's rule, or by the particular provisions of the Treaty, or by the general principles of international law.

to that right is exactly the same as was your title to the authority which you forfeited through misrule. That is, it rests upon favour shown to your Highness by the British Government, in its mode of dealing with other rights which it had acquired by conquest."

12. "The good faith of that Government towards your Highness is inviolate. Its justice can as little be called in question. After *patiently permitting for twenty years an administration which culminated in insurrection,* and rendered necessary the intervention of British troops to suppress anarchy, the British Government was imperatively called upon to vindicate its own character for justice, and not to permit its name or its power to be identified with misrule. It had a duty to fulfil towards the people of Mysore, and for thirty years, under the able and honest administration of British Officers, that duty has been efficiently performed. Solvency has been restored, and order is now maintained in Mysore. So far the immediate purpose of the resumption has been obtained. But when your Highness proceeds to state that the native system of government has produced these results, and that you will provide an administration for the future as good as that which you would supersede, your Highness seems to forget the material fact that the para-

PARAGRAPH 12.

That the Government of India "patiently permitted" the maladministration of Mysore for twenty years, which the writer of this despatch strangely enough seems to consider a proof of graceful forbearance, is, as I have already shown, an example of inexcusable neglect of duty, which might be much more deservedly, and much more appropriately stigmatised as a breach of solemn obligations, than the untutored extravagance of the young Prince's career. (*Ante,* p. 16.)

There is, and always was, an ample security for the good government of Mysore,—including, if thought necessary, the employment of English officers, —in the proper application of Article XIV of the Treaty, declaring the authoritative nature of British counsels.

mount authority of British Officers is the safeguard, and the very essence of the good which is manifest in the present administration. Your Highness *fails to offer any security upon a point not inferior in importance to the restoration of order and solvency, namely, the future maintenance of good government in Mysore.* This was one of the avowed purposes of the resumption of authority by the British Government; and I say frankly to your Highness that it is my conviction, founded on experience of the past, that if the authority of the British Officers was removed, or even hampered, the peace and prosperity of Mysore would be at an end. The justice of the British Government might indeed be open to question, if, without the fullest security that the measure would not be synonymous with a return to oppression and misrule, the province of Mysore was replaced under its former Head."

13. "The obligations of the British Government to the people of Mysore, are as sacred as its self-imposed obligations to your Highness, which alone form your Highness's title to any rights under the Subsidiary Treaty.

When in that Treaty the British Government *reserved to itself the reassumption at its own discretion of the dominions entrusted under conditions to your Highness*, it thereby acknowledged the obligation by which *conquest* had been accompanied, and admitted its responsibility for the enduring welfare of *the people over whom it had become Sovereign*. And whilst the British Government has been careful to satisfy the right which it originally conceded to your Highness, and certainly not the less careful because *the concession was made spontaneously, and without its being in your Highness's power to offer any consideration of the smallest political value as an equivalent*, it is equally alive to its obligations to the people of Mysore, and to the responsibility for their prosperity and welfare, of which it cannot divest itself. It has been and will continue to be scrupulously just to both parties."

PARAGRAPH 13.

The British Government did *not* "reserve to itself the reassumption at its own discretion of the dominions entrusted under conditions" to his Highness. The Treaty simply empowered the Honourable Company to assume management of such a portion of the Rajah's territories as might be sufficient to supply funds for the Subsidy, "whenever" and "so long" as there should be "reason to apprehend" a failure in the funds so destined. This is very far from amounting to the "re-assumption" of dominions held merely as a trust by the Rajah.

When the writer of the despatch states that the Rajah's sovereignty in Mysore was a "concession made spontaneously" by the British Government, and that it was not in the Rajah's power "to offer any consideration of the smallest political value," the statement is in direct contradiction of the opinions of Lord Wellesley as to the political theory and expectations of 1799, and to the opinions of such men as the Duke of Wellington, Sir John Malcolm, the Marquis of Hastings and Sir Mark Cubbon, as to the practical results from 1799 down to 1860.

14. "Your Highness has pressed upon my consideration your advanced age, and your desire that the stigma which attaches to

your name might be removed by a restoration to the position you formerly held. These are pleas to which in themselves I desire to show respect, and all practicable indulgence, but accompanied as they have been by pretensions based upon erroneous assumptions, and leading as they have led to an imputation upon the fair dealing of the British Government, it has been incumbent on me to correct the errors into which your Highness has fallen; and to put upon record, that in my opinion your Highness was very ill-advised, when upon the grounds of assumed ancestral and hereditary rights which have no existence, and of admissions and promises which never were made, you permitted yourself to forget the generosity of the British Government, in order to call in question its good faith and justice.

"I beg to express the high consideration I entertain for your Highness, and I beg to subscribe myself,

"Your Highness's sincere Friend,

"CANNING.

"*Fort William, 11th March, 1862.*"

This letter is well known not to have been of Lord Canning's composition, though he sanctioned and signed it at the last moment, when enfeebled by illness, and glad to dispose in any way of an irritating and perplexing subject that had long pressed for settlement, and which he felt ought not to be handed over to Lord Elgin, after a year's delay, in an undetermined state. The Calcutta Secretariat could not forgive the Rajah for having so signally discomfited their confident anticipations of the forthcoming bequest of the Principality, "in free will and full sovereignty", and "in a spirit of loyal attachment", by its "venerable Sovereign", —"more than sixty years of age, and of a family notoriously short-lived". From this source seems to have been infused that otherwise unaccountable acrimony which pervades the whole letter.

Captain W. J. Eastwick makes the following observations in his Minute of Dissent, with reference to this stage of the case :—"It thus appears, that while we believed that the Maharajah intended to give his country to the British Government he had entire liberty to bequeath it 'in full sovereignty;' but when this illusion is dispelled, we find out that he has not the right to bequeath it to any one, even to a natural or adopted heir. In the same spirit we appeal to the conditions of the Treaty when we wish to divest the

Rajah of his dominions; and we ignore the Treaty when called upon under its conditions to restore the country to the Rajah."*

Within a month from its receipt the Rajah sent a rejoinder to the newly arrived Governor-General, Lord Elgin, as an appeal to the Home Government against Lord Canning's decision.†

For nearly a year and a half the Rajah heard nothing officially on the subject of this appeal; though rumours, supposed to be authentic,‡ more than once reached India, of great differences of opinion and animated discussions in the India Council as to the Hindoo Sovereign's rights, as to the duty of the British Government towards him and towards the people of Mysore, and as to the general policy of restoration. And at one period the Rajah was positively assured—and the assurance was not, I believe, founded on error—that the Secretary of State had consented to reinstate his Highness at the head of the Mysore Government on certain conditions, and that a draft despatch to that effect had been actually prepared, and was under consideration at the India Office. All his hopes, however, were damped for the present at the conversation with the Commissioner of Mysore described in the following Memorandum.

"At an interview which Mr. Bowring had with the Rajah of Mysore on the 14th September 1863, the following conversation took place:—

"Mr. Bowring.

"A private letter has been received by me from Lord Elgin, the Viceroy, stating that a despatch from the Home Government contains an unfavourable decision with regard to your Highness's appeal for the restoration of the government of your country. His Lordship has desired me to inform him of the whole of your Highness's desires, and to report to him my own sentiments regarding the promotion and advancement of your Highness's dignity and comfort.

"The Maharajah.

"The British Government considering me as the sole and rightful owner of this Kingdom—a Kingdom which from antiquity belonged to my ancestors—established me on the throne.

---

* Mysore Papers, 1866, p. 77.
† Ibid., 1866, p. 8.
‡ Known to be authentic since the appearance of the Parliamentary Papers Relating to Mysore of 1866.

"You must be aware that I myself ruled this country for a space of twenty-two years with absolute power. I now firmly assert that I now am what I have been through life, a humble Ally, a staunch friend and well-wisher to the British Government. Moreover you must consider that I am the very person who was proclaimed by the Treaty of 1799 to be the rightful heir. I am no one else, but the same man, who is by the blessing of God still alive, and whose privileges and titles have from time to time been fully acknowledged and upheld by the British Government. It would undoubtedly be as well consistent with the principles of justice, as it would be gratifying to myself and to all my subjects, should the British Government, honouring the solemn provisions of the Treaty of 1799, restore me in my old age to the government of my country, which was declared to be assumed only for a certain time. But I have noted down on this paper all my sentiments, and I particularly desire you to hear me read it; or I shall be glad to have it translated, if you will give me the services of one of your Assistants for a few minutes.

" Mr. Bowring.

" As your Highness's case has been finally settled by the Secretary of State, there could be no advantage in my hearing anything more regarding the restoration of the government; but if there be any suggestion for the improvement of your Highness's dignity and comfort, your Highness can express yourself verbally with perfect freedom.

" The Maharajah.

"It is my wish that the British Government should make it known by proclamation throughout my Kingdom that the country has been restored to me. Hereafter I wish that the Commissioner of Mysore may be designated the Resident and Minister at my Court,—the government being still administered by him, but in my name, and with my voice in all matters of importance. The balance now in the Treasury should be made over to me, and the yearly revenue also, after deducting the necessary expenses of the public establishments.* The power of Adoption must be admitted

---

* This, I must confess, is rather an alarming demand; but all alarm and anxiety on the subject ought to have been dispelled long ago, and could be dispelled before the Rajah's restoration, by "a regulation or ordinance"—to be issued as a law by the Sovereign—establishing a public Treasury and a Civil List or Privy Purse, with distinct accounts, forms and vouchers for disbursement, and under responsible officers. The organisation and control of such institutions are of course difficult at first, but not impossible; and after a time—after a succession and a minority, for instance—they would work by themselves.

During General Cubbon's administration a surplus, amounting to upwards of a million sterling, had accumulated, *in specie*, in the Mysore Treasury; part of which has been recently invested in the Indian Funds.

to rest with me. It is my earnest desire that the native State of Mysore should continue from generation to generation. If these requests are complied with it will raise me in the estimation of my brethren, the Princes of India, it would be a source of gratification to me, and fill my people with contentment.

" *Mr. Bowring.*

" Is it your Highness's wish to adopt a son to succeed to all your Highness's possessions ?

" *The Maharajah.*

" It is not only my wish to make such an adoption, but I repeat it, it is my determination to adopt a son, in conformity with the Hindoo law and the long established usages of my ancestors, to be the representative of the ancient Rajahs of Mysore.

" *Mr. Bowring.*

" What is the name of the youth whom your Highness intends to adopt,—to what line of descent does he belong; to the *Moogoor* or to the *Calola* line ?

" *The Maharajah.*

" The youth does not belong to either of the branches you mention. His name cannot be announced at present, nor until the proper time arrives; but it is my express desire that you should communicate what I have said on this point to the Governor-General."

And shortly after this, the lamented and sudden death of Lord Elgin having occurred, it fell to Sir William Denison, who as senior Governor had taken provisional charge of the Viceregal office, to communicate officially to his Highness the views taken by the Home Government on the question of his reinstatement. This was done in the following letter.

" *To his Highness Maharajah Kishen Raj Wadiyar Bahadoor,
of Mysore, etc., etc., etc.*

" My honoured and valued Friend,

" It is my duty to inform your Highness that your appeal against the decision of the Government of India which was conveyed to you in Lord Canning's Khareeta dated the 11th March 1862, was duly forwarded to the Secretary of State in Council, and that the commands of Her Majesty's Government on the subject of the administration of the Mysore Territories, have now been received.

" Her Majesty's Government, in arriving at their decision, have

been influenced by an anxious desire to do justice to all those
who would be affected by it, and have felt that every consideration
is due to your Highness on account of your age and your loyalty
to the British Government. At the same time Her Majesty's
Government, after weighing fully and carefully all the arguments
adduced by your Highness have decided that your title to the
territories of Mysore rests solely upon the exercise by the British
Government, in your favour, of an undoubted right of conquest;
that the Subsidiary Treaty of the 8th July 1799 contains no conditions under which the administration of your Highness's possessions, if once assumed by the British Government, was to be
restored to you; that while the orders from time to time issued
by the Government of India and the Home Government, indicate
a wish that no steps should be taken or expressions used which
would interfere with the free exercise of their discretion in any
future circumstances which might arise, the expression of these
sentiments constitutes no obligation on the part of the British
Government to reinstate your Highness and gives your Highness
no right to such restoration.

"Her Majesty's Government are of opinion that the assumption
of the administration of your Highness's Territories in 1831, was
in accordance with the provisions of the Subsidiary Treaty; that
your Highness cannot, as of right, now claim its restoration; and
that the reinstatement of your Highness in the administration of
the country is incompatible with the true interests of the people
of Mysore.

"I am therefore commanded by Her Majesty's Government to
inform your Highness, that Her Majesty's Government have determined not to interfere with the decision which was communicated to your Highness by Earl Canning and confirmed by Lord
Elgin, and that the administration of Mysore shall continue to
be conducted as at present by the British officers.

"I beg to express the high consideration I entertain for your
Highness, and to subscribe myself,

"Your Highness's sincere friend,

"W. DENISON."

"Fort William, the 31st December 1863."

There is nothing contained in this letter that will be new
to my readers, nothing that demands any lengthened comment. In terms more guarded and courteous than those
used in Lord Canning's letter, the Rajah's title to the territories of Mysore is said to "rest solely upon the exercise by
the British Government, in his favour, of an undoubted
right of conquest". To this, after again observing that the
conquest and the cession were made not by the British

Government solely, but by the British Government and its Ally the Nizam, I can only once more append the question,—What better title could the Rajah possibly have ? The Rajah certainly desires no better title than the cession of 1799, and has never repudiated his obligations to the British Government, although he alludes with very natural pride to the antiquity of that legitimate title which Lord Wellesley himself professed to respect, and which is recorded in the Partition Treaty.

The Rajah's claim to reinstatement is explicitly and decidedly rejected in this despatch—for the first time be it observed since 1832—on the ground that the Subsidiary Treaty "contains no conditions under which the administration of his Highness's possessions, if once assumed by the British Government, was to be restored to him." There are indeed no particular conditions mentioned, no peculiar formality or process is laid down in the Treaty by which the restoration is to be accompanied ; but at the same time it certainly does not appear to contemplate the perpetual retention of the government in our hands, since all the provisions of the Articles authorising British management, are expressly stated to be applicable only "*so long* as any part or parts of his Highness's territories shall remain under" our " exclusive authority and control."

In Article V of the Subsidiary Treaty it is expressly provided, that " whenever and so long " as any part of Mysore remains in our hands, we are to " render to his Highness a true and faithful account of the revenues and produce of the territories so assumed." This stipulation is now, and has been always, fulfilled by the British Commissioner. The accounts are regularly furnished to the Rajah up to this day.

The Treaty undoubtedly leaves the execution of the two corrective Articles, IV and V, both as to commencement and as to duration, to the discretion of the British Government. But this discretion, being of necessity so placed in the hands of that one of the two contracting parties which alone possesses the power of enforcing the provisions of the Treaty, the heaviest moral obligation is imposed upon it to be cautious as to the commencement of such an execution, and to make its duration as brief as possible—to treat

the weaker party with good faith and generous consideration, so long as he conducts himself with loyalty and deference towards his powerful Ally and Patron. This the Rajah
of Mysore has always done, and he has never been accused
of doing otherwise. But we were *not* cautious in commencing the execution ; having previously neglected to
train the Rajah and to organise his administration, we overlooked, when it fell into disorder, the milder plan of introducing regulations and ordinances, and at once rushed to
the extreme process—that "harsh and unprovoked measure,"
as Lord Metcalfe called it, of setting the Prince entirely
aside, and putting the management exclusively in the hands
of English officers. And we have certainly not, in any way
or at any time, tried to shorten the duration of our interference. I cannot but come to the conclusion that the Subsidiary Treaty has been infringed by the stronger party,
both in letter and spirit, and that the weaker party is entitled to a signal and complete reparation The Subsidy,
which Lord William Bentinck admitted had "never been in
jeopardy," having been punctually paid for sixty-five years
in monthly instalments according to the terms of the Treaty ;
there is no reason to doubt that the funds of the State are
efficient and available in time of peace or war ;" and, consequently, no cause remains, under the strict terms of the
Treaty, for any longer retaining the Rajah's dominions
under the "exclusive control and direct management" of
British Commissioners.

But the question of partially restoring a native government during the reigning Prince's life-time, sinks into insignificance before the imminent prospect of the whole frame-
work of the protected State being swept away at the reigning Prince's demise, and of Mysore being incorporated in
the Madras Presidency. The future maintenance of this
allied and tributary State, of that "separate Government"
in Mysore for which the Partition Treaty stipulates, and of
the rights of the Rajah's heir, now depend entirely upon the
wisdom of the Home Government. If the professional
rulers at Calcutta are allowed to have their own way in
these matters, they will soon make short work of them.

CHAPTER V.

THE ADOPTION AND SUCCESSION.

THE hopes entertained and expressed by two successive Governors-General that the Rajah would never adopt a son, were undoubtedly based upon nothing but Residency gossip, and never ought to have been officially recorded in any more serious light. The importance attached to them is an evident proof of the absence of any fair and reasonable impediment to the ordinary course of the Hindoo law of inheritance. But there is seldom smoke without fire ; rumours of this description are seldom quite unfounded. There really was for several years a very prevalent report, which spread a panic throughout Mysore, and for the first time in his life brought the Rajah into such personal unpopularity that he was more than once very badly received by the inhabitants of his capital,—that the Rajah had refused to adopt a son, and that at his death the Kingdom would lapse to the Honourable Company. The truth is, that in addition to that natural aversion to adopt an heir during Lord Dalhousie's career of annexation, to which I have referred, other influences were occasionally brought to bear upon his Highness which led to doubt and procrastination. An adoption being usually the selection of a successor from among the junior ranks of the family, and tending to enhance the rank and importance of a more distant branch at the expense of nearer relatives, a good deal of jealousy and opposition is frequently excited, and various devices and intrigues are sometimes employed, before the irrevocable step has been taken, to induce a postponement, in the hope that the choice may be altered. At one time the same notion was assiduously inculcated in the Rajah's mind as had been used, with a similar object, to deter the Rajah of Nagpore from concluding an adoption*

---

* Papers relating to the Rajah of Berar, 1854, p. 17.

—it was suggested that an heir might be used to effect his deposition, if he were to persist in demanding his reinstatement, or in any other way to be importunate and troublesome to the Commissioner.

·At another period a rumour was spread abroad, and conveyed to the Rajah's ears, that some Brahmin soothsayers had positively ascertained that his own death would follow, very closely, his adoption of an heir to the throne. It is highly probable that these alarming prognostications may have caused the Rajah to dislike the idea of concluding an adoption, and to defer it as long as possible, just as an Englishman may sometimes evade and defer the execution of his last will. But he never faltered in his determination ; and it is creditable to his good sense and steadiness of purpose, that his Highness overcame all his misgivings, and on the 18th June, 1865, publicly adopted a son at the Palace of Mysore, in the presence of a large and enthusiastic assemblage of all classes of his subjects. Major Charles Elliot, C.B., the Superintendent of the Mysore Division, specially summoned by the Rajah, was present on the occasion and witnessed the whole ceremony, and to this officer his Highness handed a letter to the Viceroy and Governor-General, announcing the completion of the measure that had been so long meditated. In this letter the Rajah writes to Sir John Lawrence :—"I have this day, the 18th June, 1865, according to Hindoo law, the usage of my ancestors, and in virtue of Her Majesty's Proclamation, adopted a son as successor to all my rights under the Partition Treaty·of 1799 between the East India Company and the Nizam, and under my Subsidiary Treaty of the same year with the East India Company, both of which are in full force."

The boy whom the Rajah has adopted, and who has received the name of Cham Rajyendra Wadiyar, was two and a half years of age at the time of the ceremony, and is of the Raj-bindee or Royal blood, descended from the same stock with the Rajah, although their common ancestor can only be found in a very distant generation : he is the grandson of Gopaul Rajah Urs,* the brother of Her High-

* *Urs* is the Canarese for Prince, and the title is given to all the members of the Rajah's family.

ness the Ranee Luchmee, who, as Regent and guardian during the Rajah's minority, signed the Subsidiary Treaty of 1799. The young Prince was a child of the Bettada Kotay House, one of the thirteen branches of the family most nearly related to the reigning Rajah. He is now by Hindoo law the Rajah's son.

The Rajah of Mysore has outlived by more than eleven years the family limit of sixty prescribed by the seers of Calcutta. He has also outlived the short interval which certain Brahmin astrologers predicted would separate the day of an adoption from the day of his own death. He is said to be in excellent health and spirits, determined to maintain the rights of his son and of his throne to the last moment of his existence, and expressing the most perfect confidence in the justice of Her Majesty the Queen.

The question of the Rajah's reinstatement has thus become complicated with one of much higher and more lasting importance, that of the future destiny of the ancient Hindoo State of Mysore, of which His Highness is the reigning representative, and his adopted son the lawful heir. The object of His Highness's temporary suspension from power, as declared to him by Lord William Bentinck, in his letter of 7th September, 1831, viz. :—" the preservation of the State of Mysore," and "the permanent prosperity of the Raj," or dynasty, is now completely dropped by the authorities at Calcutta ; and arguments are now employed to justify a persistence in the suspension, and the non-recognition of the recent adoption, which point to the subversion of the State of Mysore, and the extinction of the Raj at the decease of the present Sovereign. All those public men, therefore, who look to the maintenance of a system of protected, reformed and tributary native States as the best constitution for the British Empire in India, both as a pacificating and as an educating Power, ought to demand the restoration of the Rajah of Mysore to the functions of royalty,—not merely in submission to the faith of Treaties and the abstract justice of the claim, not merely to remove an unjust personal stigma from a friendly and faithful Prince, but as the best proof that can be given that the preservation of the Raj is still intended, and not its speedy destruction.

The Rajah having previously communicated to the Commissioner of Mysore, for the information of the Viceroy, his intention of adopting a son, a reply was sent from the Foreign Office of Calcutta, (No. 333, 29th March, 1864,) in which the following sentence occurs :—"The Rajah has a full right to adopt so far as his private property is concerned; but his Highness must be distinctly informed that no authority to adopt a successor to the Raj of Mysore has ever been given him, and that no such power can now be conceded to him."

But no such concession is necessary to give legal effect to the adoption. It is true that no copy of the circular of 1860, permitting the Hindoo Princes to adopt successors, was sent to the Rajah of Mysore; but this arbitrary or accidental exclusion is of no disinheriting effect, by any law or custom, Asiatic or European, municipal or Imperial.

The general plan and object of Lord Canning's circular may well be applauded, as a graceful retreat from an offensive and untenable position, but there are absolutely no grounds for maintaining that the Rajah of Mysore, or any other Hindoo Sovereign, ever had, or has now, any need of the Viceroy's permission, in any form, as the preliminary or as the ratification of a fully effective adoption.

Adoption is no peculiar or exceptional privilege: it is the specific principle of the Hindoo law of inheritance. The right of adoption is that of nominating an heir in cases where *actual issue* has failed—not necessarily, or even usually, a remedy for lack of heirs, but the selection of one from a number of possible heirs, often from a long list of agnates and cognates, to be not merely *an heir* but *a son*.

The British Government has never possessed the right of disallowing adoptions for its own purposes: even where it has retained or acquired from its predecessors the prerogative of investiture over minor Principalities, it has no more right to forbid the succession of an adopted son than of a lineal male descendant. The prerogative of investiture gives jurisdiction in disputed successions, asserts supremacy, and enforces subordination, but does not justify the refusal of investiture to a lawful heir. But in the case of a Hindoo Prince, with whom a treaty of perpetual friendship and alliance has been contracted, not even the prerogative of investiture exists. Nothing but the moral duty of protection and pacification authorises any intervention to control and regulate the course of inheritance.

Lord Canning himself, in that same Adoption Despatch of 1860, fully acknowledged that, notwithstanding all the previous assertions to the contrary, no precedent could be found for declining to recognise a succession by adoption to territorial and princely rights :—" We have not shown," he says, " so far as I can find, a single instance in which adoption by a Sovereign Prince has been invalidated by a refusal of assent from the Paramount Power." And he adds :—" I believe that there is no example of any Hindoo State, whether in Rajpootana or elsewhere, lapsing to the Paramount Power, by reason of that Power withholding its assent to an adoption."*

Yet, by a singular series of gradations, the Mysore question has come to this unhealthy complexion at last, and if the declared intentions of the Calcutta authorities are approved and confirmed at home, the British Government will be openly committed to the violation of two Treaties, to the destruction of another friendly State, and to a direct contradiction of both the Queen's Proclamation and Lord Canning's Adoption Despatch. It is a sufficiently dangerous state of things, when the name or the memory of some particular Viceroy or Governor, living or dead, is the object of popular execration. But much more solemn sanctions are now assailed. It would be an incurable wound to British honour and influence, if the Princes and people of India should be practically taught that the word of the Queen of Great Britain, never pledged before 1858, is not to be trusted,—that Treaties are waste paper, and a Royal Proclamation merely idle words, when they stand in the way of the acquisition of more territory.

Sir Charles Wood, in his reply of the 26th of July, 1860,

* Sir John Willoughby writes as follows in one of his Dissents :—" In my opinion, prohibiting an adoption would be a grievous violation of Lord Canning's pledges and proclamation on the subject." " On the general question of adoptions in India, my opinion varies in some respects from that of Sir F. Currie, and more especially as regards the case of Sattara ; but my views, shared by many others, were authoritatively set aside by the late Lord Canning's manifesto on the subject" (Mysore Papers, p. 47). Sir John Willoughby's former views were founded on imaginary precedents, and Lord Canning, in the sentence just quoted, admits their imaginary nature.

cordially agrees with Lord Canning's Adoption Despatch, and says :—" In the sentiments expressed in your Excellency's letter of the 30th of April I entirely concur. It is not by the extension of our Empire that its permanence is to be secured, but by the character of British rule in the territories already committed to our care, and by practically demonstrating that we are as willing to respect the rights of others as we are capable of maintaining our own."

But if the declared intentions of the present Calcutta authorities with regard to Mysore are allowed to be realised, it will be a practical demonstration that we are *not* willing to respect the rights of others, that we are resolved to treat with contempt the rights of the Rajah of Mysore, the rights of our Ally the Nizam, the feelings and interests of the people of Mysore, and of the Princes and people of all India.

CHAPTER VI.

TREATY RIGHTS OF THE NIZAM.

The threatened absorption of Mysore, on the demise of the present aged Rajah, is calculated to disgust and alarm all the Princes of India, as the first infraction of the general pledge in favour of native sovereignties, the promise to respect existing Treaties, and to abstain from territorial extension, contained in Her Majesty's Proclamation of 1858, and confirmed by Lord Canning's latest public measures ; but it is more particularly calculated to disgust and alarm the Nizam, because it would constitute a direct and most contemptuous violation of our engagements with him, and would involve a direct menace against some of his most valued possessions, which, like the Mysore country, are at present confided, under Treaty, to our exclusive management.

Sir Frederick Currie observes in his Minute dissenting from one of the despatches adverse to the Rajah's claims :—

" I think the decision impolitic, also, as likely to lead, when the permanent exclusion of the Maharaja from the possession of Mysore is promulgated, to inconvenient questions with the Nizam, whose treaty rights in Mysore, though kept out of sight in this Despatch, and the proceedings of Lords Dalhousie and Canning referred to in it, cannot be ignored."*

In the conquest of Tippoo Sultan's dominions, and in the establishment or revival of the Hindoo State of Mysore, the Honourable Company did not act alone, but in concert with the Nizam. The Nizam, besides providing and forwarding immense supplies, had sent an army of his own into the field—including a large body of Cavalry, the arm in which we were most deficient—who received their full share of the prize-money after the storm of Seringapatam. Two Treaties were then concluded, one called the *Partition Treaty*, and dated 22nd June, 1799, between the East

* Mysore Papers, p. 25.

India Company and the Nizam—the other, called the *Subsidiary Treaty*, and dated the 8th July, 1799, between the East India Company and the Rajah of Mysore.

The two victorious Allies agreed to a certain division and settlement of the conquered territories; and under the Partition Treaty, portions equal in revenue, and conveniently situated with reference to their respective frontiers, were "retained in sovereignty" by the Company and the Nizam, while the central districts, forming a compact Principality, were allotted to the Rajah of Mysore. Three Schedules attached to this Treaty specify minutely the limits and subdivisions of this triple distribution. Lord Wellesley, however, reserved to the Company, "as a just indemnification for their superior share in the expenses and exertions of the war, the principal benefit of whatever advantages might flow from any engagements to be contracted with the new Government of Mysore."* The Rajah was to be placed in a tributary and dependent position to the British Government, in return for its military protection, and as security for the regular payment of a fixed military Subsidy, and of additional contributions in time of war.†

In the last words of the Preamble to the Partition Treaty of Mysore, it is declared that all its Articles, "by the blessing of God, shall be binding upon the heirs and successors of the contracting parties as long as the sun and moon shall endure, and its conditions shall be reciprocally observed by the said contracting parties."‡

One of those conditions is thus stated in Article IV of the Treaty :—

"*A separate Government* shall be established in Mysore; and for this purpose it is stipulated and agreed that the Maharajah Mysoor Kishna Rajah Oodiaver Bahadoor, a descendant of the ancient Rajahs of Mysore shall possess the territory hereinafter described."

And in Article V, " the contracting partices mutually and severally agree that the districts specified in Schedule C, hereunto annexed, shall be ceded to the said Maharajah Mysoor Kishna Rajah, and shall form *the separate Government* of Mysore, upon the conditions hereinafter mentioned."§

The only subsequent condition of this Treaty, referring to the Rajah of Mysore, is contained in Article IX :—

"It being expedient, for the effectual establishment of Maharajah Mysoor Kishna Rajah in the Government of Mysore, that his Highness should be assisted with a suitable Subsidiary Force, it is stipulated and agreed that the whole of the said Force shall be furnished by the English East India Company Bahadoor, according to the terms of a separate Treaty, to be immediately concluded between the said East India Company and his Highness the Maharajah."*

And as if to mark by a conspicuous ceremony the concerted action and equal participation of the two Allies in restoring the ancient Hindoo sovereignty, the infant Prince was carried to the ivory throne of his ancestors, and publicly installed, by the officers of the highest rank belonging to both Governments, eight days after the Partition Treaty was signed. The circumstance is thus described by the Mysore Commissioners in their Report to the Governor-General, dated the 30th of June 1799 :—

"The ceremony of placing the Rajah on the Musnud was performed by Lieut.-General Harris, as senior member of the Commission, and by Meer Allum, each of them taking a hand of his Highness on the occasion."†

And Lord Wellesley himself records the same incident in his despatch to the Court of Directors of the 3rd of August :—

"On the 30th June" (1799) "the Rajah of Mysore was formally placed on the Musnud by the Commissioners, assisted by Meer Allum."‡

And in the same letter we learn that the Subsidiary Treaty with the Rajah was not concluded until the 8th July, and was not ratified by Lord Wellesley until the 23rd July, more than three weeks after the Rajah had been publicly enthroned.

Meer Abool Cassim, better known by his abbreviated title of Meer Allum, was the Dewan or Prime Minister of Hyderabad, who had been present with the Nizam's army throughout the campaign and siege of Seringapatam, and who, as his master's Plenipotentiary, concluded and signed the Par-

---

* Appendix B.   † Wellesley's Despatches, vol. ii, p. 736.   ‡ Ibid., p. 85.

tition Treaty of 1799.* "I found in Meer Allum, the Commander," wrote Sir John Malcolm, who acted as Military Commissioner with the Nizam's troops, "a man whose heart and soul were in the cause ; and the advance of this force was so rapid, that it was obliged to halt some days for the advance of the Grand Army."†

No step in the negotiations and settlement had been taken without the knowledge and consent of Meer Allum. Lord Wellesley, in the despatch appointing the Commissioners for the affairs of Mysore, and giving the outline of the arrangements he wished to be adopted, concludes with this injunction :—"The contents of this despatch must not be communicated to any person who may not have taken the oath of secrecy prescribed in the Commission, excepting Meer Allum."‡

And in a letter to the Court of Directors, dated the 3rd of August 1799, he observes :—

"On the 5th of June I had furnished the Commissioners with the first draft of a Treaty between the Company and his Highness the Nizam, for the partition of Mysore, and having received the fullest communication of their sentiments, and of those of Meer Allum, on the subject, I made such alterations as appeared to be advisable."§

One very distinguished and highly trusted officer who was employed in the settlement of Mysore, Major Munro— afterwards General Sir Thomas Munro and Governor of Madras—gave a very decided opinion, as in the following extract, that the conquered territories ought to be equally divided, and that the installation of the infant Rajah would be both impolitic, and unfair to our Ally :—

"In making this partition, we have only to consult our own advantage and that of the Nizam.

"As I am convinced that the Mahrattas will not dare to give any interruption to the partition of the Mysore dominions between the Company and the Nizam, I do not know a single argument against it, unless it may be thought that it would make the

---

* The Present Prime Minister of Hyderabad, the Nawab Salar Jung, is great grandson to Meer Allum ; his paternal grandfather, Mooneer-ool-Moolk, having married Meer Allum's only daughter. This lady's son, Meer Mahomed Ali, was the Nawab Salar Jung's father.

† Kaye's Life of Malcolm, vol. i, p. 84.

‡ Wellesley's Despatches, vol. ii, p. 23.   § Ibid., p. 84.

Nizam too powerful; but this is an objection without much foundation.

"We may assert that the Nizam's army has not contributed so much as the Company's to the conquest of Mysore; but he has done all that he could; his troops have done more than was expected; and had they done less, still every principle of good faith demands that both parties should share alike; but if we only divide with him a part of the territories of the late Sultan, and set up a pageant over the rest to pay a British garrison in Seringapatam, and subsidise a large body of our troops, he must see and feel that we have infringed upon our engagements with him."*

And he writes as follows in a familiar letter to his father:—

"You will see in the papers how the Partition Treaty has been made. I believe that it has not met with general approbation here. Had I anything to do in it, I would certainly have had no Rajah of Mysore, in the person of a child, dragged forth from oblivion, to be placed on a throne on which his ancestors for three generations had not sat more than half a century. I would have divided the country equally with the Nizam, and endeavoured to prevail on him to increase his Subsidy, and take a greater body of our troops; but whether he consented or not, I would still have thought myself bound by treaty to give him his fair half of the country."†

The principle of the original offensive and defensive alliance between the Company and the Nizam, was that of "an equal division of conquered territory," as stated in Article VI of the Treaty of 1790;‡ and although Lord Wellesley ruled that this engagement was not permanently obligatory, and that, according to the letter of the new Treaty of 1798, the Nizam could not demand a share in the territorial acquisitions beyond his relative proportion in the expenses and exertions of the campaign,§ yet the principle of equal division was in fact adopted as the basis of the new arrangements. Indeed, so clearly was the spirit of the long standing engagements between the Allies in favour of the Nizam's claim, that the same plan of equal partition was laid down in a Treaty concluded the very year after these transactions. In the third "separate and

---

* Gleig's Life of Sir T. Munro, vol. ii, p. 231, 234.
† Ibid., vol. i, p. 222.
‡ Volume of Treaties, 1853, p. 133.
§ Wellesley's Despatches, vol. ii, p. 77.

secret" Article of the Treaty of 1800, it is agreed as follows :—

" If, contrary to the spirit and object of this defensive Treaty, war should hereafter appear unavoidable (which God avert !) the contracting parties will proceed to adjust the rule of partition of all such advantages and acquisitions as may eventually result from the success of their united arms. It is declared that in the event of war, and of a consequent partition of conquests between the contracting parties, his Highness the Nawab Asoph Jah shall be entitled to participate equally with the other contracting parties, in the division of every territory which may be acquired by the successful exertion of their united arms."*

And the same course was pursued in the Treaties of 1804 and 1822, after the first and second Mahratta wars.† By the Treaty of 1822 the Nizam not only gained an exemption from debts which he owed the dethroned Peishwa, amounting to about sixty millions of rupees (six millions sterling), but cessions of territory which gave him at least eighteen lakhs (£180,000) of additional revenue. On both occasions the Nizam received rather more than his fair share of the territories conquered by the allied forces.

The provinces at present forming the Principality of Mysore were thus ceded to the Rajah, not by the East India Company alone, but,—as stated in Article V of the Partition Treaty, and in Article V of the Subsidiary Treaty,—by the two allied and conquering Powers, the East India Company and the Nizam. If therefore, by "right of conquest," the British Government has any reversionary claim upon those provinces, the reversionary claim of the Nizam must be equally strong.

The following extracts from the contemporary despatches will prove that Lord Wellesley fully admitted the equal right and interest of the Nizam, in the disposal and settlement of the provinces conquered from Tippoo :—

" It is almost superfluous to state to you that the whole Kingdom of Mysore, having fallen to the arms of *the Company and the Nizam,* is at present to be considered as a part of their dominions by right of conquest."‡

" From the justice and success of the late war with Tippoo Sultan, *the Company and the Nizam* derived an undoubted right

---

* Volume of Treaties, 1853, p. 151.   † Ibid., pp. 157-159.
‡ Wellesley's Despatches, vol. ii, p. 13.

to the disposal of the dominions conquered by their united arms. The right of conquest entitled *the Company and the Nizam* to retain the whole territory in their own hands; the cession of it to any other party, might be a consideration of policy or humanity, but could not be claimed on any ground of justice or right."*

"To have divided the whole territory *equally between the Company and the Nizam*, while it would have afforded strong grounds for jealousy to the Mahrattas, would have aggrandised the Nizam's power beyond the bounds of discretion."†

"The Rajah of Mysore will therefore be restored to the throne, and maintained on it, *under the protection of the Company, the Nizam*, and I trust also of the Mahrattas, who certainly all have a concurrent and common interest in the exclusion of Tippoo's family."‡

And writing to the Commissioners who were engaged in negotiating the Subsidiary Treaty with the relatives of the infant Rajah, on the absolute necessity of one particular Article being maintained without any alteration from the original draft, he says :—

"This is a point I hold to be so essential to the very existence of the new arrangement, that if it should appear objectionable, (on grounds of which I am not aware), I see no alternative but that of dividing the whole territory between the Allies."§

It surely might be supposed, when a Principality had thus been constructed or reconstituted out of territories conquered by two Allies, and in consequence of the stipulations of a Treaty between them, that this settlement ought not to be disturbed, that this Principality ought not to be summarily appropriated by one of those two Allies, without the other's consent having been asked, without any previous consultation having taken place, without any explanation or notice having been given. The impropriety and irregularity of such a proceeding do not seem to be lessened in the present instance, when we recall to mind that for ten years before and for twenty-three years after that settlement, those two Powers had continued to act upon that principle of equal partition which was the basis of their original alliance ; that Lord Wellesley himself declares that the only alternative to the Hindoo restoration, would have been to divide the conquered country with our Ally ; and

---

* Wellesley's Despatches, p. 72.   † Ibid., p. 36.
‡ Ibid., p. 38.   § Ibid., vol. ii, p. 49.

that he anticipates the maintenance of the Mysore State under the protection of the Company and the Nizam. And this reliance on the Nizam's concurrent protection, which I have quoted, is not stated in a document intended to persuade or flatter that Court, but in a private despatch addressed to Dundas (Lord Melville), then President of the Board of Control, where no empty compliment to the Nizam could possibly find a place, and where, on such a point, Lord Wellesley would be sure to express himself frankly.

Three great objects were settled by the Partition Treaty between the East India Company and the Nizam :—(1) the allotment of certain portions of the conquered country in full sovereignty to the Allies ; (2) the establishment of a separate Government in Mysore under a descendant of the ancient Hindoo dynasty; (3) a suitable provision for Tippoo Sultan's family.

Besides those outlying provinces of Tippoo's Empire which were acquired by the British Government as its share of the conquest, one small piece of territory within the frontiers of Mysore Proper was specially transferred to its keeping by the contracting parties, "for the preservation of peace and tranquillity, and for the general security." By Article III of the Partition Treaty, "it is stipulated and agreed that the Fortress of Seringapatam, and the island on which it is situated, shall become part of the dominions of the said Company, in full right and sovereignty for ever."*

This Article constitutes the sole and sufficient title of Great Britain to the possession of this celebrated stronghold. Without the express consent, thus given, of the Nizam, our Ally and partner in the conquest and its advantages, Seringapatam would have become part of the separate State under the Rajah of Mysore. Without the Nizam's consent, no other place or district within the limits of that separate State could have then become British territory, or can ever become British territory, by any legal title, "as long as the sun and moon endure."

The emphatic and special grant of the "sovereignty" in the little river island of Seringapatam to the Company by this Article, proves that the claim to sovereignty over the

---

* Appendix B.

whole of Mysore by right of conquest, advanced in the Calcutta letter of the 11th of March 1862* is quite unfounded.

And it is worthy of remark that by a Supplemental Article to the Partition Treaty, it is agreed, " with a view to the prevention of future altercations," that so far as the third great object of that Treaty—a suitable provision for Tippoo's family—extended, " the contracting parties shall not be accountable to each other on this head."† The least important of the three objects, an object merely of personal interest, being thus by a separate Article specially exempted from future inquiry and expostulation, and left to the discretion and good pleasure of the contracting parties, it is quite clear that the more important and fundamental objects of the Treaty were *not* by any means to be exempted from future inquiry and expostulation, and were *not* left to the discretion and good pleasure of either party, but that on these heads both parties would " be accountable to each other," " as long as the sun and moon should endure."

Thus not only would the Nizam have a good cause of protest against the appropriation of Mysore by the British Government for its own aggrandisement, as an unauthorised reversal of the settlement of 1799, as a measure opposed to the traditional policy of his House, but even in the case of a genuine and unavoidable " lapse," by the extinction of the reigning family, his claim to a partition would be irresistible. If, on the contrary, the " lapse," pronounced or predetermined, were not genuine, but, as I contend, factitious and unfounded, the protest and remonstrance of the Court of Hyderabad would be still more formidable and embarrassing.

If, in reply to the Nizam's objections, the Government of India were to appeal, as they could hardly avoid doing, to the only plausible extenuation,—to the thirty years of British management, to the prosperity and contentment of the people during that period, and the duty of securing the permanence of the reformed institutions of Mysore,—the Nizam might well inquire, with very reasonable solicitude, how many years of British management would suffice to

---

* Ante, p. 68.   † Appendix B.

extinguish the sovereignty of his family in the two Provinces of Berar.

Just as the Nizam concurred with the Honourable Company in 1799 in recognising the young Rajah as the Sovereign of Mysore, so had the Nizam concurred with the Honourable Company in 1768 in recognising the Nawab Mahomed Ali Wallajah, previously his own feudatory, as the Sovereign of the Carnatic. And just as the Nawab Azeem-ood-Dowlah, the acknowledged Sovereign of the Carnatic, by the Treaty of 1801, entrusted to the Company "the civil and military administration" of his territorial possessions, so did the Nizam of Hyderabad in 1853 assign Berar and other provinces to "the exclusive management" of the British Government.* In neither case was there any cession, or any relinquishment of sovereignty. After two hard diplomatic struggles, one in 1853, the other throughout 1859 and 1860, the Nizam still retains the sovereignty of those provinces, and has avoided assigning their management in "perpetuity" to the British Government.

We received the Carnatic from the Nawab, as we received Berar from the Nizam, as *a trust* on certain conditions, and not as an absolute possession. And at the present day we ought to hold the Carnatic, as we still profess to hold Berar as a trust,† and on no other terms. But instead of doing so, since the demise of the Nawab of the Carnatic in 1855, we have refused—on the preposterous plea that the Treaty of 1801 was only "personal", or for one life, and that the two subsequent successions were merely by "grace and favour"—to recognise the lawful heir and successor, Prince Azeem Jah, a son of the Nawab with whom the Treaty of 1801 was concluded.‡

The Nizam, having been already sufficiently alarmed and affronted by the Carnatic spoliation, now sees the

---

* Parliamentary Papers, Nizam's Debts, 1854, p. 144.

† This very term is used by Lord Clive, the Governor of Madras, in the Proclamation of 31st July 1801 :—"His Lordship, in accepting the *sacred trust transferred to the Company by the present engagements*, invites the people of the Carnatic to a ready and cheerful obedience to the authority of the Company."—*Carnatic Papers*, 1861, p. 105. The same term is used in the Nizam's Treaty of 1860.—*Collection of Treaties*, Calcutta, 1864 (Longman & Co., London), vol. v, p. 114.

‡ For a full account, see *The Empire in India*, Letter III, p. 47.

annexation of Mysore impending; a transaction so hostile to his rights and dignity, so manifestly injurious to his interests, that it would be difficult, if not impossible, to evade or resent his demand for explanations. If, after managing Mysore in the Rajah's name, and rendering annual accounts, for thirty-five years, we claim the sovereignty of his dominions, and decline to recognise his heir; if after fifty years of uninterrupted "*civil and military administration*,"* and after two successions, we were entitled —without form, apology, or public notice—to confiscate the Carnatic, and to refuse the stipulated share of the revenues to the Nawab—after how many years of "*exclusive management*,"† and after how many successions, shall we be entitled to appropriate the Nizam's two provinces of Berar, and to refuse any longer to "make over the surplus revenues"† to the Sovereign of Hyderabad? How these questions can ever be answered, how any distinction can ever be drawn between the cases, so as to reassure the Nizam's Government, appears to me to be quite an insoluble problem. To meet expostulations from that quarter with a contemptuous reprimand, to refuse explanations, to decline discussion, and to threaten coercion, would be a much easier task, and one much more congenial and familiar to the powers that be—at Calcutta.

Sir Frederick Currie in his first Minute, dated 17th July 1863, dissenting from the despatch refusing to replace the Rajah at the head of his Government, makes the following remark:—"I think the decision impolitic, also, as likely to lead, when the permanent exclusion of the Maharajah from the possession of Mysore is promulgated, to inconvenient questions with the Nizam, whose treaty-rights in Mysore, though kept out of sight in this despatch, and the proceedings of Lords Dalhousie and Canning referred to in it, cannot be ignored."‡

* The words used in the Treaty of 1801 with the Nawab Azeem-ood-Dowla, Collection of Treaties, 1812, p. 467.

† Terms used in the Treaty of 1853 with the Nizam Nasir-ood-Dowla, Volume of Treaties, 1856, p. 70, and in the Treaty of 1860 with the Nizam Afzool-ood-Dowla, Collection of Treaties, Calcutta, 1864 (Longman and Co., London), vol. v, p. 114.

‡ Mysore Papers, p. 25.

Nor was this inconvenient question long kept out of the discussion. The Rajah himself raised this very obvious objection in his letter to the Governor-General, Sir John Lawrence, of the 25th January 1865, printed among the Mysore Papers (p. 61). His Highness argues that the conquest of Tippoo's dominions was the joint conquest of the Company and the Nizam, that the cession to himself of his territories was the joint cession of the same parties, and that if those territories should ever "lapse," they would not lapse to the British Government, but to the Allies who shared in the conquests and arranged the partition of 1799. In paragraph 33 of his letter, the Rajah thus briefly sums up his position :—"I claim for my heirs the same rights as I shall have died possessed of ; and should I have no heirs, then, for the first time, those who gave me my dominions will become absolutely entitled to them."*

If peremptory language and sweeping denials could overturn the embarrassing obstacle thus raised by the Rajah's remonstrances, it would have been effectually overturned by Sir John Lawrence's reply of the 5th May 1865. In this he says :—

"I must point out to your Highness that, in treating the conquest of Mysore as the joint conquest of the British Government and the Nizam, and the cession thereof as the joint cession of both parties, your Highness has allowed yourself to fall into an error which it is my duty to correct. The Nizam, at the time alluded to, was in the condition of a purely dependent ruler, and in a state of subordinate alliance with the British Government."†

Abundant quotations have already been given to prove that the Rajah, in speaking of the joint conquest and joint cession of Mysore, has simply repeated the words of Lord Wellesley and of all the contemporary documents.‡

As to the Nizam having been "a dependent ruler" in 1799, it may be sufficient to reply that in 1853 Lord Dalhousie declared him to be "an independent Prince."§ There is no foundation or pretext whatever in Indian history or diplomacy for asserting that the Nizam was either dependent or subordinate ; unless, indeed, mere inferiority of material strength could degrade an ally into a position of dependence and subordination.

* Mysore Papers, p. 67.   † Ibid., p. 69.   ‡ Ante, p. 88-93.
§ Papers relating to the Nizam, 1854, p. 39.

The Governor-General, pursuing and expanding the same argument in his despatch to the Secretary of State, also dated the 5th May, 1865, in which he forwards his correspondence with the Rajah, endeavours to make out the Nizam's subordination and dependence from the larger numbers of the British army engaged in the campaign, and from Lord Wellesley having exercised "plenary powers" throughout the expedition and in the settlement of the conquered territories. Sir John Lawrence omits to mention that the Nizam had specially conferred those plenary powers upon Lord Wellesley ; he very much underrates the numbers of the Hyderabad troops that cooperated in the campaign, and seems to have overlooked entirely the large force of Irregular Cavalry, without whose aid our communications could not have been kept up, nor our supplies secured. It is not denied that the Nizam's own army cooperated in the conquest, but the Governor-General objects that it was not so large or so efficient as that of the Company, and that its movements were directed by British Officers. The relative numbers and efficiency of the two armies is really a matter of indifference. There is nothing unusual in the forces of one Ally being placed by mutual consent under the command of a General nominated by the other. When there is a great inequality of power between two Allies, such an arrangement becomes most natural ; when military science and the munitions of war are almost in the exclusive possession of one Ally, such an arrangement becomes inevitable. At various periods the troops of foreign States have been incorporated in a British Army; while at other times British forces have served under a foreign Commander-in-Chief. The army of Portugal during the Peninsular War, and a considerable Turkish force during the Crimean Campaign, were placed entirely under British officers. But I have never yet heard that such a military Convention impairs the independence or entails the subordination of any State, beyond the terms and purposes of the Convention, however small in extent that State may be, however weak in material resources.

The Governor-General thus continues his argument :—

"Lord Mornington with plenary power controlled the proceedings of the expedition. The conquest was therefore really a

British one; and although from courtesy and views of expediency, the Nizam's Government was spoken of as conjoint in the operations against Tippoo, and was allowed to share with the British Government in the advantages accruing from the successful termination of the contest, yet such phraseology was conventional, and misled no one, and least of all the Nizam. For the Governor-General, whilst prepared to treat his subordinate Ally with the utmost liberality, resented any pretension at interference in or with his arrangements, and, dictating to the Nizam the terms of the Treaty of Mysore, intimated, with stringent plainness, that if the Nizam should object to the basis and fundamental principles of the Treaty, Lord Mornington was perfectly prepared to carry the new settlement into effect by the aid of British arms alone."*

Sir John Lawrence misrepresents Lord Wellesley's views when he says that "the conquest was really a British one." No such language was used at the time. The Nizam's share in the operations, and right to participate in the consequent advantages, though not rated equally with those of the Company, were never denied or despised.

It is true that Lord Wellesley expressed a firm intention, as we and the Nizam may have learned from certain confidential papers which were published thirty-five years after the fall of Seringapatam,† of carrying the new settlement into force by the aid of British arms alone, should the Nizam object to the terms of the proposed Treaty. I do not see, however, that Lord Wellesley's firm determination to re-establish the Hindoo State of Mysore, and to make it tributary to the British Government, even at the risk of hostilities with his Ally, can tend to weaken the rights of sovereignty conferred upon the Rajah, or to threaten the separate existence of the re-established State. The very improbable contingency of hostilities with the Nizam did not occur; no objections were made to the triple partition designed by Lord Wellesley; and the Treaty was concluded after consultation with the Nizam's Plenipotentiary, Meer Allum, at Mysore, and duly ratified by His Highness at Hyderabad. It surely cannot be said that this cordial and prompt concurrence in the establishment of a separate Government in Mysore, under a descendant of the ancient Rajahs, can lessen the Nizam's right and interest in the permanent maintenance of that separate Government.

* Mysore Papers, p. 55.
† The Marquis Wellesley's Despatches were published in 1836.

Sir John Lawrence's argument is worth nothing, unless he means to say that because Lord Wellesley "dictated" the terms of the Partition Treaty, and was prepared, if necessary, "to carry the new settlement into effect by the aid of British arms," therefore Lord Wellesley's successor has a right to disregard the terms of Partition, and to break up the settlement for his own exclusive advantage.

Sir John Lawrence then urges that besides the

"absolute negation of any claim on the part of the Nizam to an equal partition of territory, Lord Mornington was studiously careful to be perfectly explicit in placing the cession of Mysore to the Rajah on a footing which should exclude any territorial claim of the Nizam, whether actual or reversional, present or future. Accordingly, with reference to the 4th Article of the Treaty of Mysore, which laid down that a separate government was to be established for Mysore, under Kistna Raj Oodiaver, Lord Mornington issued these further commands to the Resident at Hyderabad :—

"The 4th Article contains the basis of an arrangement founded on the strongest principle of justice, humanity, and policy. It does not appear to me necessary to state anything further on this or the 5th Article; you will naturally observe that if the Nizam's claim to an equal partition of territory had been founded on right, and consequently admitted by me, this adjustment, so honourable to the moderation, generosity, and wisdom of the British character, would not have taken place."*

But while Lord Wellesley, in order to secure his point at Hyderabad, instructed his representative at that Court to adopt this high tone, he acknowledged in the directions given to the Commissioners at Mysore, that if this adjustment could not be effected, the Nizam's claim to an equal partition would become irresistible, that there would be "no alternative but that of dividing the whole territory between the Allies."†

Although Lord Wellesley at the critical moments of negotiation, assumed an imperious and determined style in dealing with the Nizam, he well knew the immense value of his past and continued cooperation, and the impossibility of slighting his just pretensions. He writes as follows in one of those demi-official letters to Dundas

---

* Mysore Papers, p. 56.
† Wellesley's Despatches, vol. ii. p. 49 ; ante, p. 93.

President of the Board of Control, which are certain to reveal his real sentiments :—

"I trust in God that before this time my brother Henry's arrival in England has satisfied your expectations respecting the settlement of Mysore. To have retained the whole territory for ourselves would have raised such a flame both at Hyderabad and Poonah, as could hardly have been extinguished without another war. Henry will have informed you of the difficulties which delayed even the settlement as ultimately effected at Hyderabad. The Nizam's pride would not have been satisfied without a considerable cession of territory."*

This is very different from the supercilious and over-bearing tone which Sir John Lawrence assumes, and attributes to Lord Wellesley.

The Governor-General then flies to another fallacious argument, utterly inconclusive and irrelevant, even if it were not based, as it is, on the misquotation of a Treaty. He says :—

"So far from preferring any claims, such as his Highness the Maharajah seeks to suggest and to evoke in support of his own pretensions, the Nizam afterwards ceded in perpetuity to the British Government, not only all the territories acquired under the Treaty of Seringapatam of 1792, and the Treaty of Mysore of 1799, but also whatever other territory he possessed, or was dependent on his Government South of the Toombuddra and the Kistna."†

It is not, perhaps, very important to remark—except as an illustration of the careless statements of fact which abound in the Calcutta despatches—that the Nizam, under Article VI of the Treaty of 1800, retained a portion of these acquisitions from Mysore, the districts of Copal, Gujjinderghur, and others, and still retains them.‡ But the Governor-General has not explained how these cessions and exchanges can touch either the sovereign rights of the Rajah of Mysore or the reversionary claims of the Nizam.

Not that the question to be decided is merely that of the Nizam's "reversionary claims," as the Calcutta despatches assume. The Nizam as yet has advanced no such claim. He does not wish to disturb the settlement made by the Partition Treaty of 1799, but he is not likely to admit the right

---

* Wellesley's Despatches, vol. ii, p. 202-3.   † Mysore Papers, p. 56.
‡ *Collection of Treaties*, Calcutta, 1864 (Longman & Co.), vol. v, p. 71.

of the other contracting party to disturb it ; and the question is whether this ought to be done without his concurrence. The question of his reversionary claims would only be raised if such claims were advanced or enforced by the other contracting party.

In paragraph 14 of this same despatch from the Governor-General to the Secretary of State, we read :—"It has been shown that the acceptance of the Treaty of Mysore was a distinct admission on the part of the Nizam, that the sovereignty of Mysore rested with the British Government."[*] Nothing of the sort has been shown ; on the contrary, the terms of the Partition Treaty of Mysore expressly negative any such view. There is not one single phrase or word in the Treaty that claims any superiority for the Honourable Company, or any exclusive share in the conquest or its fruits.

Far from " the sovereignty of Mysore" being admitted to rest with the British Government, the "sovereignty" of one very small portion of Mysore, the river island of Seringapatam, is, as I have before pointed out,[†] expressly granted to the British Government by a distinct Article (III) of the Partition Treaty.

At the end of the twenty-third paragraph of the same Despatch of the 5th May, 1865, the Maharajah is said to have been designated in the Partition Treaty with the Nizam as " the contemplated recipient at the hands of the British Commissioner of the Raj of Mysore."[‡] And in the same way the Rajah himself was told in the letter from Calcutta, dated the 11th March, 1862, that in the Partition Treaty " your Highness was not otherwise a party concerned than as the notified future recipient of the liberality of the British Government."[§] These are complete misrepresentations : the Rajah is not once designated or notified in the Partition Treaty as the recipient of liberality or of anything " at the hands" of any " British Commissioner," or of the British Government. I am compelled to meet these unwarrantable assertions with somewhat wearisome iteration. The Preamble of the Partition Treaty declares that—

" It has pleased Almighty God to prosper the just cause of the

---

* Mysore Papers, p. 57.   † Ante, p. 95.   ‡ Mysore Papers, p. 60.   § Ibid., p. 5.

Allies, the Honourable Company, and his Highness the Nizam, with a continual course of victory and success, and finally to crown their arms by the reduction of the capital of Mysore, the fall of Tippoo Sultaun, the utter extinction of his power, and the unconditional submission of his people ; and the said Allies, being disposed to exercise the rights of conquest with the same moderation and forbearance which they have observed from the commencement to the conclusion of the late successful war, have resolved to use the power which it has pleased Almighty God to place in their hands, for the purpose of obtaining reasonable compensation for the expenses of the war, and of establishing permanent security and genuine tranquillity for themselves and their subjects, as well as for all the Powers contiguous to their respective dominions ; wherefore a Treaty, for the adjustment of the territories of the late Tippoo Sultaun between the East India Company and the Nizam is now concluded, according to the under-mentioned Articles, which, by the blessing of God, shall be binding upon the heirs and successors of the contracting parties, as long as the sun and moon shall endure, and of which the conditions shall be reciprocally observed by the said contracting parties."*

Articles IV and V of the Partition Treaty are as follows :

"IV. A separate Government shall be established in Mysore; and for this purpose, it is stipulated and agreed, that the Maha Rajah Mysore Kishna Rajah Oodiaver Behauder, a descendant of the ancient Rajahs of Mysore, shall possess the territory hereinafter described, upon the conditions hereinafter mentioned.

"V. The contracting Powers mutually and severally agree, that the districts specified in Schedule C, hereunto annexed, shall be ceded to the said Maha Rajah Mysore Kishna Rajah, and shall form the separate Government of Mysore, upon the conditions hereinafter mentioned."†

Nothing in this Treaty is done by the British Government alone ; the "rights of conquest" are exercised by "the Allies ;" the cession is made "mutually and severally" by "the contracting Powers."

If we now turn to the Subsidiary Treaty with the Rajah, to which the Nizam was not a party, but which was concluded eight days, and ratified twenty-three days, after the Rajah had been placed on the throne by the Plenipotentiaries of the Company and the Nizam, we shall find that in Article V the Rajah's dominions are defined as "the territories ceded to him by the Fifth Article of the Treaty of

* Appendix B.   † Ibid.

Mysore," the Partition Treaty ; and that in Article XV that Treaty is again mentioned as the authority, declaring the districts which " belong respectively to the English Company and to his Highness."

The cession was thus effected by the Partition Treaty. The Subsidiary Treaty, to which the Nizam was not a party, solely relates, as its name implies, and as its contents prove, to the conditions and securities of the British Subsidy, and to the relations between the two States. No cession is made by the Subsidiary Treaty,—on the contrary, it declares the cession to have been effected by the Partition Treaty,—no grant is made in it, except that of the Subsidy to the British Government. The Subsidiary Treaty, as was most inconsistently admitted in the Calcutta letter of the 11th March, 1862, is " ancillary and subordinate"* to the Partition Treaty, and is, in fact, inseparable from it.

It is erroneous, therefore, to represent, as the Governor-General does in his letters both to the Secretary of State and to the Rajah, that the cession of Mysore to the Rajah was effected by the Subsidiary Treaty, or that his Highness was the recipient of anything under that Treaty.

The Governor-General in his letter of the 5th May, 1865, impresses on the Rajah that " it was clearly understood by the Nizam that his accession of territorial rights was limited to the districts specifically assigned him in Schedule B of the Partition Treaty."† And in his despatch of the same date to the Secretary of State, Sir John Lawrence, referring to the transactions of 1799, observes :—

" The Governor-General caused to be distinctly signified to the Nizam that if he elected to accept the Treaty, it was on the clear understanding, and the precise condition that his accession of territorial rights was limited to the districts specifically assigned to the Nizam in Schedule (B.) of the Treaty, and that the Nizam abjured all claim to the territory which the British Government was about to confer on the youthful Maharajah."‡

The frequently repeated mistake as to the British Government conferring territory on the Rajah, has already been sufficiently exposed. The British Government, acting alone, took nothing and conferred nothing. Whatever was

---

* Mysore Papers, p. 5.　　　† Ibid., p. 69.　　　‡ Ibid., p. 56.

conferred upon the Rajah was conferred by the Allies. And of course when the Allies conferred territory upon the Rajah, to form "a separate Government," they *ipso facto* abjured all claim to it themselves. But there was no more abjuring, expressed or implied, on the part of the Nizam, than on the part of the Company.

It was, no doubt, clearly understood by the Nizam, that his accession of territorial rights was limited to the districts specifically assigned him in Schedule B of the Partition Treaty. But the territorial acquisitions of the East India Company were also limited to the districts specified in Schedule A, and to the fortress of Seringapatam and the small tract of land assigned by Article III ; while the provinces intended to form the separate Government of Mysore, and ceded to the Rajah, under Articles IV and V, are in like manner defined in Schedule C of the same Treaty.

The right of conquest empowered the Company and the Nizam to make a partition and settlement of the territories held by Tippoo. Whatever was acquired by the British Government, whatever was acquired by the Nizam, whatever was conferred upon the Rajah, are all clearly defined in the Partition Treaty. By that Treaty his sovereignty and his territories were conferred upon the Rajah ; by virtue of that Treaty he was enthroned by the Allies. Under the subsequent Subsidiary Treaty the British Government holds its annual Subsidy, its neglected prerogative of authoritative supervision, and its abused prerogative of temporary management.

CHAPTER VII.

RIGHTS OF THE RAJAH AND HIS HEIRS.

I HAVE heard that in a certain voluminous work—age and author unknown—descriptive of Northern Europe, there is one Chapter with this remarkable heading,

"ON THE SNAKES IN NORWAY."

The whole Chapter however only consists of these words :—

"There are no snakes in Norway."

A singular parallel to this negative specification is to be found in the Administrative Report of the Government of India for 1860 on Mysore. In the general Table of Contents, in company with JUDICIAL, REVENUE, and PUBLIC WORKS, there is a special department for

"MARINE,"

And a Section with the same heading is duly placed in its proper order; but contains only the following information :—

"MARINE.

"Mysore is without any sea-board or navigable river."

If the present Chapter were to be written, in this peculiarly exhaustive style, by any one imbued with the doctrine and spirit of the Calcutta letter of the 11th March, 1862, it would be very brief, and might stand thus :—

RIGHTS OF THE RAJAH AND HIS HEIRS.

The Rajah has no rights, and his heirs cannot be recognised. Or, if we expand our summary a little, and adopt the very words of that extraordinary communication, it might run as follows :—

The Rajah of Mysore enjoys the personal provision—an ample provision for his comfort and dignity—made for him when the British Government, as Conqueror and Sovereign, cancelled the authority it had conferred, and reentered upon the possession of the Mysore territories. This provision is a personal right, not heritable even by a natural-born heir; and his title to that right rests upon favour shown to his Highness by the British Government.[*]

A personal right, resting upon grace and favour, seems to me to be little better than no right at all. But I trust I have given sufficient reason in the last two Chapters for not accepting the conclusions of the Calcutta letter, and for disapproving entirely of its spirit. I believe that the Rajah and his heirs for ever, have the right of sovereignty in Mysore, and that this right is secured and guaranteed to them by the Partition Treaty of Mysore, between the Nizam and the British Government.

In their determination not to allow the coveted reversion of Mysore to escape, the Calcutta officials were driven at last to threaten the annihilation of the Rajah's dynasty with a very cruel weapon—the weapon used by Lord Dalhousie in the Carnatic spoliation, and displayed in his Minute on Mysore[†]—to deny that the sovereignty of Mysore was hereditary even to direct lineal descendants, to declare the Subsidiary Treaty of 1799 "a personal Treaty," made only for one life, and renewable merely at the good pleasure of the British Government, as a matter of grace and favour. The intention of using this plea is evident in that passage of the letter to the Rajah, in which the Rajah is told that his personal provision "is not a heritable right, and would not be claimable even by a natural born heir.[‡] This reserved plea of a personal or life Treaty is utterly untenable and groundless.

. The Subsidiary Treaty of 1799 with the Rajah of Mysore is declared in the Preamble to be "a Treaty of perpetual friendship and alliance," concluded in consequence of what was "stipulated in the Treaty of the 22nd of June 1799" (the Partition Treaty) "between the Honourable East India Company and the Nawab Nizam-ood-Dowla ;"—" for effecting a settlement of the territories of the late Tippoo Sultan,"

---

[*] Ante, p. 71.

[†] Ante, p. 41. The iniquitous Carnatic case is quoted by Mr. Mangles as an available precedent !—Mysore Papers, p. 84 (*note*).

[‡] Ante, p. 71.

—and "in order to carry the said stipulations into effect ;"* and the Preamble closes with the asseveration that it "shall be binding upon the contracting parties as long as the sun and moon shall endure."†

Two preliminary points of great importance come out very clearly in the terms of this Preamble. Firstly, although the Nizam is not a party to the Subsidiary Treaty with the Rajah, his equal action and interest in establishing the separate State of Mysore, are therein fully admitted ; the Subsidiary Treaty is concluded in order to carry out the stipulations of the Partition Treaty with the Nizam. Secondly, as the Treaty is stated to be perpetual," and to be of binding force on both parties " as long as the sun and moon shall endure," it is not a personal but a real Treaty ; and therefore, although the usual words, " his heirs and successors," are not appended to the Rajah's name, hereditary succession is effectually maintained.

The Treaty declares itself to be perpetual, and to be made for important public objects ; it is therefore a real and not a personal Treaty.‡ The Rajah of Mysore was certainly recognised by the terms of this Treaty, as the reigning Sovereign of Mysore, and an Ally of the British Government. The dignity of a reigning Sovereign is essentially hereditary in India, as in Europe. If the Rajah had been a person arbitrarily selected for this dignity by the East India Company alone, of its own good pleasure, as a reward for his services, or in consideration of his eminent personal qualifications, this Treaty collated with the Partition Treaty, would still have transmitted the sovereignty to his heirs. But it was not so : the Rajah's position is much stronger ; he was selected by the two Allies, the East

---

    * Appendix B.   † Ibid.

‡ " Treaties, properly so called, are either personal or real. They are personal, when their continuation in force depends on the person of the Sovereign (or his family), with whom they have been contracted. They are real, when their duration depends on the State, independently of the person who contracts. Ali Treaties made for a time specified, or for ever, are also real."—*Law of Nations*, translated from G. F. von Martens, London, 1803, p. 54. " Treaties," says Vattel (book II, chap. xii, § 187), " that are perpetual, and those made for a determinate time, are real ; since their duration does not depend on the lives of the contracting parties." And Grotius points out that it is not necessary that the words " heirs and successors" "should be introduced in order to make the Treaty *real.*"—*De Jure Belli et Pacis*, lib. II, c. xv.

India Company and the Nizam, disposing of territories conquered by their united arms, to be the Sovereign of "a separate Government;" and he was expressly so selected as the "descendant of the ancient Rajahs of Mysore," as the representative of a royal family whose hereditary succession had been preserved for upwards of three centuries, which had only been excluded from power, during the military usurpation of Hyder and Tippoo, for the comparatively short space of thirty-eight years, and which had only been excluded from the representative sovereignty for the still shorter space of sixteen years. Lord Wellesley himself, while declaring that the ancient family could assert no absolute right; that the whole settlement must be based on the conquest by the Allies, and that "their cession must be the source of the Hindoo Prince's dominion,"* still always spoke of the Rajah's enthronement as a restoration, and alludes to "the antiquity of his legitimate title." And Lord William Bentinck, in his severe letter of the 7th September 1831, informing the Rajah that he was about to assume the management of Mysore, thus describes what took place after the fall of Seringapatam :—"Your Highness is well aware of the generosity displayed by the conquerors upon that occasion. Instead of availing themselves of the right of conquest, and of annexing the territories of Mysore to those of the Honourable Company and of the Nizam, the sovereignty was *restored* to the family of the ancient Rajahs of the country, who had taken no part in the contest, and your Highness was placed on the musnud."† And all the conditions of the Partition Treaty, providing for this restoration, and making the detailed allotment and cession of the provinces "to form the separate Government of Mysore," are also said to be binding upon "the heirs and successors of the contracting parties as long as the sun and moon shall endure."

The Partition Treaty, as I have stated in the last Chapter, divided the dominions ruled by Tippoo Sultan into three parts, and the Schedules attached to that Treaty define the respective acquisitions of the Honourable Company and the Nizam, and the limits of the Rajah's dominions. No

---

* Wellesley's Despatches, vol. ii, p. 26.   † Appendix C.

Schedule is attached to the Subsidiary Treaty ; the frontiers and extent of the Mysore State are not in any way indicated therein, except in the Preamble as "the territories specified in Schedule C, annexed to the said" (Partition) "Treaty," and in Article V, as "the territories ceded to him" (the Rajah,) "by the 5th Article of the Treaty of Mysore" (the Partition Treaty).* Thus, without a reference to the Partition Treaty with the Nizam, the representatives of the Rajah would never have known what districts were comprised in the Mysore country. Again, in Article XV of the Subsidiary Treaty, providing for subsequent exchanges of territory (which for convenient reference will be found entire in a note to this page†), allusion is made to "the districts declared by the Treaty of Mysore" (the Partition Treaty), "to belong respectively to the English Company Behauder and to his Highness ;" so that the titles of the Company and the Rajah to their respective possessions are referred to the same document, the Partition Treaty. And, therefore, although the Rajah was not a party to the Partition Treaty, nor the Nizam to the Subsidiary Treaty, it is manifest that the one cannot be read without the other ; that the two are inseparably bound up together ; that the Rajah of Mysore is entitled to point equally to both Treaties in support of his sovereign rights.

All the conditions which were imposed upon the Rajah of Mysore by the Subsidiary Treaty of 1799, slightly modified by the additional Articles of 1807, may be concisely stated as follows :—He was to receive a military force furnished by the East India Company, for the defence and security of his dominions, and to pay the annual sum of seven lakhs of star pagodas (£245,000) as a Subsidy‡ (Article II); he was to maintain at all times fit for service, and ready

---

* **Appendix B.**

† "xv. Whereas it may hereafter appear, that some of *the districts declared by the Treaty of Mysore to belong respectively to the English Company Behauder and to his Highness* are inconveniently situated, with a view to the proper connection of their respective lines of frontier, it is hereby stipulated between the contracting parties, that in all such cases they will proceed to such an adjustment, by means of exchanges or otherwise, as shall be best suited to the occasion."

‡ In addition to this, the Rajah, by a subsequent arrangement, pays £5,000 per annum, as *rent* for the river island of Seringapatam, held in sovereignty by the British Government, making £250,000 per annum in all.

to serve with the Company's army, a body of 4,000 effective Horse (Additional Article I); to hold no communication or correspondence with any foreign State (Article VI); to admit no European into his service, or into his territories, without the consent of the Company (Article VII); to make a suitable provision for certain officers of rank in the service of Tippoo Sultan (Article XI): and lastly, Article XIV contains a declaration on behalf of the Rajah that he will "pay at all times the utmost attention to such advice as the Company's Government shall occasionally judge it necessary to offer to him, with a view to the economy of his finances, the better collection of his revenues, the administration of justice, the extension of commerce, the encouragement of trade, agriculture, and industry, or any other objects connected with the advancement of his Highness's interests, the happiness of his people, and the mutual welfare of both States." (Appendix B.)

It is with reference to this last Article only that the Rajah has been most unfairly charged with an infraction of the Treaty, or in the words of the Calcutta epistle, with its "flagrant and habitual violation." Every stipulation of that Treaty providing an equivalent in money and military aid for general protection, has always been fulfilled to the letter, and the British Government has thereby profited largely. The Rajah has never been accused of hostile or sinister intrigues against the dominant Power, either within or without his own territories. His Highness's hearty allegiance to British supremacy, his loyal demeanour, his beneficial influence and useful services during the crisis of rebellion, have been the recent subject of grateful acknowledgments by the Viceroy, the Secretary of State, and—it is understood—by the Queen herself. The slightest dereliction within this sphere of duty, might well be charged as an infraction of the Treaty. But the obligations of Article XIV must be placed in quite another category. In the first place, they do not relate to any promised advantages or service that could be improperly withheld from the British Government, and which the Rajah might be called upon, under penalty, to make good. They relate to "the mutual welfare of both States" in a general way, but more particularly to "the advancement of his Highness's interests, and the happiness of his people,"—in short, to the welfare of the State of Mysore. This Article was meant to promote the good order and stability of the separate Government of Mysore, and was never intended to prove a trap, or to furnish a pretext for its destruction. The obligations are mutual, the dominant Power undertaking to offer good advice, the dependent Prince promising to pay the utmost attention to it. But the British Government could not possibly have the right of complaining that its advice was not followed, unless the Rajah displayed the most open and defiant contumacy, because it held the corrective remedy for the inattention or disobedience of the Mysore State in its own hands.· The British Government having confined its controlling action to vague and loose reproof, and to the remonstrances of the Resident in particular cases ; having neglected to make its advice efficacious by establishing general principles and substantive law ; having neglected to make its advice authoritative by the imposition of ordinances, or even by the firm presentation of specific measures of reform, is completely debarred from accusing the Rajah of an infraction of the Treaty. With much more·reason the Rajah of Mysore might accuse the British Government of infringing the Treaty, in not having pressed its good advice upon him at the proper time, and in the most effectual form.*

The Subsidiary Treaty of 1799 is what is called by writers on public law "a Treaty of unequal alliance." Grotius says that in a Treaty of unequal alliance, "where the terms of the compact give a permanent precedence to one of the parties,"—"where the greater share of power goes to the stronger,"—"the King" (or State) "preserves his sovereignty." And "in unequal alliances the words *command* and *obedience* are sometimes used with reference to transactions between the superior and the inferior ; but this does not refute what I have said." "The payment of money to the superior, as a consideration for protection, does not destroy sovereignty."† And Wheaton says :—"Treaties of unequal alliance, guarantee, mediation, and protection, may

* As Sir Frederick Currie and Sir Henry Montgomery point out, ante, p. 16.
† *De Jure Belli et Pacis*, Dr. Whewell's edition, 1853, lib. I, chap. ii, pp. 152, 153, 157, 160.

I

have the effect of limiting and qualifying the sovereignty according to the stipulations of the Treaties."*

The sovereignty of the Rajah of Mysore is, therefore, undoubtedly limited and qualified by the stipulations of the Subsidiary Treaty, under which the power of making war, and of communicating with other States is resigned, and an authoritative right of counsel is conceded to the British Government; but it is limited by nothing beyond those stipulations, and no provision is made in that Treaty for the suppression, under any circumstances, of the Rajah's sovereignty, or of that "separate Government" of Mysore constituted by the Partition Treaty with the Nizam.

The suppression of the Mysore State was first distinctly threatened by the fact that the Rajah was tacitly excepted from the benefit of the *amende honorable* to Hindoo Sovereigns, which were based on that Adoption despatch of the 30th April 1860, approved in Sir Charles Wood's reply of the 26th July of the same year, to which I have so often referred.† In this despatch Lord Canning strongly reprobated the caprice and mutability of our former practice with regard to regulating successions in the minor Principalities, and absolutely abandoned that pretended prerogative of rejecting adopted heirs, by which so many annexations had been effected, and to which the acquisitive school of Calcutta mainly trusted for pursuing future appropriations. But even while recommending the policy of maintaining a system of Native States, while repudiating the imaginary precedents which had been evoked for their destruction, Lord Canning—misled by the superficial temptations and supposed facilities of acquiring another rich province—sent no copy of the circular letter declaring Her Majesty's intention to recognise all future adoptions, to the Rajah of Mysore, who thus, at first sight, seems to have been purposely excluded from the operation of this conservative and restorative measure.

But it must be noticed here that Lord Canning, having on the 30th of March, 1860 (Ante, p. 54), told the Secretary of State that the Rajah was willing to bequeath his Kingdom to the British Government, and having referred to the

* *Elements of International Law*, Boston, 1855, p. 45.   † Appendix A.

fact that his Highness had not adopted an heir, as a satis-factory point in the situation, could hardly be expected on the 30th of April—just one month later—to write to the Secretary of State, proposing to encourage the Rajah to adopt, and to follow that up by inviting that Prince himself to take the very step which, in Lord Canning's opinion, was so strongly to be deprecated, and which step—relying upon the Residency gossip of Lord Dalhousie's time, and upon the further instalment of the same in 1858,—Lord Canning seriously believed the Rajah did not wish to take.   It must have seemed quite evident to Lord Canning that if he pressed the Rajah, he would either induce an adoption, and thus preclude the desired bequest, or he would cause the aged Sovereign's last days, in the event of his refusal to adopt, to be embittered by family dissensions, and by the general execration of his courtiers and subjects, and of all good Hindoos.   The invitation to adopt was therefore not extended to the Rajah of Mysore.   But there is great reason to doubt whether, in omitting to send a copy of the circular letter to the Rajah, Lord Canning, however desirous of se-curing the reversion of Mysore, had any hostile intention towards his Highness.   He clearly believed at that time that the Rajah and himself were both of one mind on the subject.   Sir John Willoughby states as follows in one of his Minutes :—" By a comparison of dates, it seems to me clear that Lord Canning had no idea of excluding the Rajah from the benefits of his adoption policy by resorting to such a quibble as that the Rajah is not 'now governing his own territory'."[*]

It is very remarkable that neither Lord Canning, in his despatch to the Secretary of State of the 30th March, 1860, nor even Lord Dalhousie, in his Minute of the 14th of January, 1856,[†] directly impugns the Rajah's right of adoption.   Indeed, from their both noticing as a gratifying circumstance that he had not adopted a son, one would rather be justified in assuming that they could not deny his right to adopt—in Sir Mark Cubbon's words :—"As for the adoption, they dare not refuse it."[‡]

I regret that a copy of the circular letter to the Princes

* Mysore Papers, 1866, p. 31.   † Ante, p. 41.   ‡ Ante, p. 51.

of India, promising to recognise adopted successors, was not sent to the Rajah of Mysore ; but I cannot allow that his rights, or the rights of his family, are in the least diminished by that omission. The Rajah's act of adoption conveys to any person legally eligible an indefeasible title to the sovereignty of Mysore. In the event of his Highness's demise without having adopted a son, the right and duty of adoption would have devolved upon his senior widow. To the many authorities on this point, quoted by me in a recent publication,* I may add the testimony of Sir John Malcolm :—

"The first in rank among the Princesses of a Hindu Ruler or Chief who has no issue, becomes on his death a personage of great consequence in the State, from her acknowledged right of adoption, and the claims upon the power and property of her husband, which this choice confers. It is generally conceived a duty to choose from the least objectionable among the near relations of the deceased ; but the obligation is not imperative, and the consequences of the exercise of this right too often produce family feuds and disputed successions."†

The "ruling sanction" of the Paramount Power, however amplified and abused during Lord Dalhousie's sway, properly extends only to the prevention of these family feuds, to the ultimate decision in disputed successions, and no farther. If annexation is decreed, it may as well be done boldly, on the plea that the Raj is not heritable even to a natural-born heir ; for it is impossible to show that any Paramount Power in India has ever possessed any more right to refuse succession to an adopted son than to a lineal male descendant.

* I have recently argued the general question of Adoption so fully, that I do not consider it necessary to go over the same ground here, but must refer to *The Empire in India*, Letters on " The Right of Adoption," and " Sattara."
† *Central India*, vol. i, p. 484.

CHAPTER VIII.

IMPERIAL RIGHTS, DUTIES, AND INTERESTS.

WHETHER we consider this Mysore case as a legal question, as a matter to be decided by a strict interpretation of covenants ; or from a moral point of view with special reference to the good of the people ; or in relation to what may be called sentimental ideas of progress ; or with sole regard to our own political and material interests,—it will equally appear, in every aspect, that the projects of the Calcutta Government are alike unjust and inexpedient.

The legal situation of the case, considered as one of abstract justice and fidelity to contracts, may be very briefly summed up. The Partition and Subsidiary Treaties of 1799, except where they are expressly modified by subsequent engagements, are still in full force.*

The Mysore Subsidy, which Lord William Bentinck admitted had "never been in jeopardy", having been uninterruptedly paid for sixty-five years in monthly instalments according to the terms of the Treaty, no cause remains, under the strict terms of the Subsidiary Treaty, for any longer retaining the Rajah's dominions under the "exclusive authority and control" of the British Government.

For refusing to recognise the Rajah's adopted son and lawful successor, no honest excuse or pretext can possibly be brought forward. Such a refusal is simply a perverse reassertion of that imaginary and pretended prerogative which Lord Canning, in the Adoption Despatch of 1860, expressly and publicly rejected and abandoned.

Regarding the question again as a matter of moral obligation to the people of the country,—looking merely to the

---

* A new Treaty was made with the Nizam in 1800, by which the greater part of the territories acquired from Tippoo under the partitions of 1792 and 1799, were ceded to the East India Company, to provide for the Subsidiary Force ; but in this, as well as in the later Treaties of 1822 and 1853, all previous engagements were expressly renewed and confirmed.

broad general case of the former misgovernment of Mysore during the Rajah's personal rule, it has been proved that the Honourable Company was primarily and mainly blameable for it.   If Mysore was badly governed in the past, it was our own fault; and if Mysore were in the future to be badly governed under the restored rule of its Sovereign, the faithful Ally and attached feudatory of the British Crown, it would be equally our own fault.   Ample securities can be obtained, under the provisions of the existing Treaty, for the due administration of justice, and for the economical management of the finances.   No valid objection can be made, therefore, under that head to the Rajah's immediate restoration.   No valid excuse can be found, under that head, for the rejection of the Rajah's heir.

Extending the power of our Government under the Treaty to the utmost limit, granting that having once assumed the management, and having retained it for thirty-four years, we are morally bound not to relinquish it until we have obtained the best security for "the welfare of the people" (one of the objects mentioned in Article V), there is no such difficulty in obtaining a full security, as can justify us in having turned the temporary interference contemplated by the Treaty into such a persistent sequestration.   Still less could the British Government be justified in turning this administrative sequestration, existing professedly under the Subsidiary Treaty, into a territorial appropriation in defiance both of this Treaty and of our engagements with the Nizam.

The political stability of our Empire and the progressive instruction of India, would equally be impaired and retarded by an unjust settlement of this Mysore question.   And it is a most extraordinary fact that Lord Canning, though misinformed and misled in this solitary instance, was fully convinced, and expressed the soundest views on the general aspect of the question.   Arguing for the proposed policy of no longer interfering with the succession of adopted heirs, he says in his Despatch of the 30th April, 1860 :—

"The proposed measure will not debar the Government of India from stepping in to set right such serious abuses in a Native Government as may threaten any part of the country with anarchy or disturbance, nor from assuming *temporary charge* of a Native

State when there shall be sufficient reason to do so. This has long been our practice. We have repeatedly exercised the power with the assent and sometimes at the desire of the chief authority in the State, and it is one which, used with good judgment and moderation, it is very desirable that we should retain. It will, indeed, when once the proposed assurance shall have been given, be more easy than heretofore to exercise it without provoking jealousy of any designs upon the independence of the State."

Now most certainly the power of "assuming temporary charge of a Native State," with the object of establishing a system of law and order, is a power which the Government of India might most beneficially hold in reserve, and employ to a much greater extent than has been hitherto attempted. But if the reformed State of Mysore were to be appropriated by the protecting Government, the power of assuming temporary charge of any other State could never be exercised without provoking jealousy and alarm to the highest possible degree.

In this most conspicuous instance of Mysore we have effectually reformed the administration of the country, but have signalised our management by the complete exclusion of the Rajah from all share in the government; and an intention is now very plainly shown of making our administrative possession at once the opportunity and the pretext of absorbing the State and abolishing the sovereignty. If this contemplated breach of trust and violation of Treaties be allowed to proceed to the final extremity, what reliance can hereafter be placed in our moderation and good faith?

As Captain W. J. Eastwick remarks in his Minute against the annexation of Mysore :—

"An eminent and lamented statesman" (Sir G. C. Lewis) "justly writes : 'The only stable foundation for a Government is its moral authority : so long as it is looked up to with respect, confidence, and esteem by the body of the people, it stands on a rock.' These essentials wanting, it is an edifice built on sand."*

In another part of the Adoption Despatch of 1860, Lord Canning wrote as follows :—

"It is certain that objection to the proposed measure will be taken on the ground that it will cut off future opportunities of accession of territory, and that it is our duty not to forego these.

* Mysore Papers, 1866, p. 79.

" I regard this not as an objection, but as a recommendation ; and I cannot take that view of our duty.

" Our supremacy will never be heartily accepted and respected so long as we leave ourselves open to the doubts which are now felt, and which our uncertain policy has justified, as to our ultimate intention towards Native States.

"We shall not become stronger so long as we continue adding to our territory without adding to our European force ; and the additions to that force which we already require are probably as large as England can conveniently furnish, and they will certainly cost as much as India can conveniently pay.

"As to Civil Government, our English officers are too few for the work which they have on their hands, and our financial means are not yet equal to the demands upon us. Accession of territory will not make it easier to discharge our already existing duties in the administration of justice, the prosecution of public works, and in many other ways."*

The last paragraph in this extract shows that Lord Canning had become well acquainted with the immense fallacy of those hopes of augmented financial resources which had animated the advocates of annexation. He knew that the acquisition of territory had always brought with it the necessity of increased establishments, civil and military, on a more expensive scale than that which sufficed for the native government, that contented submission was turned into dangerous disaffection, and that instead of receiving tribute the Imperial Treasury was called upon to supply deficiencies. He knew that every Province absorbed by Lord Dalhousie had proved a burden on the revenues of our older possessions, and he therefore adduces the inadequacy of our "financial means" as one of the reasons for avoiding accessions of territory.

And this leads us to consider the question as it affects the material interests of Great Britain. Even by those who in a general way acknowledge the iniquity and impolicy of persistent and systematic annexation, the question of absorbing Mysore has been represented as quite special and peculiar. It has been urged, in addition to arguments drawn from the growing value and capabilities of this country, that it is so completely encircled by British provinces, that it would be highly impolitic and unadvisable to

---

* Appendix A.

perpetuate a separate jurisdiction. It is chiefly to these considerations that Lord Canning may be supposed to have been adverting, when he wrote in the following terms to the Secretary of State for India, in that letter of 30th March, 1860, from which we have already quoted (p. 55, 58):—

"It may be very little desirable that more provinces should be added to those which are already under the absolute rule of the Queen in India; but the case of Mysore, lying in the midst of the Madras Presidency, and already bound to us in a way which is not convenient or satisfactory, is quite exceptional; and the bequest of that country in full sovereignty to the Crown, by the free will of the ruler, and in a spirit of loyal attachment to the British power, is a consummation which, in the interest of all concerned, no one would wish to see defeated."

If there were any weight in the considerations founded on the geographical position of Mysore in relation to our immediate possessions, it would not be difficult to show that there is nothing exceptional in that position. If the course of annexation were to be resumed in the tempting instance of Mysore, a long series of similar temptations would be re-opened, and every little sovereignty, embedded in the British dominions, would feel itself to be doomed to assimilation in its turn, at the first plausible opportunity. For although the large revenue of Mysore makes it appear a more than usually desirable acquisition, there is really no special cause that can render its appropriation more defensible than that of any other State in India.

There is nothing inconvenient or unsatisfactory in the way in which Mysore is legally connected with the British Government. On the contrary, it would be much better for the Imperial Power, for the Princes and for the people, if all the Native States of India were connected with the British Crown by such well-defined ties and obligations as those of the Subsidiary Treaty of 1799. There is nothing inconvenient or unsatisfactory in the way Mysore is at present bound to us, except that obstacle to its full development as a reformed Native State, offered by the needless and unjust suspension of its legitimate Sovereign. But when Lord Canning penned the lines which we have just quoted, in his Despatch of 30th March, 1860, he was, as we know, still under the mistaken impression that the Rajah would never adopt a son, and would actually prefer the absorption of Mysore in the British dominions to the maintenance of his hereditary throne. Without our knowledge of this erroneous belief, we should find it very difficult to account for the strange inconsistency that on the 30th March, 1860, the Governor-General should deem the case of Mysore, "lying in the midst of the Madras Presidency", to be "quite exceptional", and such that its "bequest in full sovereignty to the Crown," is "a consummation which no one would wish to see defeated", while on the 30th April, 1860,—just one month later,—in his admirable Adoption Despatch, he declares that all who "remember the condition of Upper India in 1857 and 1858" must be "thankful that in the centre of the large and compact British province of Rohilcund there remained the solitary little State of Rampoor, still administered by its own Mahomedan Prince, and that on the borders of the Punjab and of the districts above Delhi, the Chief of Puttiala and his kinsmen still retained their hereditary authority unimpaired."*

In this Despatch Lord Canning most emphatically pronounced this maxim of Imperial policy :—

"The safety of our rule is increased, not diminished, by the maintenance of the Native Chiefs well affected to us."*

What Native Prince is more well-affected to us, what Native Prince has proved himself to be more faithfully attached to the British Crown, than the Rajah of Mysore—"that venerable and loyal Prince", as Lord Canning termed him, "the oldest and staunchest Ally of Her Majesty in India", as the Secretary of State observed, and who, again in the words of Lord Canning, "possesses a very strong claim to have his wishes and feelings consulted by us"? He does indeed possess a strong claim, although he asks for nothing but bare justice ; for those who can appreciate the terrible results that must have followed, if the contagion of the revolt in Northern and Central India had spread to the Southern Presidency and the Madras Army, may well maintain, as many experienced officials have done, that not even the Nawab of Rampoor or the Rajah of Puttiala deserved so much the gratitude of the British Government for their con-

* Appendix A.

duct during the rebellion, as did the Rajah of Mysore for "the ready and useful assistance which he rendered to the Queen's troops," and for his personal efforts "in preserving peace and encouraging loyalty."*

There is nothing but disgrace and loss of moral influence to be got by denying the Rajah's just claim ; and every evil effect would be enormously and irretrievably increased by refusing to recognise his lawful heir. Beyond the miserable patronage, nothing whatever is really to be gained from this unjust confiscation. The Mysore State now pays a much larger sum as tribute applicable to Imperial purposes than could ever be shown as a surplus under our immediate rule, besides being bound to furnish a body of four thousand Irregular Horse, most useful troops, whenever required for our service. Altogether the direct contributions payable by Mysore, out of its revenue of one million sterling, cannot be computed at less than £300,000 per annum. No Presidency, no Collectorate in India pays so well. And the British Government is subject to no burden, is placed under no obligations in return, beyond those of general guaranty and protection. The Viceroy is not bound to station a single soldier, European or native, within the frontiers of Mysore, if he does not choose. All our troops may be withdrawn on an emergency.

The continued acquisition of territory—even by fair means and with a just title—can no longer be advantageous to Great Britain, or beneficial to India. But every district that is acquired by foul means and with a bad title, is a burden and an injury to the Empire. However strong, however well administered, the Government of India may be, it is not, and never will be so strong, and so well administered, as to be able to trust to physical force and organised establishments, and to dispense with moral superiority. There is still immense scope for the exercise of our authoritative counsels. I would rather see one reformed native State than a dozen model Presidencies. We may want some of our seventy thousand soldiers nearer home one of these days. I should prefer the power of calling them in, on an emergency, to the privilege of being

* Lord Canning to the Rajah, 28th June, 1860, ante, p. 48.

incessantly called upon to send out more Cadets, or more
Competition Wallahs.

If the great aim and object of British supremacy in India
be the reform of native institutions, and the mental and
moral improvement of the native races, I cannot doubt that
the permanent civilisation of a people will be more advanced by the development of their capacity for self-
government, than by a stereotyped system—be it ever so
benevolent—of exotic and exclusive management.   In the
cause of progress not less than in the cause of peace, I
should plead for the maintenance of Native States, and for
the elevation of Native Princes and ministers.   If our Government declares that it can devise no substantial reforms
for Mysore as a dependent Principality ; that it knows not
how to impose such " ordinances and regulations" as would
form a constitutional protection to the people ; that it can
prescribe no remedy for the defects of this, or any other
native State, except extinction ; then I say that it is not
proclaiming the incapacity of the minor Princes, but its own
incapacity as an Imperial and Paramount Power.

For many years past very confused and erroneous notions
have extensively prevailed, as to the absolute rights or strong
claims of Great Britain to the possession of Imperial or
Paramount supremacy over all the native Sovereigns of
India.   I do not think that any such claim was ever advanced, in any official document or in any historical work,
before the complete subjugation of the Mahratta Princes, and
the general pacification of India, by the Marquis of Hastings
in the year 1819 ; and no such general claim can be found,
expressed or implied, in the Treaties of that critical period.
It would be immaterial, even if it were possible, to trace the
exact date, or the particular authority, from which this claim
originated ; but we find it asserted and enforced, in its
fullest development, with ruinous results to several native
dynasties, and with the effect of a general menace to all,
during Lord Dalhousie's eight years' tenure of the Vice-
royalty, from 1848 to 1856.

As the British dominions were extended and consolidated,
and British domination became more and more an indis-
putable fact, a gradual approach seems to have been made
to the demand of Imperial prerogatives, while the limits of

those prerogatives were at every step progressively expanded.

These assumed prerogatives have been strained in two directions, and with two purposes : in the direction of Feudal Suzerainty, with the alleged purpose of consolidating our Empire ; in the direction of Administrative Dictatorship, with the alleged purpose of protecting the people. Both these purposes are good ; both these pretensions are based on truth and reason ; but they have unfortunately been pushed far beyond their legitimate scope, until their ordinary statement, official and literary, has become false in letter and spirit ; until their origin has become obscure, and their future inscrutable ; until the native Princes and their subjects have learned to dread every allusion to these prerogatives as the prelude of insidious aggression.

To regulate the successions in minor Principalities is a natural attribute of Imperial authority ; and although the East India Company, which, like the Nawabs and Rajahs, had been a vassal of Delhi, never could or did pretend to occupy the throne of Timour, the duty of deciding in cases of doubtful or disputed succession has devolved upon Great Britain, as a moral result of her immense material strength, and of her pre-eminent interest in the preservation of the general peace and good order of India.   This duty was not assumed by our Government without many misgivings and much hesitation.   It was declined on two remarkable occasions by Lord William Bentinck,* and the manifest disorder and discredit arising from the over-scrupulous non-interference of that nobleman's administration had probably the greatest effect in determining his successors to adopt a bolder policy.   But we did not know where to stop.   The moral duty of pacification, imposed upon Great Britain by her overwhelming power in India, naturally extended to all cases of disputed inheritance ; while over a large class of petty Princes she had acquired, by conquest, treaty or patronage, an unquestioned supremacy and the privilege of investiture. But the duty of investing feudatories, of superintending and controlling successions in Hindoo royal families, was by degrees exaggerated into the right to *divest*

* *The Empire in India*, Letter on " Jhansi."

feudatories, and to abolish royal families, by refusing to recognise adoptions.   The adoption of an heir, which among
the Hindoos is not only a religious and social obligation, but
is an ordinary, essential and incessantly recurring incident
of their law of inheritance,—without which, on the failure
of lineal descendants in the male line, even the nearest collateral cannot claim by virtue of his consanguinity,—was
declared to be an extraordinary and special boon, to be
granted or withheld at the choice of the dominant Power.
This new doctrine, resting on no historical or legal foundation, was first applied in 1841, in Lord Auckland's time, to
bar a succession to the petty State of Colaba, over which
" the entire supremacy", and "right of investiture", were expressly reserved by Treaty to the British Government ; and
in 1848 it was employed for the extinction of the Sattara
family, although its head had always been treated by us
with great form and ceremonial as a royal personage, with
whom, "his heirs and successors", "in perpetual sovereignty",
we were connected by a Treaty of "friendship and alliance".
On this critical occasion the new destructive heresies, forti-
fied by an audacious assertion of utterly imaginary precedents,* were exalted into political maxims, formally ratified
and confirmed by the conclusion of the Court of Directors,
that " a dependent Principality cannot pass to an adopted
heir without the consent of the Paramount Power ; that we
are under no pledge, direct or constructive, to give such
consent ; and that the general interests committed to our
charge are best consulted by withholding it".†   In accordance with this judgment, and as natural consequences of
the approved annexation of Sattara, the extinction of the
important State of Nagpore, and the small Principality of
Jhansi, followed in the year 1854.

And thus, with the purpose in view of consolidating the
Empire, one of the chief prerogatives of Imperial Suzerainty,
which might have been exercised with the cheerful and
unanimous acquiescence of the Princes and people of India,
was perverted and prostituted to the lust of territory.

Our first encroachment, in the case of Colaba,—far from
being a proper and opportune assertion of Imperial rank

* *The Empire in India,* " Sattara."   † Sattara Papers, 1849, p. 8.

and functions, as some have argued,—was an absolute abdication of that federal rank, and a repudiation of those functions of protection and reforming control, which alone could entitle the *de facto* Paramount Power to be recognised and obeyed as the Imperial Sovereignty of India. By this new policy our Government has denied its origin and history, contradicted all its precedents, renounced the beneficent duties of *Empire*, and assumed the offensive and defiant position of an all-absorbing acquisitive *Kingdom*. And the consequence is that our territorial acquisitions in India have already overstepped the limits of profit, utility, and safety.

Between the years 1848 and 1856 the doctrine had become universally accepted at Calcutta, that the native Princes were disqualified for any good purpose, useless as allies, impotent as enemies, and yet capable of being very troublesome, and that our only true policy was, in Lord Dalhousie's own words, that of "getting rid of those petty intervening Principalities, which may be made a means of annoyance, but which can never be a source of strength".* Mr. George Campbell wrote as follows in 1852, alluding to the case of Sattara :—

" One right of Lord Paramount we have unequivocally established, that of succeeding to the estates of Princes who die without legitimate heirs; yet that right has not always been exercised. In former times, when it was the policy of the Government to maintain and even to create subsidiary States, heirs were generally found or created; but latterly, better understanding our position, we have been more inclined to insist on our rights. It is indeed only in this way that we can hope gradually to extinguish the native States, which consume so large a portion of the revenues of the country, and so prevent us from lightening the burdens and improving the condition of the mass of the people."†

The rights of Princes, represented by certain musty old parchments called Treaties, were allowed to weigh as nothing

---

* Sattara Papers, 1849, p. 83.

† Campbell's *Modern India*, 1852, p. 169. This plausible and smartly written book represents very fairly the ordinary views of Indian affairs held by the Bengal Civil Service, of which Mr. Campbell, now a Judge of the High Court of Calcutta, is a very able and distinguished member. The book contained a great mass of information, was favourably received, and much read ; and it was published just in the nick of time, as if to serve as an exponent and defence of Lord Dalhousie's policy of annexation.

against the "real good" of their contented subjects, "whose
best interests, we sincerely believe," says Lord Dalhousie,
"will be promoted by the uniform application of our system
of government."*

This alleged desideratum—"the uniform application of
our system of government"—appears to me to be the extreme abuse and perversion of what I have called the second
assumed prerogative of Imperial power, Administrative
Dictatorship.   Based, like the claim to regulate successions,
on truth and reason, on the dominant power and dominant
interests of Great Britain throughout the continent of India,
it has been pushed, beyond all bounds, to a climax of exaggeration and falsehood.   Confined to a fair supervision of
public affairs in the secondary States, to the reproof and
correction of scandalous misrule, to the inculcation of sound
general principles, and the deprecation of barbarous prejudices, the reforming action of the *de facto* Paramount
Power has effected great and beneficial changes in their laws
and customs, and in the prevalent tone, temper and opinions,
both of rulers and subjects ;† and would have been capable
of indefinite extension, without infringing any engagement,
without exciting any dissension or mistrust.   Every step
gained in this way is a substantial and permanent advance
in the course of civilisation and progress.   But when, according to recent practice, the defects of native institutions
are not only denounced, but deplored as being quite incurable by native and natural means, and the introduction
of English officers into every place of authority is pre-

---

* Sattara Papers, 1849, p. 83.

† I allude particularly to the prohibition of Suttee ; the resolutions against
female infanticide among the Rajpoots, and the combined plan for relaxing
the restrictions on marriage connexions and the enormous expense attending
them, which were the chief incentives to that horrible crime ; the suppression
of Thuggee, and consequent disappearance of the superstitions which tended
to its concealment and toleration; the cessation of torture, cruel punish-
ments, the arbitrary infliction of death, and imprisonment without trial ; the
abolition or mitigation of transit duties, and other impediments to trade ; and
in more complete protection to the accumulation of wealth and its transmis-
sion by inheritance. Some of these reforms are as yet but partially secure ; and
it is above all to be regretted that our Government should have struck the
heaviest blow possible against that last mentioned—the inviolability of property—by its recent inroads upon the jewel-rooms and wardrobes of mediatised
royal families.   Native Princes and Ministers were already but too prone to
similar high-handed acts, on due provocation ; and needed no such example of
confiscation in cold blood.   See *The Empire in India*, "The Bhonsla Fund."

scribed as the only panacea, there is an end of harmonious co-operation; advice appears as an insult and a menace, and the very idea of reform becomes detestable. During the last twenty years, while the prerogative of regulating successions has been vitiated by the lust of territory, the prerogative of correcting abuses has been vitiated by the lust of patronage; the one assumed prerogative has been employed to prove, explain and strengthen the other, and the two together have been made the pretext and justification for destroying Principalities and extinguishing dynasties, for abolishing native nobility and proscribing native talent.

A reconstructive policy for the Indian Empire can never grow out of a series of illicit assumptions and silent encroachments: any apparent gain that can be traced to no other source than that, must always be illusory and precarious; there is nothing to show for it; it is matter neither of record nor of repute. A solid and permanent Imperial fabric can only be built on explicit, acknowledged and recorded declarations, preceded by general confidence, followed by general consent. Our relations with the native States have been reduced, legally and morally, to a stagnating Chaos of confusion and contradiction. Is it possible to evoke a Cosmos out of this Chaos? I think it is possible.

Up to this time, the British Government has done nothing to deserve the general confidence, or to secure the general consent. The two great Imperial prerogatives which naturally devolved upon our Government, and which, if fairly exercised, would have been gladly conceded by all, have been turned into weapons of offence and destruction, until the only chance of honour and security for a native Prince appears to lie in denying those prerogatives to the utmost limits of subordination, and in evading their operation by every practicable device. Our counsels and our assistance are seen to be fatal, not only to the independence, but to the very existence of the most friendly and submissive Principalities. In one most conspicuous and important instance—that of Mysore—we have effectually reformed the administration of the country, but have signalised our management by the complete and permanent exclusion of the Rajah from all voice and share in the government, and by giving all places of high trust and emolument to English officers ; and an intention is now very plainly shown of making our administrative possession at once the opportunity and the pretext of absorbing the State and abolishing the sovereignty. If this contemplated breach of trust and violation of Treaties—as I think I have shown it to be —be allowed to proceed to the final extremity, what reliance can thereafter be placed in our moderation and good faith ?

In order that we may be able to undertake the reform of the native States, in order that the native States should accept our instruction and guidance, it is necessary not only that our moral influence should be restored to its former height, but that it should rise to a revolutionary strength. Three great political operations appear to me to be required to produce this full effect :—(1) a Golden Bull, or declaration of paramount authority over all the Princes of India, explaining the Imperial principles, and the reciprocal rights and duties of the secondary Powers ; (2) a demonstration of good will and liberal intentions towards native Princes in general, which should precede or accompany, and thus illustrate the Golden Bull ; (3) the exhibition—as an example, model and encouragement—of one or more native States, reformed under British tutelage, and then re-established in their former dimensions, or aggrandised by the Paramount Power, as active members of the Federation.

These measures would be intelligible and acceptable to all, would involve no embarrassing confessions, would not openly break the continuity or consistency of our political action, but would vindicate, to a certain extent, the severities of the past, while removing all menace from the future.

One very plausible objection might be brought against the fundamental notion of an Imperial manifesto or Golden Bull : it might be denounced as being after all an arbitrary usurpation of prerogatives and functions not lawfully appertaining to the British Government, as being, in wholesale and with the widest extension possible, just one of those high-handed "acts of state" against which, in detailed and particular instances, I have myself protested. But this is a complete misconception of my views.

I have not protested, and do not protest against arbitrary acts of state in general, any more than I protest against war, conquest, revolution or rebellion in general. An act of state, however arbitrary and rigorous, may or may not be justifiable, just as in the case of war, conquest, revolution or rebellion. I have protested against certain transactions in which the British Government has violated solemn treaties, while professing by sophistical arguments to respect their provisions, has repudiated treaties in full force as if they were waste paper, has claimed Imperial prerogatives, which not only it had never acquired, but which never existed in any age or country, and has not employed those assumed prerogatives for the protection, instruction or reform of friendly and orderly Native States, but for their confiscation and destruction.* And in those cases to which I refer, the British Government did not pretend to act under any sense of revolutionary or belligerent necessity, did not admit that its action was abnormal or extraordinary, but asserted its legality ; appealed, without a shadow of right, to "the universal and immemorial custom of India," and invoked a visionary series of precedents, which were said, without a vestige of proof, to have come down from "the Imperial House of Delhi," and the other "Governments which preceded us."† These are not legitimate acts of state, these are not acts of war, these are not conquests,—they do not present themselves as such,—they are simply appropriations on false pretences. They do not command the respect, assent or approval of any native party or of any native interest, either in our long settled possessions or in the newly acquired provinces, or in the allied Principalities that are still preserved. They are utterly unintelligible to the native mind, except when viewed as despotic equivocations, as disingenuous pretexts for predetermined violence. Such transactions as these can give no valid title, can destroy no adverse right ; they do not even produce terror and submission, but simply exasperate, and generate permanent conspiracies.

Open undisguised conquest is an intelligible process ; and the title to possessions so gained is not, within certain limita-

* *The Empire in India*, Letters on the Carnatic, Sattara, Nagpore, and Jhansi, and *passim*.
† Ibid., " Adoption" and " Sattara."

tions, impugned even by modern international law, while, according to the popular conceptions of the East, the right of conquest is a sufficient plea before God and man. The lapse of time, general acquiescence and content, may confirm a conquering Power in dominions that were originally acquired by an unprovoked aggression. Nor is it necessary that a conquest should be consecrated with blood : overwhelming force may produce all the effect of conquest without a sword being drawn. But there must be a visible process, and an open avowal.

It is not then against high-handed acts of state that I protest, but against the underhand and undeclared proceedings of a secret Executive. I do not protest against conquest in hot blood, but against the cold-blooded denial of rights, without even the form of a proclamation, in contempt both of a lawful and unoffending claimant, and of an unwilling and bewildered people.

A war, a conquest, a revolution, a rebellion, an act of state, may be justifiable, when international discussion or municipal law affords no prospect of redress or remedy. There must be a beginning to every political constitution, and to every constitutional change. The most Pragmatic of Pragmatic Sanctions becomes good public law, if it is founded on truth and justice, if it supplies a great political want, if the promulgating Power is manifestly competent to enforce its provisions, and if a great majority of the secondary Powers, and the people of the Empire, accept it with joy and gratitude. All these conditions could, I believe, be fulfilled in Queen Victoria's Imperial manifesto ; and therefore I think that all objections to its issue on grounds of international law or public faith, can be fully refuted.

From the following passage in the Adoption despatch of the 30th of April 1860, Lord Canning would seem to have been partially conscious that a clear definition of Imperial pretensions was required under the altered circumstances of British rule :—

"The last vestiges of the Royal House of Delhi, from which, for our own convenience, we had long been content to accept a vicarious authority, have been swept away. The last pretender to the representation of the Peishwah has disappeared. The Crown of England stands forth the unquestioned Ruler and Paramount Power in all India, and is, for the first time, brought face to face with its feudatories.   There is a reality in the suzerainty of the Sovereign of England which has never existed before, and which is not only felt, but eagerly acknowledged by the Chiefs."

But this despatch, confined to the subject of succession in certain States, is addressed, not to the Princes and people of India, but to the Secretary of State.   It contains no sufficient avowal of principles, even within its limited scope, and was followed up by no precise and public declaration of Imperial supremacy.

We have hitherto failed to appreciate the sources of power that lie hidden in the peculiar civilisation and social life of India.   We have hitherto neglected to guide, to mould or to encourage the political sentiments of the natives, which are thoroughly monarchical and conservative, but have left them to brood over the memories and glories of bygone days and fallen dynasties.   It is our fault that both Princes and people have learned to gaze for the centre of their national existence, interests and honour, anywhere but towards the British Throne.   In order to authenticate a thorough change in the legal relations between the British Government and the minor States of India, to make the transition harmonious, and to place the Imperial constitution on a secure basis, the evident stamp of Royal Personality, a distinct assertion of the Royal will, should characterise each document, and dignify each transaction.   Were attempts to be made to institute a general reform of the native States merely by the ordinary official means, by a greater stringency of local interference, the movement would be opposed and hampered in every direction by the terms of existing Treaties, by the irresistible mistrust which our past dealings have generated, and even by our own recorded practice and precedents. Without the avowed assumption of Imperial supremacy, inaugurated and exemplified by Royal acts of restoration and re-assurance, our reforming propensities will merely provoke native Princes to antagonism, and us to annexation.

For until an Imperial Constitution for India is solemnly proclaimed and acknowledged, the British claim to paramount authority over the more important States will rest upon nothing but a silent usurpation, unjustified, unrecognised and undeserved.

When in consequence of Napoleon's conquests, and his alliances with the minor Princes of Germany, the Holy Roman Empire was dissolved in 1805, and the Emperor Francis assumed the hereditary title of Austria, the Electoral and Feudal Principalities were transformed into independent and sovereign States, and were ultimately so recognised by the Treaties of Vienna, and the Acts constituting the German Confederation.

The practical dissolution of the Mogul Empire, and the reduction of its political elements, some into British provinces and British dependencies, others into protected, allied and independent States—begun by the Mahratta Confederacy, and perfected by British victories—was definitely registered and recorded in our long series of treaties with the Princes of India of every degree. We maintained —as the supposed medium of political influence—an outward ceremonial and verbal deference towards the Great Mogul, down to a later period than even any of our native Allies ;* but when in all our negotiations we had entirely ignored and set aside his Imperial pretensions, and dealt on terms of equality and alliance with the Princes who, from his point of view, were undutiful vassals, it was clear that the throne of Delhi had fallen, and that the ancient constitution of the Empire had fallen with it. That shadowy succession to the Mogul Emperor, which has been sometimes attributed to the East India Company, rests upon no basis either of inheritance or of testament, of ancient forms or of modern compact.

It is true that some of the Indian Princes, with whom treaties were made, or their ancestors, had been tributaries, feudatories or provincial Governors under the Great Mogul, the Rajah of Sattara or the Peishwa : some of them had no better original title than that of a rebellious vassal or con-

* The Nawab of Oude, hereditary Vizier of the Empire, openly renounced his ancient allegiance to the throne of Delhi in 1819, by assuming the title and insignia of King, and coining money in his own name. This was undoubtedly done with the consent and approval of the British Government ; but, as Sir John Malcolm observes, "no alteration was made in the relations subsisting between the Company's Government and the Imperial family." And the Honourable Company continued for some years longer " to coin money in the name of the Emperor of Delhi, and to style itself, upon the face of that coin, the servant of a monarch who owed his daily subsistence to its bounty." —Malcolm's *Political History of India*, vol. i, pp. 536, 540.

tumacious Lieutenant; but then the East India Company —in whose name, and not in that of the British Sovereign, all the treaties were concluded—entered upon the field of negotiation with no more secure footing, with no more valid pretensions.

The English Authorities avowed themselves to be vassals of the King of Delhi, tenants and tributaries of the Nizam and the Nawab of the Carnatic, and entered into various complicated relations of joint management, partnership and assignment, with Chieftains of inferior rank. At successive political conjunctures these embarrassing engagements were, for the most part, shaken off or commuted; the ambiguous tenures were simplified or converted into cessions; but whatever new rights of sovereignty and independence may have been gained by the East India Company, must have been equally conceded to those confederates and to those defeated adversaries with whom treaties were concluded.

The British Government having made treaties of "perpetual friendship and alliance," in which the reciprocal position of both parties is strictly defined; having received cessions of territory from these Princes as the consideration for military defence; and having thus generally, and with more or less precision, recognised them as the absolute masters of their dominions and subjects, has acquired no right to term them or treat them suddenly as feudatories, or to assume over them the prerogatives and functions of a dictatorial Suzerain.

That right, those functions and prerogatives, may be acquired, but not without an open assertion and justification, not without fair limitations and compensations; and this acquisition will never be advanced by a contempt for existing treaties, or by destroying Mysore, a reformed Principality, the work of our own hands, before the face of those whom we wish to subject to a similar reforming process, but only by measures of persuasion and encouragement, and by the offer of reciprocal advantages.

By very simple and equitable means, as I believe, the Nizam, and other Princes who are, equally with him, left, under the terms of their treaties with the East India Company, in the possession of absolute local power, might be induced not only formally to acknowledge the Queen as their Imperial Suzerain, but to adopt, under Her Majesty's guidance and example, constitutional government, judicial reform, and a sound financial system.

The Nizam of the Deccan, who rules over ten millions of subjects, had asserted and secured his independence of Delhi for upwards of forty years before our first Treaty with him in 1766.* The English have never known the Nizam, have never had any dealings or any communications with him except as an independent Sovereign. Lord Dalhousie himself, while aiming to deprive the Nizam of a large portion of his dominions,† observed that he was "an independent Prince,"‡ and that "the British Government was bound by the solemn obligations of a Treaty to abstain from all interference in his Highness's internal affairs," and "had guaranteed to him the exercise over his own subjects of his own sole and absolute authority."§ The obligations referred to are contained in Article XV of the Treaty of 1800 :—

"The Honourable Company's Government, on their part, hereby declare that they have no manner of concern with any of his Highness's children, relations, subjects or servants, with respect to whom his Highness is absolute."‖

And in another part of the same Minute Lord Dalhousie says :—

"Were it not for the existence of the Subsidiary and Contingent Forces, our relations with the State of Hyderabad would be merely those which usually are found between two independent Powers, and the position of the Resident at Hyderabad would correspond in all respects with that of any accredited Minister of a foreign State."¶

It is expressly stipulated in Article VIII of the Treaty of 1804 with Maharajah Dowlut Rao Scindia of Gwalior,

---

* Grant Duff's *History of the Mahrattas*, 1826, vol. i, p. 478; Volume of Treaties, 1853, p. 116.

† Papers relating to the Nizam, 1854, p. 107. See also the *English in India*, p. 79.

‡ Papers relating to the Nizam, p. 39.　　　　　§ Ibid., pp. 38, 39.

‖ Volume of Treaties, 1853, p. 149.

¶ Papers relating to the Nizam, 1854, p. 37. Lord Dalhousie's words in 1853 suffice to contradict the assertion of Sir John Lawrence in 1865, that " at the time of the fall of Seringapatam and of the conquest of Mysore, the Nizam was in a state of subordinate alliance with the British Goverument, and had passed from the condition of an independent to that of a purely dependent ruler."—Mysore Papers, 1866, p. 55.

confirmed by the subsequent engagements of 1805, 1817 and 1844, that "the Honourable East India Company's Government have no manner of concern with any of the Maharajah's relations, dependents, chiefs or servants, with respect to whom the Maharajah is absolute; and it is further agreed, that no officer of the Honourable Company shall ever interfere in the internal affairs of the Maharajah's Government."*

The British Government obtained, under Article IX of the Treaty of 1817 with Maharajah Dowlut Rao Scindia, freedom from those restrictions of the former Treaty which prevented alliances being formed with the States of Oodeypoor, Joudpore and Kota, which had hitherto paid tribute to Scindia; but a condition is added, "that nothing in this Article shall be constructed to give the British Government a right to interfere with States or Chiefs in Malwa or Guzerat, clearly and indisputably dependent on or tributary to the Maharajah; and it is agreed that his Highness's authority over those States or Chiefs shall continue on the same footing as it has been heretofore."† The suzerainty of Scindia over certain petty States is hereby clearly recognised; but no suzerainty or right of superintendence over the State of Gwalior is claimed for the British Government in this or any other Treaty.

In Article X of the Treaty concluded in 1818 with Maharajah Mulhar Rao Holkar of Indore, " the British Government declares that it has no manner of concern with any of the Maharajah's children, relations, dependents, subjects or servants, with respect to whom the Maharajah is absolute."‡

And " the English Government engages," in Article XVI of the same Treaty, " that it will never permit the Peishwa, nor any of his heirs or descendants, to claim or exercise any sovereign rights or power whatever over the Maharajah Mulhar Rao Holkar, his heirs and descendants."§

The dissolution of the Mahratta Confederacy, and the cessation of the Peishwa's authority, are thus admitted by both parties : complete independence is guaranteed to the Rajah of Indore, but none of the Peishwa's prerogatives are transferred to the East India Company.

* Volume of Treaties, 1853, p. 357.   † Ibid., p. 365.
‡ Ibid., p. 410.   § Ibid., p. 411.

By Article III of the Treaty of 1803 the British Government agreed, "never to interfere in the concerns of the Maharajah of Bhurtpore's country, nor to exact any tribute from him."* And after the outbreak of hostilities, the unsuccessful siege of Bhurtpore, and the submission of the Rajah in 1805, this condition was repeated in Article V of the new Treaty :—" The Honourable Company, in consideration of the friendship now established, will not interfere in the possession of this country, nor demand any tribute on account of it."†

There is a similar provision in Article III of the Treaty of 1803 with the Maha Rao Rajah of Alwur, that "the Honourable Company shall not interfere with the country of the Maha Rao Rajah, nor shall demand any tribute from him."‡

The Rana of Dholepore, a small Principality with about one hundred thousand inhabitants, is the only Indian Sovereign who retains the full power of declaring war and peace, and of establishing diplomatic relations with all the potentates of the world. Article IV of the Treaty of 1806 provides that this State " will remain exempt from all orders of the Adawlut, and other demands of the Honourable Company, and the Maharajah Rana hereby agrees to take upon himself the responsibility of adjusting all disputes which may arise, either external or internal, and no responsibility for assistance or protection remains with the Honourable Company."§

" The Honourable East India Company engages," by Article II of the Treaty of 1833, " never to interfere with the hereditary or other possessions of the Nawab of Bhawulpoor." And Article III declares that "as regards the internal administration of his Government, and the exercise of his sovereign rights over his subjects, the Nawab shall be entirely independent, as heretofore."‖

Many other States of Rajpootana and Central India,—of which the more important are Oodeypoor, Jeypoor, Jodhpoor, Kota, and Bhopaul,—are bound by their treaties " to act in subordinate co-operation"¶ with the British Govern-

---

* Volume of Treaties, 1853, p. 471. † Ibid., p. 473.
‡ Ibid., p. 468. § Ibid., p. 384. ‖ Ibid., p. 502.
¶ A reference to the original negotiations, and to the position of this en-

ment, and to acknowledge its supremacy ; but the British Government on its part, agrees that the Princes, their heirs and successors, " shall remain absolute rulers of their dominions, and that the British jurisdiction shall not be introduced."*

The Principalities of this numerous class, acknowledging their subordination to the one Great Power of India, are true feudatories of the British Crown. But the very fact of their acknowledged subordination—of British supremacy over them being expressly admitted in their treaties,—contributes to prove that the Principalities of that more important and less numerous class, such as the Nizam, Scindia, and Holkar, in whose contemporaneous treaties subordination is not promised, and British supremacy is not admitted, are not feudatories, but independent States.

There are thus two classes of native States, those which are independent sovereignties, connected with the dominant Power by treaties of friendship and alliance only ; and those which are confessedly dependent. All those of the former, and many of the latter class, are left, by the terms of their engagements with the East India Company, in possession of the absolute and uncontrolled power over their own subjects and revenues. They have renounced for themselves all the prerogatives of external action, and we, on our part, have repudiated all pretensions to interfere with their internal affairs.

But it may be objected that it is useless at this late period to claim perfect administrative freedom for the petty States of India ; that the practice of many years sanctions our supervision ; that, in the interests of humanity, and for the good of trade, we have constantly interfered with beneficial effect in their internal concerns, and that we must continue to do so. It is true that we have frequently interfered with our advice, for the protection of individuals, for the improvement of public communications, and for the removal of objectionable imposts,—such as transit duties—which had been found burdensome on commerce, or injurious to some of our own sources of revenue ; and when

gagement among the terms of the Treaty, will prove that it invariably applied to military and diplomatic " cooperation" only.

* Volume of Treaties, 1853, p. 420, 426, 430, 435, 441.

our suggestions have been steadily pressed upon a native Court, regardless of evasions and delay, they have at last produced the desired result: but, however sound in principle and advantageous in practice such changes may be, they are hardly calculated to work a permanent reform in the local system, or to create an impression of our disinterested intentions. They generally appear to the native Prince as proposals that he should incur additional expenses, abandon some profitable tax or monopoly, or even prohibit some produce or manufacture within his dominions—such as salt or opium—for the benefit of his gigantic friend. These proposals are recommended by no prospect of gain to the Prince himself, are not even demanded by his own people, and are dreaded more especially as pretexts and precedents for further encroachments and for continued dictation.

The truth is, that except by an intrusive regard for the protection and advancement of individuals,—which in its best aspect resembles jobbery and favouritism, and in its worst, approaches the confines of corruption—and an intermittent mediation in favour of those peculiarly British objects to which I have alluded, our Residents and Political Agents have seldom brought their influence to bear either upon the general form of administration, or upon any particular measures of the Princes to whom they are accredited. Our own Government has never enjoined or encouraged such interference, nor would it be easy in most cases to interfere with effect. Those very clauses of treaties which I have just cited stand in the way of such schemes of reformation; and even if not firmly insisted on by a Prince or Minister of some talent and resolution, (as has often been done,) they would not fail to supply the means of obstruction and delay. A Resident has neither resources at his disposal for enforcing his suggestions on a friendly native Court, so long as the country is peaceable and orderly, nor has he always any adequate sources of information to assure him whether his suggestions are actually adopted, or whether their adoption is really practicable. Unless during a minority, when a struggle for power has induced an appeal or an intrigue for British support, or during some crisis of political danger and disorder—not always of provincial origin—it is seldom that any pretext or opportunity has been afforded for directly assuming or controlling the management of one of those Principalities which are entitled to internal independence.

What the votaries of annexation considered the most splendid opportunity possible, not merely for interference but for acquiring territory, was offered to Lord Ellenborough in 1843, by the open contumacy and formidable warlike preparations of Scindia's Government. But having been compelled to invade Gwalior, to fight two pitched battles, and to occupy the capital, Lord Ellenborough replaced the Rajah on the throne ; imposed very moderate conditions of peace ; and though he secured, by the new Treaty, a certain control over the Regency during the reigning Prince's minority, no steps were taken to subvert the native administration or the established usages of the State. This equitable and considerate settlement had a most reassuring effect throughout India—soon, however, to be effaced by Lord Dalhousie—and secured to us a most faithful and serviceable ally at Gwalior, whose loyal and gallant conduct in 1857, went very far to prove how much a native Prince's influence could contribute to the stability of our Empire.

In this instance the Resident's supervision was imposed as a consequence of the recent hostilities, by virtue of a special Article in the Treaty of peace, and only for the minority of the Rajah then reigning ;* so that, as the former Treaties were expressly confirmed in the new one, the general principle of the autonomy of Gwalior was not attacked or questioned.

During the last twenty-five years, however, we have exerted our practical supremacy very seldom to persuade and improve, but very often to coerce and destroy. A notion seems gradually to have become established, and to have been accepted as a political maxim during the progress of Lord Dalhousie's acquisitive operations, that we were on every occasion reduced to an absolute choice between the complete abandonment and the total abolition of

* Article VIII. "Inasmuch as it is expedient to provide for the due administration of the government during the minority of his Highness the Maharajah, which shall be considered to terminate when his Highness shall

a native State.　This is very clearly stated in a Minute by Mr. Dorin, who was a member of the Supreme Council when the annexation of Nagpore was carried out :—

"If it were possible to withdraw British influence entirely from any Native State, so as to leave its Government to stand or fall on its own merits, there might be reason for trying the experiment of self-government; but in the position in which the British Government, as paramount in India, stands to Nagpore, this isolation is not practicable.　Between the two extremes of entire neutrality, or entire possession, I see no justifiable cause of interference for the Government of India."*

Mr. Dorin could write in these terms, and the Governor General in Council could endorse them with approval; and the Bhonsla dynasty was extinguished, and the Nagpore territories were annexed, mainly on the plea of incorrigible misrule : although it was quite manifest that the real and ultimate blame of the alleged misrule must rest with the Government of India, since the Treaty of 1829 conferred upon it full power to dictate, through the Resident, such administrative measures as it pleased, and in case of extreme disorder to assume the entire management of the Nagpore country for so long a period as it might deem necessary.†

No such necessity ever did arise.　The State of Nagpore was certainly so far well governed, that our active and open interference was never once required, during twenty-five years of purely native administration, to check oppression, to keep the peace, or to restore order.　That this Principality was not very badly managed, may be fairly inferred from the following words, in which Lord Hardinge, warning the King of Oude in 1847 of the inevitable consequences of his continued misrule, holds up the case of Nagpore before him at once as an example and an encouragement :—

---

have attained the full age of eighteen years, that is, on the 19th January, 1853, it is further agreed that during such minority the persons entrusted with the administration of the government shall act upon the advice of the British Resident in all matters whereon such advice shall be offered, and no change shall be made in the persons entrusted with the administration without the consent of the British Resident, acting under the express authority of the Governor-General."　*Volume of Treaties*, 1853, p. 373.

* Papers relating to the Rajah of Berar, 1854, p. 38.

† "It shall be competent to the British Government, through its local re-

" The Nagpore State, after having been restored to order by a British administration of the land revenue, is now carried on under native management, with due regard to the rights of the Prince and the contentment of the people."*

Lord Dalhousie refused to undertake the temporary management of Oude, which Lord Hardinge had intended, and which was proposed by Sir William Sleeman and Sir Henry Lawrence, the two wisest and most successful officials of the time ; he refused to take measures for reforming the administration of the Nizam's Dominions which were pressed upon him by General Fraser, the able Resident at Hyderabad in 1851.   He did not wish for the reform of the minor States, but rather for that rottenness that might lead to their fall or justify their extirpation.

The true cause of such defects as really existed in the Government of Nagpore and of Oude, may be easily divined from the following remarks by Mr. Mansel, an officer of great distinction and long experience, and the last Resident at Nagpore, in a despatch to the Government of India, dated the 14th December, 1853 :—

" This oscillation of interference, and of principles by which people of a country are to be guided, is a most serious evil.   The Chief who to-day is subject to the control of a strict Resident, is amused by his flatterers with the prospect of a successor of a wholly different character.   The advice of to-day is disarmed of half its force if it can be expected to be followed by a different course of policy on the morrow ; and when the season of indifference and ease has produced its natural effects of misgovernment and debt, the reaction must needs be violent and doubly distasteful to an arbitrary Prince, on the appointment of an officer impelled by duty to enforce a general reform.   It has frequently been a subject of astonishment to me that so much difficulty should exist in forcing a Mahratta Chief to follow out the views

presentative, to offer advice to the Maharajah, his heirs and successors, on all important matters, whether relating to the internal administration of the Nagpore territory or to external concerns ; and his Highness shall be bound to act in conformity thereto.   If, which God forbid, gross and systematic oppression, anarchy, and misrule, should hereafter at any time prevail, in neglect of repeated advice and remonstrance, the British Government reserves to itself the right of reappointing its own officers to the management of such district or districts of the Nagpore territory, in his Highness's name, and for so long a period as it may deem necessary, the surplus receipts in such case, after defraying charges, to be paid into the Rajah's treasury." *Volume of Treaties*, 1853, p. 404.

* Oude Papers, 1858, p. 63, 64.

of the Resident, as I have found at Nagpore with this Rajah. But after long thought upon this subject, I am convinced that the main cause of the difficulty lies in the system of filling up diplomatic appointments. It seems to be quite a chance if the system of the officer who precedes, and of the officer who follows, agrees. The Rajah and his Ministers speculate on this difference of action or opinion. Honesty is lukewarm and roguery is fearless, as there is no certainty or no permanence in the policy to be enforced."*

Mr. Mansel speaks of the oscillation of the *Resident's* policy and system, in a style that clearly indicates that our Government had no system or policy whatever of its own, and furnished its diplomatic agents with no definite instructions as to their control over the local administration.

The last Rajah of Nagpore and his Ministers were always submissive and well affected to British supremacy ; during his reign upwards of two millions sterling were paid to our Government as tribute, and his troops marched four times across the frontier to the assistance of his powerful Ally. On his death, however, in December, 1853—though his grandnephew, Janojee Bhonsla, was well known to be his intended successor and was adopted by the widow†—the Bhonsla family was declared to be extinct, and the Nagpore country annexed to the British dominions. And thus disappeared from the political scene one of the few native States that were really well affected and accustomed to our principles, amenable to our guidance, and capable of indefinite improvement.

By Article VII of the Treaty of 1837, the King of Oude promised " to take into his immediate and earnest consideration, in concert with the British Resident, the best means of remedying the existing defects in the police, and in the judicial and revenue administration of his dominions," and the following arrangements were made :—

" If his Majesty should neglect to attend to the advice and counsel of the British Government or its local representative, and if, (which God forbid) gross and systematic oppression, anarchy and misrule should hereafter at any time prevail within the Oude dominions, such as seriously to endanger the public tranquillity, the British Government reserves to itself the right of appointing

---

* Papers relating to the Rajah of Berar, 1854, p. 17.
† *The Empire in India*, " Nagpore."

its own officers to the management of whatsoever portions of the Oude territory in which such misrule may have occurred, for so long a period as it may deem necessary."

And in Article VIII :—

" It is further agreed that in case the Governor-General should be compelled to resort to the exercise of the authority vested in him by the preceding Article, he will endeavour, as far as possible, to maintain, with such improvements as they may admit of, the native institutions and forms of administration within the assumed territories, so as to facilitate their restoration to the Sovereign of Oude when the proper period for such restoration shall have arrived."*

But besides this very explicit provision for the restoration of the Oude territories to native rule when an improved system should have been established, there was also a stipulation in Article VII, that during the time of British management, "the surplus receipts, after defraying all charges, should be paid into the King's Treasury, and a true and faithful account rendered to his Majesty of the receipts and expenditure of the territories so assumed."†

By the cession of nearly two-thirds of his possessions, made in the Treaty of 1801, the Nawab Saadut Ali Khan, crushed by arbitrary exactions, purchased exemption from all further pecuniary demands, and "paid such a price for it as no other native ruler ever did," as General Low, when negotiating the Treaty of 1837, wrote to the Government of India.‡   But the Treaty of 1801, according to Lord Dalhousie's interpretation, gave us no right of interference, except as friendly advisers, and "peremptorily and insurmountably barred the employment of British officers" in the administration.§   The Treaty of 1837 was concluded with the express object of supplementing these supposed defects, and of giving us the positive right to interfere effectually and to assume the management of the country, in case of "gross and systematic oppression and misrule."

* Volume of Treaties, 1853, p. 93-94.
† Ibid., p. 93.
‡ Oude Papers, 1858, p. 19.
§ Oude Papers, 1856, p. 182.   See also the Proclamation, p. 256.

When, however, the assumption of the Government of Oude began to be a practical and urgent question in 1854, it was perceived by the Governor-General and his advisers that these two Articles (VII and VIII) in the Treaty of 1837, providing for the ultimate restoration of native rule, and for the intermediate payment of all surplus receipts to the native Sovereign, would deprive the British management of that permanent and profitable character which, under Lord Dalhousie's acquisitive maxims, was now invariably contemplated, when any disorder in the affairs or break in the direct lineal succession of a native Principality, appeared to afford an opening for our " paramount" claims. Therefore Lord Dalhousie proposed that this Treaty, although duly ratified by both the contracting parties, and officially published as a valid engagement, should be declared null and void by the perverted interpretation of a *secret letter* from the Court of Directors in 1838.*

In Nagpore we had a right to interfere ; no occasion for interference arose, yet we seized upon the first plausible, though false pretext—the death of the Rajah without male issue—to destroy the native State, and we justified our proceedings by alleging defects and corruption in its internal affairs, that could only have arisen from the neglect, connivance, or incompetency of our own accredited agents.

Thus in Oude we had a right to interfere ; the very best justification for our interference arose, but we rejected alike the right and the justification, and violently extinguished, instead of reforming, another friendly native State.

In Mysore we had a right to interfere. A fair occasion for such interference presented itself. A rebellion broke out in one of the provinces, and the management of Mysore was assumed in 1832 by the Governor-General Lord William Bentinck, avowedly for a temporary purpose,—to introduce order into the finances and a regular system for the good government of the State. But according to the spirit of the Treaty, and the declared intentions of Lord William Bentinck, of several of his successors and of the Court of Directors, order and regularity having been estab-

---

* *The Empire in India*, " Lord Dalhousie."

lished in every department, and ample guaranties existing for their continuance, no cause remains for any longer retaining the Rajah's dominions under the exclusive authority and control of the British Government. On various pretences, however, the restoration of the Rajah to his proper position has been postponed and evaded; until now, in his old age, this unfortunate Prince finds, from the manner in which his last urgent appeal is treated, not only that he is to remain degraded in his forced retirement, but that a private decree has been registered for the annexation of his country and the extinction of his family at his death. Long and uninterrupted possession has produced the usual effect. The fancied power and the real patronage derived from the sequestration, are too precious to be relinquished; the contemplated sacrifice is too much for the virtue of the Calcutta Foreign Office.

And thus another friendly and influential native State is threatened with destruction, the native State of all others that is certain to afford us invaluable material and moral support, and to relieve us of all risk and responsibility over a large area in any time of political or military danger, and which, in ordinary days of peace and tranquillity, pays handsomely for our general protection. As a British Province, filled with bitter regrets and reminiscences, where no one would be responsible and no one would have anything to lose, Mysore could never be denuded of troops, it could never be relied on, and might at any time become a centre of hostility, or the scene of anarchy and confusion.

The flourishing existence of Mysore as a separate though dependent Principality, must always be creditable and profitable to Great Britain, and might be held up to the other Sovereigns of India as an example of our beneficent influence, as an encouragement for them to submit to our tuition and guidance. As an annexed Province it would constitute a flagrant instance of British duplicity; it would prove to the native Princes and statesmen that all their suspicions of advice from Calcutta were well founded; that the first suggestion of reform must be resisted as a malignant encroachment, and that the control or management of their administration by English officers would be merely the first step towards the extinction of the dynasty, the absorption of the State, and the proscription of all native talent.

The acquisitive proceedings of the last twenty years have made native Princes and Ministers averse to our laws and institutions, and have served to render our principles of government more conspicuously offensive to the higher classes, even in our own Provinces, as the cause and badge of their degradation and ruin. But if British good faith and the majesty of the British Throne were vindicated by gracious acts of restoration and restitution, royally decreed and royally performed; if the era of annexation were manifestly closed for ever, and a proposal of innovations were seen not to be an insidious encroachment, but the preliminary step to territorial aggrandisement and admission to the security and dignity of a place in the Imperial Federation—reform would appear in a much more favourable light.

Peaceful reforms can never flourish or take permanent root in an atmosphere of distrust and hatred. The alienation of the Princes, the nobility, and all the conservative classes and interests, will never tend to the conciliation and improvement of the mass of the population. If, in spite of its own professions and promises, our Government is to be quietly allowed to recommence the career of annexation, under the pretence of reforming native institutions, by first assuming or accepting a trust and then playing the part of a fraudulent trustee—we shall soon discover that an army of even 100,000 British soldiers will be insufficient to prevent a second great rebellion, in which we might find most of the native Princes ranged against us, instead of their co-operating with us, as they did in 1857. If the new system of *management* is permitted to succeed and to spread, such a hostile coalition of native Princes could hardly be considered either morally unjustifiable or politically imprudent. Extinction being the inevitable fate of our best friends, our worst enemies could anticipate no more dreadful doom for themselves, in the event of their bold attempt failing.

In 1858-9 there were 122,000 British soldiers employed in India. A special return, showing the casualties among our troops during the hottest year of the insurrection, 1858, would present a fearful picture,—would prove that 35,000 men, or thirty per cent. of those engaged, disappeared entirely in that year, from death or ruined constitutions, while a large proportion were always in hospital. But the rebellion was nothing to what it would have been if a coalition of native Sovereigns had been in the field against us, or even if one of the more important Princes—Scindia, Holkar, the Nizam, or one of the leading Rajpoot Rajahs—had entered with heart and soul into the movement, instead of assisting us as most of them did, and discountenancing the rebellion as they all did.

Undoubtedly, better sanitary appliances, and less intemperance, have lowered the percentage of deaths in our tropical stations in time of peace ; and greater attention to the soldier's requirements will make a still more marked improvement ; but little or nothing can be done, I fear, to lower the mortality in time of war, which, as is well known, arises from fatigue, over-crowding, exposure to the sun and rain, and malarious epidemics, and depends to a very slight extent upon the deaths in action.

The following extract—very ordinary in its purport—from the military intelligence of the *Times*, October 25th, 1864, will give some idea of the human expenditure in Eastern service :—

" New colours for the 31st Regiment have arrived at Aldershot, and will shortly be presented. The Regiment has seen much service in India, the Crimea, and in China. In 1860 it left India for China over 1,100 strong, and received during its stay in that country a draft of 102 men. It embarked from the latter place for England only 642 strong, having experienced a total loss of 588 of all ranks, or nearly one-half of its strength, in the space of three years and a half."

This is a loss of 15 per cent. per annum. In all probability not fifty of these men were killed or died of wounds. It is thus, that on an average of twenty years, the percentage of deaths in India appears so high, although during the last two or three years of quiet garrison duty a favourable return may be made.

And if the disaffection of the people, and the area of our

military occupation and civil responsibility, are to spread
and widen progressively by this new process of annexation,
we shall soon find that the demand for European troops
will far exceed the present enormous establishment of
75,000 men.   At the rate of average casualties which prevailed from the first year of this century up to 1857,*
fully 10,000 would be required *yearly* to keep up the present force in India.   Double that number would be wanted
in one year of war or rebellion.   Recruiting is becoming
more difficult every day.   The standard height of the
infantry has been gradually lowered.   Our army grows
more expensive as the condition and prospects of the soldier require and receive more attention.   Emigration, steadily operating on Great Britain, has, within twenty years,
drained away an entire generation of able-bodied men from
Ireland, once the most fruitful source to fill the ranks of
the army, and the exodus has scarcely slackened yet.   The
day may come when we shall want some of those men
from India, and wish for them in vain.   It may then be
no comfort or consolation whatever to know that this large
force is paid for from the Indian revenues.   We may want
British soldiers in Europe at any price ; and the absence in
India of 75,000 men of the age, class, habits, and temperament of which soldiers are made, must lead to the offer of
larger inducements to the limited number of that class that
remain in the country.

In the midst of a general war, when the national honour,
great interests, and great principles were at stake, we should
of course make efforts that would astonish the world.   We
might, for a time, find it difficult to raise our armies to the
numerical strength we required, but in a crisis of great
importance and difficulty we should certainly do it, because we are a nation of thirty millions, and because we
can afford to pay whatever may be found absolutely necessary to attract recruits and to keep veterans in the ranks.
We have the population to furnish the men,† and we have
the wealth to supply the cost, and for a limited time and a

---

* 69 per 1000 by death, 82 by invaliding ; total 151 per 1000 per annum.
† The last returns, however, show that the population of Great Britain is
now nearly stationary, increasing only at the rate of about 80,000 per annum,
and the rate of increase perceptibly diminishing.

definite object the prospect of a great war charge and a highly-paid army is not so alarming to our old-fashioned statesmen as the younger school of Liberals might desire. When the crisis is passed, it will be said, the army may be diminished. But in India there is not merely a crisis to be passed; it is a permanent occupation with 75,000 men that is contemplated.

When it has become necessary to raise the pay and per-quisites of the troops required for European service, the same advantages will at once be extended to those in India and the Colonies. And no emoluments or privileges granted to our army can ever be retracted. It appears, therefore, to me that the entertainment of a permanent force in India of 75,000 men, and a permanent force of 40,000 men at home solely to relieve and recruit this great army of occu-pation, is likely to prove a rapidly progressive strain on our military resources. And when we perceive how the numerical demand upon a population which is at once prosperous and drained by emigration, and the natural aversion to a long tropical service, are combining to hasten the period when the pay and pensions of the entire army must be enhanced, I think the formidable menace to the finances both of Great Britain and India, can scarcely escape observation, and ought not to be treated with levity by any section of British politicians.

If we can devise no plan for ruling India except that of retaining and extending our direct possessions; if we can offer our good offices to India only on condition of taking all the good offices in the country for our sons and nephews, then two great objects must be abandoned by English statesmen—the one (with which I have myself but little sympathy) that of maintaining what is called our just influence in Europe by the display of an imposing force at home, as desired by the two old established parties —the other, that of reducing our armaments so as to mi-nimise taxation and expenditure—the cherished aim of our social and financial reformers. These two great objects, if the first be kept within bounds, are by no means irre-concileable with each other; for by judiciously organising the Militia, a reserve of veterans, and the newly-acquired defensive arm, our noble Volunteers, nearly all the regular troops in Great Britain might be made disposable for foreign service ; but both objects are utterly incompatible with the reluctant subjection of India.   I do not hesitate to say that so long as the present repulsive, contemptuous and hopeless plan for governing India continues, neither of these two great objects can ever be fully attained.   Should a general war break out in Europe, a desperate war of principles, when Great Britain ought to strike an effectual blow for the good cause,—or even an aggressive coalition against us —no troops could be safely withdrawn from the East, our vulnerable point.   Nor could our force in the East be easily sustained or relieved: while in a time of general tranquillity, the Indian depôts and relieving reserves at home —useful as they may be for defence—could neither be reduced nor made available for the contingency of active operations.

It appears to me to be a manifest and incontrovertible fact that it is only by organising an Imperial Federation, by trusting, reforming, and strengthening the native States, that the actual and prospective strain on our own military resources can be relieved, and those of India made available for Imperial objects.   Wherever there is a native State, there is a competent and visible authority, responsible for for the peace and good order of a certain area, and of a certain population.   Even now we could, on an emergency, march all our troops out of Mysore, or out of the Nizam's dominions, with much more confidence, and with much less anxiety, than out of any part of our immediate possessions.

Lord Dalhousie was enabled to keep up the temporary and superficial appearance of not having entailed a heavy burden both on India and on the Imperial resources, solely by not calling for a proper and reasonable augmentation of European troops to occupy his territorial acquisitions.   Had he demanded, as he should have done, the reinforcement of 15,000 British soldiers required for the Punjaub, Nagpore, and Oude, the expense would have opened all eyes to the ruinous nature of his policy.*

---

* He did ask for two or three battalions, but did not insist upon the reinforcement as a precaution that was urgently and imperatively required ; and this very moderate request leaves my statement intact.

" Lord Dalhousie," said a writer in the *Saturday Review*, by no means an advocate for annexation,* " can scarcely have been mistaken in the inference that the pressure of a fixed charge would be lightened by an extension of the area of taxation." The inference is quite correct ; but where is the " fixed charge" ? Lord Dalhousie undoubtedly *thought* there was a fixed charge ; he thought that he could occupy the Punjaub, Nagpore, Oude, and Scinde, enlarged by confiscating the greater part of Ali Morad's possessions, with the same force of 40,000 Europeans that had sufficed before those acquisitions were made. He seems even to have thought that in certain cases the acquisition of territory enabled him to diminish the number of occupying troops. Thus, he writes in a Minute dated the 5th of February, 1856, paragraph 27 :—

" Scinde would be perfectly safe with one European corps, now that Meer Ali Morad has been deprived of even the semblance of power, while the Punjaub has become a British Province."†

Unquestionably Scinde might well be considered more secure—though I doubt if it was ever in danger from the Scikhs—after the Punjaub had become a British possession, garrisoned by an army of 60,000 men, including 13,000 Europeans, besides an Irregular Force of 15,000 men, at an expense of £2,100,000 per annum, equal to the entire revenue of the Province !‡ The cost of this additional security may appear rather heavy, but the whole charge of the Regular troops was laid on the Bengal Presidency ; and Scinde, I may admit, reaped a part of the benefit. But that Scinde was more safe, more able to dispense with European Regiments after Meer Ali Morad had been deprived of his richest districts than it was before, I cannot admit at all. Surely Lord Dalhousie did not mean that he had been accustomed to regard Meer Ali Morad, whom we had set up as Räis of Khyrpoor, in despite and at the expense of his brethren, as a Prince likely to commit some aggression or to engage in some conspiracy against us ! Ali Morad was not

---

* *Saturday Review*, February 26th, 1859.
† Parliamentary Papers, East India, Additional Troops, 1858, p. 16.
‡ First Punjaub Report, p. 95.

the man to be a popular leader. But still, such as he was, he would obviously have had a much greater inclination for mischief, and, I believe, quite equal power for mischief, when injured and disaffected by a partial confiscation, than when enjoying, undisturbed by us, the increased wealth and dominion which he owed to our patronage.

But this was always Lord Dalhousie's argument, brought forward in every case of annexation, that by destroying the native Princes and disbanding their armies, all the hostile and dangerous elements in the country were to be dissipated, and none but external enemies would remain,—the truth of which may be estimated by comparing the work cut out for us in Oude and Jhansi, recently annexed, and in our older provinces of Rohilcund and Bahar, by discontented pretenders and adventurers, like the Nana, Khan Bahadoor Khan, Kooar Sing, and Tantia Topee, with the moral and material assistance we received from native Princes and Chieftains of every class, during the rebellion of 1857. The very reverse of Lord Dalhousie's theory is true : no Sovereign in India is so foolish as to think of committing any aggression against us ; we require literally *no* troops for the special duty of watching the little armies of native States ; every native Prince is a conservative agent, who knows himself to be bound over under heavy penalties to keep the peace ; and whenever we extinguish a Principality, we not only let loose all the swash-bucklers and fanatics who have hitherto been harmlessly employed and amused within its precincts, but we rouse the spirit which makes the men of that class powerful and popular.

The idea that the great use of our army is to protect the frontiers, and that our " settled" provinces may almost be left to take care of themselves, pervades all the writings of the acquisitive school. Thus Mr. George Campbell, perhaps the most able advocate of consolidation, wrote in 1852 :—

" The army heretofore employed in guarding our frontiers has only been moved forward —and, in fact, instead of being increased in number and expense, has rather been diminished since the conclusion of the war."*

* G. Campbell's *Modern India*, 1852, p. 430.

The force in Hindoostan was indeed diminished; important stations were denuded to garrison the Punjaub; and the consequence was that in 1857 the great strategic points and centres of political influence, the cities of Delhi and Agra, and Bareilly, the chief town of Rohilcund, with the surrounding districts, at once fell into the hands of the mutineers and rebels, and were not recovered until after several months of marching and fighting.   And again :—

"It is perfectly clear that our older territory must require fewer troops than it did in 1835-6, now that the frontier is advanced many hundred miles, (!) that the Gwalior army is transformed into a British force, and that the country has in every way become more settled."*

A great part of the Gwalior army *was* transformed into a British force, and although restrained and delayed for some time by the Maharajah Scindia, took the field against us in 1857, and gave a great deal of trouble ; while that part of the Gwalior army which did *not* become a British force, but remained in the native Prince's service, *though equally ill-disposed*, was perfectly inactive and innocuous throughout the rebellion.

It must also be remarked that at the outbreak of the mutinies in 1857, the native army was not only unnecessarily large and expensive,—the lust of patronage having swelled the local Contingents, providing good places for English officers, without diminishing the Staff or the number of the Regular Regiments,—but it was dangerously large.   Every one who has observed the habits and sentiments of the Indian soldiery can testify to the accuracy of Lord Ellenborough's opinion :—

"It was impossible for me not to see the respect which our own soldiers entertained for native Princes.   I felt satisfied that I never stood so strong with our own army as when I was surrounded by native Princes.   They like to see respect shown to their native Princes."†

Recruited, in the various arms of the service, from all the most warlike tribes of India, animated with recent and tra-

* G. Campbell's *Modern India*, 1852, p. 431.
† Evidence before the Select Committee of the Lords on Indian Territories, June 18th, 1852,—Question 2305.

ditional achievements, and yet alienated by the exclusion of
their race from even the lowest military command and distinction ; stationed, frequently for years, within the limits
of the allied States, the Sepoys took the deepest interest in
the fate of the native Princes ; and they were peculiarly
exposed to be personally taunted in places of public resort,
with being accomplices in the destruction of all the historical dignities and ancient institutions, which every native
with a spark of honour and national pride, was bound to
admire, to love, and to respect. The same temper, the same
passions exist now-a-days. Sir Mark Cubbon, a very shrewd
and practised observer of native character and feelings,
wrote as follows in a private letter to a friend, dated the
22nd of May, 1859 :—

" There never was such a mistake as to suppose that the
hostile spirit has been extinguished or cowed by the suppression
of the mutiny, and that we can safely do now what would have
been dangerous in former times."

It is as true now as it was in 1857, that every extinction
of a friendly Principality at once adds to our immediate
responsibilities, burdens our military strength, and lowers
our moral dignity before the people of India. Not only
does that grasping and greedy policy cause an ever increasing demand for European troops, but it prevents us from
having a trustworthy native army,—it deteriorates and de-
moralises the best native soldiers in the service. Maintain
the allied States in willing allegiance, and the native army
may be safely recruited from the most warlike races in
India to any strength required, trusted with the most
efficient arms, and (a great part of them) employed, for
occasional and emergent service, in almost any part of
the world. But turn those States into British Provinces,
and then, besides British troops being required for their
occupation, the necessity for cautiously raising and arming
native Regiments, and for balancing their numbers by a
certain proportion of European soldiers, will be indefinitely
enhanced.

It is strange to see how Lord Canning, led away by the
particular temptation of Mysore, could yet express himself
with such force and decision on the general question of
extending our territorial limits. He writes to the Secretary

of State, in paragraph 33 of the Adoption despatch of the 30th April 1860, to the following effect :—

" We shall not become stronger so long as we continue adding to our territory without adding to our European force ; and the additions to that force which we already require, are probably as large as England can conveniently furnish, and they will certainly cost as much as India can conveniently pay."

CHAPTER IX.

BRITISH ADMINISTRATION.

BUT presuming that I have successfully established my two points,—firstly, that on grounds of legal right, and according to the terms of Treaties, the State of Mysore ought to be preserved as a separate Government, and not incorporated in our immediate possessions,—and, secondly, that its distinct preservation is the most prudent and advantageous policy for the British Empire,—there is still a class of objections to a course of mere abstract justice, that has considerable weight both in India and at home, that deserves our notice, and even demands our respect.

It is asked whether the British Government having *de facto*, if not *de jure*, attained to the position of Imperial Suzerain of all India, is to exercise its immense power for the benefit of the Princes and nobles, or for the benefit of the people at large ; whether a native administration can possibly be as good as ours ; and whether we are not bound —even at some risk and sacrifice—to take every fair opportunity of extending the uniform application of our system of government to those whose best interests will be thereby promoted. " The obligations of the British Government to the people of Mysore," said the memorable Calcutta letter of 11th March, 1862, to the Rajah, "are as sacred as its self-imposed obligations to your Highness."*

Many people would point to the Rajah's misrule of Mysore, or to the acts of oppression and cruelty that were perpetrated in Oodeypoor,† and ask whether it is advisable that the native Princes of India should be everywhere released from British control. I do not wish to emancipate the Princes from British control. I complain—more especially in this particular case of Mysore—that control has

---

* Ante, p. 73. † *The Empire in India*, p. 393.

never been properly or steadily applied, that we have always neglected general principles and meddled in obscure particulars: and that after finding our intermittent and desultory dabbling in details to be utterly unproductive of substantial reform, we have pressed that false and fruitless method to its extreme, by deposing all the local dignitaries, sweeping all the patriarchal institutions into the dustbin, and distributing English officers over the country in every place of honour and emolument.

Thus in Mysore, as in our own possessions, although we have indeed introduced order and regularity into every department, we have done very little to initiate or instruct the rank and wealth of the country—the old governing classes, or the new class of educated natives,—in the practical working of the reformed administration.

We have stopped the independent development of the Hindoo races, by taking the management of every detail of their affairs upon ourselves, and condemning their best men to an insignificant and humilitating position, or to a discontented inactivity. All the progressive energy and ambition of India is forcibly turned by our exclusive policy into the direction either of fanaticism, or of conspiracy,—or of both combined. We have carried the system of class-government to the greatest extreme, retaining the entire and distinct series of superior offices—all access being denied to natives,—in the hands, not only of a class, but of foreigners,—not only of foreigners, but to a great extent of inefficient and unqualified foreigners.

Of course I would not be understood to make any comparison, either as to moral end and aim, or as to beneficial results, between our Government and that of Tippoo Sultan in Mysore ; and yet we seem to have fallen into the very error attributed by Sir John Malcolm to that bigoted Mahomedan Prince, with the same effect of a positive deterioration in the character of our native coadjutors. In a Report to the Governor-General on the state of Tippoo's dominions, Malcolm comments on the Sultan's want of success in the administration of Mysore, as compared with what had been done by his father, Hyder Ali, and says that " it may be ascribed to his chiefly employing Mussulman Asofs and Amildars, which Hyder seldom did. The Hindoos still do the business, *but are more venal, from having less responsibility."*

While the founders of our Indian Empire were maintaining and strengthening a precarious position, controlling and conciliating allies, and contending with powerful enemies, the English in India continued to place a high value on the good will and good opinion of the natives. While they were evoking peace and order out of a chaos of conflicting interests, they learned at every step to appreciate the value of native tact in negotiation, and of native skill and experience in the settlement of districts. And, as in all times of real difficulty, the work was done by a few men : our most celebrated tasks of pacification and organisation were effected by one or two able and experienced English officers in each province, by means of some special native agency. No doubt on many occasions, at a very early period in the process of conversion, the ignorance and prejudices of the local authorities whom our officers found in the districts, induced some of that passive obstruction and counteraction, of which General Cubbon, as we have seen, had reason to complain in Mysore, and necessitated for a time the employment of European Assistants, who could understand what was required of them, and could be trusted to obey orders. But there was no wish to bring the natives back to their old places, or to train up a new generation to succeed to them. Every appointment gained for the dominant race was permanently appropriated, if it was worth having.

As our supremacy became every day more surely established and acknowledged, the immediate obvious necessity for reliance on native agency rapidly diminished, and the stream of patronage, swelled by private interest, by national and professional pride, and by official pedantry, has filled the country with English gentlemen, to be provided for, with apparent functions to be performed, and with ever increasing claims for promotion or pensions. The mass of English idlers and nonentities in the civil and military services certainly do not add to the physical strength of the British Empire in India, while they detract from its

---

* Wellesley's Despatches, vol. i, p. 655.

moral strength, lower the native ideal standard of English ability and dignity, and introduce those constant provocations of levity, insolence, and contempt, which are so dangerous to our power, and derogatory to our national reputation. The same great vice pervades the whole organisation ; an unnatural and degrading rule of exclusion is manifest in all our establishments ; appointments for Englishmen are multiplied ; and young Englishmen without any peculiar qualifications are placed even in minor positions, the duties of which could be fulfilled in a much more efficient manner by natives, with the great advantage of their improvement in knowledge, in self-respect, and in attachment to British institutions.

Just in proportion as our direct possessions have been extended by annexation, competent English officers have been more thinly scattered over the country. The Civil Service has been largely supplemented by the Army. Even that source has frequently seemed to be exhausted ; and promotions of Englishmen from the " uncovenanted " ranks have been occasionally made to appointments that had been previously reserved for commissioned and covenanted servants ; but all natives were, and are still, consigned to an inferior range ; they are destined to remain Deputy Collectors and Deputy Magistrates for ever, subordinate and inferior to the youngest newly-arrived covenanted Assistant or military officer, and incapable of attaining to any post where distinction may be won by original and independent action.

It is the greatest mistake to suppose that our elaborate arrangements have put an end to corruption in high places. What with the confusion of tongues, and the want of a public opinion, it is generally impossible to prove or to disprove particular cases ; but with well-informed and experienced persons there is no doubt as to its prevalence. The corruption is still in high places, although among a different set of persons from those who would have been the recipients under native rule. The class of officials that is really tainted with corrupt and fraudulent malpractices, is chiefly to be found among the *Amla*, the wretchedly paid ministerial officers of the Courts and of the Collectors' offices, those who too often can retard or expedite business, and bar access to their superiors, at their will ; and who, in the worst instances, absolutely pull the wires of an indolent or incapable principal, who shields them from view, and relieves them from responsibility. Our English hierarchy, with all its symmetrical procedure, with all its apparatus of checks and balances, is too often the whited sepulchre of administration, beautiful on the outside, but within which are dead men's bones and all uncleanness.

An English public servant in India is perfectly secure and comfortable so long as he preserves amicable relations with his official superiors. By keeping up his monthly returns, annual reports, and English correspondence, and keeping down the arrears of current business with the aid of clever native subordinates, a smooth appearance can be easily maintained before the higher authorities. However incapable and indolent, however dependent on his underlings he may be, so long as he is popularly reported to have a good name at head-quarters, no native will undertake the Quixotic task of denouncing him or his adherents. All open scandal may be avoided, and with a little good luck and prudence, he may safely and successfully float and rise far above the highest point attainable by the ablest and most deserving native. How he stands with the people of his district, how they speak among themselves of his public conduct or private character, is a matter of very little moment, and can neither injure his prospects nor affect his social position.

On the other hand, a native Judge or Prefect is sure to find his own level ; he would be fully subjected, in all the intercourse of life, to the public opinion of his town or district ; and if he became justly obnoxious to the community, not only might he be visited with those legitimate social penalties from which the European in a similar position is perfectly exempt, but there would be none of that despair of being heard, and dread of the consequences of such audacity, which too often prevents a complaint being made against an English Civilian, and there would be no compunction, on the part of Government, as to his removal, reduction, or dismissal.

And while it is notorious that in our own Provinces corrupt practices are very seldom detected or punished, except in petty and trifling cases, the highest offenders in native States are exposed to summary and exemplary correction, if popular indignation is roused to the pitch of clamour by their extortion, or if by any other means the scandal is forced upon the Prince's attention. No doubt the inquisition would be conducted without any regular arraignment, and with a complete disregard of the rules of evidence ; even if no specific charge could be proved, the possession of unaccountably large private funds would probably be held to criminate the accused sufficiently to warrant his degradation and the forfeiture of his goods. Unquestionably this check is intermittent and capricious in its performance ; but, maintained and set in motion by public opinion—of which the Prince himself is susceptible—it does constitute a check more effective, as every native will tell us, than any that has been devised by the British Government.

We are not, in short, justified in concluding either that official oppression and corruption reign unbridled and unpunished in the normal and unreformed native Principality, or that these evils are expunged, or even materially lessened, on the introduction of British rule. Matters are neither so bad in native States, nor so good in the British dominions, as is commonly represented.

The English Government has attempted by merely penal measures, to obtain the irreconcileable advantages of the cheapness of Oriental, and the purity of European, administration. Very insufficient pay, and but little confidence and encouragement have been hitherto afforded to native officials. Not only are they badly paid, but no amount of ability and faithful service can secure their advancement to places of consideration and profit for which they may be well qualified. It is not reasonable to expect honour and loyalty to spring up and flourish as the return for neglect, contempt, and humiliation. Hopeless exclusion and proscription will not produce a reformation, but something very different.

It has been argued, from the results of the attempt in Mysore, that native agency, except in subordinate places, is a failure under our legal and orderly system, and that all the superior officers of every department in provinces under our control must be European. Now, so far as the experiment was a failure, I believe that the failure was inevitable, that the experiment of native administration in the higher ranks under British supervision, was never fairly tried, was never allowed a fair chance of success in Mysore. We tried at first to work our civilised machinery, requiring punctuality, patience, and assiduous attention, and presupposing the equality of all before the law, with the instruments we found to our hand, with the old set of prejudiced and uneducated native officials. We tried to keep a complex and delicate engine at work with unskilled and unwilling labour. We did not try very long. No opportunity was lost of getting rid of the Foujdars, the higher officials whom we found in charge of districts, and as they were removed their places were taken by English Superintendents. No attempt seems ever to have been made to obtain natives of English education, judicial training and established character, for such offices. No one ever thought of strengthening the local administration by bringing a single well educated and trained native Judge or Collector from Calcutta, Bombay, or Madras. No one ever thought of turning to such men for assistance. No one thought of finding an appointment for any one who was not an English gentleman, a "covenanted" Civilian, or an officer in the Army.

I deny that it is impossible or even difficult, now-a-days, to find a certain number of native gentlemen morally and mentally competent to execute the duties of the highest posts in the civil government of India, in conformity with our own principles and practice. There are literally *no* grounds—and I challenge contradiction on this point—for casting the slightest general aspersion on the honour and probity of the higher class of our native public servants, either in the Judicial or Revenue Departments—the Sudder Ameens and Deputy Collectors. They are, for the most part, fairly, though not handsomely, paid ; and notwithstanding their subordinate functions, undefined rank, and circumscribed prospects, their credit for efficiency and integrity stands deservedly high, both with the Government and the people.

Now let us inquire what has been done for this deserving

class in Mysore, where Lord William Bentinck, in assuming the charge, desired that "the agency should be exclusively native; indeed, that the existing native institutions should be carefully maintained."*   Here, at least, in this reformed native State, we might expect to find that during our thirty years' management, a body of native gentlemen had been educated and trained to the public service, and would be capable of undertaking many, if not nearly all of the important posts throughout the country,—the power of supervision and control, and the highest executive authority being vested in the hands of three or four British officers. But no! ever since 1832 the natives have been steadily losing, and English gentlemen have been continually gaining ground in the field of civil employment.   There has been a constantly recurring tendency to a more elaborate organisation of departmental establishments, sometimes with good reason, but always with the same result,—more appointments for European officers.   Not a single native has ever been promoted to the charge of a district, although, in spite of the small encouragement offered to educated men, there are many fully competent for such duties.

The details of the Mysore Educational Department, as given in Mr. Bowring's Administration Report for 1862-3, afford a good epitome of the scope and effect of the educational operations of Government throughout India,—a fair example of that shallow, showy, and fussy misdirection of the public resources, which we call civilisation and progress, and for which we claim so much credit.

The population of Mysore is nearly four millions.   The number of scholars in the schools maintained or aided by the local Government during the official year, was 2317. Of these it is said that 1450 are learning the English language, and 722 are educated up to the University entrance standard—evidently belonging to an urban class whose parents are well able to pay for their education, most of whom would do so if the Government would leave them alone, but who certainly have no claim whatever to an education for their children — the school-fees being

* Ante, p. 30.

quite nominal—at the expense of the agricultural population.

But out of these 2317 scholars, we find that 434, or about one-fifth, are of English or East Indian parentage, and that the schools they attend receive fully one-fourth of the public money expended as grants in aid. The people of this description may perhaps be able to muster, at the very most—exclusive of the military, who have their own schools—two thousand out of the four million inhabitants of Mysore, and they are all located in the town and cantonment of Bangalore. By no means a poor class, as compared with others, utterly insignificant in numbers, and consisting chiefly of British military pensioners and their descendants, they are yet allowed to swallow up one quarter of the funds allotted for the encouragement of Education.

The total expenditure of the Mysore Educational Department for the year 1862-3 was, in round numbers, £5,000. Of this, £2,000 went in the salaries of the Director and Inspectors; and of the remainder, two-thirds, or £2,000 more, were devoted to schools at the official capital, Bangalore—population under 100,000—leaving just one-fifth, £1,000, for the schools of the 3,900,000 provincials.*

Doubtless the highly respectable gentleman who perhaps receives a better income as Director of Public Instruction than he could earn in his legitimate sphere of an independent schoolmaster, does his work most conscientiously, and sends in a most satisfactory annual Report of his labours, with the prettiest tabulated statements; but with the doubtful exception of himself and his inspecting colleagues, I do not believe that any man, woman, or child in Mysore, derives any real benefit from this absurd misapplication of the public funds—certainly no one who has the slightest claim to assistance from the State. I believe that if the Government of Mysore—and my remarks are intended to apply equally to the Government of India—were to give up meddling with the details of education, and were to confine its action to providing the machinery, either by Universities or by boards of examiners, for ascertaining and declaring the qualifications of candidates for the public service, and

* Administration Report of Mysore for 1862-3, paragraphs 111 to 118; and Appendix D.

for granting degrees and certificates of proficiency in Law and Medicine, it would undertake quite as much as any Government legitimately and fairly can, and would promote education much more effectually than by sustaining or assisting any number of schools. I believe that Government schools and stipendiary instruction attract the wrong sort of students, and obstruct the efforts of the right sort of teachers. If proper inducements were held out to persons of recognised position and ample fortune to give their children a good English education—if a fair field to all qualified natives were opened by Government—the greatest possible encouragement would be given both to schoolmasters and scholars.*

I would exclude no person from employment, or from competition for employment, on account of his caste or connections in India, any more than I would in England ; but I believe that those who can qualify themselves without any extraneous aid, will in general be found to be better qualified, both morally and intellectually, than those who have been raised above their ordinary sphere by charity schooling, public or private, by Government scholarships or other factitious means, or who have sought for education merely as a stock in trade. Men of decided genius, and even of extraordinary talent, may be left to work their way upwards ; most certainly the Government has no special faculty for drawing them from their obscurity in their early youth. The connection between the Government and education in India, hampers the progress of reform by rendering education unpopular and unfashionable, and by discouraging natural enterprise and individual self-reliance.†

It must not be supposed that I attach any very great importance to this particular topic ; that I consider a very grievous injury to be inflicted on Mysore by this annual prodigality of five thousand pounds; that I burn with indignation against so very harmless a hobby as Government education. The reason of my expatiating so far on this

---

* What deters men of rank in India from entering the British service, or bringing up their children with that object, is that, whether in Civil or military employ, a native has been hitherto compelled to commence life in a position little, if at all, raised above that of a menial servant.

† Appendix E.

question is, that this fallacious system of public instruction is one of those "inestimable blessings of British rule", that would most certainly be declared to be imperilled by the restoration of the Rajah's Government.

An altered distribution of the territorial divisions of Mysore and a comprehensive revision of establishments, mainly after the pattern of the Punjaub, was recommended by the present Commissioner, Mr. Bowring, in June, and sanctioned by the Government of India in September, 1862 ; and the complete inauguration of the new arrangements is announced in the Administration Report of Mysore for the official year 1862-3. The general effect of the revised organisation may be briefly summed up as follows :—the number of appointments in the Executive and Judicial Departments, filled by English gentlemen, is raised from twenty-one to twenty-seven, their aggregate salaries from £28,000 to £40,000, and the average annual salary—from the Commissioner's £5,000 down to the junior Assistant's £500—is increased from £1,300 to £1,500.*   "The good work which had been so well begun" in Lord Dalhousie's time is still carried on !

But the higher native officials participate very moderately, if at all, in the benefits of this revision of establishments. Some of the changes are not as fully explained as could be wished ; but, on the whole, it appears to me that this body of public servants gains a little in position and prospects—though even that is doubtful—but loses decidedly in the number of superior appointments open to the class, and in the aggregate of its emoluments.†

This latest inroad upon the constitution of Mysore—though introduced merely as a revision of establishments, and evidently considered as a mere matter of routine—strikes me as being a very remarkable disclosure, after a thirty years' probation, of the utter inability or unwillingness of our authorities in India, according to the maxims which prevail at Calcutta, to carry out the reform of a native State with the express object, loyally avowed and loyally fulfilled, of replacing the administration in native hands.

---

* Administration Report of Mysore, 1862-3, paragraph 181.
† Appendix F.

If the present administration of Mysore is of such a nature that it cannot be maintained without a full complement of English officers, and without the constant support of British troops, then I say it is not an administration that is really suited to the country or to the people. It may last for a time, it may be compatible with a high state of social order and material prosperity, it may have been a necessary stage in the production of that state of order and prosperity, but on the face of it such an administration is temporary and provisional, and it ceases to be a reforming or progressive agent when its temporary nature is forgotten, when class interests and national arrogance suggest that it should be perfected and perpetuated.

By the opposite policy which I recommend, British authority would be greatly strengthened. In that diplomatic reconstruction of the Empire in India, which I believe is now urgently required, I would not resign an atom of Imperial power; I would more openly assert it. I would cause it to be more distinctly acknowledged, and more generally understood and respected—I would give up no means of influence, I would strengthen those that exist already, and I would acquire more. Our influence—political, moral, and social—is at present quite as strong in the native States of Mysore or Hyderabad, as it is in our own districts of Bellary, Kurnool, or Cuddapah, which fell to the Nizam's share in the partition of Tippoo's dominions, and were eventually ceded to us in 1800, to provide for the expense of our subsidiary troops. Indeed on the proverbial grounds of *omne ignotum pro magnifico*, I believe that the reputation and authority of the British Government and nation stand much higher in the more remote native States, than in those under direct control, or in our own immediate possessions, where familiarity with our institutions and manners has dispelled awe and blunted admiration.

And I totally and emphatically deny that by anything I have said in this Chapter, or in any part of this book, I have depreciated the achievements, or cried down the just fame of those eminent public servants, who during the last half century, have raised the stately structure of our Indian Empire, and have adorned it with so many enduring trophies of humane and peaceful progress. The great names

of the past generation, and the greatest who yet survive—
such men as Mountstuart Elphinstone, Malcolm, Metcalfe,
St. George Tucker, General Briggs, and Sir George Clerk—
are all on my side. And though many of the new school
are, I fear, at present opposed to that policy by which alone,
as I believe, the Indian Empire can be long preserved by
Great Britain as a beneficial and honourable charge, I am
neither hopeless of seeing them converted, nor blind to
their great merits. I do not presume to disparage a Lawrence, a Temple, or an Edwardes ; I feel myself unworthy
and unqualified to express the admiration that I feel for
their unrivalled labours. The mistake against which I contend is that of assuming, as the indiscriminate eulogists of
" the services" and the system sometimes appear to do, that
every English official who supplants a native in a recently
annexed Province, or excludes one in a settled district, is
necessarily a Lawrence, a Temple, or an Edwardes.

What I desire, and venture humbly to recommend, is that
we should endeavour to gain the confidence of the Princes
and their advisers; that we should aim at the instruction
and not at the destruction of native administrators; and that
whenever and wherever the local abuses are so rooted and
inveterate, the local magnates so ignorant and depraved,
that the only possible cure consists in radical extirpation
and removal—and this may have been the case in Mysore—
we should never lose sight of what ought to be the chief
end and object of our most rigorous measures, the installation, one by one, as soon as may safely be, of trained native
statesmen and magistrates in the place of their British
teachers and precursors. This plan may seem to the bureau-
cratic mind to savour too much of a self-denying ordinance,
and to endanger the official fabric : but I am convinced that
the happiness and permanent civilisation of a people will
be more advanced by the development of their capacity for
self-government, than by a stereotyped system—be it ever
so symmetrical and ever so benevolent—of foreign and exclusive nepotism.

Even if there were the greatest reason to dread that a
large proportion of native officials, when installed in the
higher posts after an apprenticeship in our schools, would
prove intriguers, tyrants, and corruptionists—I should still

say that it would be better to leave the Hindoo to stagger and struggle through the bogs and thickets of bribery and oppression, than to keep him for ever cramped and constrained in the strait-waistcoat of foreign management. Having once placed him in the right way, we need not abandon him to his fate ; we may still give him a helping hand in his difficulties.

There will always be work enough in India for our Lawrences and Temples; but a great part of the work that has now fallen—through patronage, official pedantry, and national arrogance—into the hands of Brown, Jones, and Robinson, ought to be transferred cautiously and gradually to the hands of educated and trained natives, by whom it could be executed in a style and with actual results more genuine, more finished, and more popularly acceptable than can ever be expected under existing arrangements. And the proportion of higher appointments, the positive share in the Government of India, that may be safely entrusted to natives—in the Principalities as well as in British Provinces—is an increasing proportion, and the demand for its concession will every day become more irresistible.

It is in the reform of the native States, and in that direction alone, as I believe, that the regeneration of India, including our own immediate possessions, can be pursued. And if the most sanguine expectations of political success and material prosperity should be realised ; if by sheer dint of a long peace and administrative skill, the resources and revenues of our Government should continue to increase, and British capital continue to be more largely invested in works of productive utility, and railway communications become perfected throughout India; our provocations and our obligations to interfere with the administration of native States will become more frequent. I wish to make our interference more easy and more efficient. I am by no means of opinion that our power should be timidly exerted in controlling and superintending the government of native States. I should rather complain that it has not been used sufficiently, and not in the most effectual and acceptable manner and direction. Hitherto we seem to have aimed more at extending our boundaries than our laws and customs, more at enlarging our patronage than our moral influence.

Hitherto we have seldom exerted our vast and irresistible authority in India to transmute Asiatic despotism into limited and legal monarchy. Still, enough has been done in that direction to furnish a precedent and an example; and this good work could have been, and still can be, as well done in Mysore, as it has been in the less important State of Travancore, under the auspices of the Madras Government, and with the hearty approval of the present enlightened Rajah, and by the Government of Bombay in the small Principalities of Kolapore and Sawunt Warree.

Undoubtedly much remains to be done in Travancore; but, on the whole, this Principality is decidedly more advanced than any one of those in direct subordination to the Calcutta Foreign Office, and the condition of the people, and their feelings towards the Government, may be favourably compared with the state of affairs in the adjoining districts of the Madras Presidency.

Travancore pays an ample Subsidy to the Government of Madras; and yet both Prince and people would cheerfully acknowledge how much it owes to British protection and guidance. But they certainly do not see, and I cannot see, that any benefit would accrue to them by its becoming a province of Madras. I cannot see that the annexation of Travancore in 1809 would have been advantageous to the British Empire. And I cannot see that any benefit or advantage would be conferred, either upon the people of Mysore or upon the Imperial Government, by the annexation of that Principality. On the contrary, for manifold reasons, already stated, I believe the change would be injurious to all classes, and, sooner or later, most damaging and burdensome to us; while the restoration of native rule—which might be brought about by a very gradual process,—would greatly redound to the honour of Great Britain, would immensely augment our moral influence, and our means of extending reform; and might almost immediately be turned to account as a relief to our military expenditure.

The question of the relative advantages to the people, and to the Imperial power, of provincial uniformity, administered by Englishmen, and of the greatest possible development of native rule,—both in subordinate States and in British territories,—is not settled by proving—if it could be proved,—that all the English gentlemen employed in the public service in India, are certain to be more talented and better educated and more high-principled, than any native gentlemen that are available for the same duties—that a British Governor or Commissioner must necessarily be a more wise and a more able ruler than a Hindoo Prince. No one but a professed Republican would think of setting up such a comparison between a European Sovereign and an eminent Statesman,—of comparing and contrasting, for instance, King Victor Emmanuel with Count Cavour, and condemning the former as an expensive superfluity. No Bengal Civilian, whether he be the " highly distinguished" offspring of Haileybury, or the winner of untold " marks" in open competition, can ever supply—even with twenty years experience—the twenty generations of the Mysore Raj.

We can appreciate in Europe the value of a hereditary Monarchy, and a hereditary Peerage, without wishing to subject either Prince or Peer to a competitive examination, —but in India the alleged incapacity of a Sovereign or Chieftain is made the pretext, not for limiting his power, but for abolishing it altogether, and for degrading the family to stipendiary insignificance. We can give due weight at home to the claims of wealth and rank; but in India, far from admitting the great proprietors to participate in the management even of communal or civic affairs—instead of enlisting them on our side,—we have done everything to injure the property and the prospects of the class, to outrage their keenest susceptibilities, and to reduce them to a social position even lower than that of our secondary officials. Even if I admitted in full the arrogant pretensions of professional administrators, I should not believe in the efficacy of a system of Government and of society under which there are to be great establishments, but no great estates; no privileges, except official privileges; no prescriptive rights, except those of the " covenanted Services"; no subordination, except official subordination, to which Princes must daily bow down; no dignity, except official dignity; no access to even the lowest share in public life, except through a competitive examina-

tion. The ideal of Indian officials has never been brought
to perfection : the greatest servants of Government in
India, and the Home Authorities, have, from time to time,
opposed its full realisation ; but the inevitable tendency of
our system has been just what I have described. This has
been, and continues to be, the tendency of our operations
in Mysore ; and the consummation would be much facili-
tated by the disappearance of the Rajah and his Court.

I can place no hope or reliance upon such a system, either
as a Conservative power or as a reforming agent, when once
the point of good order and a working administration has
been gained. Perhaps we are entitled to a full acquittance
for the past ; perhaps we could not have instituted order
and progress without territorial possession, without exclusive control. But if repression and proscription are maintained too long, and pushed too far, I believe that the system
will be found—not only in Mysore, but all over in India,— .
to be ephemeral and explosive.

It is an extraordinary thing that any English statesman
should be found to speak of the supposed deficiencies of an
Indian Sovereign, as if, according to the best theory of
government extant, the Prince was bound to be the ablest
and most active administrator in his dominions.

There have been native Princes who completely answered
to that description ; we might find some now, if we cared
to look for them ; but, if a sound and practical form of
government were fairly established in each important State,
it is very doubtful whether the all-accomplished, all-inquiring,
all-seeing Prince would be the best ruler. We ought not
to expect or wish a native Prince to be the best possible
financier, legislator and judge in the country. On the contrary, Oriental Sovereigns must be taught to do less, rather
than to do more, than they attempt or assume to do, under
the maxims and canons of ancient state-craft.

A Hindoo Prince, such as the Rajah of Mysore, is not
wanted to be an accomplished administrator, not to be a
profound statesman, but to be the living symbol of authority
and order, the visible and avowed representative of allegiance and obedience to Her Majesty's Imperial Crown, an
indispensable connecting link and medium of communication between the Teacher and the Pupil.

There cannot be a greater mistake than to set up that invidious comparison which is so often made, between a British Commissioner and a Hindoo Prince. Their attributes and functions are quite distinct. With a native Prince on the throne, and in the full possession of every befitting prerogative, all the influence of a British Commissioner may be maintained in the person of a Resident, exercising with more or less stringency, according to time and circumstances, the right of authoritative counsel. But no British Commissioner or Governor can, on the extinction of a native Sovereignty, fill the Prince's place, exert the same influence, or wield the same moral authority. A certain moral force is destroyed, and physical force must supply the loss. The most energetic Commissioner would not undertake to govern Mysore without the constant support of British troops. More especially at any period of great national excitement—during an actual or impending invasion, or extensive rebellion—a British Commissioner, though burdened with full responsibility, would be absolutely powerless unless backed by European soldiers. A British Resident in a native State of similar area, with less responsibility, would have more power and influence ; for he could bring all his representative authority and all his personal talents, to bear with full force upon the Sovereign, his Ministers and nobles, upon the most intelligent, the most deeply interested, and most influential personages in the country, upon six or eight persons who have the most to lose, and who know that they can be individually identified, and made to answer for their conduct. But no British Commissioner could bring his own influence, his own powers of persuasion, to bear upon four millions or ten millions of people without a recognised leader, or led by a deposed Prince, or a desperate pretender.

At such a time,—when a British Commissioner, without adequate military support, would be a laughing-stock, a victim, or fugitive—a Hindoo Prince, such as the Rajah of Mysore, unaided by our troops, with or without the countenance and advice of a Resident, in the face of much local opposition, might, by lifting up his finger, preserve the peace, not merely in his own dominions, but over a large area of adjacent British territory ; and would, to say the least, neutralise or impede a considerable part of the hostile resources, which, if unrestrained, would be arrayed against us. Such has ever been and, I believe, always will be, the general effect of an allied native State, as a conservative power in the Empire.

And in peaceful times, the beneficial effects of an allied native State, as a reforming agent throughout the Empire, ought, in my opinion, to be equally conspicuous. A British Resident, properly instructed, can bring all his representative and personal influence to bear upon the Sovereign and his Ministers, upon six or eight persons with whom he is in close communication, and who are connected by innumerable ties with all the great interests and centres of thought of the country. When these are gained the battle is won ; but until they are gained, the British Instructor cannot hope to make a very deep or permanent impression upon the millions of an Indian Principality.

So long as the Princes, and all those to whom the people look up as their national and social leaders and celebrities, regard our political system with distrust and disaffection, so long will every reform, every material improvement, even in our longest settled Provinces, rest upon a precarious foundation, so long will our Government continue to be not an organism in India, but a mechanism ; not rooted in the soil, not vitally connected with the population, but loosely attached to localities, running smoothly in the presence and by the authority of English officers, liable to sudden and total disarrangement when military force is withdrawn. I believe that India under the existing course and practice of our rule is very much over-administered, and that if a great crisis and time of trial were to come upon us, while we still adhere to Calcutta principles, she would be found not to be governed at all.

It is a fact—very deplorable, perhaps, but not the less true—that men, even in a very advanced stage of civilisation, are not guided entirely by reason, but to a great extent by their affections and their imagination. Men, also, in some strange countries, are known to have a certain regard to their own interests and their own worldly enjoyments, and even to such intangible considerations as a love of excitement, loyalty to a Prince, national pride and personal vanity. Of course these untutored feelings may be considered to be very unphilosophical, but still it cannot surely be advisable to overlook the fact of their existence. Perhaps a judicious ruler might detect their hidden meanings, divine their tendency, and turn their forces to some good purpose. Up to the present day we have ventured, as it seems to me, to navigate the vessel of the State in India too much by the compass and the dead-reckoning, without allowing for the force of the wind and the current, without observing the clouds by day or the stars by night. We have trusted too much to rule and plumb-line, without paying attention to those invisible and imponderable elements which are as potent in social and political action, as the physical imponderables are in physical dynamics.

Man cannot live on bread alone ; and even with an ample supply of bread, man cannot be made happy by administrative tidiness, or by the perfect punctuality of returns and reports. The most striking effect of Sir Mark Cubbon's improved management in the eyes of the agricultural population, is the vast increase in the revenue, which has risen from what may be roughly stated as an average of £600,000 under the Rajah's rule, to its present annual amount of £1,000,000. This great augmentation has been chiefly produced by the gradual commutation of the *Battoya* land-assessment, or equal division of crops between the tenant and the Sovereign, into a money payment, which has been steadily carried on for upwards of thirty years, concurrently with a constant rise in the prices of all agricultural produce. The vexatious imposts, upwards of sixty in number, abolished by General Cubbon, were not very heavy in their aggregate amount, were levied chiefly from special classes and professions, and their remission was not felt as a boon to the bulk of the population—to the occupants and cultivators of the soil. I have no doubt myself that the people are much better able to pay the present land-assessment than they were to pay the nominally smaller amount demanded thirty years ago ; owing to higher prices, and access to markets by good roads, the relative burden of taxation, has, I believe, been lightened. But we must not be suprised or indignant if the farmers,—proverbially *laudatores temporis acti*,—are not nearly as grateful as they ought to be for the

abolition of transit duties and petty cesses, while they are
fully alive to the fact that they are paying a much higher
land-tax than they did under native rule,—that they no
longer share a bad crop with the Sircar, but have to find
cash on the day of reckoning, whatever the past season may
have been.   In short, they do not feel at all satisfied that
they get more "*panem*" under the Commissioner's, than they
did under the Rajah's auspices ; while they know for a certainty that on the extinction of the Raj, their loved "*cir-
censes*" would for ever disappear.

Is it surprising that the natives should perversely prefer
a Rajah to a Commissioner ?   A considerable share of the
public revenue is allotted to the Rajah,* which doubtless
stirs the spleen and rouses the cupidity of our Financial
Department ; but this large income is all expended in Mysore ; the Rajah's patriarchal bounty supports thousands
who would find no place at our board ; and the splendour
of his genial hospitality, public ceremonies and processions,
is a constant source of pride, entertainment and excitement,
to all ranks and classes.   All this must cease on annexation ;
all encouragement to native art and learning ceases ; the
manufacture of many fabrics and articles of luxury falls
off ; all public pomp, state, and general amusement disappear ; the sting and vivifying charm of life is gone ; everything is doomed to settle down to a dead, dull, and uniform
level.† . The stately dinner-parties and gay balls, in which
English officials and their families take delight, may be
highly civilised and intellectual recreations, worthy of
general respect and admiration ; but these festivities can
hardly be expected to rouse much popular interest, for they
take place in private houses, and natives, even of the highest
rank, are very seldom invited to them.   The diversions of
the British hierarchy being of this exclusive nature, the
current rumours of their ordinary expenditure can scarcely
call forth any warmer sentiment than that of cold esteem.
No doubt it is very proper that the Commissioner and his

---

* About £140,000 per annum. His successor might probably be persuaded
to manage with a smaller Civil List.

† On this aspect of the case, see a curious article, " Christmas in Bombay,"
from a native newspaper, the *Hindu Prakásh*, which will be found in Appendix G.

Assistants should remit half of their salaries to Europe, for the education of their children, and as a provision for their own retirement ; but this respectable economy, even when contrasted with the Rajah's barbaric profusion, is not calculated to raise a moral enthusiasm throughout Mysore in favour of the permanent installation of a British bureaucracy, and the permanent exclusion of a native Sovereign.

Far from desiring to see " the uniform application of our system of government" extended to every State and province, I believe that by such means the harmonious establishment of sound principles of morals and politics would be rendered impossible, that our reforms would not be really accepted and naturalised in India, but would degenerate, even to a greater extent than now, into a superficial and deceptive crust, concealing from us the volcanic elements that boil beneath it, and gather strength from the external pressure. I would rather look forward to a multiplicity of political and municipal centres, giving rise to a free and noble emulation, to a more active production of wealth, and to a more permanent type of civilisation. I believe that in a Federation of reformed native States, owning allegiance to the Imperial Crown, accepting such general rules of law and judicial procedure, and such principles of financial administration, as may suffice to make each Prince a constitutional Sovereign,—and only in such a Federation,—Conservatism and Progress may be reconciled and secured. There would be found the legitimate and benevolent application of the old Roman maxim of government " *Divide et impera.*"

I object to an extreme centralisation, even in administering our immediate possessions. I think that a larger discretion in devising improvements, and in promptly carrying them out by local expenditure,—after providing for certain Imperial disbursements and contributions,—ought to be allowed to the Viceroy, to the Provincial Governors, and by them, under analogous conditions, to their Prefects, and to Municipal Councils, both in towns and districts. But objecting, as I do, to a centralised dictation of administrative and personal details, either in the control of dependent States, or in the general control, by Her Majesty's Government, of all proceedings in India, I would yet maintain most firmly the right of supervision and ultimate decree in the hands of the Home Authorities, so as to ensure a constant application of British principles, from the purest and least prejudiced source, to the government of the Indian Empire ; so as to save the people of that Empire from the curse of professional rule, and the people of Great Britain from the consequences of that curse.

The Home Government might, I think, with much advantage to the public service, place more confidence in the Viceroy and in the Provincial Lieutenants, and charge them with a greater responsibility. The Secretary of State might relinquish—in practice, if not in theory—his power of previously sanctioning estimates, expenditure and alterations of establishments, retaining the power of criticism, correction and prohibition, as it is now exercised in Legislative matters. I have no fear that the dignity and authority of the Viceroy's office would be lowered by the rare occurrence of his orders being modified or reversed. No Minister of the Crown could be unmindful of the deep responsibility under which such a step must be taken ; and I assume that on both sides a proper understanding is to be kept up, and that good temper and all forms of courtesy are to prevail.

I think the occasional decisive intervention and peremptory explicit orders of the Secretary of State, in matters involving some broad general principle—especially in matters where great difference of opinion has existed in India, —have frequently produced a most beneficial effect, and will continue to do so. I believe that a more willing obedience and submission would be paid to the Imperial Government, if it were certain that an appeal to London against some "act of state," or departmental oppression was not a mockery; if every native Prince, and every native official were fully convinced that the Royal Government was a living reality. The consultations in London, withdrawn from contact with the strange indigenous race, unaffected by local and temporary interests and antipathies, are much more likely to be carried on with a cool and deliberate impartiality, to be characterised by a fair and generous spirit, and to lead to an impartial conclusion, than those which take place at Calcutta or Bombay. Even a

Governor-General of high rank and dignified antecedents—
even Councillors of mature years, appointed by virtue of a
distinguished career at home—must, to a certain extent,
succumb to local influences.

The Jamaica planters could never have been induced to
legislate for the emancipation of their slaves, even though
the same amount of compensation for that purpose had
been voted to them by the British Parliament. Not a
single native would have been appointed to a seat in the
High Courts or in the Legislative Council of India, had the
initiative of those conciliatory measures been left to the
local authorities.

The cry that has been from time to time raised in Calcutta, that "India must be governed in India," has never
been raised from a wish to infuse a more liberal spirit into
Anglo-Indian institutions ; but either to assert and maintain the vested rights and privileges of the "covenanted"
hierarchy, or to augment, concentrate, and strengthen the
influence of the English commercial class over the Legislative and Executive of India. This cry has never been
raised on behalf of the legitimate operations of capital—
not for any broad principle, not for any national interest,
British or native, not for the great or small landholders, not
for the toiling millions, but for the hundreds of temporary
settlers with no permanent stake in the country, encumbered
by no public duties, and restrained by no public opinion.
With very few exceptions, European capitalists are only to
be found in the Presidency cities ; the "up-country" settlers
are either their servants or their debtors. These so-called
Bengal settlers and planters, the most noisy of whom are
not settlers or planters, but *manufacturers* of indigo, their
employers and creditors, and others interested in their
operations, exasperated at the rejection in London of the
coercive Contract Law, which after a long and laborious
agitation they had carried through the Legislative Council
at Calcutta, exasperated also at the effectual modification in
London of the Rules for the Sale of Waste Land, drawn
out in the interest of their class, and too hastily published
by Lord Canning—have never ceased to pursue with their
querulous and impotent abuse the present Secretary of State,*

* Sir Charles Wood, now Viscount Halifax.

and to denounce all attempts to govern India, as they complain he has done, directly and in detail from a Council
Chamber in London. There may sometimes be a doubt
and a difference of opinion in drawing the line between
matters of detail and matters of principle ; but with ordinary prudence and moderation, there ought to be no practical difficulty. The particular cases complained of appear
to me to have involved great and fundamental principles ;
an impartial and deliberate revision in London was most
urgently required, and with the exception of the European
planting interest of which I have spoken—a party small
in numbers, but strong in speech and means of influence—
the results were most satisfactory to the public at large.

In another case, which led to a collision between the
Viceregal Government and the Home Authorities, and to a
considerable ferment for a time among the official and commercial classes in Calcutta—the grant of an increased or
more settled provision to Tippoo Sultan's family—the Secretary of State acted in consequence of an appeal to Her
Majesty's Government ; and although it was an isolated
case, and the wrong redressed had not roused much general
attention or sympathy, the decision was hailed throughout
India as an auspicious omen, as the sign of a better era
commencing.

But it must be acknowledged, in accordance with established precedents, that unless under the obligation of an
appeal in regular form, and in an affair beyond the cogni-
sance of municipal law, the Home Authorities ought not
to interfere with the proceedings of the Viceregal Government, or to issue direct orders in personal questions, or in
matters of individual grievance. For example, the Secretary of State might properly lay down the general principle
that henceforward natives were to be eligible or to be admitted in larger proportion to a certain class of appointments ; and with that object in view, Her Majesty's Government might open the door by a special order, or, if legal
obstacles existed, by an Act of Parliament ; but it would
not be advisable or right that the Secretary of State should
officially propose or forbid any particular appointment or
promotion. If the general instructions should produce very
scanty or very slow results, the proper remedy would be

found, not by tampering with the Executive power and patronage of the Indian Government, but by the installation, either at the ordinary period or immediately—as demanded by circumstances — of a Viceroy whose opinions were in accordance with those of the Ministry.

The same broad distinction between the principles and the details of Government ought to be maintained by the Imperial Power of India, in controlling and instructing a subordinate or protected State, when it has passed, or has never undergone, the probationary stage of direct tutelage or management by a Commission of English officers. For example, the British Government might very properly exert all its influence to induce or constrain a native Prince to promulgate a Code, or to limit by a law his own Privy Purse. Great judgment, tact, and patience might be required to render these reforms acceptable ; and in certain quarters, where our right of interference was least clear, and our means of control least efficient and available, it might be expedient to offer some highly coveted privileges and material advantages, such as cessions of territory, on the condition of constitutional government. In ceding territory no real power would be abandoned ; on the contrary, on giving up the administration we should retain a stronger hold on the government ; in many instances the occasion might be taken for expressly assuming Imperial supremacy; and the loss of direct possession would be a decided gain so far as it enabled us to reduce our establishments, and to consolidate our military strength.*

But however much the process for converting the disorderly and careless despotism of native States into the government of Law and Order, may be varied—under diverse circumstances and eventualities—the general object, of at once reforming the administration and strengthening the throne of an allied and friendly Prince, is, I maintain, quite within the limits of just Imperial action. But in carrying out that object,—unless it were necessary to assume the entire management for a time,—we should aim at the imposition of principles, not of persons—at the inculcation of permanent Law, not at the dictation of par-

* *The Empire in India*, p. 393-406.

ticular judgments. Thus I can conceive every possible
gradation of moral pressure, from gentle persuasion to imminent coercion —according to the urgency of the case—
being justifiably employed by the British Government, to
induce or compel a native Sovereign to institute a Code
and a sound financial system, and even to introduce a certain *class* of persons—as educated Collectors and trained
Judges—into the administration of his country. The last-
mentioned innovation would be the most delicate of all,
and by an injudicious excess or precipitancy might approach
very near to the forbidden confines ; but if the questions
of Law and procedure were first settled, and then the want
of competent initiation were demonstrated—if great care
were taken to recommend persons likely to be agreeable to
the Prince and to command respect among the people, if
the smallest possible number were brought in, and obviously
as a trained *class* to serve under the local Government, not
as personal hangers-on of the Resident, or professed adherents of the Imperial Power—the difficulty might be
easily overcome. The strangers would be employed in the
administration, not obtruded into the Government. So far,
with temper and discretion, the boundaries of a just Imperial supremacy would not be transgressed.

But while I should be prepared, in an extreme case, to
resort to the most decided measures to induce or compel a
native Prince to reform his government, I should be very
slow to exercise any moral pressure whatever, merely to
induce or compel him to dismiss a Minister, or to accept
one of our nomination. That would be quite a different
style of interference, that would be the widest departure
from what ought to be the Imperial rule—to suggest or
impose great principles, but not to dictate in personal
details. From the most aggravated form of this oppressive
supervision, where a Minister known to be offensive is
brought face to face with the Prince to overrule his wishes
and to direct his movements, no result can be reasonably
expected but the utter degradation and despair of the
Sovereign, and the complete demoralisation of all his establishments, even if it did not operate as a provocative to
intrigue and contumacy, the preliminary stages to deposition or annexation.

Yet this fruitless task of meddling with individual claims and particular grievances, of pitting the protégé of the Residency against the favourite of the Court, of interfering in details and disregarding substantive reform, has hitherto characterised our system of Political Agency in India—with this additional defect, as pointed out by Mr. Mansel,* that from our Government having had no definite policy of directing or remodelling native States, having given no consistent instructions to its diplomatic Agents, and demanded from them no precise course of action, a period of irritating importunity would often be followed by a season of indifference and repose, so that no lasting impression was ever made. In its best aspect, under the guidance of an energetic and conscientious Resident, the existing system of Political Agency merely plucks at the leaves instead of attacking the root ; while in that worst aspect which it has occasionally assumed, the noxious tree flourishes and brings forth its corrupt fruit in security and abundance.

Such has been the conduct of the Calcutta Foreign Office—such is the practice of the professional rulers of India. They are satisfied if the Resident's Diaries are regularly transmitted and contain no startling disclosures. They have devised no plan for improving a dependent State, except that of destruction.

I think I may now claim to have proved that though the Rajah's incapacity constitutes a plausible but a most untenable plea for refusing his reinstatement, it affords no plea whatever for abolishing the Principality. The plea of the Prince's personal incompetence, does in effect strike at the root of hereditary monarchy. The Rajah of Mysore, according to Calcutta doctrines, was bound to have been a benevolent and enlightened despot at the age of sixteen, and, failing that, was properly reduced to be a pensioner for life, and the last Prince of his family. And yet we may surely assume that the Rajah never was really incompetent for the duties of a limited Monarch, when we find that Lord William Bentinck, after a careful inquiry, pronounced him to be " in the highest degree intelligent and sensible," described his disposition as " the reverse of tyran-

* Ante, p. 143.

nical or cruel," and expressed his belief that he would
"make a good ruler in future."

The Rajah has repeatedly invited the imposition of regulations and ordinances ; he has often in his correspondence
with our Government, alluded to sanitary regulations that
might have been imposed upon him, and which he was
"bound by the Treaty to regard." Ample power is conferred upon the British Government by Article XIV of the
Treaty, to offer authoritative advice on all subjects " connected with his Highness's interests, the happiness of his
people, and the mutual welfare of both States." It is hard
to understand why our Government should not have introduced the first essentials of a limited Monarchy, such as a
Code, a Civil List, and a Council of State, instead of making
use of the Rajah's alleged incapacity and profusion as a
pretext for destroying the Principality.

The alleged incapacity of the Rajah is not only an anti-
quated and retrogressive objection, but it is a most unfair
and unfounded imputation. Lord William Bentinck's
opinion of his Highness's character has been already cited.
The Rajah of Mysore, if left to his own unassisted devices,
might not be found to be a very profound statesman, or a
very skilful administrator ; but, even setting aside the
powers of guidance and control retained by our Government under the terms of the existing Treaty, the Rajah
knows well where to look for good advisers, and there
would be no danger of his promoting any great alterations
in that system, towards which, as General Sir Mark Cubbon
reported in a despatch of the 2nd June, 1860, " the greatest
cordiality has been observed by his Highness for a good
many years." The Rajah has never shut his eyes to the
errors of his youth ; he has not been unmindful of the
benefits conferred upon the country by General Cubbon's
long administration, and by the existing system of European
superintendence. Hope deferred may have made his heart
sick, but it has never turned him from the firm attachment
to British supremacy and reliance on British protection,
which was the first lesson of his childhood, and has been
the guiding principle of his public life. The Rajah of
Mysore is, in fact, a Prince of more than average acuteness
of intellect, active for his years, and capable of taking a

shrewd and lively share in a discussion on public affairs ;
master of three languages spoken in his dominions, Canarese,
Mahratta, and Hindustanee ; sufficiently acquainted with
English to appreciate and control a correspondence,* and
to understand a good deal of a conversation, though unable
or unwilling to take part in it.†   At his advanced age, and
with his severe experience, there could not be a better
instrument in our hands than the present Rajah,—there
could not be a Prince more admirably adapted for our
Imperial purposes, both as a conservative power and as a
visible agent for accepting and assimilating reforms.   His
disposition is acknowledged to be humane and beneficent ;
and, apart from the general respect for his lineage and
station, the popular love and regard for the Rajah's person
and dignity, always very remarkable throughout Mysore,
have been much heightened of late years, in the midst of
conflicting rumours as to the restoration of his authority,
and with the ever approaching prospect of losing him
altogether.‡   With the government of a hundred and fifty
millions in our hands, with seventy thousand British soldiers
locked up in India, we are as little able to afford, we ought
to be as unwilling, to lose the Rajah, as are the people of
Mysore.   But if we lose him or his family by annexation,
we shall lose many other native Princes, and millions of
native hearts, by alienation.   If we regain him, or even his
successor, by restoration, we shall redouble our moral influence, we shall redouble our reforming capacity, we shall be
able to take the first steps for relieving our military strength.

* In 1844, when the Government expressed some doubt on this point, and
wished his Highness to correspond in Canarese, he gave assurance as to his
entire knowledge and approval of his own English despatches.

† In my own experience I have known several instances of native Princes
and nobles, both Hindoo and Mussulman, who, though fairly proficient in
English, had an insurmountable objection to converse in that language. There
seemed to me to be a prejudice against its use, as a *clerklike* accomplishment.
This aversion, however, is not shared, or has been overcome, by the Rajah of
Travancore and his brother, Prince Rama Vurma, both of whom are excellent
English scholars ; the latter, indeed, has published, under the modest *nom de
plume* of " A Hindoo", several remarkable letters and pamphlets on political
and religious topics.

‡ An interesting letter will be found in Appendix I, written by one who
had ample means of forming a judgment, which will give a very fair idea of
the feelings with which the threatened extinction of the Mysore dynasty is
viewed, not only by the natives, but by some of our own most experienced and
devoted officers.

The local governors of India,—the leading members of
the Bengal Civil Service,—have taken no such steps, and
they never will do so without instructions and orders from
home. They are professional administrators, and they are
English gentlemen among subservient Hindoos. The greed
of patronage, the arrogance of race, the pedantry of office,
all the evil influences of their position and training, prejudice them against the extension or restoration of native
rule, and make it impossible that they should judge such a
question impartially. Even their highest aspirations for
the good of the people are perverted to injustice by their
professional habits and predilections. Annexation, not
reform or instruction, is their political panacea for India.
They are prepared to annex the Mysore State, and they
most assuredly will do so, if they are not checked by the
Government of Great Britain. They have even had the
extraordinary imprudence to urge upon the Rajah very
recently, in reply to his unanswerable claims, that during
the last thirty years " great changes have taken place, and
new interests have grown up;"* as if it could be maintained
with dignity or with decency, that as new interests arise,
Treaties may be disregarded. The Rajah of Mysore is in
his seventy-second year, and it will be too late to interfere,
too late to remonstrate, when he is no more—when the
Calcutta professionals have committed the British Government beyond retreat by a proclamation, by preferring supposed new interests to undeniable ancient rights, by openly
rejecting the Rajah's heir, by intimidating the Nizam into
silence, perhaps by some " just and necessary" measures of
coercion and correction.

It will then be too late to reconsider either the justice or
the policy of extinguishing the Mysore Principality. The
question must be decided in England, and must be decided
without delay.

* Papers Relating to Mysore, 1866, p. 70.

CHAPTER X.

THE PARLIAMENTARY PAPERS OF 1866, AND MR. R. D. MANGLES.

THE Papers " relative to the claims of the Rajah of Mysore to be restored to the government of his territories, and to be allowed to adopt an heir," called for by Sir Henry Rawlinson, and ordered by the House of Commons to be printed on the 13th March, 1866, authenticate the more important documents published in the first edition of the Mysore Reversion, and will, I think, fully prove that I have neither overstated the case in favour of the Rajah, nor understated the adverse case set up against him. Not one of the despatches from the Governor-General in Council, or from the Secretary of State, which now see the light for the first time, nor even the hostile Minutes by Mr. R. D. Mangles and Mr. H. Thoby Prinsep, contain a single fact or allegation against the Rajah's character or conduct which I have not already noticed ; and not a single argument, whether based on right or policy, is advanced against his cause which I may not claim to have met and refuted.

On the other hand, the Papers include Minutes of Dissent from the instructions sent to India in this matter, recorded by five of the most distinguished Members of the Council of India—Sir George Clerk, Sir Frederick Currie, Sir John Willoughby, Sir Henry Montgomery, and Captain W. J. Eastwick—all of whom support the Rajah's claims, in general accordance with the views contained in my book.

The objections, urged with earnestness almost amounting to vehemence, by so many men of grave character and large experience, might well give pause to the most remorseless advocate of annexation. Even Lord Dalhousie, in his Minute of the 30th August, 1848, printed in the *Sattara Papers* of 1849 (p. 83), when recommending that no just opportunity of taking possession of Native States by the process of "lapse," should be omitted, declared that "wherever a shadow of doubt can be shown, the claim should at once be abandoned." The solemn protests recorded by the minority of the Secretary of State's Council —a minority so strong in acknowledged ability and high reputation,—ought surely to be sufficient to raise more than that "shadow of doubt" which Lord Dalhousie held should lead to the abandonment of such a design.

If the Rajah's case is so far plausible, and the adverse claim so far questionable, as to admit of the gravest scruples being entertained by five eminently competent judges, all of whose instincts and prejudices would naturally lead them to coincide with the majority, we ought seriously to reflect on the impression that must be produced in India on those who naturally sympathise with the Rajah, and who cannot help feeling that the downfall of the State may form a precedent for the ruin of their own dearest interests and for the destruction of all they hold sacred.

When Sir Henry Montgomery is seen to accuse his own Government of "*a breach of good faith*"; when Sir John Willoughby denounces "*the flagrant injustice*" of the decision; when Sir Frederick Currie declares it to be "*unjust and illegal, and a violation of special treaties, which the British Government have bound themselves to maintain inviolate;*" when Sir. George Clerk condemns it as "*the result of wild counsel, prompting the indiscriminate gratification of a selfish policy,*" "*unworthy of a great nation,*" neither "*honest nor dignified,*" and regrets that "*so loyal a Prince*" should be made "*the victim of such extreme measures;*" and when Captain Eastwick asserts that the treatment of the Rajah "*cannot be justified by our treaty obligations, nor by the law and practice of India;*" what can we expect to be said and thought on the subject by the dependent Sovereigns of India and their advisers and adherents ?

This Blue Book may do infinite good or infinite harm. If the publication does not save the Principality of Mysore, it will, by displaying the origin, progress, and pretexts of the scheme for its extinction, and the cogent reasoning by which these pretexts were refuted, aggravate and extend the worst effects of this mischievous and shortsighted measure, and remove every shadow of excuse or palliation.

The most remarkable feature of the arguments adduced in the Despatches and Minutes adverse to the Rajah's claims, is that they are invariably based upon the most obvious contradictions and misstatements of facts officially recorded.   For instance, in the despatch from the Governor-General in Council to the Secretary of State, dated 31st August, 1864, it is said that "by twenty years of misrule, by extravagance, venality, and oppression, resulting in the rebellion of his subjects, who, but for the interference of the British Government, would have shaken off his authority, the Maharajah violated the conditions which were the basis of his dominion, and forced the British Government to the exercise of the sovereign power, which, under the 4th Article of the Subsidiary Treaty, they had retained, of superseding the Maharajah's rule, and of carrying on the government of Mysore in their own name and by their sole authority."*

The terms in which the misgovernment and its results are denounced, are exaggerated far beyond what the facts warrant ; but it is simply untrue that the 4th Article of the Subsidiary Treaty gives the Honourable Company the power of "superseding the Rajah's rule, and of carrying on the government of Mysore in their own name, and by their sole authority."   There is nothing in the 4th Article that in the least resembles these terms.   That Article of the Treaty simply empowered the British Government to assume the management of such "part or parts" of the Rajah's dominions as might be sufficient to supply funds for the Subsidy, "*whenever*," and "*so long*," as there should be "reason to apprehend a failure in the funds so destined."   The powers of temporary management acquired by our Government under this Article, were hastily and harshly enforced by Lord William Bentinck,—on insufficient and erroneous grounds, according to his own candid admission,†—and since that time have been amplified far beyond the intentions and contrary to the instructions of that Governor-General and his two immediate successors, so that many apparent obstacles have now been raised against a return to native administration.   And yet the British Government

* Mysore Papers, p. 48.   † Ante, p. 22-27.

have never ventured to do what Sir John Lawrence inaccurately says they have done.   They have never carried on the government in their own name.   On the contrary, the official designation of the British officer at the head of the Mysore Commission, has always been that of " The Commissioner for the Government of the Territories of the Rajah of Mysore."*

In the same despatch from the Governor-General to the Secretary of State, dated the 31st August, 1864, the following words occur :—" By no act or promise, actual or constructive, have the British Government ever revived the Maharajah's forfeited rights, or given ground of hope that they would be revived."†

The Governor-General's assertion that the Maharajah's rights were " forfeited," is quite unwarrantable, as we see from Lord William Bentinck's own words, quoted in this passage from Sir John Willoughby's Minute :—

" We have the explicit declaration of Lord William Bentinck himself, that the assumption of the administration of the Mysore Territory in 1831 was intended only as a temporary measure. In a Minute (dated 14 April, 1834), commenting on the Report of a Commission appointed to investigate into the causes of disturbances which were the pretext for depriving the Rajah of the management of his country, Lord William Bentinck makes the following important admissions :—

" ' The entire question hinges, I think, upon this consideration; Has the Company's Government assumed the management of the Mysore country on its own account, or is that country still managed for, and on behalf of, the Rajah ?   Is the Subsidiary Treaty of Mysore virtually cancelled, or is it still in full force ?

" ' The answer must decidedly be that the management has been assumed for and on behalf of the Rajah, and that the Treaty is in full force.' "‡

Article V of the Subsidiary Treaty provides that the Governor-General shall " render to his Highness a true and faithful account of the revenues and produce of territories

<hr>

* Thus the Foreign Secretary writes to the Commissioner on the 29th March, 1864 : " The Governor-General in Council can allow of no change in the existing form of the administration, which, at the same time that it is well adapted to the best interests of the country, sufficiently consults the dignity of the Maharajah by having its head entitled, ' Commissioner for the Government of the Territories of His Highness the Maharajah of Mysore.' " Mysore Papers, p. 40.

† Mysore Papers, p. 48.   ‡ Ibid , p. 26.

so assumed," and that "in no case whatever shall his Highness's actual receipt or annual income arising out of his territorial revenue" be less than a certain sum.   How could the territorial revenue be his, and for what purpose could accounts be furnished to the Rajah, if his rights were to be forfeited, if his sovereignty were to cease in the event of this Article being enforced?   Far from there having been any intimation or intention of forfeiture, the objects of the British interference, as declared to the Rajah by Lord William Bentinck, were " the preservation of the State of Mysore," and " the permanent prosperity of the Raj."*

In the same Minute Sir John Willoughby writes as follows :—" The present decision is in contradiction of the public records, which in a continuous stream indicate the intention to restore the administration of Mysore to its native rulers at some future but hitherto undefined period. The Maharajah has never ceased to urge his claim to the restoration of his sovereign rights, and until now has never been peremptorily refused.   On the contrary, on more than one occasion, hopes have been held out to the Maharajah that restoration would ultimately be made to himself personally."

And he adds in a foot-note to this part of his Minute:—

"In the year 1844, he urged his appeal no less than five times ; namely, 15 February, 10th April, 9th May, 11th August, and 7th September.   He again appealed in June 1845, and again on the 8th August, 1848, and lastly, and more urgently than ever, on the anticipated retirement of Sir Mark Cubbon, on the 23rd February 1861.   In these appeals the Maharajah asks many perplexing questions ; such, for instance, as, ' Who was to be the judge of when the conditions for restoration prescribed by the Court of Directors have been fulfilled?   Had it ever been before heard, that because a Prince or individual had been in his youth extravagant, he should therefore be disinherited?   Have not disturbances occurred in the Company's territories, as they have done in those of Mysore, without blame being imputed to the governing authorities?   Have not the best and most upright of governments incurred, as he had done, debts ?   What proportion does my debt bear to the revenues of my country ?'   Finally, he strongly contends, and I think with success, that the original assumption of the administration of Mysore was not justified by the Treaty of 1799.

* Appendix, C.

Vide, in particular, his letters dated 7th June 1845, and 8th August, 1848, in the last of which he claims the fulfilment of Lord Auckland's promises made in 1836."*

And Sir Henry Montgomery remarks in his Minute that "it is impossible to deny that it has throughout been the professed purpose of the Home authorities to restore to the Rajah the administration of the country, and that they regarded the direct management of it only as a temporary measure."† He also objects that in one paragraph of the Secretary of State's despatch, dated 17th July, 1863, "it is said that 'the state of the finances was such as to afford no security for the punctual payment of the Subsidy;' whereas, up to that very period the Subsidy had been paid punctually in advance, and Lord W. Bentinck had subsequently recorded his belief that it was at no time in jeopardy."‡

Mr. Prinsep, in his Minute adverse to the Rajah, falls into the very same error, and, still more strangely, selects the exact term which Lord William Bentinck had employed in a negative sense. Mr. Prinsep asserts, that "the strong measure of 1832" was required "for the security of the Subsidy, which was jeopardised".‡ Lord William Bentinck expressly acknowledged that "the Subsidy was not in jeopardy."

Sir Henry Montgomery urges against the same despatch of the Secretary of State, that the harsh measure of totally superseding the Rajah's Government is justified by alleging as facts the exaggerated stories which led to Lord William Bentinck's hasty action, but were disproved by the investigations of the Special Commission of Inquiry :—"Lord W. Bentinck's letter to the Rajah, written, as admitted subsequently by Lord W. Bentinck, when he had not made himself master of the subject, is quoted. In it, it is stated, 'that the greatest excesses were committed, and unparalleled cruelties were inflicted by your Highness's servants,' such allegations of cruelties having been shown to be untrue by the Committee's Report."§

This is only one instance of the unpleasant characteristics

---

* Mysore Papers, 1866, p. 27.
† Mysore Papers, 1866, p. 20.   ‡ Ibid., p. 21.
§ Ibid., 1866, p. 89.   ‖ Ibid., 1866, p. 21.

pervading all the official documents, that while not even a specious case can be stated against the legal rights of the Rajah and his adopted heir, without re-asserting the fictitious prerogative which Lord Canning publicly repudiated, it is equally impossible for any moral grounds to be alleged for rejecting the Rajah's claims without re-asserting those fictitious accusations against him which Lord William Bentinck regretted and retracted.

We are not surprised when a journal like the *Friend of India*, representing the Calcutta Civilians and the Calcutta shopkeepers, casts a random epithet or two, such as that of " tyrannical sensualist", at the Rajah of Mysore.   Although Lord William Bentinck, after personal observation and inquiry, declared that the Rajah's disposition was " the reverse of tyrannical", that he believed his Highness was " in the highest degree intelligent and sensible", and would " make a good ruler in future",—although the slightest local research would convince even the *Friend* himself of the utter falsity of both his imputations,—we are too well accustomed to that style of discussion in the official and commercial circles which the *Friend of India* represents, to feel any extraordinary indignation.   At Calcutta it is always quite safe, and quite acceptable to an English audience, to call any Hindoo or Mussulman Prince a tyrant and a sensualist. The arrogance and prejudice of race and religion, the lust of patronage, and jealousy of any native pretensions, there reign rampant and triumphant.   The *Friend of India* has no more claim to be considered as an organ of public opinion than the *Pawnbroker's Gazette*, but it may be very fairly considered as the organ of that powerful guild of professional administrators who are allowed to rule India, and whose influence affects extensively the public opinion of Great Britain as to Indian affairs.   The intimate connection between the *Friend* and the Calcutta Secretariat* is so well known, its leading articles have so often sounded the first note of annexation, that even its most reckless calumnies, and its most improbable threats and prognostications against the

* Even more mischievous than the close tie between the *Friend of India* and the Calcutta Foreign Office, is the post of vantage occupied by its Editor as the Calcutta Correspondent of the *Times*, so that the sources of information are constantly poisoned at both fountain heads, in the metropolis of India and of the Empire.

minor States, have frequently struck terror into the hearts of our best allies and some of the best rulers in India.

We do not wonder, therefore, to encounter in the columns of the *Friend of India* a contemptuous, disingenuous, and unjudicial tone with reference to the position and claims of a native Prince, to see his character bespattered with random abuse, and his rights under treaty derided as mere matters of grace and favour, originating in temporary expediency and terminable at our own discretion.

When Mr. Bowring captiously taunts the Rajah with being " wavering, inconstant, and led away by trifles", because at the formal official communication of a message which the Rajah " had long ago learnt from other sources",* his Highness presumed " to talk jocosely"; when Mr. Bowring in two successive paragraphs (5 and 6) of a despatch, first announces the Rajah's demands that his adopted son should be recognised, that " Mysore should permanently remain a Native State", and " that a landed estate should be secured to some of his illegitimate grandchildren"—the very demands that effectually provided for all his relations and retainers,—and then immediately imputes to the Rajah " purely selfish" motives, and a total want of " anxiety about the future of his many dependants and retainers, or even of his numerous connections",† we may marvel at the blind carelessness with which the commentary is made to contradict the text, but we are not much surprised at the peevish and contemptuous spirit betrayed by the Bengal Civilian.

Mr. Bowring is, doubtless, an excellent public servant and an honourable man, but he knows the objects and wishes of his official superiors, and cannot but sympathise with them ; his own greatest success and distinction in life have consisted in his promotion to be Commissioner of Mysore, and he can hardly be expected to entertain with much complacency the notion of his functions not being permanent and indispensable. The more firmly he is conscious or convinced of his own ability and industry, the more must his personal and professional pride be outraged by the pros-

* Mr. Bowring had himself privately communicated the message several months before the interview reported in his letter of the 18th February, 1864. (Mysore Papers, p. 36.) Ante, p. 76.
† Mysore Papers, p. 37.

pect of even a partial return to native government. And possibly the natural amiability of the Commissioner's temperament may have been slightly affected for the worse by the long and unsettled controversy as to the Rajah's claims having delayed and interrupted business, causing him much annoyance and throwing additional work upon his hands. The Governor-General, clearly quoting Mr. Bowring, writes to the Secretary of State :—"Such a discussion cannot benefit his Highness, while the tendency must be to unsettle the minds of the people, and to disturb the growing prosperity of the country."* This excessively official objection evinces just that irritation at the Rajah's unanswerable claims that might be expected.

We do not, then, find fault so much with Mr. Bowring's unfair and uncivil detraction, as with the toleration and apparent approval his despatches receive from the Government of India. The honour and dignity of Great Britain are committed to so great an extent to those hands, that it cannot be a matter of indifference to us when we see them turned to iniquity. But we are still in the atmosphere of Calcutta, and the Viceroy himself is a Bengal Civilian.

For my part it is not until I arrive at the despatches from the Home Government that my heart sinks a little. Even the Minutes by Mr. R. D. Mangles and Mr. H. T. Prinsep, both of them retired Bengal Civilians, do not astonish me. The official experience of Mr. Mangles never, I believe, extended beyond the precincts of the Presidency City. It is so natural for professional administrators to be deeply impressed with the transcendent blessings conferred by their own forms and regulations, and by the employment of their own friends and relatives in every imaginable office, that the efforts of all this class may be forgiven. But to my mind it is a most painful and ominous circumstance to see the same cold shade creeping over the home despatches ; to find the Secretary of State, having deferred an explicit discussion and an absolute decision for a considerable time, reduced at last to adopt all the perversions and prevarications of Calcutta, to revive acknowledged calumnies, to reassert exploded fallacies.

* Mysore Papers, p. 54.

Mr. R. D. Mangles in 1849 acted as the spokesman of the majority of the Court of Directors in sanctioning and approving the annexation of Sattara, the first step in that systematic policy of extinguishing our best friends which culminated in the confiscation of Oude, and a year later exploded in the fire of mutiny and rebellion. The minority of the Court on that occasion, each of whom recorded a written protest, would have been almost universally acknowledged at that time as the five most able and distinguished Directors,—Messrs. H. St. George Tucker, W. Leslie Melville, and J. Shepherd, General Caulfield, and Major Oliphant. And now when, after a respite of ten years, it is proposed to recommence the extinguishing process, Mr. Mangles once more appears as the spokesman of the majority, while the five most able and distinguished Members of the Indian Council,—Sir George Clerk, Sir John Willoughby, Sir Henry Montgomery, Sir Frederick Currie, and Captain Eastwick,—record their written protests against the measure. The parallel is remarkable. It can only be hoped that the result of this second conflict may be very different from that of the first; that noise and numbers may fail this time to get the better of history, logic, and morals.

The style adopted by Mr. Mangles in his Minutes is essentially noisy and boisterous, and owes all its effect to a certain audacity of assertion and invective. In his attempt to answer one of the weightiest arguments of his eminent colleagues, Sir George Clerk and Sir Frederick Currie, he professes to "*brush away a fallacy spun to ensnare the ignorant;*" he ridicules the Rajahs of Sattara and Mysore as "*mere puppets;*" the latter Prince was "*the merest puppet,*" and "*a nominal Rajah;*" the State of Mysore always was and must be "*a sham Principality,*" and he denounces in general "*the treachery, sottishness, and imbecility of these puppet rulers.*" In short, he affords here, as he did in his too successful Minute on the Sattara succession, the most perfect illustration of the contemptuous spirit and the unjudicial disposition with which so many Englishmen, more especially if they have graduated in a Calcutta bureau, approach any claim of right on the part of a Hindoo Prince or community.

All the apparent force of Mr. Mangles's Minute is derived, as I shall show, from his loose and incorrect statement of facts, frequently amounting to a direct contradiction of the records before him, from the most cynical defiance of every dictate of good faith and public morals, and especially from his persistent reassertion of an imaginary prerogative, which after having been unjustly assumed during twelve years, the Government of India solemnly and publicly disclaimed in 1860, with the approval of the Secretary of State.

Mr. Mangles begins by "brushing away a fallacy, spun," as he says, "to ensnare the ignorant."   He says :—

"Advantage has been taken upon this, as on former occasions, to raise an *argumentum ad invidiam*, for the purpose of misleading the general public into the erroneous persuasion, that to prohibit such an adoption as that proposed to be made by the Rajah of Mysore, is not merely an act of temporal injustice, but a grievous injury extending beyond the grave, and an outrage upon the religious feelings of the whole Hindoo community; and this misrepresentation is the more mischievous, because it would be undeniably true if the British Government had really prohibited adoption, in the broad meaning of the term."*

The fallacy which Mr. Mangles professes to brush away is nothing more than a cobweb which he spins himself. Every one knows that although the term may conveniently be abbreviated into "the right of adoption," what is meant. is the right of succession by adoption.   Although we may very properly speak of the Government having prohibited an adoption, every one understands that what has been prohibited is the succession of an adopted son.   To forbid a Hindoo Prince to adopt a son, would be as futile as to forbid him to marry or to beget a son ; to interdict a Rajah's widow from performing the brief and simple ceremony of adoption, would be as futile as to forbid the birth of a posthumous son.   But to prohibit the succession of a son born in lawful wedlock, of an adopted son, or of a posthumous son, would be, in every case, and equally in each case, a prohibition utterly devoid of legal or historical warrant.   It would be no consolation to a Hindoo family to be told, after their patrimony had been confiscated, that an

* Mysore Papers, p. 83.

adoption had not been really prohibited, "in the broad meaning of the term," that the funeral rites might still be duly performed, and that there had been no interference with religious observances. The complaint would be that succession had been refused to a lawful son and heir.

But although Mr. Mangles urges that for the due performance of a Hindoo's funeral ceremonies, "it is by no means necessary that his adopted son should be a Sovereign Prince",* it is not the less certain that the refusal of succession to a Prince's adopted son is "an outrage upon the religious feelings of the whole Hindoo community", because it amounts to an assertion of the legal nullity and inefficacy of an adoption, and proclaims the illegitimacy of an adopted son. Even Mr. Bowring, the Commissioner of Mysore, admits that " the feeling of all Hindoos, whether in Mysore or in any other part of India, on the subject of adoption, is deeply rooted."† The insult and the outrage are doubly embittered when the rejected heir represents an ancient and illustrious family, and when his rejection carries with it the extinction of a Hindoo State, the ruin of many local interests, and the downfall of a respectable and influential class.

There is literally no foundation whatever in Hindoo law or in the history of India for that distinction which Mr. Mangles attempts to draw between the succession to personal property and to a dependent Principality. Ever since the annexation of Sattara in 1848, Mr. Mangles and his school have been constantly defied to show some proof of such a distinction having ever existed, to adduce one single precedent for the refusal to recognise an adoption, but they have remained silent. As Captain Eastwick remarks in his Minute :—

"It is a remarkable fact that, as far as I know, Lord Dalhousie, the originator of the policy of annexation on the plea of escheat, and its persistent upholder, has nowhere quoted any precedent for annexation in disregard of adoption, though he must no doubt have directed careful search for such precedents, which would have established his policy on something like a basis."‡

Mr. Mangles does not hesitate to charge his distinguished

* Mysore Papers, p. 84.   † Ibid., p. 52.   ‡ Ibid., p. 75.

friends with spinning a fallacy, "to ensnare the ignorant", and "for the purpose of misleading the general public",[*] and we have shown that this alleged fallacy is a mere verbal confusion of his own raising. But how shall we characterise the conduct of a judge or councillor who doggedly persists in referring to fictitious precedents, without attempting to produce them, in spite of repeated challenges from aggrieved appellants and dissentient colleagues ?

It is still more sad to find the Home Government misled by the fictitious precedents invoked by Mr. Mangles. The Secretary of State in his despatch of 17th July, 1865, writes as follows :—

"In my Despatch to you, No. 45, of the 30th July, 1864, which conveyed my approval of the course you had adopted for carrying out the instructions contained in my letter of the 17th July, 1863, I merely remarked in paragraph 5, 'with regard to the question of adoption, I will only observe, that you could not recognise more than the Maharajah's right to adopt, so far as his private property is concerned.' I have now to convey to you expressly my concurrence with your Government in the arguments you have adduced against the Rajah's claim to do more than is above specified, and my approval of your having intimated to the Maharajah, that 'no authority to adopt a successor to the Raj of Mysore has ever been given him, and that no such power can now be conceded'." [†]

The best answer to this extraordinary recurrence to the destructive prerogative disclaimed in Lord Canning's Adoption despatch, and to what are called the "arguments" by which the Governor-General, in his letter of the 5th May, 1865, reclaims that prerogative, will be found in this brief extract from Sir George Clerk's Minute :—

"This new doctrine regarding adoption is so novel and unjust, so opposed to all customs and religions in India, and so utterly inconsistent with the course of administration as previously exercised during the paramountry of Hindoos, Mohammedans and ourselves, that I can only conceive it to be the result of wild counsel prompting an indiscriminate gratification of a selfish policy, which it is endeavoured to veil under a plea of expediency." [‡]

But we will give some attention to Sir John Lawrence's

"arguments." In paragraph 21 of the letter dated 5th May, 1865 (Mysore Papers, p. 59) this passage occurs :—

"Forced to acknowledge that in the time of the Mogul emperors it was customary for vassal Chiefs to obtain the assent of the Sovereign to adoptions for state succession, the Maharajah nevertheless does not hesitate to call in question, by the line of argument his Highness advances, the rights of the British Government to limit the issue of the adoption sunnuds to Chiefs who govern their own territories. His Highness bases his reasoning partly upon an assertion, the historical accuracy of which is not only open to be controverted by the facts of both Mahommedan and Mahratta supremacy, but upon which the history of the Maharajah's own family might have suggested to his Highness a comment, how far weak Hindoo Chiefs were allowed any discretion by Moslem conquerors."

The grammar and sense of the last sentence are somewhat obscure ; but if we assume the most obvious and probable meaning, it is difficult to see how the Calcutta doctrines are advanced by it. We are not "Moslem conquerors." Moslem conquerors did not make treaties of perpetual friendship and alliance, "to be binding, by the blessing of God, as long as the sun and moon endure," with the "weak Hindoo Chiefs" whom they conquered. And, on the other hand, "the history of the Maharajah's own family" would only "suggest to his Highness" this "comment," that Hyder Ali, the "Moslem conqueror" who usurped the power of a weak Hindoo Prince" without dethroning him, *did permit an adoption to take place*, when the present Rajah's father was chosen, as in the case of the recently adopted heir, from a distant branch of the royal family.*

As to what the Calcutta authorities say the Maharajah was "forced to acknowledge,"—that the sanction of the Mogul Emperors to their adoption of a successor was always sought by dependent Princes,—the fact, though requiring much qualification, and doubtfully applicable to Princes with whom Treaties exist, may be fully admitted without injuring the Rajah's cause. The right of sanctioning and controlling a succession, even the right of investiture, does not, and never did in the days of "Mahommedan or Mahratta supremacy," involve the right of forbidding a succession. This is very clearly explained in Sir George Clerk's Minute :

* Wilks's *History of Mysore*, vol. ii, p. 163.

"A fact well known to those of us who have been much in the way of observing the circumstances of adoptions of Heirs to Chiefships, and to those who have made researches with a view to elucidate the subject, as Sir Henry Lawrence in the Kerowlee case in 1853, and Lord Canning on the general question in 1860, is that, if guided by the custom of the country and the practice of all our predecessors, our concern in adoptions consists only in adjusting the rival pretentions of two or more such heirs; a precaution which we and our predecessors have made it our duty to exercise in the interests of the peaceable public generally. Hence our sanction may in one sense be said to be necessary; for, naturally, a record of it is always sought by the rightful or by the successful claimant. Hence it is, too, that the confirmation has never been refused. Hence it is that I never found an instance on the old records at Delhi, and that I never knew one occurring within my experience of our own times, of any Chiefship, either Raj or Surdarree, great or small, being held to have escheated, excepting for felony, to the Paramount State."*

But the Governor-General proceeds thus:—"Further, it may be added that the principles of the Hindoo law of inheritance have no application to Chiefships; but, above all, none to those held under the conditions on which Mysore was conferred on his Highness." Now the principles of the Hindoo law of inheritance have application in India to everything that is heritable. It is not true that any special limitation was ever applied to the descent of Chiefships. Nor has the Governor-General attempted on this occasion to show how the Hindoo law of inheritance, which is the law of Mysore, and the main object of which is to prevent the extinction of families, can be inapplicable to the family of the Rajah of Mysore. Nor did Lord Dalhousie, or any of his school, ever attempt to show on any previous occasion how the Hindoo law of inheritance, which is the law of India, and by virtue of which every Hindoo subject can transmit to an adopted heir all his rights which are heritable, can be inapplicable to the dignity and possessions of a Hindoo Prince, who, although a tributary and dependent

* Mysore Papers, p. 71. See also *The Empire in India*, "Adoption" and "Sattara." It is really too bad that we should have again and again to put to flight these mendacious phantoms, to attack those false positions which Lord Canning expressly abandoned, although he was of course compelled to write cautiously, and to avoid directly condemning the past action of Government. It is irresistible to say of the Calcutta Secretariat:—"The dog returns to his vomit again, and the sow that was washed to her wallowing in the mire."

Ally of Her Majesty, cannot be properly included among the subjects of the British Crown. The rights, dignity, and possessions of a Sovereign in India, and throughout the world, are transmitted either by the ordinary law of the land or by some special law of royal succession. No special law, no special limitation is applicable to the Rajah's case. He is the Hindoo Sovereign of a Hindoo Principality.

But it is said that, "above all," the Hindoo law of inheritance has no application to Chiefships " held under the conditions on which Mysore was conferred" upon the Rajah. The conditions under which Mysore was conferred upon the Rajah are recorded in the two Treaties of 1799. There are no other conditions ; and no Article or Clause of those Treaties institutes any new or special law of succession, impugns or limits the operation of the Hindoo law, or declares it to have become inapplicable to a family whose successions had been regulated by its principles for many centuries.

It is very questionable whether the State of Mysore, bound to the British Government by a Treaty of perpetual friendship and alliance, can be rightly classed among "Chiefships." It is frequently termed the Kingdom of Mysore by the Marquis Wellesley, the Duke of Wellington, and many subsequent Indian statesmen ; and at the present day the Rajah is one of the few Princes of India, who sits upon a throne, and who is entitled to a royal salute of twenty-one guns. Were it not for the incessant efforts to damage the Rajah's position by depreciatory epithets, these would be matters of little or no weight, points rather of form and courtesy than of serious import ; for the pettiest Hindoo Chief is really as much entitled to adopt a successor as the most exalted and ancient Maharajah.

After declaring that the Rajah's claim to adopt an heir to the State of Mysore ought not to be sanctioned, the Governor-General says :—

"The Maharajah is not a Sovereign Prince in the sense in which he uses the term ; on the contrary, his Highness is a dependent Prince, having no rights whatever beyond those conferred upon him by the Subsidiary Treaty, and no power or authority to amplify those rights beyond the strict letter of the Treaty.

* Mysore Papers, p. 60.

That Treaty was a purely personal one with the Maharajah, and conveyed no authority to adopt, and made no mention whatever of heirs."*

The Maharajah " uses the term" Sovereign Prince in its ordinary " sense." In what sense does the Governor-General maintain that it ought to be used by his Highness ? The Governor-General would perhaps reply, in the immediately succeeding words of this passage, that " on the contrary his Highness is a dependent Prince," as if the two terms were inconsistent and contradictory, whereas they are quite compatible. Any work on International Law will explain that a Sovereign Prince may also be a dependent Prince. But in fact all the attributes and titles of sovereignty were attached to the Rajah of Mysore in the transactions and Treaties of 1799, 1803, and 1807 ; and Lord Canning, when Viceroy of India, so late as 30th March 1860, simply renewed a continuous recognition when he observed, in his despatch to the Secretary of State, that his Highness was " the Sovereign of Mysore," and that the people of Mysore were " his subjects."†

Captain Eastwick observes on this point :—

" With regard to the Maharajah not being a Sovereign Prince, we have never discovered this until lately. It is only since the absorption of Mysore has been contemplated, that we have changed our style of address to the Maharajah, and have adopted language more convenient for our purposes. Up to a very recent date, the sovereignty of the Maharajah has been uninterruptedly acknowledged by the representatives of the British Government and by the Home authorities."‡

Having thus endeavoured to cast a shade of doubt and confusion over the Rajah's sovereignty, the Governor-General then proceeds to say that his Highness has " *no rights beyond those conferred upon him by the Subsidiary Treaty.*" Here we have the indispensable misstatement of the transactions of 1799, without which it would be impossible to degrade the Sovereign of Mysore into a mere tenant for life or during good behaviour, at the discretion of the British Government. The despatch speaks of " *rights conferred upon the Rajah by the Subsidiary Treaty.*" No rights whatever were conferred upon the Rajah by the

* Mysore Papers, p. 60.   † Ante, p. 51.   ‡ Mysore Papers, p. 76.

Subsidiary Treaty, except—strange to say!—that right of
calling for the aid of British troops, (Article X) the exercise
of which, although so clearly contemplated and anticipated
when the Treaty was concluded, is now both cast in his
teeth as an extraordinary boon, and made the chief pretext
for his permanent supersession.   With this singular exception, nothing whatever is conferred upon the Rajah by the
Subsidiary Treaty.   I challenge any one to read the Treaty
through from beginning to end, and to find one word in the
Preamble, or in any one of the Articles, which purports to
grant or to concede *anything* to the Rajah.   Everything
settled by the Subsidiary Treaty is for the benefit of the
East India Company.

Sir John Lawrence in his letter to the Rajah of the 5th
May, 1865,* makes the same misstatement—a misstatement, as I have just remarked, which is indispensable for
his object.   He says :—" The Nizam was not even admitted
as a party to the Subsidiary Treaty which effected the cession of Mysore to your Highness."   The cession of Mysore
was not effected by the Subsidiary Treaty, but by the
Partition Treaty.   It is expressly stated in Article V of the
Subsidiary Treaty that his Highness's " territories" were
" ceded to him by the Fifth Article of the Treaty of Mysore" (the Partition Treaty).

Nothing was ever conferred upon the Rajah by the East
India Company acting alone.   Whatever was conferred
upon the Rajah of Mysore in 1799 was conferred by the
Partition Treaty between the East India Company and the
Nizam.   And not only is nothing conferred, ceded, or
granted in the Subsidiary Treaty, but not one single district or village that had been conferred upon the Rajah in
the Treaty of Partition is even specified or named in the
Subsidiary Treaty.   In the Preamble and several of the
Articles a simple reference is made to the Partition Treaty
with the Nizam, as the document containing both full
authority and full particulars.   Indeed, the Partition Treaty
is cited in Article XV of the Subsidiary Treaty, as constituting the sufficient title to the districts therein " declared
to belong respectively to the English Company and to his
Highness."   Both parties are referred to the Treaty with

* Mysore Papers, p. 69.

the Nizam as the ultimate record. And in Article XIII, which contemplates a commercial Treaty between the Company and the Rajah, mention is made of "their respective dominions," and of "the subjects of both Governments." In Article XIV. there is a stipulation "for the mutual welfare of both States."   It is thus impossible to deny that the Rajah is a Sovereign Prince, in every sense of the term ; and it is equally impossible to separate the two Treaties of 1799.

When the Subsidiary Treaty was about to be concluded, the cession of territory to form the restored Principality, "under a descendant of the ancient Rajahs of Mysore," and to be "a separate Government, as long as the sun and moon endure," had been already effected by the Partition Treaty ; and by its ninth Article a Subsidiary Force, for "the effectual establishment" of the Rajah's Government, was to be furnished by the Company, "according to the terms of a separate Treaty to be immediately concluded" with the Rajah.

The Subsidiary Treaty is simply supplementary to the Partition Treaty—"ancillary" and "subordinate," as was rashly acknowledged in the memorable Calcutta Letter of 11th March, 1862.*   It declares itself in the Preamble to be concluded "in order to carry out the stipulations" of the Partition Treaty with the Nizam, and "*to increase and strengthen the friendship subsisting between the English East India Company and the Maharajah*,"—words which in themselves sufficiently indicate that the Rajah's restoration to the position of a reigning Sovereign was the foregone cause and not the consequence of the Subsidiary Treaty.

The dates of the two Treaties, compared with the time and incidents of the Rajah's installation, prove clearly that the cession of territory to his Highness, and the recognition of his sovereignty, took effect from the joint action of the Allies, and were quite unconnected with the Subsidiary Treaty. The Partition Treaty is dated the 22nd June, 1799. The Rajah was enthroned on the 30th June—his right hand being taken by Lord Harris, the British Commander-in-Chief, and his left by Meer Allum, the Nizam's

* Ante, p. 66.

Plenipotentiary.   The Subsidiary Treaty, to which the
Nizam was not a party, was not signed till the 8th July,
eight days after the Rajah's public inauguration, and was
not ratified by Lord Wellesley till the 23rd July.[*]

The next assertion in the Governor-General's despatch
of the 5th May, 1865, is that the Rajah has "no power or
authority to amplify his rights beyond the strict letter of
the Treaty." Certainly not—and no more has the other
party to the Treaty. The Rajah, as we have seen, acquired
no rights, possessions, or privileges from the Subsidiary
Treaty ; but he undertook certain obligations towards the
East India Company, which have always been punctually
and faithfully performed. The Company, on the other
hand, did acquire certain rights from that Treaty ; among
others, the right to an annual Subsidy, and the right of
securing its regular payment by authoritative counsel, and
by temporary management in case of extremity. How
those rights have been amplified ; how the strict letter of
the Treaty has been interpreted by the stronger party, I
have endeavoured to show in the preceding pages.

The Governor-General thus continues : " That Treaty was
a purely personal one with the Maharajah, and conveyed
no authority to adopt, and made no mention whatever of,
heirs."

No Treaty concluded with any Hindoo Prince has ever
conveyed an authority to adopt, because treaties of perpetual friendship and alliance between two States never do
include a law of succession applicable to one of them ; and
because until the year 1848,—when, as Sir George Clerk
observes in his Minute, " the Calcutta Government led off
with the barefaced appropriation of Sattara,"[†]—no one ever
doubted that the only law of succession applicable to
Hindoo Princes was the Hindoo law, the law of the land.

But the Governor-General says that the Subsidiary Treaty
is merely "personal," and that it contains "no mention of
heirs." The absence of the words " heirs and successors,"
becomes quite immaterial, and the notion of a personal or
life grant becomes quite inconceivable, in the presence of
the fact that this document is announced as " a Treaty of

---

* Wellesley's Despatches, vol. ii, p. 85, ante, p. 89.
† Mysore Papers, p. 72.

perpetual friendship and alliance," and contains a special formula implying perpetuity in the asseveration that all its provisions are to be binding " as long as the sun and moon shall endure."

But here Mr. Mangles comes to the rescue again.   He says :—

"I am aware, of course, that the Treaty contains the expression that, ' It shall be binding upon the contracting parties as long as the sun and moon shall endure,' but I need hardly tell any one well informed in regard to Oriental phraseology, that, strange as it may appear to us, these words certainly do not imply perpetuity to Indian minds."*

And then he quotes Sir Thomas Munro as to " the terms employed in such documents, or in Hindoo grants."   The documents to which Sir Thomas Munro alluded were not treaties, but grants of land or charges on the revenue ; and if Mr. Mangles were allowed to quote and to amplify a hundred arbitrary resumptions of estates and pensions by an Eastern despot, he would be no nearer a precedent for annulling a perpetual treaty of friendship and alliance. What does Mr. Mangles mean by talking about " Oriental phraseology", and " Indian minds", and " Hindoo grants " ? The phraseology in question did not emanate from an Indian mind ; nor does it occur in an Oriental document, or in a Hindoo grant, but in two British treaties, which were drafted in the English language, and every word of which was dictated by the Marquis Wellesley himself.   . .

There really must be a lurking conviction in the minds of the most eager votaries of territorial extension, that there is something inconveniently sacred in the nature and essence of a Treaty, when we observe their evident aversion to a simple and straightforward use of the word, their efforts to avoid it altogether, to substitute some less solemn term, or to overlay it with contemptuous qualifications, even, at the last pinch, with inverted commas.†   Thus Lord Dalhousie, when arguing for the annexation of Jhansi, pronounced the Treaty between " the two Governments", to be " a grant such as is issued by a Sovereign to a subject".‡   When the

* Mysore Papers, p. 84.
† As the Duke of Argyll does in his *India under Dalhousie and Canning*, (Longman, 1865,) reprinted with additions from the *Edinburgh Review*.
‡ *The Empire in India*, " Jhansi," p. 208.

appropriation of Sattara was under discussion, Mr. R. D.
Mangles, then one of the Directors of the East India Com-
pany, attempted to disguise the "Treaty of perpetual friend-
ship" made with the Rajah, "his heirs and successors", under
the insignificant term of an "agreement," and compared it
with the grant of a sinecure office or pension.*   And Mr.
Willoughby, then a Member of Council at Bombay, whose
Minute was mainly conducive to this first step in Lord
Dalhousie's annexing career, insisted on the Principality of
Sattara having been "gratuitously conferred" on the Rajah.†
In the same way when the question of the Nagpore succession was under consideration, Lord Dalhousie made a great
point by asserting (most inaccurately) that "the sovereignty
of Nagpore was bestowed as a gift" on the Rajah.

And Mr. R. D. Mangles, in his Minute against the claims
of the Rajah of Mysore, calls the Subsidiary Treaty of 1799
"a deed of gift".‡

It is strange that any man, having any pretension to be
a statesman, should consider it politic or dignified to depreciate the value of a British gift,—to indicate as distinctly
as is done in the several instances, that the gifts of Great
Britain confer an insecure and precarious title, and, even
when confirmed by treaties, are less valid and less permanent than the grants of Delhi or Poonah!   But, as I have
just shown, there is no gift, of any sort, in the Subsidiary
Treaty; and whatever was given to the Rajah in 1799 was
given by the joint cession of the East India Company and
the Nizam.

Mr. H. T. Prinsep, the only other Member of the majority
in Council who has followed the example of Mr. Mangles by
recording an argumentative Minute, has fallen into exactly
the same mistake as his colleague.   Mr. Mangles speaks of
the Subsidiary Treaty as "a deed of gift".   No form, or
term, or word signifying a gift occurs in any part of that
Treaty.   And Mr. Prinsep says :—"A separate Treaty was
made by the British Government with the Rajah of Mysore,
to which the Nizam was no party, assigning the territory
to him personally."§   Now in the Subsidiary Treaty between
the Rajah and the East India Company, to which the Nizam

* *The Empire in India*, "Jhansi," p. 172.   † Ibid., "Sattara," p. 1 9.
‡ Mysore Papers, 1866, p. 84.   § Mysore Papers, 1866, p. 88.

was not a party, nothing whatever is assigned to the Rajah, personally or otherwise. In that Treaty there is no cession or grant of territories, no assignment of districts, no definition of the frontiers and limits of the Mysore State ; but reference is therein made to the cession and assignment of territories as having been already effected and recorded in the Partition Treaty with the Nizam, and one of his Schedules.

And on this point we are able to quote the direct testimony of the Marquis Wellesley himself, who speaks of the "country *assigned* to the Rajah of Mysore by the Partition Treaty".[*]

Mr. Mangles, having raised a dust round the question of adoption by brushing away a fallacy which no one has ever advanced, and flourishing once more his own fictitious law and precedent, five years after its public and official renunciation by Lord Canning,[†] then proceeds to argue that the Subsidiary Treaty of 1799 was intentionally made with the omission of the words "his heirs and successors", and that it was Lord Wellesley's intention "to leave his successors free to act, if the expectations with which the British Government made the experiment should be disappointed, as the circumstances of the case might demand."[‡]

All that Mr. Mangles says as to Lord Wellesley's probable intentions, is the purest effort of imagination, and utterly at variance with all that statesman's recorded intentions. Mr. Mangles speaks of the reconstruction of the Mysore State "as an experiment",—an experiment to last as long as the sun and moon endure ! Lord Wellesley speaks of it as "a settlement", as a "restoration", and not as an experiment,—as "the restoration of the ancient *family* of Mysore", not as a personal and experimental installation. In accordance with this view, and at Lord Wellesley's dictation, the Rajah is designated in the Partition Treaty as "a descendant of the ancient Rajahs of Mysore". In the same way Lord William Bentinck, in his letter to the Rajah of the 7th September, 1831, thus describes what was done in 1799 :—" The sovereignty was restored to the *family* of

<hr>

* Wellesley's Despatches, vol. ii, p. 114.
† Lord Canning's Adoption Despatch of 30th April, and Sir Charles Wood's reply of 26th July, 1860, were both published in the *Calcutta Gazette*.
‡ Mysore Papers, p. 84.

the ancient Rajahs of the country, and your Highness was placed on the musnud." Not a trace of an experiment, or of a personal Treaty, is to be found in the Marquis Wellesley's papers, or in any official document before 1856, when Lord Dalhousie, in the full career of annexation, sounded the first note of menace against Mysore.

Mr. Mangles having failed to find a single word in the Marquis Wellesley's despatches, or in the records of that period, to strengthen his argument, endeavours to set up a case of antecedent improbability, or, as he puts it, impossibility, against anything more than an experiment having been intended, and immediately involves himself in a distinct contradiction of Lord Wellesley's avowed views. He says :—"The family of this child had long been deposed, and it had not the slightest claim upon the justice or generosity of the British Government."*

In the year 1799 the family had been deposed for exactly sixteen years ; and even after their deposition by Tippoo, the British Government in 1782 had concluded a treaty with Cham Raj, father of the present Rajah.

Lord Wellesley, writing to the Court of Directors on the 3rd August, 1799, refers to "the antiquity of their legitimate title", and observes that *moral* considerations and sentiments of *generosity*, favoured the restoration of the ancient family of Mysore".†

Contrast this with the assertion by Mr. Mangles that the family "had not the slightest claim upon the justice or generosity of the British Government".

And observe that Lord Wellesley in explaining his policy, never uses one expression that denotes what Mr. Mangles calls " ephemeral political expediency"‡; he even seems to avoid the use of terms implying a mere personal arrangement. He acknowledges the weight, without admitting the validity, of " the pretensions of the ancient house of the Rajahs of Mysore", and says that " no alternative remained, but to depose the dynasty which I found upon the throne" (Tippoo's) " or to confirm the Mahomedan usurpation, and with it the perpetual exclusion and degradation of the legitimate Hindoo Sovereigns of the country".§

* Mysore Papers, p 84.   † Ante, p. 9.   ‡ Mysore Papers, p. 86.
§ Wellesley's Despatches, vol. ii, p. 78.

Undoubtedly he determined to make the Rajah so "dependant" on the East India Company, that all his "interests and resources might be absolutely identified with our own, and the Kingdom of Mysore, so long the source of calamity and alarm to the Carnatic, might become a new barrier of our defence".*   But he describes the transaction as the "restoration of the ancient *family*"; as "*their* elevation"; and observes that "by our support alone could *they* ever hope to be maintained upon the throne against the family of Tippoo Sultan".†   He speaks of "the establishment of a Hindoo State", and of "a friendly and allied State in Mysore",‡ and declares it to be a "durable settlement". And in a letter to Colonel Malcolm, the Resident at Mysore, dated the 22nd October, 1803, Sir Arthur Wellesley wrote as follows :—"The pensions were thrown upon the Rajah as so many encumbrances upon the revenues of Mysore, which was evidently occasioned by the settlement of the Government *in his family*."§   In short, a perfectly fair summary of Lord Wellesley's views is given by Captain W. J. Eastwick, in paragraph 26 of his Minute :—

"Lord Wellesley re-established 'the Hindoo State' of Mysore, with definite political objects of high importance, irrespective of the person of the Maharajah. It was intended to make Mysore entirely subordinate as to foreign relations, and to preserve a command over its resources, but there is no condition in the Treaty, and no trace in the correspondence, of any intention to make it merely a personal treaty, or to provide for the lapse of the country to the British Government."‖

Mr. Mangles having so completely misinterpreted the Marquis Wellesley's declared motives and objects, we may well refuse to accept his conjectural version of that great statesman's secret intentions. He says that Lord Wellesley was not likely to do "important business with so much haste and carelessness as to allow the accidental omission of the words 'heirs and successors' to pass without notice", and that in fact "it is quite impossible to believe that such an omission was accidental or devoid of a significant meaning".¶   But Mr. Mangles, unable to preserve a consistent line of reasoning through two consecutive paragraphs, does

* Wellesley's Despatches, p. 82.   † Ibid.   ‡ Ibid., p. 99 and 100.
§ Supplementary Despatches of the Duke of Wellington, vol. iv, p. 205.
‖ Mysore Papers, p. 77.   ¶ Ibid., p. 84.

not perceive that Lord Wellesley, if incapable of overlooking a verbal omission in the Treaty, must have been even less capable of using the affirmative words, " to be binding as long as the sun and moon endure", without " a significant meaning".   And the introduction of these words in a document declared to be a Treaty of perpetual friendship and alliance, renders the omission of the words "heirs and successors" a quite insignificant circumstance. This is the obvious verdict of common sense, as it is the unanimous and undisputed dictum of the authorities on International Law.   Perpetual treaties are of course permanent and not personal.   A " State", a " Government", when mentioned in a perpetual Treaty, signifies a sovereignty ; and the contracting party to such a Treaty, who is said to have " dominions" and " subjects", is a Sovereign.   A sovereignty is always hereditary, and a Sovereign always has heirs and successors.

I am quite willing to accept the opinion offered by Mr. Mangles that "no statesman was less likely than Lord Wellesley to do important business with haste and carelessness"; and therefore I think that if he had intended to make " a deed of gift", by way of experiment, as Mr. Mangles most unwarrantably pretends, he would have made one, and not have made " a Treaty of perpetual friendship and alliance to be binding as long as the sun and moon endure".

In a later passage of his Minute Mr. Mangles says :—" It cannot surely be pretended that such a Treaty as that which Lord Wellesley dictated to the infant Rajah of Mysore ought to constrain us" to recognise his heir. What does Mr. Mangles mean by " *such* a Treaty" ?   He forces me to reiterate that it is a Treaty of perpetual friendship and alliance.   What does he mean by referring to the undoubted fact that it was " dictated" by Lord Wellesley ?*   Does he

* Lord Wellesley himself thus describes what took place :—" On the 8th June I had forwarded to the Commissioners the first draft of the Subsidiary Treaty, to be concluded between the Company and the Rajah of Mysore. After an ample discussion with the Commissioners, who had communicated the whole arrangement to the Brahmin Poorneah and conciliated his cooperation, and after the adoption of several alterations, this Treaty was executed in the fortress of Nuzzerbagh, near Seringapatam, by the Commissioners, and certain proxies on the part of the young Rajah, on the 8th of July, and ratified by me in Council on the 23rd of July, under the title of the Subsidiary Treaty of Seringapatam."—Wellesley's Despatches, vol. ii, p. 85.

suppose that this dictation makes it less binding ? I really believe he does, because I find the same idea expressed by the Duke of Argyll, who generally agrees with Mr. Mangles, and is indeed considerably indebted to that gentleman for the arguments in favour of annexation contained in his *India under Dalhousie and Canning*, reprinted (with additions) from the *Edinburgh Review*.*   The Duke, who approves of all Lord Dalhousie's acquisitions and of the processes by which they were effected, and disapproves of the Queen's Proclamation of 1858, expresses great contempt for what he calls " the system of ' Treaties', which expressed nothing but the will of a Superior imposing on his Vassal so much as for the time it was thought expedient to require" ;† and throughout his two dissertations, when referring to our engagements with the Native Princes of India, he invariably places the word " Treaty" or " Treaties" between inverted commas.   From his employing the expression " for the time", it may also be presumed that the Duke of Argyll cares as little for the word " perpetual" as Mr. Mangles.

When the Duke writes of a Superior imposing treaties " for the time" on his Vassals, he falls into the common but quite inexcusable error of regarding the transactions of half a century ago as if the comparative power and reciprocal serviceableness of the Native States and of the British Government had been the same then as they are now.   I believe his Grace very much underrates the actual power and influence for good or evil of the tributary and protected Princes at the present day ; but even he would admit, on due consideration, that both the absolute and the relative strength of our own Government has enormously increased since 1799.   At that time the faithful alliance and co-operation of the Nizam and other minor potentates were known to be of the highest importance to us, and were therefore much more assiduously cultivated than has of late been thought necessary.   But gradually altered circumstances—altered partly in consequence of their continued and faithful co-operation—cannot convert our Allies into Vassals, change a Treaty of perpetual friendship between

---

two contracting parties into a grant or deed of gift from a
Superior, or justify the subsequent addition of inverted
commas.   And I must remind the Duke of Argyll that
there were no inverted commas to the word "Treaties" in
the Royal Proclamation of 1858.

But passing over with a renewed protest the Duke's unwarrantable application of the words "for the time", to engagements which purport to be perpetual, it is surely very
remarkable that his Grace, Mr. Mangles, and the Governor-
General, Sir John Lawrence, should all, in their endeavours
to depreciate the binding force of Treaties, lay so much
stress on the fact, or alleged fact, of their having been "dictated" or "imposed" by the stronger upon the weaker party.
This seems to be very like arguing that the stronger party
who dictates terms is only bound to observe them "for
the time", or for so long as may be "thought expedient".
Because we were able to impose our own conditions, therefore we need not abide by them!   This is very strange
doctrine.   We have heard the validity and permanence of
a contract disputed on the ground of its having been ex-
torted or imposed by compulsion ;* but here we have that
principle reversed in favour of the stronger party, who, by
the right of having used compulsion once, is only bound to
observe the conditions of his own choice "for the time" or
until he chooses to employ or to threaten another dose of
compulsion.†

We now come to deal with the question of policy ; and
although Mr. Mangles seems to me to be equally unfair in
his array of facts and equally wrong in his conclusions, as
when he was arguing against the validity of Treaties, it is

---

* Some of our Oriental Treaties might be impugned or protested against on
that score ; and we ourselves recently, and with justice, repudiated the Treaty
with Bhootan, signed on compulsion by our Envoy, Mr. Ashley Eden.

† The hideous cynicism of the following passage from the *Friend of India*,
of the 25th of October 1860 has never perhaps been surpassed :—"Annexation
is in abeyance for the hour, and it is right that Government should forswear all
approach to it now.   But the destiny of British power is in time to sweep the
effete princelings who now rule Hyderabad, Gwalior, Indore, Guzerat, and
Travancore off the face of the Peninsula."   No Machiavellian precept has
ever surpassed this unscrupulous proposal, that we should "*forswear*" for the
present that policy which it is our destiny and our firm intention to accomplish " in time," or as soon as possible.   Forswear annexation : swear eternal
friendship ; swear to respect treaties "*for the hour,*" (the Duke of Argyll says
"*for the time,*)—the pear is not ripe !

impossible to avoid respecting the convictions formed by him, and by the Calcutta Secretariat under successive Viceroys, as to the insuperable difficulty of restoring the Rajah to the head of the executive Government after thirty years of British administration. I have no doubt whatever that all of them have, in the words of Mr. Mangles, "an anxious regard for the interests of the great body of the people."* I think they very much overrate the difficulty and danger of the gradual transmutation of Mysore governed as a Non-Regulation Province into Mysore governed as a Reformed Native State ; and I cannot but attribute these doubts and fears in a great measure to official and national prejudices and interests. But such doubts and fears most naturally arise, and deserve attentive consideration.

The Governor-General writes as follows to the Secretary of State in the Despatch of the 5th May, 1865 (paragraph 20) :—

"There is no instance in which an administration, presided over by an organised executive establishment of British officers, has ever been under the direct power and control of a native ruler. His Highness asserts that, if the administration of the country were restored to him, it is not for one instant his intention to make any change in the present system, which would remain as it is now, a native administration, superintended and controlled in its every branch by English officers. Were this practicable, it is not clear what advantage would be derived from such a transfer."†

The Governor-General in alluding to "the direct power and control," "the power and administration of the Maharajah," adheres to the erroneous assumption that has so long pervaded all the doctrine and practice of the Calcutta Government with regard to native States,—the assumption that a Prince must either be a despot or a puppet. Mr. Mangles again is profuse with contempt for such "mere puppets in the hands of the British Government," as the Rajahs of Sattara and Mysore, "held in leading-strings" even when they were in charge of their own administration.‡ Would it then be such a terrible disaster for India if all the Native Princes were "held in leading-strings," and could become "mere puppets in the hands of the British Government"? In my humble opinion that would be a consummation devoutly to be wished for, enabling the Imperial

---

* Mysore Papers, p. 87.   † Ibid., p. 59.   ‡ Ibid., p. 84.

Power to wield the immense influence of ancient and popular dynasties for purposes both of order and progress, to keep the peace without bayonets or cannon, and to improve the administration without superseding and degrading all the higher classes of the country. None of the annexationists seem capable of appreciating either the advantages of monarchy or the disadvantages of despotism. They never seem to have considered the utility or the possibility of a native Prince being controlled by a Code of laws, and limited in his expenditure to a Privy Purse, under the watchful superintendence—not necessarily obtrusive or offensive—of a British Resident. Such a Prince would not, according to them, be "a real Sovereign;" he would be merely "a pageant Prince, a puppet, held in leading strings." They cannot contemplate or tolerate a constitutional and limited monarch in India; they will admit no alternative between a native despot and a British Commissioner.

Setting aside, then, this unnecessary supposition of absolute power in the Sovereign, the Governor-General is not quite right in saying that "there is no instance in which an administration, presided over by an organised executive establishment of British officers," has existed in a Native State, without the Prince being displaced or deprived of all share in the Government. There was something very like it introduced into the Nizam's dominions, when Sir Charles Metcalfe was Resident at Hyderabad, as described in the following extract from a recent publication :—

" Sir Charles Metcalfe, in the course of a few months after his arrival, discovered the total disorganisation into which every department of the State, but more particularly the revenue, had fallen before his appointment. He applied a prompt and efficient remedy by placing European officers as Superintendents in the different districts, who were entrusted with the general supervision of the subordinate officers employed by the Minister. The Nizam's Government entered into the scheme with the greatest readiness and seeming conviction of its expediency. The great object in view was to effect a general settlement of the land revenue throughout the Nizam's territories, and to afford the cultivators and other classes protection against oppression or extortion on the part of the Government or its agents. For this purpose the country was divided into several districts, to each of which was assigned an European officer charged with the general supervision of the revenue assessments and police. The executive, however, was still vested in the subordinate officers of the native Government.

"This system during the experience of eight years produced the happiest results, and the country in general enjoyed an immunity from oppression, and a state of repose to which for centuries past it had been a stranger."*

And if, after the departure of that eminent man, the first opportunity was taken to discontinue this system of supervision and gradual improvement, it is but one instance of the utter indifference of the Calcutta officials to the internal and independent reforms of a Native Principality.

What the Rajah asked for was that the British official at the head of the administration of Mysore, should be called Resident instead of Commissioner, and should be, in fact, the Prime Minister of the country,†—not, as Mr. Bowring and the Secretary to Government at Calcutta choose to misunderstand, that a separate and additional officer should be appointed, with concurrent jurisdiction, certain to lead to complications and inconvenience.‡ The Resident, at the head of the administration of Mysore, would be very much in the same position, though more firmly seated and armed with greater power, as Sir Charles Metcalfe was when Resident at Hyderabad with his staff of English Superintendents. The Rajah, like the Nizam, would be recognised and respected as the reigning Sovereign.

But the Despatch inquires :—"Were this practicable, it is not clear what advantage would be derived from such a transfer." There would be two advantages, — first, the maintenance of British honour, which is inestimable, even as an element of conservative strength ;—and second, the maintenance of a reformed and tributary Native State, of more value to us, in a political and military and even in a financial point of view, than a Province held in our immediate possession, of double its extent and revenue. The advantages to the people of Mysore and of all India, of maintaining a reformed native Sovereignty among them, I consider to be incalculably great.

The Governor-General then proceeds as follows :—

"His Highness must be well aware that it is a practical im-

* *Our Faithful Ally, the Nizam,* by Capt. Hastings Fraser (Smith and Elder), 1865, p. 232.

<table>
<tr><td>† Ante, p. 76.</td><td>‡ Mysore Papers, p. 39 and 40.</td></tr>
</table>

possibility thus to transfer a body of British officers in civil
employment, and a considerable number of European planters,
and British-born subjects, and that the reversion of Mysore to
the power and administration of the Maharajah is synonymous
with the withdrawal of the European officers, and the abandonment of a system of upwards of thirty years' growth. It is
tantamount to the collapse of order, and a rapid return to the
state of confusion and of insecurity of life, honour, and property,
from which, in 1831, the people of Mysore were rescued."*

All this inflammatory declamation is so devoid of a substantial basis, and is in some points so opposed to facts
officially recorded, that it is difficult to acquit the writers
entirely of disingenuous exaggeration. They write, no
doubt, with the strongest belief that the Rajah's reinstatement would be impracticable and injurious; but it would
really seem as if, relying on their good intentions, they felt
themselves free from all responsibility for utterly unscrupulous rhetoric. Sir John Lawrence and his colleagues at
Calcutta must know very well that the Mysore rebellion of
1830 was declared by the Special Commissioners of Inquiry,
in their Report of 12th December, 1833, to have been
"partly attributable to causes which were beyond the control of the Rajah's administration," especially "to the withdrawal of the advice of the British Resident;" and that
both by the Commissioners of Inquiry and by Lord William
Bentinck, after his own strict local investigation, the Rajah
was almost entirely acquitted of personal misconduct. The
Calcutta officials must be well aware that Lord William
Bentinck and his two immediate successors, Sir Charles
Metcalfe and Lord Auckland, were quite ready and willing
to replace the Rajah at the head of his own Government.
The Rajah has pledged himself to maintain the laws and
plan of administration approved by the British Government;
and there is as little reason to doubt the Rajah's sincerity
in giving that pledge, as there is to doubt the ample means
and appliances at the disposal of the British Government
to watch over and secure its due and exact observance.
Well knowing, as the writers of this despatch do, the unre-
stricted power held by themselves to guide and control the
Rajah, and to preserve the existing system unaltered, if
thought necessary,—fully aware of the Rajah's willingness

* Mysore Papers, p. 59.

to accept the position of a constitutional Sovereign, with the Resident as his Minister, until such time as the Imperial Government should consider it safe and advisable to entrust more freedom of action to his Highness, or his successor, or to a native Minister,—it is quite inexcusable that they should profess to believe that the reinstatement of the Maharajah would be "synonymous with the withdrawal of the European officers, the abandonment of the present system, and the collapse of order."

The rhetoric of Mr. Mangles on this part of the question, as might be expected, is even more flagrantly unfair than that of the Calcutta Foreign Office.

"Let us assume," says he, "for the sake of argument, that the remonstrances of those who insist with so much earnestness that justice and the faith of treaties should constrain us to allow the Rajah to adopt a successor were permitted to prevail. There would then be two, and only two, courses open to us ; either the adopted son must be permitted to become *the actual ruler* of his country, to appoint his own officers, *and to administer justice and the revenue according to his own views and principles*, or affairs must be carried on, as at present, by a British Commissioner, assisted by a body of British officers, who would exercise all real power, and in whose hands the *nominal Rajah* would be the *merest puppet*."*

Let me draw attention to the words which I have placed in italics. The "actual ruler" is of course the inevitable despot, uncontrolled and unimprovable. The "nominal Rajah" and "merest puppet" is that contemptible character a constitutional Sovereign. Why must a Rajah placed at the head of a reformed government, "administer justice and the revenue according to his own views and principles"? Why should he not administer justice and the revenue according to *our* views and principles, as the Rajahs of Travancore and Kolapore—no thanks to the Calcutta Foreign Office, — have learned to do? If Mr. Mangles and Sir John Lawrence do not know perfectly well that all the advantages of the present administration of Mysore could be naturalised and perpetuated under a restored native Government, then they are grossly ignorant

<hr>

* Mysore Papers, p. 85.

of the happiest and most hopeful results of our political
operations in India, and blind to the administrative ability
—sufficient though not superabundant—which lies at their
disposal. If, instead of hunting after imaginary precedents
for ignoring adoptions, counting them before they have
caught them, and constructing out of them a fictitious law
of confiscation, they would turn their attention—for no
research is required—to the real precedents for reforming
Principalities, they would find that the "schemes, which
Mr. Mangles pretends have ended in "utter and hopeless
shipwreck,"* — the "experiments" which the Governor-
General declares must be "futile and pernicious,"† *have
never failed.*

It would be useless at this time to enter into any discussion as to the alleged ingratitude and plots of the Rajah
of Sattara, which Mr. Mangles rakes up for the occasion.‡

Suffice it to say that four of the Directors of the East
India Company, Messrs. H. St. George Tucker, Cotton,
Shepherd, and Forbes, recorded Minutes of dissent against
his deposition ; that Mr. Henry Shakespear, a Member of
the Supreme Council of India, considered that " no charge
of a serious nature had been substantiated against the
Rajah ;§ that one of the Directors, Mr. Forbes, declared his
belief that all that Prince's misfortunes were caused by a
Palace conspiracy, of which, in his words, we were "the
dupes" and he was "the victim ;"|| and that many other
competent judges at the time expressed opinions equally
decided in favour of the Rajah's cause. And there is at
least this presumptive proof of his innocence, that he
steadily rejected all compromise, and when a full amnesty
was offered him, resolved to sacrifice his throne, to abandon
his treasures, to relinquish his home, and to go into exile
with his family to a distant part of India, rather than subscribe certain articles which implied a confession of his
criminality. "Guilt," said Mr. Tucker, "would have found
it easy to accept the conditions proposed, in order to escape
from the threatened penalty. The consciousness of rectitude
must be strong when it impels a man to make a great sacrifice to a sense of honour, however mistaken."¶ And in this

<hr>

* Mysore Papers, p. 87.　　† Ibid., p. 59.　　‡ Ibid., p. 85, 86.
|| Sattara Papers, 1843, p. 1260.　§ Ibid., 1255.　¶ Ibid., p. 1258.

instance the sacrifice was tremendous, and was made with perfect deliberation and great dignity.

Mr. Mangles has used the supposed treachery of the Rajah of Sattara once before, with complete success, as a plea for the extinction of that State, at the death of the Ex-Rajah's brother. He may well be satisfied with that exploit, for he not only carried his point then, but he thereby fabricated the sole precedent for the annexations of Jhansi and Nagpore. I have but a few words to add on this subject. Mr. Mangles thinks that by maintaining a native Sovereign in Mysore we run the risk of future intrigues and doubtful allegiance. It may be so. Let us consider the guilt of the Rajah of Sattara to have been as clear as day. Then during his reign we had one disaffected and intriguing tributary. Is it equally certain that we had one less when the Principality was abolished? I believe, on the contrary, that by that unjust, useless, and unprofitable acquisition we created hundreds of enemies, and excited innumerable intrigues and conspiracies. Bad news travels apace, and travels afar. Sir John Low tells us that "the confidence of our native allies was a good deal shaken by the annexation of Sattara", and that it roused feelings of discontent and alarm throughout Malwa and Rajpootana, where he was at that time Agent to the Governor-General.[*] And Sir Frederick Currie, in his Dissent from the despatch of 1864, remarks: — "The decision in the Sattara case, whatever its merits may be, undoubtedly caused surprise and alarm throughout the length and breadth of India".[†]

Mr. Mangles, though from his position at the India Office he ought to know better, may still be under the same delusion as the Duke of Argyll, who as a Cabinet Minister might have had access to the best information, that "the infection of the mutiny never reached the Presidencies of Madras or of Bombay", and that "the entire armies of Bombay and of Madras escaped the plague".[‡] The Field Forces that were actively engaged for so many months in suppressing insurrection, not without much bloodshed, in

---

[*] Papers relating to the Rajah of Berar, 1854, p. 43.

[†] Mysore Papers, p. 46.

[‡] *India under Dalhousie and Canning* (Longman and Co.), 1865, p. 118 and 92.

the Rewa Kanta, in the Satpoora district, on the Goa fron-
tier, in Kolapore, Nargoond, Shorapore, Jumkhundee, and
Kopal, and other parts of the Mahratta country ; the mutinies of the 27th Bombay Native Infantry at Kolapore,
where some of their officers were murdered, of the 21st at
Kurrachee,* the partial misconduct of the 2nd and 3rd
Bombay Cavalry at Neemuch and Nusseerabad, and of the
Golundauz Artillery in Scinde ; the disaffection and plots
among the 10th and 11th Native Infantry and the Marine
Battalion, in the city of Bombay itself, when two sepoys
were blown from guns, and others transported ; the attempted
mutiny of the 2nd Grenadiers at Ahmedabad, for which
upwards of twenty men were executed ; the notorious conspiracies throughout the Deccan ; the sixteen executions
at Sattara, several at Belgaum, and twenty-six in Nagpore,† might suggest even to Mr. Mangles and the Duke of
Argyll some little doubt whether the disappearance of the
Rajahs of Sattara and Nagpore from the political scene of
India, did actually reduce the number or lessen the probability of hostile intrigues, or whether it did not rather add
to and augment their number and their incentives.

And, therefore, while Mr. Mangles adduces for the second
time in his career as an Indian statesman, the alleged plots
of the Rajah of Sattara, for the purpose of crying down
native dependencies, as if by abolishing the Mysore Raj we
should be relieved from at least one chance of princely
treachery, I shall retain the opinion, shared by many more
competent and more entitled to speak than myself, that if
that great injustice should really be perpetrated, those
chances would be infinitely multiplied, and that in exchange
for the one good friend whom we throw away, we should
engender a hundred enemies, and justify their enmity.

Mr. Mangles has been very dexterous,—I might say, am-

* Both of these regiments were disbanded, and their numbers struck out of
the Army List.

† In the Province of Nagpore, without counting those killed in open rebellion or summarily hanged by military authority, there were nine executions
in 1857 for high treason, and seventeen for mutiny. But amid the greater
dangers and horrors further north, these trifles were little noticed. And it is
very natural that those who did their best to promote the rapacious schemes
which mainly caused the revolt, should shut their eyes to those facts which
prove a general disaffection, and should speak of the great national movement
of 1857-8 as a mere mutiny of Bengal Sepoys.

bidextrous,—in the treatment of his two illustrations. He heightens the tints of both pictures, and then produces the highest effect by their alternate exhibition. At the same time he is very careful not to display the whole of either of them. Thus he draws away our attention to the alleged disloyalty of one of the Rajahs of Sattara, without alluding to his administration, because the State was always well governed. He dwells exclusively, and in exaggerated language, on the alleged misgovernment of Mysore, because the Rajah has always been conspicuously loyal.

The administration of the deposed Rajah of Sattara was declared by the Court of Directors to be "a model to all native rulers."* The country was equally well governed by his younger brother, who was not possessed of half his abilities and energy ; one instance among many that might be given,—though none ought to be required by a statesman imbued with constitutional principles,—that the good government of a well organised State is not entirely dependent on the talents and personal character of the monarch.

Sattara was well governed, because the administration was admirably constructed, and the Rajah carefully and judiciously instructed, by an excellent political officer, Captain Grant Duff,† whose name is still revered in the Mahratta country. Mysore was badly governed, because it was disgracefully neglected. In the year 1811 the Rajah, then sixteen years of age, having received merely an ordinary Hindoo education and utterly untrained in administrative affairs, was allowed to assume absolute power. In the year 1814, when the young Prince was nineteen years old, he was encouraged by the Government of Madras to resent and resist the advice of the British Resident. Sir Henry Montgomery writes as follows in his Dissent of the 13th July, 1863 :—
"The Maharajah is declared to have failed to have fulfilled the conditions of the Subsidiary Treaty by neglecting the advice of the British Government, though it is well known and officially on record, that not only was no advice rendered, but that it was systematically and purposely with-

* Sattara Papers, 1843, p. 1268.
† Author of the *History of the Mahrattas*, (Longman, 1826).

held." And Sir Frederic Currie says :—"The conditions of the 14th Article of the Treaty the British Government had themselves, it must be admitted, 'failed to fulfil,' when they systematically withheld from the Rajah the advice which, by that Article, they are bound to give him in the conduct of every detailed department of the administration."*

This is what the Calcutta officials call "patient yet remonstrant forbearance !"† Yet Mr. Mangles, knowing all this, does not scruple to say that "it could not reasonably be expected that the adopted son should enjoy such great advantages in the way of political education as the present Rajah turned to so miserable an account."‡ I should like to hear from Mr. Mangles what his idea of political education is, and what great advantages in that respect were, in his opinion, enjoyed by the Rajah of Mysore. The obvious truth is that the present Rajah received no political education at all ; while nothing but the continued neglect of our Government could prevent his heir and successor from receiving the best possible education, both in the ordinary branches of study and in political affairs.

Mr. Mangles, however, would probably explain that in referring to "great advantages in the way of political education," he alluded to "the tutelage of a native statesman of high character and great ability," Poorniah, "who was the wise and honest guardian of the Rajah's youth."§ But Mr. Mangles must know very well, or ought to know from the records before him, that Poorniah's tutelage consisted in removing from the young Prince's reach all means of improving his mind and of becoming acquainted with public business, and encouraging him in every sort of frivolous pursuit. Poorniah's great project, in which he tried very hard to obtain the countenance of the British authorities, was to throw his Master completely into the background, and to gain for himself and his family the position of hereditary Premier.||

* Mysore Papers, p. 21-22. † Ibid., p. 59.
‡ Ibid., p. 85. § Ibid.
|| Ante, p. 14. This is referred to in the Rajah's letter (Mysore Papers, p. 63), but Mr. Mangles can see the detailed account in the Resident's reports of the time.

And Mr. Mangles must know very well that the Special Committee of Inquiry, in their Report of 12th December, 1833, include in their censure the period of Poorniah's administration, and that the "oppression and extortion," of which the Rajah is accused, was simply the continuance of Poorniah's overstrained assessment.*

Having thus made the most effective use in his power, of the alleged disloyalty in the one instance, and of the alleged misrule in the other, Mr. Mangles then inquires, " what there is in the result of these two deliberate experiments,"—those of Mysore and Sattara,—" to encourage us to convert the real Government which now exists in Mysore, as administered exclusively by British officers, into a second sham Principality, by allowing the Rajah of Mysore to adopt a successor ?"†

Before I proceed further in my answer to that question, let me ask one, viz., What is there in the result of the deliberate experiment of annexing Sattara, to encourage us to repeat it in Mysore ? Have we gained that increase of revenue that was promised ? Have we gained the military advantages that were contemplated ?‡ Have we gained

---

* Mysore Papers, p. 64, ante, p. 25, 26.   † Ibid , p. 85.

‡ General Sir John Littler, the gallant soldier who was a member of the Supreme Council in 1848, at once perceived the absurdity of the military plea for annexation. Lord Dalhousie having urged that Sattara lay " in the very heart of our own possessions," and was " interposed between the two principal military stations in the Presidency of Bombay" (Sattara Papers, 1849, p. 83), Sir John Littler remarked as follows in his Minute :—" Should it be ultimately decided that the adopted son of the late Rajah shall succeed to the sovereignty of the Sattara territory, as suggested by Sir George Clerk, I am not aware that any practical inconvenience would result, in a military point of view, from its being situated between two of our divisions. As a general rule, however, the absorption of small independent Principalities, which happen to be surrounded by our territories, will not always in my opinion tend to augment our power : on the contrary, it appears to me that such a policy would be apt to weaken it (except in special cases), by extending the British possessions beyond the limits to which our supervision could be safely and effectually afforded." (Sattara Papers, 1849, p. 86.) Yet when he was arguing for the annexation of Nagpore, Lord Dalhousie again began to urge the great advantage it would be " to absorb a separate military power," and " to combine our military strength." (Rajah of Berar Papers, 1854, p. 35, 36.) We required no European Regiment at Nagpore before the annexation ; there is one there now besides Artillery. There was not a single British soldier in the Kingdom of Oude from 1846 to 1856, when it was annexed, including the period of our Sutlej and Punjaub wars, when every man was urgently required. We have now in the Province of Oude one Regiment of Dragoons, seven batteries of Artillery, and four Battalions of Foot. And this is the way we consolidate our military strength !

the love and cheerful allegiance of the people and of the
Mahratta Chieftains?   Let Mr. Mangles turn to the records
in the India Office and answer my first question, as to the
financial gains ; I can find a full answer to the others
in those bloody events of 1857, to which I have just referred.

But why does Mr. Mangles term the existing administration of Mysore "a real government"?   It appears to me
that the British Commissioner is quite as much " in leading
strings," which Mr. Mangles seems to think such a degrading
and ridiculous position, as the Rajah of Travancore is, and
as I should wish the Rajah of Mysore to be.   Why does
not Mr. Mangles either insist on despotic powers being conferred on Mr. Bowring, or deride him as a mere puppet,
" devoid of political volition" ?*

I am very far from admitting that the Rajah of Mysore
ever was, or even that he is now devoid of political volition.
However closely a Hindoo Prince may be held in leading
strings,—whether his constitutional adviser be a Resident,
a Dewan, or a Council of State,—he will always retain that
political volition and influence which no British Commissioner can ever acquire.

Without going as far back as the eventful period between
1819 and 1825, when the Rajah, then in very loose leading
strings, received the warmest acknowledgments of his
"zealous and efficient assistance" from the Marquis of
Hastings,—which having been repeated in an autograph
despatch to the Court of Directors, can certainly not be
treated as a mere conventional compliment,† we can find
sufficient proof in the Blue-Book before us that the "political volition " of the Rajah of Mysore, now really reduced
to the position of a "pageant Prince," was of essential service to our Government during the terrible crisis of 1857.
In reply to the Governor-General's Circular, dated 26th
February, 1858, requiring a report on the conduct of parties
during the mutiny, Sir Mark Cubbon reported, that "the
Brahminical caste (very powerful), even those in the actual
employ of Government, were discontented and hostile ; the
heads of religious institutions, the great Sowcars, the petty

---

* Mysore Papers, p. 86.   † Ibid., p. 34.

Poligars and heads of villages, who subside with reluctance
into their proper and ancient position of the wealthiest and
most influential ryots of their respective neighbourhoods,
are all against our rule, and disaffected towards the British
Government." The Commissioner added : "In watching
over such a community, there had been a constant call for
information, and much had been obtained, proving beyond
doubt the existence among the classes above named, of a
spirit exceedingly hostile to the British Government; evinced
in carrying on correspondence with the malcontents in the
North, in the favourable reception of emissaries of mischief
from that quarter ; and in the convening of treasonable
meetings at their own houses, for the purpose of plotting
the subversion of our power."   At this time, said Sir Mark
Cubbon, in his letter to the Governor-General, dated 2nd
June, 1860, "to no one was the Government more indebted
for the preservation of tranquillity than to his Highness the
Rajah, who displayed the most steadfast loyalty throughout
the crisis ; discountenancing everything in the shape of
disaffection, and taking every opportunity to proclaim his
perfect confidence in the stability of the English rule."
And Sir Mark Cubbon declares that the Rajah's influence
and the display of his friendly offices, " produced great
moral effects throughout the country.   In fact, there was
nothing in his power which he did not do to manifest his
fidelity to the British Government, and to discourage the
unfriendly."*

Perhaps I can hardly expect to bring sudden conviction
to the minds of Mr. Mangles and the Duke of Argyll ; but
I hope our leading statesmen, both Liberal and Conservative,
will not remain blind, until it is too late, to the vast machinery of moral power, fitted to our hands and subject to
our guidance, which the professional administrators of Calcutta are still sedulously bent on destroying.   By twenty
years of determined hostility to native States, these worse
than Red Republicans, these Red Tape Republicans have
gained promotion and swelled their patronage, but they
have drained the military strength of the Empire almost to
exhaustion, and have left us little else to rely on in India.
Indeed, they seem every day more and more inclined to

* Mysore Papers, p. 33, ante, p. 47.

trust to nothing but material force. How much longer will British Statesmen permit their hands to be tied in Europe and their faces blackened in Asia, by the officials of Calcutta and the retired officials of the India Office ? Can they not think for themselves ? Conservatives might be supposed to set some value on monarchical institutions ; and Liberals ought to feel some compunction at the continued and extended degradation of an intelligent and docile people.

There is no reason that Mysore should become more of "a sham Principality" than it is at present ; there is no necessity for any such degeneration. I hope for better things. Without recommending any hasty measures of change, and well understanding the prudence of very cautious alterations, both during the present Rajah's lifetime and during the minority of his successor, I can see no necessity for Mysore being for ever "administered exclusively by British officers."

Mr. Bowring, the present Commissioner of Mysore, has evinced an enlightened and disinterested desire to do equal justice to all his subordinate officials, without regard to race and creed, and with a sole view to the public good, by promoting—and I believe he is the only Provincial Lieutenant in India who has ventured on such a bold step,—a Brahmin gentleman, a native of Mysore, to the charge of a District, and by what he probably has found still more difficult, maintaining him in that position for two years.* I doubt very much whether this Brahmin gentleman is the only native servant of Government in Mysore or in India, who is fit for so high or even for a higher position. And if the reigning Rajah or his successor were again permitted to take a share in the executive government of the country, it is probable that the gradual introduction of well-qualified and educated natives into posts which have been hitherto exclusively reserved for English officers, might, by the Prince's influence and in deference to his natural prepossessions, be considerably accelerated. And this is the greatest reason of all why I wish to see the native monarchy

---

* My attention was first drawn to this incident by seeing the appointment in the *Calcutta Gazette* of 3rd September, 1864 ; and I have lately ascertained that no change has taken place, though Mr. Bowring has been often importuned to remove the native in favour of an English officer.

substantially and not colourably restored. This is my greatest reason for deprecating any attempt to settle this question by a measure, however liberal, of compromise and compensation. I earnestly wish to save British honour in the face of the Princes and people of India,—I certainly do not underrate the urgency of that consideration,—but above all I want to extend our means of usefulness. It is only by employing a native dynasty as our medium that we can arrive at the most satisfactory and durable result of our struggles and labours,—a reformed native State, organised on British principles, and never released from Imperial supervision, but governed and administered entirely by its own Prince and its own Statesmen and officials. The reformed institutions that are only to be found in our own immediate possessions, under the management of English officers, are superficial and precarious, and even while they seem to work smoothly, are maintained by a disproportionate waste of life and power on our side, and at a cruel cost of humiliation and political proscription to the most advanced and most improvable classes of the native community.

The most powerful arguments against renewed annexations seem to me to spring from the impossibility that all the varying interests and requirements of an immense continent, with nearly two hundred millions of inhabitants, speaking upwards of twenty distinct languages, can be adequately watched and tended by a centralised Government of salaried officials such as now attempts to rule all India by correspondence from Calcutta. Such a Government cannot continue for an indefinite period to command respect and obedience, or to be satisfactory and improving to the people in its action. The happiness and progress of nations do not depend on forms. The best institutions are not permanently safe unless they are under the custody of men who understand them, who have a personal interest in their security, and who are bound to the soil by the ties of blood and property. The system of governing India, in every district and in every detail, by Englishmen, is open to these fatal objections, that it lowers the moral influence of the Paramount Power, that it deprives of political privileges those among the natives who, with a little help and guidance, are fit to use them, while it does not educate for political life those who are as yet unfit. And the perpetual continuance and extension of such a system can only be plausibly justified on those grounds of utter contempt for the races to be governed which consign them to perfect stagnation, or incite them to privy conspiracy.

A more hopeful and a more progressive policy will never be devised amidst the antipathies and antagonism and vested interests of Calcutta. It must originate here, and it is high time to make a beginning. Let us begin by abstaining from the unjust extinction of a reformed native State.

For it is not merely with a view to the Statics of the Empire, not merely as a guardian and guarantee of order, that we should maintain a Rajah of Mysore on the throne. We require him much more as an agent in the Dynamics of government, with a view to progress. The people will follow their leaders. We can never become popular leaders ourselves, but we can easily control, manage and direct those who are the natural leaders of the people, and who are perfectly amenable to British instruction.

And let me once more call attention to the fact that British instruction *has never failed*. It was eminently successful in Sattara, so much so that, while arguing against the recognition of the second Rajah's adopted son, Lord Dalhousie admitted "the excellence" of the deceased Prince's "administration", declaring it to have been "conspicuous for wisdom and mildness",* and only expressing a doubt whether this was not attributable rather to "the personal qualities" of the Rajah than to "the nature of the institutions of the State." But, as we have just remarked, the State was equally well governed by the elder brother; and the greater part of the credit which on this occasion Lord Dalhousie was pleased to ascribe to a Hindoo Prince, was clearly due to Captain Grant Duff's instructions, and to the institutions which he established.

Sir Charles Metcalfe's reforms, carried out by English Superintendents, succeeded in Hyderabad ;* but unfortunately on the very first application of the young Nizam, Nasir-ood-Dowla, who came to the throne in 1829, the

---

* Sattara Papers, 1849, p. 82.

system of supervision was entirely discontinued, and the beneficial results of eight years' labour, prematurely checked, were almost thrown away.

In Nagpore, during the minority of the last Rajah, from 1818 to 1829, the efforts of Sir Richard Jenkins were most successful in introducing a regular plan of administration ; and although many defects and abuses subsequently sprang up, owing to the neglect and total want of settled principles, which characterised our diplomatic relations with that State,† the good effects of British instruction were so far permanent, that during twenty-five years of purely native government, our active and open interference was never once required, to check oppression, to keep the peace, or to restore order.

The State of Travancore, now so noted for its prosperity and good government, was in the year 1808 in a much worse plight than Mysore was in 1831. There were no doubtful intrigues, as alleged against Sattara ; there was no question of fiscal extortion, paralleled and even exceeded in British districts, as alleged against Mysore,—but there was open war against the Paramount Power, and utter disorganisation throughout the country. The Subsidy due to the Honourable Company had fallen into a long arrear ; the Rajah, under the influence of an ambitious Minister, defied the injunctions of the Madras Government to reduce the number of his troops ; the Resident's house was attacked, and an attempt made to murder him. One of the chief officers of the Court, the Minister's brother, treacherously induced a party of English soldiers to come on shore from a ship for refreshment, and had them all put to death. For several months the Rajah's troops resisted in the field the military measures that were adopted for his coercion. When the Travancore army was dispersed, the Minister committed suicide ; his brother was taken prisoner and publicly executed ; and the Rajah was reduced to submission. The disorders consequent on this insurrection were so difficult of repression, and a spirit of disaffection became so manifest throughout the country, that in 1809, under Article V of the Treaty of

---

* Ante, p. 218.
† See the opinions expressed by Mr. Mansel, the last Resident at Mysore, ante, p. 143.

1805 (identical with Article IV of the Subsidiary Treaty with the Rajah of Mysore,) the management of Travancore was assumed by the British Government. For five years full authority was exercised by Colonel John Munro, the Resident, as Dewan or Minister; and in 1814 on the accession of a young Rajah, the administration of the State was transferred to a native Dewan, extricated from its embarrassments, and in a condition of great prosperity.* The good effects of this period of British instruction have never been lost; the supervision of the Madras Government has never been withdrawn; and although neither the local administration nor the exercise of the Resident's influence has been uniformly irreproachable, on the whole the progress of Travancore has been steady and satisfactory. The Maharajah and the heir apparent,† his brother, Prince Rama Vurmah, both of them accomplished English scholars, are distinguished for their exemplary conduct, and their enlightened attention to public affairs and scientific pursuits. The Brahmin Minister of Travancore, Madava Rao, is a graduate of the Madras University. In special recognition of his merits as a ruler, the Rajah has lately received an augmentation of his titles and honours, and has been invested with the Star of India; while his able Minister has been deservedly admitted to the Companionship of the same Exalted Order.

The Mahratta Principalities of Kolapore and Sawunt Warree, within the frontiers of the Bombay Presidency, were placed under the control of English officers,—the former in 1845, the latter in 1838,—in both instances after a period of rebellion and disorder of a very formidable character, directly hostile to British power, and in the suppression of which large military forces were engaged for many months, and much blood was shed. And in both instances certain members of the Prince's family were implicated in conspiracies against our Government. Sawunt Warree is still retained under British management; but the Chief has received a *sunnud* from the Viceroy, assuring

---

* Thornton's *Gazetteer of India* (compiled by authority of the Court of Directors), article " Travancore."

† According to the law of succession in the Travancore family, the Rajah's brother has the first right of succession, and then the sister's son.

him that the adoption of a successor will be recognised in his family, should direct male issue fail.   And in the mean time the Rajah's eldest son, who, scarcely emerged from boyhood, was engaged in the rebellion of 1844, and had taken refuge in the Portuguese settlement of Goa, has been restored to his forfeited birthright.   This is a generous policy, by which we shall sooner or later gain more than the revenue of this little Raj is worth ten times told.   But how strange a contrast it offers to the treatment of the Rajah of Mysore, upon whose fidelity or that of his family and adherents, no suspicion has ever been cast ; during whose reign upwards of fifteen millions sterling have been paid as tribute ; whose troops have constantly cooperated with ours on active service ; who has been repeatedly thanked by several Viceroys, by the Secretary of State and by the Queen herself, for his friendly influence on our behalf and the ready and useful assistance rendered in time of need.

After having been entirely administered under British control for seventeen years, the State of Kolapore was restored to the rule of its Hindoo Sovereign in the year 1862. The results of this transfer may be estimated from the following extract of a speech made by Sir Bartle Frere, the present Governor of Bombay,* at a public Durbar held at Belgaum on the 28th November, 1865 : —

" I had lately the pleasure of congratulating his Highness the Rajah of Kolapoor on having shown himself, after a long probation, worthy to resume the direct administration of his territories, which in the time of his predecessor and previous to his own coming of age, had, as you all know, so often been a prey to every form of misgovernment and confusion.   I found his Highness not only himself able to converse in English with English gentlemen on most topics of public and private interest, but carefully training up, under his own eye, and in his own palace, a class of young Chiefs, the sons of all the principal officers of his State, who will have the means of obtaining as good an English education as his Highness himself received under the pa-

---

* He was Resident at Sattara in 1848, and remonstrated against the annexation as much as was possible to an officer in that position. See Sattara Papers, 1849.

ternal care of the Political Agents who have been Regents of his State, from Colonel Douglas Graham and Mr. Anderson to Mr. Havelock. I found every department of the State well superintended by his Highness in person, and every visible mark of justice being duly administered, and of the people being well governed, prosperous, and contented."

Surely this reform is deeper, this progress is more permanent, than anything that could have been effected if the Kolapore State had been appropriated, and had become a Collectorate of the Bombay Presidency, But it must be remembered that in the case of Travancore the policy of reformation and restoration was designed and carried out from Madras, in the other two cases from Bombay, not from Calcutta ; and in all three instances the good work was initiated before Lord Dalhousie's arrival in India.

Without adducing any more facts and illustrations, I think I may now claim to have made out my assertion that instead of any of our " experiments" having ended, as Mr. Mangles declares, in "utter and hopeless shipwreck," they *have never failed.* Wherever British instruction has been allowed a fair trial, it has invariably succeeded. It has never been allowed a fair trial in Hyderabad ; it was relaxed too soon and too suddenly at Nagpore ; it was never tried at all in Oude. In Mysore, after that disastrous and discreditable period of neglect and indifference, which the Governor-General terms " remonstrant forbearance," we interfered and introduced a regular and orderly administration; but thenceforward we unfortunately drifted into the opposite extreme from negligence. We have carried out certain reforms most effectually : but we have signalised our management by the complete and persistent exclusion of the Rajah from all share in the government ; costly and superfluous establishments, entailing numerous lucrative offices for English gentlemen, have been imposed upon the country ; and young Englishmen without any peculiar qualifications have been placed even in minor positions, the duties of which could be fulfilled in a much more efficient manner by natives, with the great advantage of their improvement in knowledge, in self-respect, and in attachment to British supremacy and Western institutions.

These errors were not committed in Travancore and Kolapore : those Principalities were not overrun with expensive establishments, out of all proportion with the requirements of the time and people ; nor were appointments for young English gentlemen multiplied, to the detriment and degradation of native talent.   The good work was done there,—as all our more celebrated tasks of pacification and organisation in India have been done,—by one or two able and experienced English officers in each State, with the aid of some special native agency, and the existing local authorities, so far as they were amenable to improvement.   The large and growing revenue, affording so solid a basis for increased expenditure, may partly account for the progress of patronage in Mysore ; but in the early stage of British management there was good cause for the introduction of a few more English officers than was at first contemplated, in the prejudices and passive obstruction of the older native officials whom we found installed in the districts.   But nothing of the sort is now to be feared ; no counteraction could possibly take place from any quarter ; a large body of public servants have been trained in our system ; and well qualified natives, educated in our schools and Universities, are available for employment.   There is nothing now to prevent our Government from gradually restoring a native administration in Mysore.   Mr. Bowring, the present Commissioner, as already noticed,* has shown us how easy it is to make a beginning ; and if definite instructions and orders on the subject were given, and the work of reconstruction were entered upon in good faith and with a good will, it could be thoroughly completed in a very few years. The first and most essential step in the restorative process would be the public reinstatement of the Rajah at the head of his own Government, with a British Resident as his Minister.

So long as a considerable number of English officers were still engaged in the administration, it might fairly be considered advisable to maintain a provisional restraint over the executive action of the reigning Sovereign, unaccustomed as he must be to the forms and procedure of a limited monarchy.

* Ante, p. 230.

But I can see no reason why the young Prince, his adopted
son, after receiving for fifteen or sixteen years those advantages of English education and political training, which—
pace Mr. Mangles—*not* his father, but the Rajahs of Travancore and Kolapore, enjoyed, should not be admitted to
the same freedom of action as those Princes, and, with the
assistance of a native Minister, perform all the functions of
a constitutional Sovereign.

There is still one somewhat plausible argument, advanced
both in the despatches from Calcutta and in the Minute by
Mr. Mangles, which must not be passed over without a reply.
The Governor-General in that passage of the Despatch of
the 5th May, 1865, which we last quoted (ante, p. 220), declares it to be "a practical impossibility" to transfer "a considerable number of European planters" to a native Government.   And Mr. Mangles expands the same objection in the
following terms :—

"In another very important respect, the adopted son of the
Rajah would find himself beset with difficulties which did not
embarrass his predecessor, and with which, I apprehend, that no
native ruler, even with the best abilities and intentions, could
successfully cope. *Mysore is now full of European settlers, coffee
planters and others, and every day is adding to their numbers.* If
English magistrates find it no easy task to hold the balance even,
and to keep the peace between the planters and ryots of Bengal,
we might well expect that Mysore would be thrown into a state
little short of civil war and anarchy, if native officials had to deal
with differences carried on, probably with the same heat and pertinacity between the same classes with equally conflicting interests
in that Principality."*

Now the term "a considerable number," is somewhat
vague : I hardly think that a community of *five or six and
thirty individuals* in a population of about four millions,
ought to be called "a considerable number."   But perhaps
this is a specimen of what they call at Calcutta "conventional phraseology which can mislead no one."†

But Mr. Mangles employs no relative term, no vague expression, no conventional phraseology.   He boldly declares
that "Mysore is now *full of European settlers*, coffee-planters

---

* Mysore Papers, p. 85. The italics are mine.
† "Such phraseology was conventional and misled no one, and least of all
the Nizam." Ante, p. 100, Mysore Papers, p. 55.

and others, and every day is adding to their numbers." As Mr. Mangles has immediate access to the best information on this subject, it is difficult to account for his having given utterance to this extravagant statement; and leaving him to explain the origin of his error, if he thinks it worth the trouble, I shall endeavour to show how the case really stands.

My figures are open to correction; but from the concurrent testimony of several gentlemen who have recently resided in Mysore, I have no doubt that the number of European planters in that State does not amount to forty, and is probably about five or six and thirty.* And the information that I have received is fully borne out by what can be gathered from the Administration Report of Mysore for 1862-63, the latest in my possession. Indeed, from the data there given, it seems doubtful whether the number of European planters can much exceed thirty. In paragraph 219 of the Report (p. 51), the number of acres held by Europeans is stated at 22,650, with the addition of 1,800 acres from the latest returns, making a total of 24,450. And in the next paragraph the average area of holdings is given as 933 acres for each European, one of them, Mr. Middleton, being said to occupy an estate of sixteen square miles. If, therefore, we divide the number of acres, 24,450, by the average area of each estate, we obtain the quotient 26; which I believe will give a greater approximation to the truth than can be derived from the Calcutta despatch or the Minute of Mr. Mangles. And without some better evidence than the conventional phraseology of the one, and the bold assertions of the other, I am not prepared to believe that there are more than between thirty and forty European planters residing in the Mysore territories. I

---

* It is not worth while disputing about words; and this is not the occasion for entering fully on the question; but there are in fact no European "*settlers*" in Mysore or in India. The planters of coffee, tea, indigo, sugar, cotton and other valuable produce, are for the most part agents, or servants of mercantile houses at the Presidency Towns. Some, of course, are engaged on their own account and with their own capital; and in Mysore there are a few retired officers. But none of them have any intention of *settling* in India; none of them have any abiding place or permanent stake in the country; all are bent on making a fortune and going home as soon as possible. I know of one exception, and I have heard of another, but these are extraordinary phenomena; and who can answer for their sons? India can never become a Colony.

should not be surprised to hear that the number is very much less.

By his wild statement that Mysore is "full of European settlers," Mr. Mangles not only gives a very erroneous notion of their number, but an equally erroneous notion of their location. Instead of being distributed over the country, as one would suppose from the phrase that "Mysore is full of European settlers," the planters are to be found only in two small corners, in the South-West of the Ashtagram Province contiguous to the Coorg Hills, and in the Baba Booden Hills, in the North-West of the Nuggur Province, bordering on the Western Ghauts. If there were really any practical difficulty from the presence of thirty or forty European planters in a Native State, these small districts adjoining our frontiers, could easily be ceded by the Rajah, either with a corresponding deduction from the Subsidy, or in exchange for British territory.* For these hilly regions alone are suitable for coffee cultivation, which can never be extended beyond them, and their area is very limited.

Mr. Mangles having told us that Mysore is "full of European settlers", adds that "every day is adding to their numbers". If every day, or even every week added *one* to their numbers, the European planters of Mysore would long ere this have formed an important body. But notwithstanding the authority of Mr. Mangles,—and in his position he ought to know,—I am doubtful of a very rapid or continuous increase in their numbers. The Administration Report of 1862-63 (para. 220) tells us that at that time "the best land in most places had been taken up". We are also told that although the larger holdings are in the possession of Europeans, "the vast majority of grants are held by natives" ; whose aggregate estates more than double those in European hands. And the latest returns from the Ashtagram Province referred to in paragraph 219 of the Report, show that 85 per

* Some small interchanges of territory were effected by Treaty in 1804. One very convenient and obvious exchange would be that of transferring Seringapatam, (the administration of which has long been left to the Government of Mysore at an annual *rent*,) to the Rajah. The political and military advantages which were in 1799 supposed to be derived from its possession, are now quite insignificant, if not imaginary. Besides we have the right under the Treaty of occupying at our discretion any fort or position in the Rajah's dominions.

cent. of the recent increase was in native holdings. From the latest information I am inclined to believe that the number of European planters is rather on the decrease. I have been told that the great success of the early planters consisted in their obtaining large grants on very favourable conditions, stocking them with coffee-trees, and disposing of their estates on terms which are not to be obtained now, when the actual profits are more clearly ascertained, and have, indeed, become, by the rise of wages in the Hills* and other circumstances, more equalised with those of ordinary agricultural enterprise—and thus it would appear that new grants of land are chiefly made to natives, content, as they are, with a more moderate rate of profits. The Commissioner informs us, in paragraph 222 of the Administration Report for 1862-63, that the provisions of these grants and their assessment have been several times relaxed for the relief of the coffee-planters ; and that the tax levied at present, "although popular with Natives from its indirect incidence", is found to be "a heavy burden", and "is objected to by the European planters".

I believe that Mr. Bowring quite sums up the results and the future prospects of Mysore coffee-planting in paragraph 224 of the Report, in which he says that the English planters "have acted as pioneers in a new country,—a part of the country formerly considered as the least promising,—their undertaking has been shown to be successful, and the Natives of all classes are now awake to the value of land, and anxious for its possession." The original pioneers have reaped a well-deserved reward, and most of them have retired from the scene of their success ; but I question very much whether the English coffee-planters in Mysore,—though no doubt some are doing well,—form on the whole so prosperous and so contented a community at present, as to render any further increase in their number at all probable.

Perhaps Mr. Mangles, after having satisfied himself that Mysore is not yet quite full of English planters, that their number does not amount to forty among four millions, and that their numbers are not increasing "every day", might

* In Paragraph 224 of the Administration Report the rise of wages is mentioned.

be induced to modify his views as to the insurmountable objections to their residence in a Native State. He may refer at his leisure to some other facts of a reassuring tendency. Travancore is a long way from Calcutta, and possibly even the Governor General and his Secretaries may not be aware that in the Hills of that Native State there are numerous coffee-plantations belonging to English gentlemen. The Dewan, in the Administration Report for the year 1864-65, states that about 24,312 acres have already been appropriated, — about one third of the area under coffee cultivation in Mysore,—and he remarks, (paragraphs 102 and 103, page 22, 23)—

"This enterprise promises to be the means of giving employment to many subjects of Travancore."

"It is gratifying to state that the advantages held out to the labourer by this new field of industry are, so far as the experience hitherto acquired extends, quite unalloyed. All the planters are gentlemen sincerely solicitous to deal fairly with their labourers, and to rely upon good treatment and good wages alone for attracting labour."

He does not seem to anticipate that the introduction of British capital and enterprise into the Principality will produce anything like that "civil war and anarchy", which Mr. Mangles dreads ; nor have I heard that the Resident at Travancore has expressed any apprehension of that sort. And yet in Travancore the "differences" and "conflicting interests", between the planters and the ryots, which Mr. Mangles looks upon as quite irreconcileable without our own elaborate forms, must be settled by "native officials" exclusively, for there are no others. If the views expressed by Mr. Mangles were accepted by our Government, they would be bound, as soon as Travancore became "full of European settlers"—*i. e.*, when they reached the number of thirty-five, —to watch eagerly, out of a regard for this new interest, for the first opportunity to annex Travancore. And if the doctrine of Mr. Mangles and Mr. Prinsep as to "a personal Treaty", were worth anything, we should not have long to wait. The demise of the reigning Rajah would serve our turn ; for the Treaty of 1805, identical in almost every respect with the Subsidiary Treaty of 1799 with the Rajah of Mysore, is identical with it in having no mention of "heirs and successors."   It is a Treaty between the East India Company and the Maharajah Ram Rajah Bahadoor, and is declared in the Preamble to be concluded by that Rajah "for himself."*   It is true that it is to last "as long as the sun and moon endure", but Mr. Mangles tells us that is an insignificant form.   It is true that a succession has taken place since it was concluded, but Mr. Prinsep assures us that is of no consequence.†

Not only are disputes between these planters and cultivating occupants settled by the native authorities in Travancore, but even in Mysore, under the existing administration, nearly all the differences between the planters and the ryots are actually disposed of by native officials, whose duties, it is true, are carried on subject to an appeal, and to the revision of English Superintendents.   But this supervision and protection of the planters' interest, would equally exist if a native government under the Rajah were restored in Mysore.   Mr. Mangles knows perfectly well, and so do the Civilians at Calcutta, that English planters and British born persons in a Native State are never made subject to the local magistrature in criminal matters, and only to a certain limited extent to the local civil jurisdiction ; but that under special capitulations with the Native Princes, of which one was concluded with the Nizam in 1861,‡ the Resident is constituted the judge in crimes and disputes arising among Europeans and descendants of Europeans.

Many experienced persons, both among the planters and the English official class, are of opinion that the interests and enterprise of a few scattered individuals of the dominant race can be much more effectually fostered, and their peculiar relations with the labouring occupants more fairly regulated, by a machinery like our Consular system in the East, than by that ostensible equality before the law which, as Mr. Mangles seems more than half to understand, has failed and still fails grievously to secure even-handed justice and good order in our own long settled province of Bengal.

One thing is very certain, that the idea of a European

---

* *Collection of Treaties*, Calcutta, 1864 (Longman and Co.), vol. v, p. 311.

† Mysore Papers, p. 90.

‡ *Collection of Treaties*, Calcutta, 1864 (Longman & Co., London), vol. v, p. 117.   This concession was, I believe, made by the Nizam, chiefly on account of the Railway passing through his dominions.

planter or merchant being oppressed or persecuted by a native official, or even a Native Prince, or by a British Resident, is so utterly preposterous and incredible, that it will never meet with anything but ridicule from persons acquainted with life and manners in India. The independent and non-official Englishman belongs to a very visible and a very audible class. Even the Thugs never ventured to operate on a European.

It is clear, therefore, that either by the transfer of two small hilly districts to the British Government, or by about three dozen European planters being left subject to the judicial control of the same English official, under another designation, to whom they are ·now subject, the "practical impossibility", denounced by the Calcutta Government, would disappear. For it must be remembered that legally Mysore is still a foreign State, that British law cannot be administered there,* and that the Commissioner is the supreme authority over the English planters, as the Resident would be if the Rajah were reinstated.

Although I consider the question of right to have been adequately treated by me before I turned to that of policy, some remarks by Mr. Mangles towards the close of his Minute, compel me once more to revert to it. The Calcutta officials did not fail to perceive the obstruction offered by Lord Canning's Adoption Despatch, but they endeavour to remove it in the following fashion :—

" Nor, it is plain, can the Maharajah have any claim under the general right of adoption guaranteed by Lord Canning to Hindoo Chiefs governing their own territories. · For thirty years the Maharajah had ceased to govern; and while, in accordance with the expressed intention of Lord Canning's Despatch that the assurance should be conveyed to each Chief individually, a sunnud guaranteeing the right to adopt was granted to every Chief governing a State 'no matter how small,' a sunnud was advisedly withheld from the Maharajah of Mysore."†

But even granting what is quite inadmissible, that it could be legal or equitable in certain cases to exclude Princes who were not then governing their own territories,

---

* All these inconveniences, and even the difficulties arising from British process not running in a foreign State, could easily be remedied, partly by British legislation and partly by treaty with the native Princes.

† Mysore Papers, p. 48.

it would, in the instance of the Rajah of Mysore, be taking advantage of our own wrong, to exclude him.   For the strongest points of his appeal are that we were too hasty and sweeping in assuming the management of his country; and that we have retained the management in our hands long after the declared object has been attained, and far beyond what was contemplated by the Treaty.

There is no principle or consistency of purpose visible in the exclusion of the Rajah of Mysore; and it is impossible to believe that Lord Canning purposely, and with a hostile intention, gave him no written notice that his adoption would be recognised, when we observe that such a written notice was sent to the Rajahs of Kolapore* and Sawunt Warree, neither of whom, as already observed, were then " governing their own territories."

As to Lord Canning having " advisedly" withheld a sunnud from the Rajah, the Governor-General and his Secretaries know perfectly well that Lord Canning did so, not from any doubt of the Rajah's right to adopt, but because he was labouring under the erroneous impression that the Rajah did not wish to adopt, and that therefore it would be equally impolitic and inconsiderate to encourage or urge

---

* Since the first part of these pages was printed, the news has arrived of the sudden death of the Rajah Sivajee of Kolapore on the 4th August.   It is thus noticed in the *Times* of India :—" The announcement of the death of the Rajah of Kolapoor in the prime of life, and in the midst of many plans of usefulness for the well-being and advancement of his people, has been received with unfeigned regret by all classes in Western India, and many in England also will share in this regret.   The Rajah was a representative of the younger branch of the House of Sivajee, the founder of the late Mahratta dynasty, whose name he bore, and was looked up to in the Deccan as the head of the Mahratta chiefs and nobility.   He succeeded to the Kolapoor Principality in 1838 when quite a child, and a Council of Regency was formed to administer the country during his minority.   The members of this Regency quarrelled among themselves, and by their misgovernment compelled the British Government to interfere.   This was followed by an insurrection in 1844-5, which was put down at considerable expense to the State.   On the restoration of order the British Government assumed the entire administration of the country and placed it under the control of a political officer, to whom the care and education of the young Rajah was specially entrusted.   During the mutinies the Rajah behaved with conspicuous fidelity, while his half-brother Chimna Sahib (now a state prisoner at Kurrachee) threw all his influence into the opposite scale.   The loyal example of the Rajah, and his acknowledged fitness to rule, induced Her Majesty's Government, in 1862, to invest him with the management of his Principality.   The Rajah's administration since this period has afforded many proofs of his being one of the most enlightened among the native Princes of Western India."

him to take that step.*   Sir John Willoughby states as
follows in one of his Minutes :—"By a comparison of dates,
it seems to me clear that Lord Canning had no idea of excluding the Rajah from the benefits of his adoption policy
by resorting to such a quibble as that the Rajah is not
'governing his own territory'."†

On this point, however, Mr. Mangles says :—

"The name of the Rajah of Mysore is not found in those lists,
and no sunnud was addressed to him. Can it be believed that
these were accidental omissions, and that Lord Canning, if he
had not forgotten for the time the existence of such a person,
would have treated the Rajah on the same footing as the hereditary Princes of Rajpootana, or of what were formerly called
'the protected Sikh States'? I cannot give credit to such an
hypothesis, and, therefore, I must believe that Lord Canning intentionally omitted the name of the Rajah of Mysore from the
list of those to whom 'the assurance' of his Government was to
be conveyed, because he was satisfied, as I am satisfied, that,
under the circumstances of his case, he had no just or reasonable
claim to the privilege in question."‡

But if Mr. Mangles is not aware of the fact, some of his
colleagues, and the two last Secretaries of State, are well
aware that Lord Canning, though anxious to obtain Mysore
by bequest from the Rajah (which in itself is a full admission
of his Sovereignty), has left in writing the most distinct
avowal that the Rajah's right of adopting a successor could
not be disputed.

Mr. Prinsep, like Mr. Mangles, has "no doubt whatever"
that the omission of the words "heirs and successors" in
the Subsidiary Treaty was intentional on the part of the
Marquis Wellesley. I have already shown that this omission could not have been intentional, and that in "a perpetual Treaty to be binding as long as the sun and moon
endure", such an omission is quite insignificant.§   But Mr.
Prinsep endeavours to prove Lord Wellesley's intention by
adducing another case in which he supposes that statesman
to have excluded the words "heirs and successors" from a
Treaty, in order to convert it into a merely personal grant.
And here he has only afforded one more instance of those
misquotations of public documents and misstatements of

* Ante, p. 115.   † Mysore Papers, 1866, p. 31.
‡ Ibid., p. 86.   § Ante, p. 213.

officially recorded facts, without which it seems impossible to make even a semblance of assailing the Rajah's rights. He says :—" In the case of Arcot, this Governor-General specifically erased the words 'heirs and successors' from the Treaty with that Prince when it was sent up to him for approval and ratification."*

Mr. Prinsep, a Member of the Council of India, with all the records at hand, is entirely wrong. ;The Governor-General did *not* " specifically erase" the words " heirs and successors" from the Treaty as sent up to be ratified ; and he did not do so for the simple reason that those words were not in the Treaty. All that Lord Wellesley did was to have the word " established" substituted for the word " acknowledged." The passage in the original edition of the Treaty to which Lord Wellesley objected, had no reference to the future descent of the Nawab's dignity, but to his accession to the throne by " the hereditary right of his father, the Nawab Ameer-ool-Omrah Bahadoor." Instead of this right being " *acknowledged* by the East India Company", the new Preamble, drafted by Lord Wellesley, announced that the Nawab had been " established by the East India Company in the rank, property and possessions of his ancestors, heretofore Nabobs of the Carnatic."

Lord Wellesley attached so little importance to the alteration, that he expressly cautioned Lord Clive that it should not be proposed to Azeem-ood-Dowlah " *at the hazard of exciting any alarm or jealousy in his Highness's mind*", or of incurring his " *dissent or displeasure*."† And in the meantime, anticipating the possibility of Azeem-ood-Dowlah's objections, Lord Wellesley ratified the original Treaty. But the modified Preamble was accepted by the Nawab without discussion.

There was no necessity for inserting the words " heirs and successors" in the Carnatic Treaty of 1801, because its second Article expressly " renewed and confirmed" all the former Treaties, which contained ample guaranties of hereditary succession. And the alteration suggested and carried out by Lord Wellesley was not aimed at hereditary succession, but against the inherent and independent right and power of the Nawab to succeed to the throne, at a

* Mysore Papers, p. 90.   † Carnatic Papers, 1861, p. 109, 110.

political crisis, without British sanction and support. I am fully convinced that Lord Wellesley had no more notion of making a personal Treaty with the Nawab of Arcot than with the Rajah of Mysore. But having pointed out that Mr. Prinsep's citation of the Carnatic case is completely erroneous and unfounded, consisting in fact of a misquotation, I am relieved from any call to notice it further.

I may mention, however, that Mr. Mangles also refers to the Carnatic case as "a precedent."* I can only say that it is fully as worthy of being a precedent as the case of Sattara.

Before finally concluding my task I must ask Mr. Mangles whether he can, on serious reflection, reconcile it with his notions of public duty to have failed so flagrantly in accuracy and precision of statement and reference, throughout his Minute of Consultation, as I have proved him to have done. He was selected for the honourable position of a Councillor to her Majesty's Government in a special department, from trust in his professional experience, and his long familiarity with bygone transactions recorded in the voluminous chronicles of the India Office, with which no Secretary of State can become immediately conversant. If the Minister can place no reliance on statements of fact and quotations of public documents laid before him by his confidential advisers, the Council will be a snare to him rather than an assistance. He had much better trust to humbler aid. No clerk, no *précis* writer, no Under-Secretary would venture to mislead the head of his Office as Mr. Mangles has done, and would certainly not be allowed to do so twice. For the worst derelictions with which I have charged Mr. Mangles are not to be palliated by a plea of carelessness or inadvertence. The best sources of information, the best means of verification lay within his reach, and the specific assertions of which I complain, can be found nowhere at the India Office, except in his own Minute.

And in my humble opinion it is just because Mr. Mangles is not open to reproof and correction as a subordinate official, but is invested with the sacred and judicial character of a Councillor, and associated as a colleague with

---

* Mysore Papers, p. 84 (*note*). I have discussed the Carnatic case in *The Empire in India.*

the Secretary of State, that he should be held to a stricter account by the Government and by the country. Although not a subordinate official, he is now a salaried public servant. In his former capacity as a Director of the East India Company, he was not exactly a servant of the public, owing merely a nominal responsibility to his constituents in the Court of Proprietors. And in the House of Commons, a few occasional loose assertions and rash contradictions may be excused, in a man of a certain temperament, from considerations of the heat of debate, the urgency of immediate reply, and the absence of the records required. If Mr. Mangles, as Member for Guildford, had assured the House of Commons that " Mysore was now full of European settlers, and that every day was adding to their numbers", the enormity even of this exaggeration might have been passed over or pardoned, as a sudden flight of rhetoric called forth in the excitement of a party struggle, or in defending the credit of the Court of Directors. But what might be tolerated and forgiven in a speech, is quite inadmissible and inexcusable in a consultative Minute, penned in cold blood, in the calm retirement of a room at the India Office, with access to every piece of information connected with the subject, and every opinion that has ever been passed upon it.

Notwithstanding the good intentions for which Mr. Mangles may receive full credit, it must not be forgotten that he is committed beyond retreat to a policy of unrelenting annexation, by his active participation in all the territorial acquisitions of the last twenty years, from Sattara to Oude. He could not spare Mysore without condemning all his previous utterances and exertions. In truth Mr. Mangles has always manifested, and manifests most signally in this particular case, that unjudicial frame of mind which seems the peculiar growth of those Calcutta bureaux to which his Indian experience was confined. From extensive research among the Minutes and Despatches of Indian Governors and Councillors in the leading political cases of the last twenty years, I have been struck with the general prevalence of the same unjudicial method. Instead of starting with a straightforward determination to settle the points of right and wrong, with few exceptions each Councillor has evidently begun by deciding what arrangement will be the most advantageous for all parties, with especial regard to the supposed interests of his own Government, and has then set to work to concoct ingenious and elaborate pretexts for carrying out the desired arrangement. There is no actual insincerity, no disingenuous perversion of the truth, but an unmistakeable subordination of judgment, logic and law to the political and social results that are expected and desired, and a dexterous adaptation of the premisses to meet the required conclusion. And when I see plain evidence both of national prejudice and professional bias, I neither question nor value benevolent motives.

I have pointed out some errors of fact into which Mr. Prinsep has fallen. Himself an old Bengal Civilian, he betrays in his Minute the characteristic want of personal and class sympathy for those who are to be despoiled and degraded, and an utter contempt for the feelings and wishes of the people of Mysore. And moreover it would hardly be consistent with human nature if Mr. Prinsep were entirely free from a very strong though probably unconscious bias against the Rajah. Mr. H. T. Prinsep, as Foreign Secretary, signed all the despatches in 1831, by which the suspension of his Highness's authority was explained and carried out. Even the severe letter from Lord William Bentinck to the Rajah, of September 7th, 1831, announcing that he was about to assume the management of Mysore,—that letter which contains at least two erroneous charges against the Rajah, first, that *the Subsidy had not been paid monthly according to the Treaty,** and second, that "*the greatest excesses were committed and unparalleled cruelties inflicted by his Highness's officers,*"†—was issued from his office, and according to the ordinary routine must have been drafted by himself. Of course these charges were brought against the Rajah, probably in stronger terms, in all the despatches home. In his Minute of the 1st August 1865, Mr. Prinsep does not repeat these accusations, but he does not withdraw them. When the Report of the Special Commissioners of Inquiry, dated the 12th December, 1833, which dispelled

---

* The Subsidy was proved not only never to have been a month in arrear, but to have been paid in advance (Mysore Papers, p. 64).

† Ante, p. 25, 27, and 194. The letter will be found entire in Appendix C.

several of the imputations cast upon the Rajah's rule and personal conduct, and opened Lord William Bentinck's eyes to the wrong that had been committed, was submitted to the Government of India, Mr. Prinsep was no longer Foreign Secretary, but had been replaced by Mr. (afterwards Sir W. H.) Macnaghten, who was always favourable to the Rajah's reinstatement.

In conclusion I would say, if the Rajah is ever to be reinstated, it should not be done as a half measure, but with a definite purpose and policy. The object should not be that of pleasing, consoling, and flattering an aged Prince, and smoothing the transition of Mysore into an ordinary British Province. The ultimate object, even though postponed till the young Prince's majority, should be that of preserving the Principality, and maintaining the Treaties of 1799 inviolate. No measure of compensation and compromise, however liberal, will save the honour of Great Britain, relieve the alarmed and outraged feelings of the Princes of India, or secure to the Imperial Power the full advantages of a reformed Native State. We do not want the Rajah of Mysore as a pageant, or as a nobleman, or as a pensioner, but as a tributary and protected Sovereign, ruling his own territories according to our views and principles, acting for us as a Conservative agent, as the symbol of law and allegiance.

The policy and practice of the rulers of India have been necessarily modified by circumstances. The experiment even of unrelenting appropriations was perhaps inevitable for a time; nor do I think it was carried too far, until we began absorbing friendly and faithful dependencies,—until, as Sir George Clerk says, "the Calcutta Government led off with the bare-faced appropriation of Sattara".* We need not condemn or deplore the exploits of our predecessors. It was necessary to restore order; it was necessary to produce submission. The rule, the very idea of law—unmixed with religious and ceremonial sanctions and exemptions,—was introduced, and could only have been established by the hands of our countrymen. But the perpetual degradation of our docile pupils cannot be essential to British supremacy. Slavery, or polygamy, or the feudal system may have been

* Mysore Papers, p. 72.

necessary to human progress in a certain age and region, and may therefore have been justifiable ; but it does not follow that these historical conditions are either necessary or justifiable now.

We want the Native Princes of India much more than they want us. We cannot get near the people without the good will of their natural leaders. We want them both for the discipline and the education of that vast population. Mr. Gladstone eloquently observed in his speech of the 12th March last :—" When we are told that affairs are managed more economically, more cleverly, and effectually in foreign countries, we answer, 'Yes, but here they are managed freely ; and in freedom, in the free discharge of political duties, there is an immense power both of discipline and of education for the people'." The nearest approach to political freedom that the people of India can make in their present phase of civilisation, must be made by means of reformed Native States, owning allegiance and subordination to the Imperial Power. The British Government of India should not attempt to be ubiquitously executive ; it should be constructive and critical, not operative ; it should everywhere contrive and control the organisation, but wherever native agency is available, it should not undertake more than the superintendence of functions.

Even if natives administer judicial and financial affairs worse than English officers,—which I do not admit,—Native Princes, when once put in the right way, can govern much more effectually and economically for themselves as well as for us, than English Commissioners. And even if we are not at present prepared to increase the number or the area of our reformed Native dependencies, let us not, at an immense sacrifice of honour and moral influence, strike out of our system the most prosperous and to us the most profitable of them all, by reverting to an abandoned policy, and reasserting a usurped and disclaimed prerogative.

APPENDIX.

(A.)

THE ADOPTION DESPATCH.

Foreign Department,
Simla, 30th April 1860 (No. 43a).

Sir,

In accordance with the intention expressed in my Despatch No. 16, of the 6th of December last, I desire to bring to the notice of Her Majesty's Government the general subject of adoption as affecting the succession to the Native States and Principalities of India.

2. I have, in the course of my recent march to Upper India, been forcibly struck by the want of some clear and well understood rule of practice in our dealings with the Princes and Chiefs upon this subject.

It is not that the measures taken under the orders of the late Court of Directors, in dealing with doubtful or lapsed successions, have not in many instances been liberal and even generous, and certainly there is, at the present moment, an indisposition on the part of the Native States to doubt the general good-will towards them of the Paramount Power. But there appears to be a haze of doubt and mistrust in the mind of each Chief as to the policy which the Government will apply to his own State in the event of his leaving no natural heir to his throne, and each seems to feel, not without reason, that in such case the ultimate fate of his country is uncertain.

3. It is to this alone that I can attribute the extraordinary satisfaction with which my assurance to Scindia that the Government would see with pleasure his adoption of a successor if lineal heirs should fail, and that it was the desire of the Paramount Power that his House should be perpetuated and flourish, was accepted by those attached to his Court, to the extent that at Gwalior the news was received with rejoicings very like that which would have marked the birth of an heir. For there is not a State in India which has had stronger or more practical proofs of the wish of the British Government that its integrity should

be maintained than Gwalior, from the time when, in 1826-27, the then Maharajah was, in his last illness, perseveringly pressed by Lord Amherst to adopt an heir, and was assured that nothing could be further from the wish and intention of the Government than to exercise then or thereafter any intervention in the internal administration of his country or to pretend to control the succession to his State, down to 1843, when the present Maharajah, then a child, was placed upon his throne and confirmed in the possession of it by Lord Ellenborough in person.

4. To the same cause I ascribe the manifest pleasure of the Maharajah of Rewah, when a like assurance was given to him. He said to me that his family had been in Rewah for eleven hundred years, and that my words had dispelled an ill-wind that had long been blowing upon him. A son had lately been born to him, but if any Prince might reasonably expect his adoption of a successor to be respected, without a special promise to that effect, it would be one who is bound to us by treaty, and who can show an unusually long and uninterrupted descent from an ancient Rajpoot stock, which for centuries has steadily held its own against all intrusion, whether by Mahomedans, Mahrattas and Pindaries, as is the case with the Maharajah of Rewah.

5. I could adduce other instances, such as those of the Maharajah of Cashmere, the Maharajah of Puttiala, and the Chiefs of the Cis-Sutlej country, in which the value attached to the announcement, and the eagerness to have it solemnly recorded, were strongly marked.

6. I believe that the chief cause of this feeling is the vagueness that has prevailed in our policy respecting adoptions. That policy has not only been incoherent, but even when an adoption has been admitted there has often been long discussion in India, and references to the Home Government, before a final decision has been taken, thereby giving rise to doubts of our real desire to admit it.

7. But it is not only through what has passed between the Government of India and Native Courts that our hesitation and uncertainty have been made manifest to the latter. Within the last ten or twelve years the discussions between the Government of India and the Home Government, and the keen conflict of opinion between the individuals of experience and of the highest authority in India and in England, upon this question of adoption, have been laid bare to all who have chosen to examine them. Since 1849, the official correspondence on not less than sixteen or seventeen cases of doubtful succession and of adoption have been printed by orders of Parliament. In these papers there is every variety of opinion as to the claims of Native States on the one hand, and as to the duty, rights, and policy of the British Government on the other.

And it must not be supposed that because these documents are published in Blue Books and in English they are beyond the knowledge of Native Courts. They are, on the contrary, sought for and studied by those whose dearest prospects they so closely affect. It is not many months since I was informed, by the Governor General's Agent in Central India, that a native Court had received from England the Parliamentary Papers on Dhar before they had reached my own hand.

Papers relative to the Rajah of Sattara, printed by order of the House of Commons, March 1st, 1849.

Papers respecting the succession and adoption of Sovereign Princes in India, printed by order of the House of Commons, February 15th, 1850.

Papers on the annexation of Jhansie, printed by order of the House of Commons, July 27th, 1855.

Papers on the annexation of Kerowlee, printed by order of the House of Commons, August 3rd, 1855.

8. A brief examination of the papers named in the margin will show how irreconcileably at variance with each other are the views which the highest authorities have taken of a subject which lies at the very root of the future existence of Native States.

9. There is disagreement even on the first fundamental point of all,—our own duty.

See Minute of Lord Dalhousie on Sattara, August 30th, 1848, paras. 25 to 30, and on Kerowlee, August 30th, 1852, para. 7.

Minute of Mr. Lowis on Kerowlee, September 2nd, 1852.

Minute of Mr. Willoughby on Sattara, May 14th, 1848.

In one place, it is urged that we are bound not to neglect rightful opportunities of acquiring territory or revenue by refusing to permit adoption in independent States, where there has been a total failure of all heirs; and that we should take these opportunities of consolidating our territories and of getting rid of petty intervening Principalities.

See Minute of Sir J. Littler on Sattara, September 5th, 1848.

Dissent of Mr. Shepherd on Sattara, January 6th, 1849.

Dissent of Mr. Tucker on Sattara, January 3rd, 1849.

In another place, and by other authority, it is contended that the absorption of small independent Principalities, which happen to be surrounded by our own territories, will not always augment our power, but will be a source of weakness to ourselves, without being a benefit to the people.

10. Neither is there agreement on the subject of our own rights. On this head there arise, as might be expected, many complications from differences of origin, of race, and of tradition amongst the various Native States. Some are designated "independent," as having maintained their existence under successive paramount dynasties, and having suffered comparatively little interference in their internal affairs from any. Such are the Rajpootana States, some of the Bundelcund States, and

others. Some are called "dependent," as having been created or re-established by the Moguls, or the Peishwa, or ourselves, and as having been invested, in some instances, with authority short of sovereign authority. Such were Sattara, Jhansi, Jaloun. Then there are disputed points arising out of race and usages; whether, in a Rajpoot State, the widow of a Rajah may adopt a son without having received her husband's permission. To what extent, in a Rajpoot State, the voice of the principal officers of the State is necessary to the recognition of the succession. Whether, in a Bundeela State, the Chief may adopt a stranger, to the exclusion of collaterals. Whether, in Hindoo States generally, the senior widow of a Chief is allowed to adopt unreservedly, or is limited to a choice within certain degrees of affinity. These are points of nicety which, probably, it would be impossible to rule absolutely and with satisfaction to all, but putting aside for the present all small complications, remain broad and important questions of right on our part, upon which the very highest of our officers are at issue.

See Minute of Lord Dalhousie on Sattara, paras. 8, 9, and 30.

Minute of Mr. Willoughby on Sattara, para. 10.

11. In one paper, it is maintained to be beyond doubt that a Prince's adoption of any individual does not constitute the latter heir to the Principality, or to sovereign rights, until the adoption has received the sanction of the Sovereign Power; and that this sanction may be withheld even from independent States.

See Minute of Lord Metcalfe, October 20th, 1837.

Minute of Lord Auckland on Oorcha, January 2nd, 1842, para. 4.

Elsewhere, it is confidently laid down that Hindoo Sovereign Princes, on failure of heirs male of the body, have a right to adopt to the exclusion of collateral heirs, and that the British Government is bound to acknowledge the adoption, provided that it be regular and not in violation of Hindoo law; and further, that even in the case of a fief or dependency, a legal adoption cannot be barred by the Government or Lord Paramount.

See Minute of Sir George Clerk on Sattara, April 12th, 1848, paras. 11, 12.

12. It is impossible that the minds of native rulers and of their people should not be disquieted so long as such a question as this, bearing as it does upon every class of State, independent and dependent, is allowed to remain in doubt; for the doubt has been only partially resolved by the decisions of the Court of Directors on the cases at issue. The Court "were fully satisfied that by the general law and custom of India a dependent Principality, like that of Sattara, cannot pass to an adopted

See Despatch from the Court of Directors to the Government of India, January 24th, 1849.

heir without the consent of the Paramount Power." But this decision extends only to dependent Principalities, and not even to these unreservedly, for all dependent Principalities are not like that of Sattara, which was created, or resuscitated, by the British Government, upon conditions framed by that Government, and of which that Government might, perhaps, be assumed to be the rightful interpreter.

See Despatch from the Court of Directors to the Government of India on Kerowlee, January 26th, 1853.

In another place, the Court of Directors draw a marked distinction between the case of Sattara, a State of recent origin and of our own creation, and that of Kerowlee, an old Rajpoot State, which had existed long anterior to our rule in India. But there is no admission that, even in such a case as that of Kerowlee, we are bound to recognise an adoption. It is rather implied that the question is one of expediency, and that, even in that case, there might have been grounds for taking the opportunity to substitute our own Government for that of a native ruler.

13. Another point upon which strong difference of opinion will be found in the papers referred to, and which has a most important bearing upon the claims of many Native States, is the meaning of the words "heirs and successors" in the several treaties and grants in which we find them used.

The instances in which the Government of India has bound itself by engagements or concessions to a Chief and his "heirs and successors," or to his heirs for ever, without explanation of what is to constitute the right of succession or inheritance, are very numerous. The question arises whether the expression is to be interpreted according to our own sense, which would limit it to heirs and successors by blood, or to be extended to heirs and successors by adoption, when the adoption has taken place in accordance with Hindoo law and with the custom of the other party to the engagement.

14. This question has never, so far as I know, received an authoritative answer; perhaps the decision of the Court of Directors on the case of Sattara may be regarded as having determined it against the admission of an adopted heir and successor where a dependent Chiefship is concerned; but this is not clear, for other considerations were mixed up in that case.

It is a question which is sure to recur. There are several of the Hill States, the possession of which was confirmed to their respective Chiefs by special grants after the Ghoorka War of 1814, and in dealing with which a decision upon it may any day be called for, owing to the terms in which the grants are couched.

15. Whilst there has been so much doubt as to the duty and rights of our Government in India, there has not been less as to its policy.

16. Probably that view of our policy which would prescribe

the retention in our hands of the power to disallow adoption, and thereby to secure to ourselves an accession of territory, could not be expressed in terms more moderate or less calculated to alarm Native States than those used by Lord Auckland, when, in reference to the Colaba succession, he declared that we ought to "persevere in the one clear and direct course of abandoning no just or honourable accession of territory or revenue, while all existing claims of right are at the same time scrupulously respected."

But this declaration contains nothing reassuring or clear to those who will be most affected by it. It has been shown that the opinions of the very highest authorities in India and in England, of those in fact with whom alone the decision of such matters rested, have differed widely as to what accessions of territory would be just, and as to what claims of right do exist, and do deserve our respect. .

17. Nor does it appear possible to lay down these points with certainty by any declaration, however detailed and elaborate.

We profess, indeed, to be guided by the Hindoo law, and by the practice of those who have preceded us as rulers in India; but as to what that practice has been we are not agreed amongst ourselves. If, indeed, we never referred to it but for the purpose of avoiding carefully all new encroachments upon the liberties of Native States, and with the determination that our authority in questions of succession should be exercised with at least as much forbearance as was shown by the Mahomedans and Mahrattas, a little uncertainty would be immaterial. We would easily make sure of erring only on the right side. But it has even been appealed to in support of a pretension to withhold our assent to adoption, even in the case of independent States, thereby making the State a lapse to the British Government; and yet we have not shown, so far as I can find, a single instance in which adoption by a Sovereign Prince has been invalidated by a refusal of assent from the Paramount Power.

18. I venture to think that no such instance can be adduced, and that the practice which has prevailed is truly described by Sir Henry Lawrence, where he says:—"The confirmation of the Suzerain is necessary in all cases. He is the arbitrator of all contested adoptions; he can set aside one or other for informality, irregularity, or for misconduct; but it does not appear, by the rules or practices of any of the sovereignties, or by our own practice with the Istumrardars of Ajmere, that the Paramount State can refuse confirmation to one or other claimant, and confiscate the estate, however small."

See letter from Sir H. Lawrence on Kerowlee, November 17, 1853.

I am aware that Sir H. Lawrence, who, when this was written, was the Agent of the Governor-General in Rajpootana, speaks only of that part of India; but although the strong brotherhood of the Rajpoot States, their geographical position, and other circumstances caused their relations with the Emperors of Delhi to be more clearly defined, and less subject to capricious change than those with other feudatory States, I believe that there is no example of any Hindoo State, whether in Rajpootana or elsewhere, lapsing to the Paramout Power, by reason of that Power withholding its assent to an adoption.

19. It has been argued that the right to grant sanction implies the right to withhold it. This, however sound logically, is neither sound nor safe practically. The histories of feudal Governments furnish abundant examples of long-established privileges habitually renewed as acts of grace from the Paramount Powers, but which those powers have never thought of refusing for purposes of their own, or upon their own judgment alone.

See Minutes of Mr. Reid and Lord Falkland on Sattara, April 25th and July 28th, 1848.

20. Then as regards our other rule of guidance, the Hindoo law, it has been said, by one who is well competent to speak on the subject, that "it is hunting after a shadow to search for laws of inheritance to Chiefships in India so fixed as the Government desires to obtain."

See letter of Sir George Clerk on the Chiefship of Bughaut, November 10th, 1842.

* * * * * *

"The Hindoo law, which is comprehensive regarding rights to private property, does not provide distinctly for Chiefships. It is not fair, therefore, to desire a claimant to support his pretensions by adduced fixed laws." And in the same letter it is observed, in reference to certain views of the right of succession amongst the Hill Chiefs, "that it is the inconsistency, caprice, and mutability of our opinions regarding all great principles that is the bane of our supremacy in India." I fear that as regards the matter now under consideration, this is too true.

21. And now I would beg Her Majesty's Government to consider whether the time has not come when we may, with advantage to all, adopt and announce some rule in regard to succession in Native States, more distinct than that which we have been seeking to derive from the sources above mentioned; not by setting aside the Hindoo law wherever that avails, and not by diminishing in the least degree the consideration which the feudatory States have experienced at the hands of former ruling dynasties, but, on the contrary, by increasing this consideration, and at the same time making our future practice plain and certain.

22. A time so opportune for the step can never occur again. The last vestiges of the Royal House of Delhi, from which, for our own convenience, we had long been content to accept a vica-

rious authority, have been swept away. The last pretender to the representation of the Peishwah has disappeared. The Crown of England stands forth the unquestioned ruler and Paramount Power in all India, and is, for the first time, brought face to face with its feudatories. There is a reality in the suzerainty of the Sovereign of England which has never existed before, and which is not only felt but eagerly acknowledged by the Chiefs. A great convulsion has been followed by such a manifestation of our strength as India had never seen, and if this, in its turn, be followed by an act of general and substantial grace to the native Chiefs, over and above the special rewards which have already been given to those whose services deserve them, the measure will be seasonable and appreciated.

23. Such an act of grace, and in my humble opinion, of sound policy, would be an assurance to every Chief, above the rank of Jagheerdar, who now governs his own territory, no matter how small it may be, or where it may be situated, or whence his authority over it may, in the first instance, have been derived, that the Paramount Power desires to see his Government perpetuated, and that, on failure of natural heirs, his adoption of a successor, according to Hindoo law (if he be a Hindoo) and to the customs of his race, will be recognised, and that nothing shall disturb the engagement thus made to him, so long as his House is loyal to the Crown and faithful to the conditions of the Treaties or Grants which record its obligations to the British Government.

24. The effect to be expected from this measure may be shortly described.

25. To the old Principalities of Rajpootana it would be of no direct importance. There adoptions have been hitherto generally respected by all Ruling Powers, and if any class of Chiefs feel secure that we shall not question their claims to adopt successors, it is probably the Princes of Rajpootana.

To the great Houses of Scindia, Holkar, Rewah, Puttialla, and to other smaller ones to whom the promise has already been made, it would be no new concession.

But to all other Chiefs, to the Guicowar and others in Western India, to those in Central India, in Bundlecund, and in the Hill States, it would be a most welcome assurance.

26. It would reassure them upon a matter on which they are especially sensitive, the continuance of the representation and dignity of their families.

It would remove a distinction already adverted to, which has been drawn between independent and dependent States, founded (though I venture to think not quite correctly founded) upon Lord Metcalfe's Minute of October 28th, 1837, and would do away with the difference of treatment between the independent Chiefs, and the Chief of a State like Jaloun and Jhansie, who, although he and his forefathers may have exercised for more than a century the full functions of government, is not considered entitled to adopt a successor, because the Peishwah had recognised his ancestor only as a Soubadar.

It would show at once, and for ever, that we are not lying in wait for opportunities of absorbing territory, and that we do deliberately desire to keep alive a feudal aristocracy where one still exists. It would establish this more conclusively, and bring it home to many more minds, than the promises and declarations recently made in Durbar to the powerful Chiefs to whom we are under special obligations.

27. I have proposed that the assurance should be given to every Chief who now governs his own territory, and who holds a position higher than that of a Jagheerdar.

This will mark a line which will be generally clear and intelligible, and it will accord with the one main distinction drawn by Lord Metcalfe between Chiefs who are, and Chiefs who are not, entitled to adopt.

Nevertheless, I think that some exceptions in favour of Jagheerdars should be made. A Jaghoer is usually an assignment of land or revenue, in consideration of services, and not hereditary, or hereditary only for a generation or two. But, as Lord Metcalfe observes, there are in Bundlecund Chiefs whom it is difficult to place in either of the classes which he describes; and it is clear that he alludes to some who are there called Jagheerdars.

See De Cruze's Political Relations, p. 39, *et seq.* In their case the word means much more than in other parts of India. Their territories and the administration thereof have been granted to them and to their successors in perpetuity, so long as certain obligations are observed, and the concession of the privilege of adoption to the most influential among them would have a beneficial effect, not only in that disjointed Province, which, whatever may be our desire and however stringently we might enforce lapses, we could not hope to consolidate under our own administration for many generations to come, but throughout India.* In these last men-

---

* These Jagheerdars resemble those of whom Sir John Malcolm wrote as follows :—

" Adoptions which are universally recognised as legal among Hindoos are not a strict right (any more than direct heirs) where grants of land are for service.   *   *   *

" But we have received the submission of the Jagheerdars, confirmed their estates, honoured them, and have continued to do so, by treating them as Princes ; but while a few have been permitted to adopt, others are denied the privilege ; and while we declare their direct heirs are entitled to succeed, we lie in wait (I can call it nothing else) to seize their fine estates on failure of heirs, throwing them and their adherents and the country into a state of doubt and distraction. These families should either never have been placed in possession of these countries, or never have been removed from them."— *Life and Correspondence of Sir John Malcolm*, Nov. 14th, 1829.

tioned cases it would be expedient to require Nuzzerana whenever adoption took effect. From a fourth to a third of a year's revenue would, I think, be a fitting amount.

28. The case of the Mahomedan Chiefs remained to be considered.

Adoption in the full sense in which it is exercised by Hindoo Chiefs they cannot claim. But adoption of one collateral in preference to another of closer affinity, has been allowed to them where lineal heirs have failed; and it seems that it is also in accordance with Mahomedan law and usage that the Sovereign should select from among his sons the one whom he may desire to succeed to him. The King of Delhi exercised this right shortly before his rebellion.

See Papers on the Bhopal Succession, 18, 19, 20.

To the Mahomedan Chiefs, then, the assurance to be given would be that the Paramount Power desires to see their Governments perpetuated, and that any succession to them which may be legitimate according to Mahomedan law will be upheld.

See Minute of Lord Metcalfe, Oct. 28th, 1837, para. 6.

29. I recommend that in every case, Mahomedan or Hindoo, the assurance should be conveyed to each Chief individually, and not by a general notification addressed to all. This would be necessary, in order to avoid future claims from petty Jagheerdars or others whom it is not intended to include in this measure.

30. The proposed measure will not debar the Government of India from stepping in to set right such serious abuses in a Native Government as may threaten any part of the country with anarchy or disturbance, nor from assuming temporary charge of a Native State when there shall be sufficient reason to do so. This has long been our practice. We have repeatedly exercised the power with the assent and sometimes at the desire of the chief authority in the State, and it is one which, used with good judgment and moderation, it is very desirable that we should retain. It will, indeed, when once the proposed assurance shall have been given, be more easy than heretofore to exercise it without provoking jealousy of any designs upon the independence of the State.

31. Neither will the assurance, if worded as proposed, diminish our right to visit a State with the heaviest penalties, even to confiscation, in the event of its disloyalty or flagrant breach of engagement.

Upon this point, I beg to refer to the following passages in papers by Sir George Clerk :—

See Minute on Sattara, April 12th, 1848, para. 26.

"We should look for escheats not from such a source as the doubtful meaning of the stipulation of an agreement, but from the incorrigible misconduct of allies when thrown back, as they should be, on the responsibilities of the Sovereign rights relinquished to them, rendering punishment in such cases signal and salutary, by abstaining from half measures, such as largely pensioning or managing for the delinquent, or substituting his child, wife, or minister."

And again,—

See Letter on Chiefship of Bughat, November 10th, 1842.

"The proper punishment for the Paramount State to inflict for gross mismanagement and oppression, such as prevails to a considerable extent in these Hills, would be sequestration of the Chieftaincies; but this would not be fair until we had revived their interest in their ancestral territories, by manifesting the same respect for their rights, founded on a possession of many centuries, as is entertained by the people in general. Could we inspire them with confidence in our general disinterestedness, our severity, when called for, would be rightly and beneficially understood; and for the most part, that confidence would correct the motives to neglectful or tyrannical conduct requiring punishment."

I consider those views to be sound, not only in the cases to which they refer, but in those of Native States generally; and I would apply them generally, with this single limitation—that the penalty of sequestration or confiscation should be used only when the misconduct or oppression is such as to be not only heinous in itself, but of a nature to constitute indisputably a breach of loyalty or of recorded engagement to the Paramount Power.

32. It is certain that objection to the proposed measure will be taken on the ground that it will cut off future opportunities of accession of territory, and that it is our duty not to forego these.

I regard this not as an objection, but as a recommendation; and I cannot take that view of our duty.

33. Notwithstanding the greater purity and enlightenment of our administration, its higher tone, and its surer promise of future benefit to the people, as compared with any Native Government, I still think that we have before us a higher and more pressing duty than that of extending our direct rule, and that our first care should be to strengthen that rule within its present limits, and to secure for our general supremacy the contented acquiescence and respect of all who are subjected to it.

Our supremacy will never be heartily accepted and respected so long as we leave ourselves open to the doubts which are now felt, and which our uncertain policy has justified, as to our ultimate intentions towards Native States.

We shall not become stronger so long as we continue adding to our territory without adding to our European force; and the additions to that force which we already require are probably as large as England can conveniently furnish, and they will certainly cost as much as India can conveniently pay.

As to Civil Government, our English officers are too few for the work which they have on their hands, and our financial means are not yet equal to the demands upon us. Accession of territory will not make it easier to discharge our already existing duties in the administration of justice, the prosecution of public works, and in many other ways.

34. The safety of our rule is increased, not diminished, by the maintenance of Native Chiefs well affected to us. Setting aside the well known services rendered by Scindia, and, subsequently, by the Maharajahs of Rewah, Chirkaree, and others, over the wide tract of Central India, where our authority is most broken in upon by Native States, I venture to say that there is no man who remembers the condition of Upper India in 1857 and 1858, and who is not thankful that in the centre of the large and compact British province of Rohilcund there remained the solitary little State of Rampoor, still administered by its own Mahomedan Prince, and that on the borders of the Punjab and of the districts above Delhi, the Chief of Puttiala and his kinsmen still retained their hereditary authority unimpaired.

In the time of which I speak, these patches of Native Government served as breakwaters to the storm which would otherwise have swept over us in one great wave. And in quiet times they have their uses. Restless men, who will accept no profession but arms, crafty intriguers bred up in Native Courts, and others who would chafe at our stricter and more formal rule, live there contentedly ; and should the day come when India shall be threatened by an external enemy, or when the interests of England elsewhere may require that her Eastern Empire shall incur more than ordinary risk, one of our best mainstays will be found in these Native States. But, to make them so, we must treat their Chiefs and influential families with consideration and generosity, teaching them that, in spite of all suspicions to the contrary, their independence is safe, that we are not waiting for plausible opportunities to convert their country into British territory, and convincing them that they have nothing to gain by helping to displace us in favour of any new rulers, from within or from without.

25. It was long ago said by Sir John Malcolm, that if we made all India into Zillahs, it was not in the nature of things that our Empire should last fifty years ; but that if we could keep up a number of Native States, without political power, but as royal instruments, we should exist in India as long as our naval superiority in Europe was maintained.

Of the substantial truth of this opinion I have no doubt, and recent events have made it more deserving of our attention than ever.

I have, etc.

CANNING.

(B.)

PARTITION TREATY OF MYSORE, 1799.

*Treaty for strengthening the Alliance and Friendship subsisting between the English East-India Company Behauder, his Highness the Nabob Nizam-ul-Dowlah Asoph Jah Behauder, and the Paishwah, Row Pundit Purdhaun Behauder, and for effecting a Settlement of the Dominions of the late Tippoo Sultaun.**

Whereas the deceased Tippoo Sultaun, unprovoked by any act of aggression on the part of the Allies, entered into an offensive and defensive alliance with the French, and admitted a French force into his army, for the purpose of commencing war against the Honourable English Company Behauder, and its Allies, Nizam-ul-Dowlah Asoph Jah Behauder, and the Paishwah Row Pundit Purdhaun Behauder; and the said Tippoo Sultaun having attempted to evade the just demands of satisfaction and security made by the Honourable English Company and its Allies, for their defence and protection against the joint designs of the said Sultaun and of the French, the allied armies of the Honourable English Company Behauder and of his Highness Nizam-ul-Dowlah Asoph Jah Behauder proceeded to hostilities, in vindication of their rights, and for the preservation of their respective dominions from the perils of foreign invasion, and from the ravages of a cruel and relentless enemy.

And whereas it has pleased Almighty God to prosper the just cause of the said Allies, the Honourable English Company Behauder and his Highness Nizam-ul-Dowlah Asoph Jah Behauder, with a continual course of victory and success, and finally to crown their arms by the reduction of the capital of Mysore, the fall of Tippoo Sultaun, the utter extinction of his power, and the unconditional submission of his people; and whereas the said Allies, being disposed to exercise the rights of conquest with the same moderation and forbearance which they have observed from the commencement to the conclusion of the late successful war, have resolved to use the power which it has pleased Almighty God to place in their hands, for the purpose of obtaining reasonable compensation for the expenses of the war, and of establishing permanent security and genuine tranquillity for themselves and their subjects, as well as for all the powers contiguous to their respective dominions; wherefore a Treaty, for the adjustment of the territories of the late Tippoo Sultaun between the English East-India Company Behauder and his Highness the Nabob Nizam-ul-Dowlah Asoph Jah Behauder, is now concluded by Lieutenant General George Harris, Commander in Chief of the Forces of his Britannic Majesty and of the English

---

* The Paishwah refused to accede to this Treaty.

East-India Company Behauder in the Carnatic and on the Coast of Malabar, the Honourable Colonel Arthur Wellesley, the Honourable Henry Wellesley, Lieutenant Colonel William Kirkpatrick, and Lieutenant Colonel Barry Close, on the part and in the name of the Right Honourable Richard Earl of Mornington, K.P., Governor General for all Affairs, civil and military, of the British Nation in India; and by the Nabob Meer Allum Behauder, on the part and in the name of his Highness the Nabob Nizam-ul-Dowlah Asoph Jah Behauder, according to the under-mentioned Articles, which, by the blessing of God, shall be binding upon the heirs and successors of the contracting parties, as long as the sun and moon shall endure, and of which the conditions shall be reciprocally observed by the said contracting parties.

I. It being reasonable and just, that the Allies by this Treaty should accomplish the original objects of the war (*viz.* a due indemnification for the expenses incurred in their own defence, and effectual security for their respective possessions against the future designs of their enemies), it is stipulated and agreed, that the districts specified in the Schedule A, hereunto annexed, together with the heads of all the passes leading from the territory of the late Tippoo Sultaun to any part of the possessions of the English East-India Company Behauder, of its Allies or tributaries, situated between the Ghauts on either coast, and all forts situated near to and commanding the said passes, shall be subjected to the authority, and be for ever incorporated with the dominions of the English East-India Company Behauder, the said Company Behauder engaging to provide effectually out of the revenues of the said districts, for the suitable maintenance of the whole of the families of the late Hyder Ali Khan and of the late Tippoo Sultaun, and to apply to this purpose, with the reservation hereinafter stated, an annual sum of not less than two lacs of Star Pagodas, making the Company's share as follows:

Estimated value of districts enumerated in the Schedule
     A, according to the statement of Tippoo Sultaun
     in 1792   -   -   -   Canterai Pagodas   7,77,170
Deduct, provision for the families of Hyder Ali Khan
     and of Tippoo Sultaun, two lacs of Star Pagodas,
     in Canterai Pagodas   -   -   -   -   -   2,40,000

Remains to the East India Company   -   -   -   5,37,170

II. For the same reason stated in the preceding Articles, the district specified in Schedule B, annexed hereunto, shall be subjected to the authority, and for ever united to the dominions of the Nabob Nizam-ul-Dowlah Asoph Jah Behauder, the said Nabob having engaged to provide liberally, from the revenues of the said districts, for the support of Meer Kummer-ud-Dien Khan Behauder, and of his family and relations, and to grant him for this purpose a personal Jaghire in the districts of Gurrum-condah equal to the annual sum of 2,10,000 rupees, or of 70,000 Canterai Pagodas, over and above and exclusive of a Jaghire, which the said Nabob has also agreed to assign to the said Meer Kummer-ud-Dien Khan, for the pay and maintenance of a proportionate number of troops to be employed in the service of his said Highness, making the share of his Highness as follows :

Estimated value of the territory specified in Schedule
        B, according to the statement of Tippoo Sultaun
        in 1792   -   -   -   Canterai Pagodas   6,07,332
Deduct, personal Jaghire to Meer Kummer-ud-Dien
        Khan, 2,10,000 rupees, or   -   -   -   -   70,000

Remains to the Nabob Nizam-ud-Dowlah Asoph Jah
        Behauder -   -   -   -   -   -   -   5,37,332

III. It being farther expedient for the preservation of peace and tranquillity, and for the general security, on the foundations now established by the contracting parties, that the fortress of Seringapatam should be subjected to the said Company Behauder, it is stipulated and agreed that the said fortress, and the island on which it is situated (including the small tract of land, or island, lying to the westward of the main island, and bounded on the west by a Nullah, called the Mysore Nullah, which falls into the Cauvery near Chenagal Ghaut) shall become part of the dominions of the said Company, in full right and sovereignty for ever.

IV. A separate Government shall be established in Mysore; and for this purpose, it is stipulated and agreed, that the Maha Rajah Mysore Kishna Rajah Oodiaver Behauder, a descendant of the ancient Rajahs of Mysore, shall possess the territory hereinafter described, upon the conditions hereinafter mentioned.

V. The contracting powers mutually and severally agree, that the districts specified in Schedule C, hereunto annexed, shall be ceded to the said Maha Rajah Mysore Kishna Rajah, and shall form the separate Government of Mysore, upon the conditions hereinafter mentioned.

VI. The English East India Company Behauder shall be at liberty to make such deductions, from time to time, from the sums allotted by the first Article of the present Treaty, for the maintenance of the families of Hyder Ali Khan and Tippoo Sultaun, as may be proper, in consequence of the decease of any member of the said families; and in the event of any hostile attempt, on the part of the said family, or of any member of it, against the authority of the contracting parties, or against the peace of their respective dominions, or the territories of the Rajah of Mysore, then the said English East India Company Behauder shall be at liberty to limit or suspend entirely the payment of the whole, or any part of the stipend hereinbefore stipulated to be applied to the maintenance and support of the said families.

VII. His Highness the Paishwa Row Pundit Purdhaun Behauder shall be invited to accede to the present Treaty; and although the said Paishwah Row Pundit Purdhaun Behauder has neither participated in the expense or danger of the late war, and therefore is not entitled to share any part of the acquisitions made by the contracting parties (namely, the English East India Company Behauder and his Highness the Nabob Nizam-ud-Dowlah Asoph Jah Behauder), yet for the maintenance of the relations of friendship and alliance between the said Paishwa Row Pundit Purdhaun Behauder, the English East India Company Behauder, his Highness the Nabob Nizam-ud-Dowlah Asoph Jah Behauder, and Maha Rajah Mysore Kishna Rajah Behauder, it is stipulated and agreed that certain districts, specified in Schedule D, hereunto annexed, shall be reserved for the purpose of being eventually ceded to the said Paishwah Row Pundit Purdhaun Behauder, in full right and sovereignty, in the same manner as if he had been a contracting party to this Treaty; provided, however, that the said Paishwa Row Pundit Purdhaun Behauder shall accede to the present Treaty, in its full extent, within one month from the day on which it shall be formally communicated to him by the contracting parties, and provided also that he shall give satisfaction to the English East India Company Behauder, and to his Highness Nizam-ud-Dowlah Asoph Jah Behauder, with regard to certain points now depending between him, the said Paishwa Row Pundit Purdhaun Behauder, and the said Nabob Nizam-ud-Dowlah Asoph Jah Behauder, and also with regard to such points as shall be represented to the said Paishwah, on the part of the English East India Company Behauder, by the Governor General or the British Resident at the Court of Poonah.

VIII. If, contrary to the amicable expectation of the contracting parties, the said Paishwah Row Pundit Purdhaun Behauder shall refuse to accede to this Treaty, or to give satisfaction upon the points to which the Seventh Article refers, then the right to, and sovereignty of, the several districts hereinbefore reserved for eventual cession to the Paishwah Row Pundit Purdhaun Behauder, shall rest jointly in the said English East India Company Behauder and the said Nabob Nizam-ud-Dowlah Asoph Jah Behauder, who will either exchange them with the Rajah of Mysore for other districts of equal value, more contiguous to their respective territories, or otherwise arrange and settle respecting them, as they shall judge proper.

IX. It being expedient for the effectual establishment of Maha Rajah Mysore Kishna Rajah in the Government of Mysore, that his Highness should be assisted with a suitable Subsidiary Force, it is stipulated and agreed, that the whole of the said Force shall be furnished by the English East India Company Behauder, according to the terms of a separate Treaty, to be immediately concluded between the said English East India Company Behauder and his Highness the Maha Rajah Mysore Kishna Rajah Oodiaver Behauder.

x. This Treaty, consisting of ten Articles, being settled and concluded this day, the 22d of June, 1799 (corresponding to the 17th of Mohurrun, 1214 Anno Hegiræ) by Lieutenant General George Harris, the Honourable Colonel Arthur Wellesley, the Honourable Henry Wellesley, Lieutenant Colonel William Kirkpatrick, and Lieutenant Colonel Barry Close, on the part and in the name of the Right Honourable Richard Earl of Mornington, Governor General aforesaid; and by Meer Allum Behauder on the part and in the name of His Highness the Nabob Nizam-ud-Dowlah Asoph Jah Behauder; the said Lieutenant General Harris, the Honourable Colonel Arthur Wellesley, the Honourable Henry Wellesley, Lieutenant Colonel William Kirkpatrick, and Lieutenant Colonel Barry Close, have delivered to Meer Allum Behauder one copy of the same, signed and sealed by themselves; and Meer Allum Behauder has delivered to Lieutenant General George Harris, the Honourable Colonel Arthur Wellesley, the Honourable Henry Wellesley, Lieutenant Colonel William Kirkpatrick, and Lieutenant Colonel Barry Close, another copy of the same, sealed by himself; and Lieutenant General George Harris, the Honourable Colonel Arthur Wellesley, the Honourable Henry Wellesley, Lieutenant Colonel William Kirkpatrick, and Lieutenant Colonel Barry Close, and Meer Allum Behauder, severally and mutually engage, that the said Treaty shall be respectively ratified by the Right Honourable the Governor General, under his seal and signature, within eight days from the date hereof, and by his Highness the Nabob Nizam-ud-Dowlah Asoph Jah Behauder, within twenty-five days from the date hereof. Ratified at Hyderabad, by his Highness the Nizam, on the 13th day of July, Anno Domini 1799.

(Signed)   J. A. KIRKPATRICK, Resident.

Schedule A (The Company's Share).
*   *   *   *
Schedule B (The Nizam's Share).
*   *   *   *

Schedule C (Districts ceded to Maha Rajah Mysore Kishna Rajah Oodiaver Behauder.
*   .   *   *   *

SEPARATE ARTICLES OF THE TREATY WITH THE NIZAM.

Separate Articles appertaining to the Treaty of Mysore, concluded on the 22nd of June, 1799 (corresponding to the 17th of Mohurrum, Anno Hegira 1214) between the Honourable English East India Company Behauder, and the Nabob Nizam-ul-Dowlah Asoph Jah Behauder.

i. With a view to the prevention of future altercations, it is agreed between his Highness the Nabob Nizam-ud-Dowlah Asoph Jah Behauder and the Honourable English East India Company Behauder, that to whatever amount the stipends appropriated to the maintenance of the sons, relations, and dependants of the late Hyder Ali Khan and Tippoo Sultaun, or the personal Jaghire of Meer Kummer-ud-Deen Khan, shall hereafter be diminished, in consequence of any one of the stipulations of the Treaty of Mysore, the contracting parties shall not be accountable to each other on this head.

ii. And it is further agreed between the contracting parties, that in the event provided for by the Eighth Article of the Treaty of Mysore, two-thirds of the share reserved for Row Pundit Purdhaun Behauder shall fall to his Highness the Nabob Nizam-ud-Dowlah Asoph Jah Behauder, and the remaining third to the Honourable English East India Company Behauder.

Ratified at Hyderabad by his Highness the Nizam, on the 13th day of July, Anno Domini 1799.

(*Signed*)   J. A. KIRKPATRICK, *Resident.*

SUBSIDIARY TREATY OF SERINGAPATAM, 1799.

A Treaty of perpetual Friendship and Alliance, concluded on the one part by his Excellency Lieutenant-General George Harris, Commander in Chief of the Forces of his Britannic Majesty and of the English East India Company Behauder in the Carnatic and on the Coast of Malabar, the Honourable Colonel Arthur Wellesley, the Honourable Henry Wellesley, Lieutenant Colonel William Kirkpatrick, and Lieutenant-Colonel Barry Close, on behalf and in the name of the Right Honourable Richard Earl of Mornington, K.P., Governor General for all Affairs, civil and military, of the British Nation in India, by virtue of full powers vested in them for this purpose by the said Richard Earl of Mornington, Governor General; and on the other part by Maha Rajah Mysore Kistna Rajah Oodiaver Behauder, Rajah of Mysore.

Whereas it is stipulated, in the Treaty concluded on the 22nd of June, 1799, between the Honourable English East India

Company Behauder, and the Nabob Nizam-ud-Dowlah Asoph Jah Behauder, for strengthening the alliance and friendship subsisting between the said English East India Company Behauder, his Highness Nizam-ud-Dowlah Asoph Jah Behauder, and the Peshwa, Row Pundit Purdhaun Behauder, and for effecting a settlement of the territories of the late Tippoo Sultaun, that a separate Government shall be established in Mysore, and that his Highness Maha Rajah Mysore Kistna Rajah Oodiaver Behauder shall possess certain territories, specified in Schedule C, annexed to the said Treaty, and that, for the effectual establishment of the Government of Mysore, his Highness shall be assisted with a suitable Subsidiary Force, to be furnished by the English East India Company Behauder; wherefore, in order to carry the said stipulations into effect, and to increase and strengthen the friendship subsisting between the said English East India Company and the said Maha Rajah Mysore Kistna Rajah Oodiaver Behauder, this Treaty is concluded by Lieutenant-General George Harris, Commander in Chief of the Forces of his Britannic Majesty and of the said English East India Company Behauder in the Carnatic and on the Coast of Malabar, the Honourable Colonel Arthur Wellesley, the Honourable Henry Wellesley, Lieutenant Colonel William Kirkpatrick, and Lieutenant Colonel Barry Close, on the part and in the name of the Right Honourable Richard Earl of Mornington, Governor General aforesaid, and by his Highness Maha Rajah Mysore Kishna Rajah Oodiaver Behauder, which shall be binding upon the contracting parties as long as the sun and moon shall endure.

I. The friends and enemies of either of the contracting parties shall be considered as the friends and enemies of both.

II. The Honourable East India Company Behauder agrees to maintain, and his Highness Maha Rajah Mysore Kistna Rajah Oodiaver Behauder agrees to receive, a military force, for the defence and security of his Highness's dominions; in consideration of which protection, his Highness engages to pay the annual sum of seven lacks of Star Pagodas to the said East-India Company, the said sum to be paid in twelve equal monthly instalments, commencing from the 1st of July, Anno Domini 1799. And his Highness further agrees, that the disposal of the said sum, together with the arrangement and employment of the troops to be maintained by it, shall be entirely left to the Company.

III. If it shall be necessary for the protection and defence of the territories of the contracting parties, or of either of them, that hostilities shall be undertaken, or preparations made for commencing hostilities against any State or Power, his said Highness Maha Rajah Mysore Kistna Rajah Oodiaver Behauder, agrees to contribute towards the discharge of the increased expense incurred by the augmentation of the military force, and the unavoidable charges of war, such a sum as shall appear to the

Governor General in Council of Fort William, on an attentive consideration of the means of his said Highness, to bear a just and reasonable proportion to the actual net revenues of his said Highness.

iv. And whereas it is indispensably necessary, that effectual and lasting security should be provided against any failure in the funds destined to defray either the expenses of the permanent military force in time of peace, or the extraordinary expenses described in the Third Article of the present Treaty, it is hereby stipulated and agreed between the contracting parties, that whenever the Governor General in Council of Fort William in Bengal shall have reason to apprehend such failure in the funds so destined, the said Governor General in Council shall be at liberty, and shall have full power and right, either to introduce such regulations and ordinances as he shall deem expedient for the internal management and collection of the revenues, or for the better ordering of any other branch and department of the Government of Mysore, or to assume and bring under the direct management of the servants of the said Company Behauder, such part or parts of the territorial possessions of his Highness Maha Rajah Mysore Kistna Rajah Oodiaver Behauder, as shall appear to him, the said Governor General in Council, necessary to render the said funds efficient and available either in time of peace or war.

v. And it is hereby further agreed, that whenever the said Governor General in Council shall signify to the said Maha Rajah Mysore Kistna Rajah Oodiaver Behauder, that it is become necessary to carry into effect the provisions of the Fourth Article, his said Highness Maha Rajah Mysore Kistna Rajah Oodiaver Behauder shall immediately issue orders to his Aumils, or other officers, either for carrying into effect the said regulations and ordinances, according to the tenor of the Fourth Article, or for placing the territories required under the exclusive authority and control of the English Company Behauder. And in case his Highness shall not issue such orders within ten days from the time when the application shall have been formally made to him, then the said Governor General in Council shall be at liberty to issue orders, by his own authority, either for carrying into effect the regulations and ordinances, or for assuming the management and collection of the revenue of the said territories, as he shall judge most expedient for the purpose of securing the efficiency of the said military funds, and of providing for the effectual protection of the country and the welfare of the people. Provided always, that whenever, and so long as any part or parts of his said Highness's territories shall be placed, and shall remain under the exclusive authority and control of the said East India Company, the Governor General in Council shall render to his Highness a true and faithful account of the revenues and produce of the territories so assumed; provided also, that in no case whatever shall his Highness's actual receipts or actual income, arising out of his territorial revenue, be less than the sum of one lac of Star Pagodas, together with one-fifth of the net revenue of the whole of the territories ceded to him by the Fifth Article of the Treaty of Mysore; which sum of one lac of Star Pagodas, together with the amount of one-fifth of the said net revenue, the East India Company engages, at all times and in every possible case, to secure and cause to be paid for his Highness's use.

VI. His Highness Maha Rajah Mysore Kistna Rajah Oodiaver Behauder engages, that he will be guided by a sincere and cordial attention to the relations of peace and amity, now established between the English Company Behauder and their Allies, and that he will carefully abstain from any interference in the affairs of any State in alliance with the said English Company Behauder, or of any State whatever. And for securing the object of this stipulation, it is further stipulated and agreed, that no communication or correspondence with any foreign State whatever, shall be holden by his said Highness without the previous knowledge and sanction of the said English Company Behauder.

VII. His Highness stipulates and agrees, that he will not admit any European foreigners into his service, without the concurrence of the English Company Behauder; and that he will apprehend and deliver up to the Company's Government all Europeans, of whatever description, who shall be found within the territories of his said Highness, without regular passports from the Company's Government, it being his Highness's determined resolution not to suffer, even for a day, any European foreigners to remain within the territories now subjected to his authority, unless by consent of the said Company.

VIII. Whereas the complete protection of his Highness's said territories requires that various fortresses and strong places, situated within the territories of his Highness, should be garrisoned and commanded, as well in time of peace as of war, by British troops and officers, his Highness Maha Rajah Mysore Kistna Rajah Oodiaver Behauder engages, that the said English Company Behauder shall at all times be at liberty to garrison, in whatever manner they may judge proper, all such fortresses and strong places, within his said Highness's territories, as it shall appear advisable to them to take charge of.

IX. And whereas, in consequence of the system of defence which it may be expedient to adopt, for the security of the territorial possessions of his Highness Maha Rajah Mysoor Kistna Rajah Oodiaver Behauder, it may be necessary that certain forts and strong places, within his Highness's territories, should be dismantled or destroyed, and that other forts and strong places should be strengthened and repaired, it is stipulated and agreed, that the English East-India Company Behauder shall be the sole judges of the necessity of any such alterations in the said fortresses; and it is further agreed, that such expenses as may be incurred on this account, shall be borne and defrayed, in equal proportions, by the contracting parties.

x. In case it shall become necessary, for enforcing and maintaining the authority and government of his Highness in the territories now subjected to his power, that the regular troops of the English East-India Company Behauder should be employed, it is stipulated and agreed, that upon formal application being made for the service of the said troops, they shall be employed in such manner as to the said Company shall seem fit: but it is expressly understood by the contracting parties, that this stipulation shall not subject the troops of the English East-India Company Behauder to be employed in the ordinary transactions of revenue.

xi. It being expedient for the restoration and permanent establishment of tranquillity in the territories now subjected to the authority of his Highness Maha Rajah Mysoor Kistna Rajah Oodiaver Behauder, that suitable provision should be made for certain officers of rank in the service of the late Tippoo Sultaun, his said Highness agrees to enter into the immediate discussion of this point, and to fix the amount of the funds (as soon as the necessary information can be obtained) to be granted for this purpose, in a separate Article, to be hereafter added to this Treaty.

xii. Lest the garrison of Seringapatam should, at any time, be subject to inconvenience from the high price of provisions and other necessaries, his Highness Maha Rajah Mysore Kistna Rajah Oodiaver Behauder agrees, that such quantities of provisions and other necessaries, as may be required for the use and consumption of the troops composing the said garrison, shall be allowed to enter the place, from all and every part of his dominions, free of any duty, tax, or impediment whatever.

xiii. The contracting parties hereby agree to take into their early consideration the best means of establishing such a commercial intercourse between their respective dominions, as shall be mutually beneficial to the subjects of both Governments, and to conclude a Commercial Treaty for this purpose, with as little delay as possible.

xiv. His Highness Maha Rajah Mysore Kistna Rajah Oodiaver Behauder hereby promises to pay at all times the utmost attention to such advice as the Company's Government shall occasionally judge it necessary to offer to him, with a view to the economy of his finances, the better collection of his revenues, the administration of justice, the extension of commerce, the encouragement of trade, agriculture, and industry, or any other objects connected with the advancement of his Highness's interests, the happiness of his people, and the mutual welfare of both States.

xv. Whereas it may hereafter appear, that some of the districts declared by the Treaty of Mysore to belong respectively to the English Company Behauder and to his Highness are inconveniently situated, with a view to the proper connection of their respective lines of frontier, it is hereby stipulated between the contracting parties, that in all such cases they will proceed to such an adjustment, by means of exchanges or otherwise, as shall be best suited to the occasion.

xvi. This Treaty, consisting of sixteen Articles, being this day, the 8th of July, Anno Domini 1799 (corresponding to the 3rd of Suffur, Anno Hegiræ 1214, and to the 7th of the month Assar, of 1721st year of the Saliwahan era) settled and concluded at the fort of Nazzerbagh, near Seringapatam, by his Excellency, Lieutenant-General George Harris, Commander-in-Chief of the Forces of his Britannic Majesty, and of the Honourable English East India Company Behauder, in the Carnatic and on the Coast of Malabar, the Honourable Colonel Arthur Wellesley, the Honourable Henry Wellesley, Lieutenant-Colonel William Kirkpatrick, and Lieutenant-Colonel Barry Close, with the Maha Rajah Mysore Kistna Rajah Oodiaver Behauder, the aforesaid gentlemen have delivered to the said Maha Rajah one copy of the same, in English and Persian, sealed and signed by them, and his Highness the Maha Rajah has delivered to the gentlemen aforesaid another copy, also in Persian and English, bearing his seal, and signed by Luchuma, widow of the late Kistna Rajah, and sealed and signed by Purnia, Dewan to the Maha Rajah Kistna Rajah Oodiaver. And the aforesaid gentlemen have engaged to procure and to deliver to the said Maha Rajah, without delay, a copy of the same, under the seal and signature of the Right Honourable the Governor General, on the receipt of which by the said Maha Rajah, the present Treaty shall be deemed complete and binding on the Honourable the English East India Company and on the Maha Rajah Mysore Kistna Rajah Oodiaver Behauder, and the copy of it now delivered to the said Maha Rajah shall be returned.

· Witnessed   *(Seal of the Maha Rajah)*

(Signed)   EDWARD GOLDING,   and the

       Assistant Secretary.   *(Rance's Signature.)*

                      (Seal and Signature of Purniah.)

    A true Copy,

       (Signed)   G. BUCHAN,

                   Sub-Secretary.

ARTICLES EXPLANATORY OF THE THIRD ARTICLE OF THE SUBSIDIARY TREATY, 1807.

Additional Articles for modifying and defining the Provisions of the Third Article of the Treaty of Mysore, settled and concluded between the English East India Company Behauder and Maha Rajah Mysore Kishen Rajah Oodiaver Behauder, Rajah of Mysore.*

Whereas it is stipulated by the Third Article of the Treaty of Mysore,* that in the event of hostilities, or of preparations for hostilities, against any State or Power, Maha Rajah Mysore Kistna Rajah Oodiaver Behauder shall contribute towards the discharge of the increased expenses thereby incurred, a sum to be eventually determined by the Governor General in Council of Fort William; and whereas it has appeared expedient to the contracting parties, that the provisions of the said Article shall now be rendered specific, and that the said indefinite contributions in war should be commuted, for the fixed maintenance of a certain body of Horse in peace and war, wherefore these additional Articles, for modifying and defining the provisions of the Third Article of the said Treaty, are now concluded, on the one part, by Major Mark Wilks, in the name and on behalf of the Honourable Sir George Hilaro Barlow, Baronet, Governor General for all affairs, civil and military, of the British Nation in India by virtue of full powers vested in him for the purpose by the said Sir George Hilaro Barlow, Baronet, Governor General, and on the other part, by Maha Rajah Mysore Kistna Rajah Oodiavur Behauder, Rajah of Mysore, in his own behalf.

I. It is agreed and stipulated, that his Highness Maha Rajah Mysore Kistna Rajah Oodiavur shall be relieved from the pecuniary contribution to which he was liable, by the provisions of the Third Article of the Treaty of Mysore: in consideration whereof, his Highness engages to maintain, at all times, fit for service and subject to muster, a body of (4,000) four thousand effective Horse, of which number about (500) five hundred shall be Bargeer, and the rest Silladar Horse.

II. Such portion of the said body of (4,000) four thousand Horse as, in the opinion of the British Government, shall not be necessary for the internal protection of the country of Mysore, shall be, at all times, ready to accompany and serve with the

---

* By a singular mistake in drafting these Additional Articles, the Subsidiary Treaty is called the Treaty of *Mysore*. The Partition Treaty was the Treaty of Mysore; the Subsidiary Treaty the Treaty of Seringapatam,—see Wellesley's Despatches, vol. ii, p. 44, 45.

Honourable Company's army, and while employed beyond the territory of Mysore, the extra expenses of their maintenance, or batta, at the rate of (4) four Star Pagodas per month for each effective man and horse, after the expiration of one month from the date of their crossing the frontier, shall be regularly paid by the Honourable Company. The extra expense of any casual service beyond the frontier, not exceeding in duration the period of one month, shall be borne by the Government of Mysore.

III. If it should, at any time, be found expedient to augment the Cavalry of Mysore beyond the number of (4,000) four thousand, on intimation to that effect from the British Government, his Highness the Rajah shall use his utmost endeavours for that purpose; but the whole expense of such augmentation, and of the maintenance of the additional numbers at the rate of (8) Star Pagodas for each effective man and horse, while within the territory of Mysore, and of an additional sum, or batta, at the rate of (4) four Star Pagodas a month, after the expiration of one month from the period of their passing the frontier of Mysore, as described in the Second Article, shall be defrayed by the Honourable Company.

IV. Whereas, in conformity to the wish of the Governor General, a body of (4,000) four thousand Horse and upwards has been provisionally maintained by his Highness the Rajah, from the period of the conclusion of war in the Deccan until this time, it is hereby declared, that his Highness has fully and faithfully performed the obligations of the Third Article of the Treaty of Mysore until this day, and is hereby absolved from all retrospective claims on that account.

These four additional Articles, which, like the original Treaty of Mysore, shall be binding on the contracting parties as long as the sun and moon shall endure, having been settled and concluded on this 29th day of January, Anno Domini 1807, corresponding to the 19th of Zilcaad, Anno Hegiræ 1221, and to the 21st day of the month of Poosh, of the year 1728 of the Shaliwahan æra, at Mysore, by Major Mark Wilks with the Maha Rajah Kistna Rajah Oodiavur Behauder, Major Wilks has accordingly delivered one copy of the same, in Persian and English, signed and sealed by him, to his Highness the Maha Rajah, and who has likewise delivered to Major Wilks another copy, in Persian and English, bearing his Highness's seal and signature, and signed by Lutchuma, widow of the late Kistna Rajah, and sealed and signed by Poornia, Dewan to his Highness Maha Rajah Oodiavur Behauder; and Major Wilks has engaged to procure and deliver to the said Maha Rajah, without delay, a copy of the same, under the seal and signature of the Honourable the Governor General, on the receipt of which by the Maha Rajah the present additional Articles shall be deemed complete and binding on the Honour-

able East India Company and on the Maha Rajah Mysore Kistna
Rajah Oodiavur Behauder, and the copy now delivered to the
said Maha Rajah shall be returned.

A true Copy,

(*Signed*)   N. B. EDMONSTONE.

Secretary to Government.

(Collection of Treaties, 1812, p. 441-459, and 302-304.)

(C.)

LETTER OF LORD WILLIAM BENTINCK, GOVERNOR GENERAL, IN 1831, ANNOUNCING HIS INTENTION OF ASSUMING THE MANAGEMENT OF MYSORE.

To the Rajah of Mysore.

September 7th, 1831.

After Compliments,—It is now thirty-two years since the
British Government, having defeated the Armies and captured
the Forts and overrun the Territory of Tippoo Sultan, laid Siege
to Seringapatam, and that city being taken, the dynasty and the
power of Tippoo was brought to an end.   Your Highness is well
aware of the generosity displayed by the Conquerors upon that
occasion.   Instead of availing themselves of the right of conquest and of annexing the Territories of Mysore to those of the
Honourable Company and of the Nizam, the sovereignty was
restored to the family of the ancient Rajahs of the country, who
had taken no part in the contest, and your Highness was placed
on the Musnud.   But your Highness being then but a child of
three years old, Poorniah was appointed Dewan of the State,
with full powers, and, with the aid and countenance of the Officers
of the British Government, he conducted all affairs with exemplary wisdom and success.   Up to the period when your Highness approached the years of maturity, through his good management, and as the consequence of his measures, the country
prospered, and the State of Mysore attained splendour and ex-
altation, and the population of all ranks were contented and
happy.   Further, at the time of his resigning the Government
to your Highness, after having conducted its affairs for ten
years, he gave proof of the wisdom and correct integrity of his
management by leaving in the Treasuries, for your Highness'
use, no less than seventy-five lacks of Pagodas in cash, which is
a sum exceeding two Crores of Rupees.

From that time, which is now more than twenty years, your

Highness has been vested with all the powers and authorities of the Rajah of Mysore, and still exercise the rights of sovereignty in the Territory of the State. But I am sorry to be compelled to say that the former state of things no longer exists, and that the duties and obligations of your Highness' position appear to have been greatly neglected; for it seems that, besides the current revenue of the State, the treasure above stated to have been accumulated by Poorniah has been dissipated on personal expenses and disreputable extravagance; an immense debt has been incurred, and the finances of the State have been involved in extricable embarrassment: and although Sir Thomas Munro, the late Governor, as well as the Right Honourable S. R. Lushington, the present Governor of Madras, frequently remonstrated with your Highness on the subject, and obtained promises of amendment and of efforts to reduce your expenditure within your income, it does not appear that the least attention has been paid to their remonstrances or advice. The Subsidy due to the British Government has not been paid monthly according to the Treaty of 6th July 1799. The Troops and Soldiers of the State are unpaid, and are compelled, for their subsistence, to live at free quarters upon the Ryots. The debt is represented to be greater than ever; and so far from its being possible to entertain, from past experience, the smallest hope that these evils will be corrected under your Highness' management, more extensive deterioration and confusion can alone be anticipated.

My Friend,—there are stipulations in the 4th and 5th Articles of the Treaty above alluded to, of which it may be useful to quote at length the substance. These provisions are in effect as follows :—

"Art. 4. And whereas it is indispensably necessary that effectual and lasting security should be provided against any failure in the fund destined to defray either the expenses of the permanent military force in time of peace, or the extraordinary expenses described in the 3rd Article of the present Treaty, it is hereby stipulated and agreed between the contracting parties, that whenever the Governor General in Council at Fort William in Bengal, shall have reason to apprehend such failure in the funds so destined, the said Governor General in Council shall be at liberty, and shall have full power and right, either to introduce such regulations and ordinances as he shall deem expedient for the internal management and collection of the revenues, or for the better ordering of any other branch and department of the Government of Mysore, or to assume and bring under the direct management of the Servants of the said Company Bahadoor, such part or parts of the territorial possessions of His Highness Maharaja Mysore Kistna Rajah Oodiaver Bahadoor as shall appear to him the said Governor General in Council, necessary to render the said funds efficient and available in time of peace or war."

"Art. 5. And it is hereby further agreed that whenever the said Governor General in Council shall signify to the said Maharaja Mysore Kistna Rajah Oodiaver Bahadoor that it is become necessary to carry into effect the provisions of the 4th Article, His said Highness Maharaja Mysore Kistna Rajah Oodiaver Bahadoor shall immediately issue orders to his Amils or other officers, either for carrying into effect the said regulations and ordinances according to the tenour of the 4th Article, or for placing the Territories required under the exclusive authority and control of the English Company Bahadoor, and in case His Highness shall not issue such orders within ten days from the time when the application shall have been formally made to him, then the said Governor General in Council shall be at liberty to issue orders by his own authority, either for carrying into effect the said regulations and ordinances, or for assuming the management and collection of the revenues of the said territories, as he shall judge most expedient for the purpose of securing the efficiency of the said Military Fund, and of providing·for the effectual protection of the country and the welfare of the people. Provided always that whenever and so long as any part or parts of His said Highness' Territories shall be placed and shall remain under the exclusive authority and control of the East India Company, the Governor General in Council shall render to His Highness a true and faithful account of the revenues and produce of the Territories so assumed; provided also, that in no case whatever shall His Highness' actual receipt, or annual income arising out of his territorial revenue, be less than one lakh of Star Pagodas, together with one-fifth of the net revenue of the whole of the Territories ceded to him by the 5th Article of the Treaty of Mysore, which sum of one lakh of Star Pagodas, together with the amount of one-fifth of the said net revenues, the East India Company engages, in all times and in every possible case, to secure and cause to be paid for His Highness' use."

These stipulations were intended to provide for the specific evils which I have described, and to the consequences, I lament to say, your Highness has made yourself justly liable.

Moreover, from the time when your Highness assumed the management of the affairs of Mysore, every symptom of maladministration and misgovernment began to appear. The collection of the revenues has failed through the choice of improper and incapable officers for the charge of districts; alienations have been made of villages and public lands to a great extent, not in reward for public services, but to favourites and companions of your Highness, so that the resources of the State have been greatly diminished. As a means of raising funds for temporary purposes, to the neglect of future prospects and of the good of the country, state offices of all descriptions have been sold, and privileges of exclusive trade, whereby the Ryots and subjects of the State were made over to needy and greedy adventurers. This mismanagement, and the tyranny and oppression that resulted, came at length to such a pass, as to be no longer bearable by the inhabitants of the Territory of your Highness: and for the past year, the half of your Highness' entire dominions have been in insurrection in consequence. The troops of your Highness were first sent to bring the insurgents to subjection, the greatest excesses were committed, and unparalleled cruelties were inflicted by your Highness' officers; but the insurrection was not quelled. It became necessary to detach a part of the armies of the British Government to restore tranquillity and take part against the insurgents. Tranquillity has for the present been restored, but the British Government cannot permit its name or its power to be identified with these acts of your Highness' misrule; and while it cannot escape from the necessity of putting an end to insurrection, although justifiable, which should lead to general anarchy and confusion, it is imperiously called upon to supply an immediate and complete remedy and to vindicate its own character for justice. I have in consequence felt it to be indispensable, as well with reference to the stipulations of the Treaty above quoted, as from a regard to the obligations of the protective character which the British Government holds towards the State of Mysore, to interfere for its preservation, and to save the various interests at stake from further ruin. It has seemed to me that in order to do this effectually, it will be necessary to transfer the entire administration of the country into the hands of British officers; and I have accordingly determined to nominate two Commissioners for the purpose, who will proceed immediately to Mysore.

I now, therefore, give to your Highness this formal and final notice, and I request your Highness to consider this letter in that light; that is, as the notice required by the Treaty to be given to your Highness of the measure determined upon for the assumption and management of the Mysore Territory in the case stipulated. I beg of your Highness, therefore, to issue the requisite orders and proclamations to the officers and authorities of Mysore within ten days from the date when this letter may be delivered to your Highness, for giving effect to the transfer of the Territory, and investing the British Commissioners with full authority in all departments, so as to enable them to proceed to take charge and carry on affairs as they have been ordered, or may be hereafter instructed.

My Friend,—it is stipulated in the Treaty that one lakh of Star Pagodas per annum shall be provided for the expenses of your Highness, with your family and dependants. This shall be paid by monthly instalments from the British Treasury; besides which, after providing for the charges of administration, any surplus revenue shall be accounted for according to the stipulations of the

Treaty, and one-fifth shall further be paid to your Highness. I write this for your Highness' full assurance on the point. This letter will be transmitted to your Highness through the Right Honourable Stephen R. Lushington, the present Governor of Madras, to whom I have fully explained all my views and wishes. The Right Honourable the Governor will either deliver the letter in person, or cause it to be presented to your Highness by the Resident at Mysore, who will offer any further explanations that may be necessary.

Your Highness may be assured of the extreme reluctance under which I find myself compelled to have recourse to a measure that must be so painful to your Highness' feelings, but I act under the conviction that an imperative obligation of a great public duty leaves me no alternative. I entreat your Highness to review your past conduct, and calmly to consider the discredit of your own administration, and the deep injury to the population entrusted by the British Government to your care and protection, which have been produced by unworthy advisers and favourites. And I trust that the result of your patient and deliberate reflection may be that, however afflicting to your own personal feelings the consequences must be, the permanent prosperity of the Raj will be best promoted by an adherence to the course which the wisdom of the Marquess Wellesley established for a crisis like the present.

True copy,

(Signed) H. T. PRINSEP,

Secretary to Government.

(D.)

GOVERNMENT EDUCATION.

(Page 166.)

The following extracts from an article in the Bombay *Times of India* of the 13th of August 1864, so exactly convey my views on the general question, that I cannot refrain from bringing them forward to my aid :—

"The annual charge for 'Education' on the revenues of India has come to be a very heavy one. In the Budget Estimate for the current year, it stands at £561,175. * * * * It is a charge, moreover, which has doubled itself since 1861-62, and which bids fair to annually, and considerably, increase in amount. * * * * According to the latest returns at hand, there are attending Government schools, or schools under Government inspection, in the Punjab, 59,990 pupils ; in Bengal, 71,699 pupils ;

in the Central Provinces, 21,353 pupils ; in the North-Western
Provinces, about 110,000 pupils ; in the Bombay Presidency,
about 50,000 pupils ; and in the Madras Presidency, about 30,000
pupils ; or a total for all India of 343,042 pupils receiving instruction either at Government schools or Government aided
schools. Now, comparing this total number of pupils with the
total estimated expenditure of the Education Department for the
current year, as given above, it will be seen that each pupil costs
the state between £1 and £2 per annum, the precise cost being
much nearer the latter than the former sum. * * * * If
the Education Department continues to be fed with the public
money on the same scale as at present, ten years hence it will be
a greater burden on the tax-payers than a treble income-tax
would be just now. But if we look closer into the present expenditure, we shall find that it is mainly devoted, not to the enlightenment of 'the people,' but to the superior education of
classes who should have required no pecuniary aid at all, and the
corresponding classes to which in Europe never dream of obtaining or seeking for any State educational aid whatever. If the
truth were made apparent, it would become but too clear that up
to the present, the educational operations of the Government of
India have touched neither the highest, nor the lower and most
numerous grades of the population. The Government Colleges
and schools have been mainly attended by pupils whose parents
would have provided an English education for them, had there
been no Government Education Department at all. It is the
children of traders and native officials, or of parties ambitious that
their sons shall become officials or pleaders, who constitute the
great bulk of the pupils at the Government schools. And it is
because the institutions seem as if wholly intended for such
classes, that the Rajahs, Jaghirdars, and other Chiefs, will not
send their children to them ; while, on the other hand, the high
schooling fees charged, effectually prevent the poorer natives from
sending theirs. A result is that the entire educational expenditure is practically devoted to cheapening the cost of 'schooling'
to a class who would provide good schools for themselves were
there no Government education whatever. There is a well
grounded belief that a sufficing number of good private schools for
the instruction of the children of respectable natives of the middle
class, would now be in existence, and flourishing, but for a consciousness of the hopelessness of their competing with institutions
supported by Government funds, and the certificates of whose
masters and professors are, to the pupil, a kind of diploma of
eligibility for State employment.

The average cost of each pupil to Government does not at
present exceed £2 per annum ; but if from the aggregate number
of pupils be excluded those of the merely "aided" schools, the
cost per head becomes something actually astounding to contem-

plate. Some of the Government Colleges have comparatively few pupils, yet have a most costly educational staff. But putting the Colleges out of the account, the cost per pupil at the mere schools is startling. We have before us a General Statement of the Progress of Education in the Punjaub, during 1862-63, and therein we find that, excluding 'General establishment and charges,' and all charges for 'buildings,' the expense of instructing 1,969 boys at 22 Zillah schools was Rs. 87,258, or Rs. 44-5-0 per pupil per annum !"

(E.)

NATIVE PROMOTIONS.

(*Page* 168.)

The Commissioner of Mysore, in his Administration Report for 1862-3, after describing the new appointments and increased salaries for English officers under the revised arrangements, tells us that a corresponding amelioration has also been made in the position of the native officials :—

"The new and honourable post of Native Assistant has been created. The number of superior appointments opened to natives has been increased from thirteen to fifteen, and the average salary raised from Rs. 342 to Rs. 440 per mensem." (Par. 182.)

If an acceptance of this statement were to be the termination of our inquiry the result would be that while the body of English officials was augmented by six, and their annual receipts by £12,000, the body of superior native officials would be augmented by two, their receipts by £2,500, and their average salary raised just to the level of that allotted to the junior European Assistant. And although the Report dignifies the new offices with the title of "superior appointments," they are still placed in an inferior category, out of the line of ordinary promotion, and subordinate to that allotted to the youngest English officers.

But this statement requires a little closer examination. Although the Commissioner, who admits (par. 179) the propriety of a "due advertence to the claims of the native officials," declares that "the number of superior appointments opened to natives, has been *increased* from thirteen to fifteen," it is somewhat remarkable that the details given in that very paragraph would lead us to suppose that the number had been *decreased* from nineteen to fifteen. We are told that "of the principal native officers affected by the new arrangements," there were selected for the post of Native Assistant, "two Judges of the Hoozoor Adawlut (the Court being abolished), three Head Sheristadars of the former Divisions, and eight Moonsiffs." And then it is added that "six individuals who were found ineligible for the new class of appointments, were permitted to retire on suitable pensions." These pensioners seem to make up a list of nineteen "principal native officers," who are now succeeded by fifteen Native Assistants.

I cannot offer an explanation of the apparent discrepancy, with any degree of certainty, for want of the requisite particulars ; but, from the context of the Report, I believe it to arise from four of the pensioners, whose former offices were abolished and who were not considered qualified for the new posts, having been Head Sheristadars of the old Divisions. The other two pensioners had been Moonsiffs (Judges), only eight out of ten of that class having been made Assistants under the new organisation. Now while the writer of the Report includes the Head Sheristadars among the "principal native officers," of the old list, he does not choose to classify them as "superior officials." And though I think that the distinction is over-strained and calculated to mislead, it is not entirely without meaning or pretext. The Sheristadar of a Division, though occupying a post of great indirect influence and power, was merely a ministerial officer, exercising no judicial functions, entrusted with no ostensible authority, while the Native Assistant is a Magistrate, Judge and Collector, whose orders in every department, though subject to appeal, are valid and decisive. But as the Head Sheristadar's salary ranged from £300 to £480 per annum, the distinction seems to be almost without a difference, and the substantial gain in "superior" appointments to the class of native officials, sinks—if I am not very much mistaken—into a clear loss.

<hr>

(F.)

PUBLIC WORKS AND POLICE.

Lord Dalhousie, contrary to Sir Mark Cubbon's opinions and wishes, insisted on a Public Works' Department being cut out for Mysore, on the model of that which he had then lately framed for our own provinces, and which has long been a reproach to our Government, and a jest among all intelligent natives, on account of the large number of highly salaried English officers permanently maintained—out of all proportion to the work executed—the very indifferent style in which much of that work is executed ; and the gross peculation which pervades the Department, in spite of all the complicated safeguards of sanctioned estimates and audited accounts. Previously to this unwelcome innovation, Sir Mark

Cubbon had, through the agency of one Engineer officer, the Superintendents of Districts, their local subordinates, and native contractors, provided a much more complete system of roads throughout Mysore, than existed in any British province of the same extent; and always kept the irrigation works of the country in good order, at a very much smaller outlay for construction and repairs, than could have been shown in similar instances by our own elaborate accounts. The formation and maintenance of roads, tanks, and channels, and other simple engineering operations, upon which the public revenue and the profits of agriculture so greatly depend, have been from time immemorial familiar to Hindoo experts. A very little supervision would enable these men to carry out all the ordinary work of a district, and to execute almost all the plans of our scientific Engineers. They are quite competent to render all the necessary returns and accounts, and if properly remunerated would be as trustworthy as most people. The native architects and engineers, worthy of culture and instruction at our hands, are dying out in our older possessions, and their craft, from disuse, is becoming forgotten; but some of them, and many of a similar standing, are employed on the Public Works, and being, as in other departments, badly paid and not burdened with responsibility, have not, as a class, the highest character for purity, are popularly supposed to accumulate small fortunes in a wonderfully short time; and these scandals are often most unfairly brought forward as examples of what must be expected whenever natives are employed.

On the other hand, the English Engineers of districts, who by mere position, relieve their subordinates of responsibility, and unwittingly screen them from observation, are almost entirely occupied in clerical duties, upon the accuracy and regularity of which, their official reputation depends. Although invested, in theory, with the executive charge of all the works within their range, the close application to accounts and correspondence imposed upon them, frequently keeps them tied to the desk for months together, so that they may never, or very seldom, have seen the works they are nominally constructing.

Since the newly modelled Public Works Department of Mysore commenced to act, its operations have chiefly consisted in opening and extending communications, and maintaining those already formed, in the repairs and improvement of old native works of irrigation, and in ordinary building. When plans and estimates have once been prepared and sanctioned, the cases are very few and far between in which much scientific engineering is required in completing the works. The services of English gentlemen, so-called Executive Engineers, are quite thrown away on road-making and repairing tanks, and are absurdly over-paid by salaries of £1000 a year. No practical man, undertaking the work on contract, would think of employing such expensive agency. The whole structure and system of this Department, in Mysore and throughout India, is unsound; and it affords another instance of the truth of what Sir Thomas Munro said:—

"Expensive establishments, when once sanctioned, are not easily put down. There is never any difficulty in finding plausible reasons to keep up a lucrative office."*

If the roads and tanks were re-transferred to the care of the district revenue authorities, who, with the landholders, are directly concerned and interested, and have the greatest facilities at command for prompt and constant attention to their efficiency; if a sufficient number of properly paid native Engineers were stationed over the country; the English engineering Staff might be reduced to one Superintendent with a Secretary or Assistant. The official records might not be so voluminous; there would be of necessity a certain relaxation of red tape; but by a judicious organisation, by encouraging contractors, by placing a little confidence and granting a little discretion in the right quarter, a more efficient supervision of work might be instituted, expenses greatly diminished, and peculation certainly not increased.

But then many good appointments for English gentlemen would have to be abolished.

We have already extended to the Mysore State "the inestimable blessings" of the British Public Works and Educational Departments. Mr. Bowring, the Commissioner, in the Administration Report for 1862-3 (paragraph 54), refers to "a complete and systematic reorganisation of the Police," as the next step that is to be taken. If "the good work" is to be carried on by extending the new British Police Department to Mysore, there will be an opening for eight or ten more English officers, with salaries from £2500 to £600 per annum.

The new system of Police, which has now been introduced into all the districts of the three Presidencies, is the latest and worst example of that fatal tendency to excessive organisation and extreme centralisation, which has of late years characterised the Government of India. Official pedantry and the lust of patronage have both been at work here. The general results of the new establishment,—were a public and impartial inquiry instituted,—would assuredly be summed up as follows:—vast expense, copious scribbling, general unpopularity, marked inefficiency both as a detective and a protective force. Heaps of "able" reports, and "elaborate" correspondence on controversial and personal matters, are annnally produced for the edification of Government, by three or four gentlemen enjoying splendid emoluments, the Director General, and the Inspectors General of the several minor Governments. The Police Superintendents of Districts,—military officers with salaries of from £600 to £800 per annum,—are

* Gleig's Life of Sir T. Munro, vol. ii, p. 453.

chiefly tied down to clerical duties, examining and transmitting diaries and tabular statements.

Of course the stiff regularity of the new establishment was quite incompatible and irreconcileable with the patriarchal structure of local and village Police. The two could not exist side by side. The old inexpensive system, which was susceptible of great improvement at very small cost, has lost all its own authority and influence, even where it has not been formally abolished, and cannot impart its local and traditional knowledge to the new-comers. The new Police, armed and drilled and dressed, are, in their most useful aspect, only an army of Sepoys under another name, and are actually employed on certain duties from which the native troops have been relieved. But their arms, their drill, their dress, and the escort duties which they are made to perform, simply lower their efficiency as policemen. And their pay being quite inadequate, corrupt and oppressive practices are, it is said, very generally employed to secure some additional contributions from the community among whom they are quartered. The Department, taken as a whole, is an opprobrium to British rule.

(G.)

(Page 178.)

"CHRISTMAS IN BOMBAY."

(From the Hindu Prakash, December 28th, 1863.)

"The inherent vice of all foreign rule never appears so disadvantageously, as in times like the present, specially devoted to relaxation and pleasure. The ruling race has such an awful consciousness of its own superhuman elevation, and the habits of an exclusive and single life are so studiously cherished that they never can unbend themselves nor relax the gravity of their wrinkled front, and smiling self-pleased, enjoy themselves to their heart's content. In fact, besides the hereditary element of sour melancholy which has permanently quartered itself on British character since the days of their Puritan psalm-singing fathers, their peculiar position in this country as a race of merchant rulers has served to give a sad prominence to this most unwelcome trait in their character. British rule in India has most amply vindicated the justice of Napoleon's severe distribe against their character as a European nation. In its whole aspect, it is so formal and rigid in the smallest as well as the most Imperial concerns, the one guiding principle is the expectation of money's worth for money paid. There is order, there is neatness, there is economy, there is every possible convenience and accommodation, but with all this, British rule has the appearance more of a shop, than of a splendid imperial mansion worthy of the love of millions, who might come there to honour the Sovereign Queen who sits over them enshrined in majesty. In seasons of jollity as in seasons of business, this same hateful thought of a selfish nature intrudes and spoils the cheer. It is Christmas now, and one would expect merriment and the noisy turbulence of harmless joy to bustle through our streets. But our streets look even more sombre and sadly desolate than when they are alive with the hum of business. Each man sits in his own petty self and mopes the time away; and this is our relaxation. The native population of the town, having nothing to stimulate them into the active habits of enjoying merry cheer out of doors, dissipate their means in worse than idleness.

Under native Sovereigns such times seldom would have come unattended by their train of popular attractions and enjoyments. Our temples would have blazed all night one mass of flame, and thousands would have poured there to hear some popular and favourite bard, reciting to them the pleasant stories of old days. There would have been popular masques and public theatres open to every comer. The whole public would have been freely asked to partake of their Sovereign's hospitality, and milk and sugar, in unnumbered rounds, would have infused cheer and freshness into the joyous throng. The advent of the day would have brought with it other and more martial shows. The whole city would have been invited to the Prince's Palace, and there the Sovereign would have held a magnificent Durbar in honour of the new year that was dawning on their life and fortune. The Durbar over, there would have been horse races, and foot races, there would have been fencing with the sword or the stick, there would have been bull fights and buffalo fights, there would have been wrestling and a thousand marvellous feats of agility or force. Then the whole population would have poured out in the train of their Sovereign out of the city, and having rent the air with their merriment, and tired all their capacity for enjoyment, they would have returned home and gone to rest. These are the things which forge so strong the chain of love between King and people; and in their absence the most regulated Government fails to inspire any other feeling than that of thankless content. We are sure London and Paris are not so subdued in their Christmas merriment as this city is with a Christian population of above five thousand. The people, in order to be elevated from their dreary selves, want some such machinery of popular shows and festivities, where they may catch and impart pleasure all around. The Government sadly misunderstands this popular craving for merriment and relaxation. People often feel surprised at being told that the British Government is a standing object of suspicion to its subjects; and seldom inspires any feeling of love and attachment in their bosoms. The cause, as we

have mentioned it, is obvious enough.   It treats its subjects like
severe masters, and is paid, in return for this severe formality, by
perpetual suspicion of its motives even when engaged in the
most philanthropic projects for their welfare. Bombay life is very
tiresome."

(H.)

LETTER FROM A FRIEND.

(*Page* 187.)

Dear ————   April 10th, 1863.

In the *Edinburgh Review*, just published, there is an article
headed "India under Lord Canning," which, but for the position
which the putative author holds with reference to the Government, would scarcely be deserving of notice.   As it is, however,
I suppose it must be viewed in some measure as an expression
of the sentiments of the Government, though it is hard to believe
that they would be so unscrupulous, so devoid of all honour, as
to support the monstrous doctrines put forward by the writer of
the article in question.   Most of our Governors General have
sought for and set forth some other and more specious plea than
that of mere expediency, for plundering weak Princes; but the
reviewer boldly avows that expediency should be our guide, and
some of his remarks make it quite clear that the Rajah of Mysore
is to be the next victim.   Yet he is not disloyal or disaffected.
The Commissioner, the Governor General, and the Secretary of
State have testified to the contrary.   He must therefore be sacri-
ficed on some other plea; and I know of none, after twenty years
personal experience of the Prince and his country, except that
the territory is rich, the climate good, the position eligible—and
we want it.   Add to this, that we are strong, the Rajah weak—
and what more could possibly be required to satisfy the most
delicate Whig conscience?   It is the old story of Naboth's vine-
yard once more repeated—only rather more flagrant, for we don't
propose to give anything in return to anybody.

It will be curious to see how, when the extinction of the Mysore
State has been accomplished, the claim of the Nizam to a share
of the plunder will be met.   Should we, in reference to that code
of honour which is said to be observed among thieves, give half
of the "sick" Hindoo's possessions to the Mussulman, the latter,
entertaining probably more chivalrous sentiments than at present
seem to inspire us, and feeling acutely the recent shameful attempts
to rob him of a part of his own country, might restore his share
to the Rajah or his heir, and read us a lesson of which we seem
to be sadly in want.

It is melancholy to think that in spite of all our asseverations, wrung from us in the hour of our peril, all our protestations of honesty and good faith, we should still be bent on robbing our neighbours. It has been recently avowed in the most shameless manner by a person holding high office in India, that it is our intention to deprive the Nizam, at some future period, of the territory which we seized, but were compelled to relinquish a short time ago. Meanwhile, Mysore, already in our insatiable grasp, is to be annexed, and one of the oldest Royal Houses in India obliterated. It cannot be pretended that the Rajah has committed any great crime. He is loyal, humane, generous, intelligent, hospitable; and his dignified courtesy to all classes of Europeans, strikes all who approach him. The people of the country, whose interests the author of the paper in the *Review* guards with such jealous care, look on the Rajah with the most kindly feelings, and speak of him with the deepest respect.

The whole of the Mysore country is covered with noble works, executed entirely by the present Rajah and his ancestors. The Mussulman Princes did nothing but plunder. We have done nothing but restore some of the works that had fallen into disrepair, make a fine road for our own convenience to the Hills, build Rest Houses for European gentlemen, from which Natives of all classes are carefully excluded, and construct in each station the usual Jail and Church! The Rajah's family, on the other hand, has, in the Ashtagram Division alone, constructed magnificent dams across the principal rivers, which throw water into upwards of six hundred miles of canals, excavated at a cost and with an amount of skill that throw our petty works into the shade.

At every town and almost every village there is a Chuttrum where all native travellers are housed and fed for the day, established and endowed by the Rajah. And when, in 1856, we were threatened with famine, the Rajah for months fed thousands daily, who but for his bounty might have perished. It makes one's blood boil to think that a man who has done so much good should be so shamefully maligned. His great crime, alas! is possessing a country that we covet; and that, I have learned to understand, is an unpardonable offence.

The observation that the Princes of India, with one or two exceptions, are politically ciphers, is as ungenerous as it is untrue. Had those who only remained passive in 1857, declared against us, India would have been lost, at any rate for a time. But the danger has blown over, and we, as usual, forget what we have passed through. And yet we have had some warnings that ought not to have been forgotten.

Look at the fearful catastrophes which followed our unwarrantable invasion of Affghanistan. Then retribution followed swiftly, and *one* at any rate of the instigators of that wickedness paid for it with his head. The blood, however, of the unhappy victims of this iniquitous campaign was scarcely dry, before we seized Scinde,—a country whose rulers had behaved in the most friendly manner towards us, and who could, had they been so minded, have prevented a single man of the Candahar force from ever reaching India. They helped us in every possible way, in our time of need, and they met their reward. The instant our hands were free, we conquered Scinde, plundered Hyderabad and imprisoned the Ameers. I have always looked with horror on the conquest of Scinde. I think it is perhaps the most wicked act of spoliation we have ever perpetrated; but still it is ludicrous to observe how the Whig reviewer and advocate for wholesale spoliation, carps at the single Tory acquisition of Scinde. But Whig and Tory are, I fear, alike in this accursed lust of territory; and it seems destined that robbery shall follow robbery, till India is again deluged with the blood of innocent women and children. I shared in the Affghan campaign, and escaped the fate that overwhelmed so many brave fellows. I have experienced the kindness and hospitalities of the Ameers of Scinde, and have seen them dethroned, and their country taken from them. I have seen the Carnatic, Tanjore, Nagpore, and a host of other Principalities fall before our unhallowed greed; and the only instance which I can remember when we were justified in seizing the country of a Native Prince was that of Kurnool. I have seen the terrible year 1857 pass away, and I believe that I shall live to see something similar occur again, for I do not believe that we can be permitted to continue in such a career of wholesale reckless robbery unchecked.

Before concluding these remarks, I would draw your attention to the cry that is now got up, and which the author of the paper in the *Review* put forth, about the necessity for guarding *the interests of the people*. What that may mean exactly, I don't profess to know; but we have the author's own word for it that so little sensible were the people of Oude of our tender concern for their interests, that the cultivating classes were as hostile to us during the Mutiny, as any other class of the people. As regards Mysore, you and I know from intimate personal acquaintance with the people, that however much they may fear, they neither love nor respect us, and they would joyfully see our rule changed to-morrow for that of the old Rajah. I could say much more, but you know as well as I do, how wicked and desperate is the game our rulers seem bent on playing.

Believe me, ever yours, &c., &c.

THE END.

T. RICHARDS, 37, GREAT QUEEN STREET, W.C.